THE HAND OF GOD

DARK LEGACIES
BOOK 1

YUVAL KORDOV

For my girls.
May you walk in the light.

PROLOGUE

In the beginning, there was the void.

And from the void came a heartbeat.

Proof of life was the signal.

The pain came later. Preceding it was the vague sensation of pressure: a pinprick, followed by a drowning, inescapable flood, which triggered a spark.

The creature's face—still just a suggestion—had barely formed by the time its brain was interrogated, attacked, enhanced—*accelerated*. The spark was an explosion that consumed the universe, flaying away the dark curtain of space to reveal an even darker black beneath, a black that blinded with an intensity greater than the meager flicker of distant stars.

The pink spiral canals of its blossoming ears shuddered with the noisome torrent of the flood. Its lips, a crooked molecule-thick line below the bud of a nose, turned down in an involuntary grimace, still unable to channel a scream of release. In silence it suffered each cell division, each excruciating layer of ossification as its cartilage took form.

The universe seemed to contract as the creature grew, the two competing for space in the primordial bath of darkness, which now presented the additional sensation of heat. Such heat, such incomprehensible pressure, that the creature's rudimentary biology was compressed like raw carbon into an infinitely faceted diamond.

Newly born nerve endings erupted in protest against their own premature awareness, collapsing in agony only to be resurrected by the spark, extending their reluctant tendrils deeper into the universe with each day. They whirled outward with the urgency of escape, branching into tributaries along crooked arms culminating in tiny clenched fists, the curious nub of a tail, and frail legs already withered with corruption.

The creature—now aware that *it* was a *she*—reached out with her senses, for she knew that her hands, though whole, would never be her instrument. She abandoned her shrunken limbs, recycling their genetic material into a protective carapace over her cerebral cortex instead, steeling her nervous system against the next inevitable spark.

Which came as an even greater flood.

It threatened to drown her completely, filling the minuscule cavities of her body, drenching her senses in memories not her own, catapulting her arms outward with violence. Though the flood was a torrent, she recognized motes within it: siblings lost in the void yet still alive in the substrate of the spark.

The clamor of their preanimate voices disgorged into her cells—creating, altering, destroying. Her universe erupted into war as brutal cascades of physical withering were met with a neurological hardening unmatched by each who came before. Her siblings—her sisters—died again, each in turn by sacrificial turn.

She would survive. She knew this now, as certainly as she knew that her birth was designed to cajole death from creation. She would not be the first, but she would be the last.

And so, she waited.

PART 1
ESTHER

ESTHER

1:1

The bedroom was pretty cozy considering the state of the house. This one had all its walls and even a mattress that was dry enough to sleep on, but no roof. The strange snow—she wasn't good at days of the week, but Esther was pretty sure she knew about seasons and that it didn't usually snow in summer—sprinkled down from the churning black-orange clouds high above, flecking her patchwork hair white just like her mom's "skunk streak."

She felt like the star of her very own snow globe and imagined herself being serenaded by a troupe of adorable skunks in yellow tutus, wishing her a happy birthday and new year. They spun around her in a circle, holding each other's fluffy hands and kicking up their ballet-shoed feet. She looked down at her gray cat stuffy, which had turned mostly brown and hard by now, and danced its arms to her silent song, kinking her head back and forth.

She was hungry.

Always hungry now, even more than her sister Miriam used to be. Sometimes the broken houses had canned food that she could still eat, thanks to her trusty can opener, Mr. Claw, but mostly everything was already gone or smelled really bad—worse than a real skunk must.

She hummed to Gray Cat, thinking about summer, thinking about what the distant stars in the clear blue-black sky used to look like. Every time she tried to think of them now, they seemed less real, more like something that was only ever a picture in her bedtime books. Her daddy said the sun was their planet's very own special star and that even it was millions of kilometers away, which seemed like the kind of silly joke he would tell. But maybe it explained why she couldn't see either anymore.

She missed them.

Esther hugged her knees through her torn jeans, rocking back and forth on the mattress. The wind outside howled like wolves. She used to be scared of the sound, used to stay awake at night, eyes bulging and alert, ready for something furry to sweep down from a chimney or through a shattered window. But nothing ever did, so she learned to sleep through it. Sometimes she wished a wolf *would* show up, or any creature; maybe a skunk, or a person, or her family—even Miriam.

The day had been long. Most of the houses before this one didn't have enough walls or there were too many dead people in them. It was probably bedtime by now—"*Do your pee! Brush your teeth! Pick a book already!*"

She blinked away a ridge of snow from her eyelashes and heaved her backpack from the floor onto the bed, hands gliding back and forth over the few remaining sequins of a heart pattern sewn on its front: silver, red, silver, red, silver—oops, another one fell off.

She retrieved a small plastic bag full of displaced sequins from the front pouch, carefully opening the zipper latch so it wouldn't tear this time. Pinching the new orphan with her fingers, she lifted it carefully to the bag and deposited it with the rest. Maybe one day she'd find some glue and un-break her heart. She smiled, thinking that was something her mom would say.

Esther unzipped the main compartment and peered inside. She knew there was no food tonight, but she looked anyway, just in case the tooth fairy had brought her a surprise. She rubbed absently at her gums with her prematurely calloused finger, feeling the newborn nub beside her bottom front teeth. It felt soft, like her mommy's touch on a good day.

Sighing, she closed her backpack, then her eyes, and sang to herself, back pressed hard into the wall. Behind fluttering eyelids, the band of skunks spun frantically around her, white stripes blurring, then fading completely into the pitch black of their bodies, red eyes gaping.

ESTHER

1:2

The sidewalk was caked in black ash. Like a sequin, the snow from the prior night changed color with the day, darkening everything so that night seemed like morning and morning seemed like night. Still, she made sure to skip over the cracks she could see, playing a constant game of hopscotch to remind herself that she avoided those yawning chasms not because she was scared of them but because it was more fun to jump between the smooth, predictable squares.

The broken house with the cozy room was far behind her. She might have stayed longer, might have explored in the basement even, but she was too hungry.

Sometimes the hunger just felt like a tickle in her belly, like when her dad would push her too high on the swing so he could do an under-duck. It wasn't bad then, and it also meant she wouldn't have to poop for a few days, which was nice; she could stay clean.

But other times the hunger felt like rage. The tickle turned into an itch that turned into clawing, like sharp nails dragging their way up the inside of her body, into her throat, pressing at the back of her neck. She wanted to yawn and scream at the same time. She wanted to clamp down on her teeth and break them into tiny slivers, then swallow them in revenge against her empty belly.

Esther dreamed of chocolate Os swimming happily in a bowl of milk. Or just an egg—even the yellow part. A minuscule trickle of drool formed at her lips—all that her parched mouth could spare—and she sucked it back, swallowing hard.

Every ruined house looked the same, making it hard to know which ones to look in and which ones to skip. It was usually the smell that guided her, or the lack thereof.

She hopscotched forward, sneakered feet landing with measured quiet on each step. There used to be a time that she didn't walk as quietly, and bad things happened. Now she was sure of her movements—perfect.

The road alongside her was wide and lifeless. Wrecked cars pressed against one another for warmth, their doors ajar and chattering in the wind. Its howl distorted into a tuneless elegy of remembrance as it blew through their shattered windows.

Between the sidewalk and the road, the scrabbly boulevard was a graveyard of hunched black figures that used to be trees, their crisp round canopies resembling the blackened shells of the overcooked Brussels sprouts her dad was so proud of. "Sprussel brouts" Miri called them. She loved them; Esther did not. Not then or now.

She paused to peer into a nearby canopy, wondering at the birds that once lived there and were now melted like wax into the blistered mass. Their song had been constant, a flood of chirps and whirs, the absence of which resounded through the street like a great sucking void. She even missed the obnoxious caw of the magpies outside her window as they fought over the daily roadkill.

———

They lived in the city's outermost subdivision—it was far enough away from the endless rioting of the inner city that they could walk their own streets with a reasonable assurance of safety. Being as far out as it was, her neighborhood backed directly onto the highway, separated only by a half-finished sound barrier.

Day and night, her house buzzed with the traffic of shipping drones barreling at ultra-high speed down the road. She would gaze at them from her open window, imagining what they carried within them and to whom. Girls like herself maybe, but with famous parents—"government employees," her dad called them—in safe, gated castles in the city. Ball gowns and golden slippers for their fancy parties.

It was close to the End when the autonomous trucks stopped, and with them the shaking of her house. The alien stillness unsettled her, drove her to pick at her fingernails and toenails for comfort. Her parents became distant and agitated around the same time, relegating her and Miri to their room early every night with the laptop for cartoons and boxed bedtime snacks, while they watched news in the living room. It felt special—for a while.

The whole subdivision was the same. No one went to work anymore, no one went out, no more playdates with friends. Only the magpies congregated on the streets. Everyone stayed at home, their parents watching transfixed late into the night.

She could hear the broadcasts through their thin bedroom walls, even over the loud grunting of Miri's snores, but she could never make out what the news anchors were saying. Every night, after finally shutting it off, her dad would exclaim, *"God help us!"* or words she wasn't allowed to repeat, over and over.

As though reading from a script, her mom would always try to make him feel better: *"Maybe it'll pass. Maybe they'll figure it out. Maybe it's not as bad as they say."* That was when Dad would start up about whether we should stay or go, which was the breaking point of the night.

"Where the fuck would we go?"

She blushed at the memory of her mom's curses.

The arguments, and the nights, usually ended like that: both of her parents exhausted and angry, nothing agreed on, Miriam snoring, and her tossing and turning in bed, wondering where indeed they would go. She had only ever known the subdivision.

Right before everything changed, she was awakened in the night by a familiar sound and leapt excitedly from her bed. If the auto-trucks were back, maybe it *had* passed—whatever *it* was. But the buzzing only grew louder, until her window started to rattle like an angry snake.

These trucks were different. They had headlights, and there were dozens, hundreds even, each of them a different shape, dark green, some carrying soldiers and others that just looked like giant guns. Some rode on wheels, others on tracks. She watched them without recognition, without awareness of what they meant, but an instinctual terror gnawed at her stomach. The convoy continued for what seemed like hours, until the tail-lights of the last truck faded into the horizon. She turned to see if Miriam had noticed, but her sister lay still in the bed.

A cold breeze crept into the wide sleeves of her pajama gown, prompting her to close the window when she detected a new sound. She furrowed her brow, willing more power to her ears as she struggled to recognize it. There were no headlights approaching, and her eyes strained past the noisy grain of evening, pitch black under a new moon.

It was cyclical: a long whir followed by a dull crunch. It grew louder as it approached, and the crunches turned into thuds that shook the foundation of their house.

She scrambled off the window ledge and threw open the lid of her dress-up chest. Digging past capes, swords, and masks, she exclaimed with an exuberant "aha!" as she withdrew her dad's old night-vision binoculars. They had been a special birthday present, something he said he had to sneak past his old bosses. She looped the strap around her neck, flicked on the power, and hopped back up to her windowsill.

Esther would never forget the moment she saw *it*, or that in that moment she was certain *it* also saw *her*. The only time she had ever seen anything like it before was on her father's desk after sneaking into his office one day. "Blueprints" he had called them after shooing her away, which was weird since they weren't blue.

In the middle of the highway stood what she could only describe as a giant robot, but not silly or cute like the creatures in her books. This was a "battle walker"—that was what was written on her dad's secret papers, anyway. It was all hard angles, legs jutting backward like some giant bird, upper body a vicious-looking wedge sparkling with antennae and sensors and ports. It had giant guns for arms and even more weapons in pods that ran the length of its upper body.

The machine looked at her with a single killing eye, a circular sizzle of white and green through the binoculars. She froze, held her breath, prayed for it to look away, but was unable to look away herself.

Then, with a twist of its torso, it was gone, loping after the convoy with uncanny speed. Whir, thump, whir, thump, whir, crunch...

Two nights later her dad burst into their room, saying the car was packed and it was time to go. Then the sky exploded.

ESTHER

1:3

Esther was the last one left, or so it seemed. The time right after the explosion had been mostly erased from her memory, leaving only disconnected fragments of running, screaming, separation, and heat—so much heat it felt like the whole world was on fire. Maybe it was.

Then she was wandering, too busy with the work of not dying to wonder why, or how, she survived.

She had been on the road for hours already today, placing one foot unthinkingly before the other, without aim or purpose. The hunger of the day was quickly transitioning from the okay kind to the smash-her-teeth kind, which was maybe why her legs had delivered her to the strip mall at the edge of the residential grid, nearest the city.

The brimstone boulevard steered her into the parking lot, whose wheeled carcasses looked much like those on the road. There had clearly been panic right up until the explosions. She knew there were dead people in front of her. She could see them but also not see them, pressing down the soles of her feet and curling her toes together every time her eyes skipped over a charred face or a threadbare limb.

There would have been people here that she knew, or at least that her parents knew. If she was careful to avoid accidentally seeing a familiar face—when they were still recognizable—then she might still be able to wake up from this nightmare.

She focused instead on the storefronts before her. The plastic-and-neon billboards above each store were blown out while the windows had blown in, revealing blasted debris smothered in the same monotone ash that coated the ground.

The grocery store ahead was a regular haunt. Every time they came here, she would race from her parents' hands through the doors with Miri, each pushing the other back so that they could reach the tiny shopping carts first. It always ended in a fight.

She had never dared go back before now. It was the subdivision's closest point to the city proper—to all those people. The ceaseless wind howled. If there *were* people here, she wouldn't hear them.

Esther swallowed, trying to do math in her head. She mouthed numbers while ticking off houses on her hands, swaying back and forth, toes still clenched, then did them a second and third time. She had been everywhere and really didn't want to smash her teeth, especially since the grown-up ones were finally coming in.

She reached up to pull at her lower lip, heavy eyes upon the cavern where the grocery store's front doors once resided, wishing more than ever for her daddy's hand. Instead, she gripped Gray Cat tightly under her right arm and clenched both nailless hands into fists as she stepped hurriedly forward. Each step elicited a noisy crunch as her narrow ankles twisted and popped over the rubble-strewn lot. She knew she should be looking both ways, but she looked down as she walked, still trying her best to avoid the horror of the dead.

An eternity passed before she arrived on the other side.

What looked like an open cavern from the boulevard was completely obstructed with a waterfall of stone and corrugated steel. Carefully navigating the detritus, she climbed up and through an adjacent window frame into darkness.

Dense particles swirled slowly in the air, glinting in the thin rays of light that penetrated the building's perforated roof. Esther barked out a cough without thinking, then squealed through pursed lips in protest against her carelessness. Gray Cat fell into the rubble below her as her rib cage flexed in fits.

Sinking down onto her knees, she tore at the ground in a panic. Her scrambling limbs forced plumes of ash into her eyes and nose, but she clamped her throat shut, desperate to find her companion. Frustrating piles of ruin slipped between her fingers as she dug, then at last pulled the stuffy free.

Her breath was coming in ragged huffs now, lungs burning with the intake of so much ash. Hunching down, she bit down on her lip and waited until the horrible itch of it passed, and again the muted howl of the wind outside was all anyone would hear.

Food. She just wanted some food and would leave. She promised the monsters hiding in the dark that she wouldn't take all of it and that she wouldn't be very tasty anyway in her current state.

Please, she mouthed.

With supreme effort, she continued her scramble over the rubble, moving to the middle aisles as much by memory as by sight in the minuscule luminescence.

Many of the shelves had collapsed upon one another, forcing her to walk through what seemed like an impossibly long and winding tunnel of random boxes and bottles, uninteresting things her parents would have put in the cart. Spotting a clearing ahead, she crept through with care.

Before her towered a single, perfectly undamaged metal

cabinet. It gleamed with promise, but as she approached, she saw it had been picked clean. Her eyes scanned each desolate shelf in sequence, certain that something would appear if looked for in the right order.

How could this be? How could it be empty when she had come so far? It wasn't fair!

So preoccupied was she with the impossibility of its emptiness that Esther didn't hear the crooked shuffle of footsteps behind her.

"Don't move."

The voice was harsh and mechanical, like a flap of rusted metal dragged along concrete. It had been so long since she heard someone speaking that she needed to replay the words several times over before they sank in. Maybe the speaker hadn't *spoken* in so long that it, too, was unfamiliar with language, forcing the words from a raspy, unwilling throat.

Maybe it wasn't a person at all, but the wolf on the wind.

The hair patches on her mottled scalp sprang outward, the muscles in her neck constricted, and she did in fact freeze, outwardly at least. Her bladder, however, released in a violent burst, filling her pants with a warm flood of shame. Dark amber urine dribbled in a cascade from her inseam, spilling onto the floor beneath her.

A hand pressed roughly into her back, shoving her forward into the cabinet, almost knocking them both over. She felt heat on the back of her neck: killing heat, like from the bombs, from the howling wind. But this time there was no escape. Now that everyone else was gone, the heat was here only for her.

Her thoughts raced into reverse memory: the heat, the explosion in the sky, the killing machine behind her house, the blaring news, her dad wringing his hands and crying for God to help them...

To help her.

"God help me..."

It was little more than a whisper, a discordant prayer blurted through trembling lips. The cold, empty metal of the nearest shelf dug into her forehead as the heat behind her scalded her neck.

Louder this time, she dredged up the final scraps of her will into one last forlorn plea.

"God help me!"

"I am with you."

Esther blinked in surprise. Time stopped as she grasped at the disembodied voice.

The pressure on her back released suddenly, sending her lurching backward so fast that she had to swing her arms forward for balance, hands clamping like a vise onto the shelf. The breath was still hot upon her neck, but it came in ragged bursts.

She felt every shift of movement behind her as her captor hurriedly repositioned. The sound of a bag being unshouldered, feet shifting, then the torturous crescendo of a zipper being opened. Terror washed over her.

For the first time, she wished that she had died that night with her family. She closed her eyes and waited, clutching for an intact memory of their faces. Her brain strained at the effort of it, struggling past fight-or-flight, past obscene hunger, exhaustion, and loneliness.

Only Miriam stared back at her: bright-eyed, smiling mischievously, but uncharacteristically quiet, her face ashen. Miriam reached out her little hands. Esther tried to reach her own arms forward but found herself bodiless in this void, consciousness without form. She wanted to scream.

A cool breeze blew on her shoulders.

She cracked open her left eye first, then her right, then closed both again, then opened both together. There was the impression of empty space behind her, so she turned around—very slowly. As she did, her damp foot kicked against something heavy.

Looking down, she saw two cans of food and a pristine roll of toilet paper.

With a wracking sob, body doubled over by it, she wailed for the first time since the explosions. Gray Cat fell from her armpit, and her backpack slumped to the floor.

Esther cried for her planet, cried for her home, cried for her family, but mostly cried for herself. As the tears streamed from her bloodshot eyes, her skin was cleansed of the cremated remains of the world.

ESTHER

1:4

The cozy bedroom was less cozy this time. Something had eaten away the last intact corner of the mattress, and large sections of the floor were caved in. It would be the last time she slept here.

Esther was more concerned, however, with what she saw above her than below. A vortex of clear sky had irised open above the house, like the eye of some superstorm from a nature video. All around the aperture, night-dimmed orange-black clouds continued to churn and roll, spilling over each other in an angry boil.

Beyond the hole in the sky was nothing save for half a moon, small and alone. No constellations, no distant planetary sparkles, just an endless black void. Where had all the stars gone?

Or, she thought, *where had the Earth gone?*

Esther shivered with the feeling of absolute isolation. Pulling herself away from the spectacle above, she peered at the open cans of food before her: cell-steak and corn kernels. They had been sitting there for an hour, untouched despite the hollow rumble in her belly. All she could think about was how Miriam probably wouldn't have touched them without ketchup. And where they came from—*who* they came from...

The wind was howling.

Then there was something *other* than the wind, behind it: crying—a woman's plea for help carried on the tempest. Then a scream, growing louder. It multiplied, until it became a crowd of screams, a world of people all screaming, wailing against the horror of their torture and death and torture again.

Esther's own high-pitched screaming finally joined them. Her hands slammed against her ears, eyes still fixed on the food, rocking back and forth, back and forth, back and forth, heart beating in counter-rhythm to the tumult, vision degrading into noise.

Then silence, other than the heave of her breath. Her eyelids fluttered. Her vision splintered into a kaleidoscope of swirling gray geometry before slowly refocusing. Something was there that hadn't been there before.

Sitting across from her was an angel.

The creature—male or female, she couldn't tell—stared at her from across the mattress, cross-legged, palms up, head kinked to one side. It was dressed in folds of light, had porcelain for skin and eyes of pearlescent black. A searing wreath of flame haloed its hairless, perfectly smooth scalp. It was the most beautiful thing she had ever seen.

Esther's eyelids fluttered again, slower this time. Total exhaustion swept across her body, dulling her senses, deactivating her thoughts. Her back sank into the corner of the wall.

"Rest now, Esther."

Its voice flowed like a primordial river, bathing her soul in merciful darkness.

"There's work to be done."

ESTHER

2:1

A dream.

A monotonous expanse of gray, rushing past her, tinted bloody red by the sunset.

As uniform below—for she was a machine—as it was at her bow and in her wake.

Sameness, unvarying, casting outward from the center of existence to its infinite horizons. Though her eyes were closed, her vision stretched out for kilometers, but even this afforded her no glimpse of the other side, if there was one.

Whir, thump, whir, thump—sixty tons of titanium and steel. Only the sound of her own body moving, striding with constant speed, convinced Esther that she must in fact be progressing. The miniature red orb that was once the sun hovered unmoving at her back, stuck above the western horizon like an inflamed pustule. The heavens beyond had been replaced with a black void.

Damnation lay just beyond the edges. She knew this, almost embraced it as an acceptable alternative to the psyche-shattering inanity of purgatory. Her digitigrade legs churned, cycling well past their designed tolerances. Forward, forward.

A sound: screaming. The screaming woman down the street, accelerating into a roar, then ceasing abruptly, as though shut off by a switch.

She halted her wild gait with a skid. Plumes of dust leapt reluctantly from between her mechanical toes, momentarily subject to the laws of physics before settling back down, each particle returned exactly to its original place.

She twisted her torso from left to right, scanning, seeking. A heat signature breezed into her consciousness from behind, whirling her about. As she did so, her body collapsed; armor, internal structure, all the conduits and biomechanical viscera that connected her mind to the machine deconstructing into a double helix, turning and folding, shedding itself into oblivion.

The girl looked up at the battle walker that had appeared behind her, that had watched her from the street. Her neck strained to take in its massive bulk. It stood motionless, emotionless, poised with all the abstracted violence of a war monument.

Its single eye stared back at her, inset into a head-like protrusion that jutted from its upper torso. The iris fluctuated between deep amber and pale green—pondering, calculating. Esther curled her bare toes into the hard-packed earth, scuffing the skin in an attempt to anchor herself. Retrieving Gray Cat from her armpit, she tentatively held the stuffy forward, hands vibrating, eyes unable to detach from the machine's.

Its iris rotated left to right with quick whirs before locking in at orange, and the alien mind within seemed to hesitate. With a ponderous clunk and a hum, its body lowered, squatting into its massive hawklike legs, toes as large as her whole body splaying outward to compensate.

For a timeless moment, they stood across from one another.

In the next, the machine shuddered, shaking its upper torso in refusal as it realized it had no arms with which to take what was offered. A loud hiss jetted outward from a gap in its dorsal plating, widening to reveal a launch tube.

No...

Esther's protest echoed emptily in her mind. Her throat was locked, could elicit no sound with which to express her horror.

A distant memory materialized before her: a missile, checkered yellow and black, carrying death. It vomited forth from the war machine's hunched shoulders, hurling with singular intent back the way she came.

She discarded her flesh, letting it fall away like mercury. It pooled upon the impermeable gray while her consciousness vaulted upward in pursuit.

Uniformity was all she had, her only weapon. Her mind extended forward into the synthetic brain of the guided missile, seeking, corrupting. Her own perfect flight path, forty-five degrees against the unchanging geography below, overlaid its programming, luring it into herself that she might possess it.

The checkerboard of the warhead shuddered, then segregated, unfolding into lines, giving itself up to the exactitude of her imagined edges. The missile's fuselage warped, rendering itself into a simplified facsimile of her former human body. As one they flew, bound together by her unyielding concentration.

Time passed—ostensibly, imperceptibly—until a nonuniform dark mass intruded itself upon their lovers' dance, sprawling out from the horizon onto the gray landscape. It unfurled upon the surface like an unquenchable malignancy. The mass assumed the shape of a vast city, grotesquely twisted towers and megastructures crowding upon each other, clotted streets struggling to circulate between them.

From every street, every window and rooftop, uncountable human limbs, hands, and terror-filled mouths undulated in a chorus of torment. Waves of the disembodied crashed upon the shore of the buildings, smashing at their foundations with ceaseless wailing. The song wafted up toward her, inviting Esther to ease her focus, to sink into an ocean where she would never be alone.

As she carried the missile forward, a great black geyser erupted before her, spiraling up and outward in an octagonal vortex of spires, columns, and haloed angels. Its porous surface oscillated under the fading light of the sun, withholding any reflection. The angels perched upon its terraces reached for the void with cupped hands, stretching high above the city with an absolute assertion of dominance.

Where the ocean failed to distract Esther, the immense spectacle of the cathedral completely disarmed her. It was beautiful, horrible, inevitable. A fractional shift from her flight path liberated the missile from her consciousness, separating them with a scream of thrust.

She struggled after it, surpassed it, racing to warn those below. Soaring through the columns, past the outstretched hands of the angels, she observed an array of black-robed figures, strictly aligned along the diagonals of the octagon. They stood motionless, heads bowed, hands ensconced in their sleeves.

She screamed wordlessly, desperate to rouse them from their stasis, to warn them of their imminent annihilation. But she had no body, no voice. She heard the roar of the approaching missile behind her and knew she had led it here. She had damned this place that was already damned.

As one, the figures looked up at her, and though some were young and some old, each of them had her face.

Then the sky exploded.

ESTHER

2:2

Esther's eyes shot open, seeking, straining without recognition at her surroundings. The soft tissues of her throat had glued together, blocking the oxygen flow to her brain. She was sitting up but didn't know why, or who or where she was. The entirety of her memory was the fading edges of her dream: geometry and overlapping lines falling out of alignment, portending the world's end.

Agonizing seconds passed before her throat finally released its hold upon itself, permitting her to gulp ragged, restorative breaths. Realization returned. Her sweat-soaked palms gripped the metal edge of her cot. All she could do now was wait until her self returned from the cobwebbed cellar of her brain it had retreated to.

Breaths in and out from her nose, chest pressing against the damp folds of her tank top. Her nose reactivated first, taking in the sour pungency of expired electric motors, the heady aroma of oil, the sharp jab of rusted metal. Then her eyes, recognizing the familiar confines of her utility closet bedroom, bare drywall stitched with shelves that were full and tidy, steel door slightly ajar so as not to let in the chaos of the workshop beyond. Then her skin: bare arms prickling against the still heat of the room, bare feet swollen but safe within her steel-toed tactical boots.

Esther breathed deeply, her stomach spasming and growling with the exhale. The complaint rattled loudly within her emaciated rib cage, temporarily doubling her over with discomfort. There was no escape from hunger anymore; it was a constant companion, from first light to last.

Rising ponderously from the cot, she pressed her door open and headed for the kitchenette she had set up in one of the precious metal reclamation rooms. She stepped unconsciously around heaps of abandoned junk—dozens of piles she was in the long process of sorting—focused only on watering her charred throat.

Esther had settled here a few years ago, after an excruciating age of wandering the ruins on the city's periphery. Each time another option presented itself, it inevitably proved unsuitable. Most locations were simply fouled with the residue of nuclear devastation. Others lacked necessary shelter, had no salvage, or were precariously close to other people.

Where the subdivision was empty, the city teemed with hidden life. It was to be expected, she supposed, given the millions of souls who lived there prior to the war. Thus far, she had managed to avoid all human contact. The brutal lesson of the grocery store was permanently etched in her psyche, leaving no appetite for future error.

There had been times of temptation—families, some children even, picking in the rubble for survival. She would watch them from a distance through her night vision binocs, whispering imagined conversations and finding company there. But just as often, she would turn away in revulsion as the normal ones fell prey to the *others*: packs of them, loping like hyenas, swarming and killing and eating. Night after night, there seemed to be more of these types—humans in name only.

Eventually she retreated to an industrial park only a kilometer from the subdivision, well away from the still-meaty carcass of the inner city and the predators that circled it. And close enough to her old home to suggest familiarity while still safely separated from the grocery store by the highway and a thin strip of wetlands.

Occupying more than half of the park was her new home: a shuttered electronics recycling facility consisting of a large warehouse workshop shielded by mountains of discarded machinery and well fenced against intruders. Judging by the glassy sea of inhuman faces staring out from the refuse, this one had specialized in robotics, specifically humanoids and pets. It took Esther several visits before conjuring the courage to scale the fence, shouldering her way past disturbingly lifelike body parts and what seemed like thousands of synthetic cats to gain entrance.

These former residents had since become her companions —the animals anyway. She found satisfaction in sorting them by species, ensuring the snakes were safely removed from the rodents, etcetera. Most of the humanoids were grotesquely proportioned, either with exaggerated breasts and hips or disproportionately huge genitals—in some cases both. These she still sorted, reluctantly, but they stayed stowed under opaque plastic tarps for modesty.

Two rows of phosphorescent synthetic reptiles—why anyone needed a glow-in-the-dark gecko would forever remain a mystery—guided her through the dim light of dawn to the kitchen/bathroom combo. She fumbled past the door, ignoring the light switch. Another reason this safehouse was so desirable was the functional micro-reactor that powered the industrial park's localized grid, providing lights, heat, and electricity for the workshop. But it was still too dark out—too many predators with keen eyes.

Esther leaned over the counter and squinted into the mirror, swaying sightly as her eyes adjusted to the reflection of herself therein. She stared at the rough silhouette, looking past her own gaunt features for some facet of her father or mother, some means of restoring her memory of them. Her hair had fully grown back, as black as her mother's, but she kept it sheared short. Her face may once have shared the roundness of her father's, but it was so devoid of fat now that it more closely resembled the metallic skeleton of one of her decrepit sex-bot companions.

She was so thirsty. The room spun in a wobbly, decaying orbit around her. Reaching for a stainless steel bottle by the sink, she popped its drinking spout and lifted it to her lips, carefully draining the last of her water. The solar stills she'd placed around the compound were running low, as was her filter media. Whatever meager nourishment this place had promised was on a limited timeline, which was coming to a close. She looked down at Mr. Claw, perched like a proud artisan upon a medieval castle crafted from long-ago emptied tin cans.

"Where the fuck would we go?"

The sound of her mother's words rang in her ears. As true then as they were now. Where would she go? Not back to the subdivision. Not deeper into the city. Certainly not into the country—when the stars disappeared, it left the nights far too dark to risk that. And it seemed the moon was changing too: dimmer throughout its phases, then absent for longer periods when new, as though increasingly reluctant to illuminate what lay below.

She had to eat, that much was certain. She would hunt, eat, and *then* think about her future... just as she had done every day since arriving in the city.

———

Esther scanned the compartmentalized walls of her closet bedroom, right to left, top to bottom, ensuring everything was still in its place. Such tidy, undisturbed correctness hadn't been possible in her old life, thanks to her sister. Miri was like a one-preschooler demolition crew, clawing and bulldozing her way through Esther's things, substituting her own when her many random boxes of junk started to overflow. Here, at least, the security of her possessions was assured.

The overall layout was chronological, oldest gear on the top shelf and newest on the bottom or staged for placement in an unsorted pile. Gray Cat had survived her many years on the road, minus one leg, but was now permanently relegated to first spot on the top shelf, too full of staples and duct tape to safely venture out. To its left hunched her old backpack, which had long since lost the last of its sequins and been replaced with a reinforced expedition bag she recovered from a paramilitary supply store.

Dozens of books lined the shelves: children's bedtime books she still flipped through each night but didn't dare read aloud for fear of smudging out the memory of her father's voice; a life-saving trove of printed binders rescued from an unearthed survivalist bunker; and a set of archaic encyclopedias that she found in the blasted remains of a long-ago-shuttered library. When circumstances like today's forced her to ponder the future, she would pull out one of those singed tomes and procrastinate instead, reading each entry in order.

Distributed amongst the books were various deceased robo-cats, mostly rainbow hued and all paws intact; a wide variety of primitive tools; powered survival devices, including her trusty night vision binoculars; and firearms. Guns weren't hard to find in the city, and thanks to the operation and maintenance diagrams in her binders, Esther considered herself an expert in their use, though she had yet to fire a shot. Avoidance was always the safer choice.

There were also the Bibles: Hebrew and New Testament. She recalled private holidays celebrated with candles, prayers she didn't understand, and sweet foods—and the fights she would have with her parents when they made her promise to keep their rituals secret. Her mother would become quiet, eyes haunted. *"We'll tell you when you're older,"* she always said.

Esther cradled one of the holy books in her hands, thinking back to visions half-remembered and a divine voice half-heard. Every night after finishing her bedtime books, she would pick a suitable-sounding prayer, something she could dedicate to her mother and father, and even her sister. Sometimes she would throw in a plea for acknowledgment, begging for just a word or two to let her know she wasn't alone, that the world was not alone. Then she would sleep, fitfully, reliving the horrors of her past.

Another hollow rumble cascaded across her ribs. She had to go hunting. Today.

ESTHER

2:3

Esther didn't want to wait until dusk, but she had no choice. If she hunted during the day, she was just as likely to be hunted in return.

Avoidance.

Safety.

She felt particularly uneasy about this outing, as the moon had darkened days ago and showed no sign of returning on schedule. It wasn't something she could find an explanation for in any of her books. The clear sky only seemed to enhance the encroaching darkness of night.

Her wristwatch suggested two more hours of light, though again, it could be wrong. The cycles and measures that once ruled reality seemed to be... deteriorating. It unsettled her to the core.

There was an overpass due south on the highway that marked the city boundary, with a burgeoning overgrowth below that she had scouted before. The wildlife wasn't much more robust than she was, but she had no other choice; any nonperishable goods within safe scavenging range had been exhausted years ago.

Half an hour there, an hour to hunt, half an hour back. It was doable, but perhaps she could linger a few moments more. Esther stared past the dirt road exit of the industrial park, her gloved hands clenched upon the worn rubber handlebars of the motorcycle. It was a rugged overland model: electric, two-wheel drive, ultra-light. Even still, it was more than twice her weight. Every ride was preceded by a surge of panic, the very plausible fear of an accident, followed by slow death trapped beneath its frame.

Her teeth ground noisily against one another as she warred against a heart-pounding urge to stay, to give it one more night. Gradually, the systemic chill of her own slow death by starvation loosened the grinding into a staccato chattering.

Esther compressed her abdomen, holding her breath for a moment as she flicked the motorcycle's power select switch to MAX, then depressed the start button. A steady hum cycled through its frame, resonating through her legs. The exhilaration of raw power coursing beneath her snapped Esther's procrastination loop. Her vibrating jaw quieted, switching from a chatter to a whispered prayer.

"The Lord is my light and salvation.

Whom shall I fear?

The Lord is the strength of my life.

Of whom shall I be afraid?"

With a single motion, she slammed the kickstand up and rolled the throttle, nearly careening off the seat as the instant torque of the electric motors slingshotted her forward.

ESTHER

2:4

Every minute felt like an hour, an eternity of time spent under the gaze of unknown observers on the highway. She kept to the adjacent dirt road, laser-focused on the path ahead as the knobby tires of her motorcycle kicked debris up around her. Like a silent storm cloud, she rode through the diminishing glow of the sunset.

"Just stay there," she implored under her breath, sparing a glance over her right shoulder. "Be normal, just this once."

She spoke as much to the sun as she did to the creatures in the haunted woods beyond the road. Wildlife was scarce, and the fauna that remained seemed to be changing for the worse. Sickliness was to be expected in their struggle against a countryside turned radioactive, but some of the deformities she encountered seemed impossibly exaggerated or just plain impossible.

She had witnessed a deer staggering upright across the highway, its lips blubbering out a human-sounding moan. Rodents who spun in futile combat against tails that spawned their own jaws and teeth. And wild dogs larger than any wolf, with hairless porcine skin and metal-barbed tails. They were her nightmares realized.

The sudden thrum of tires on a cattle guard snatched Esther back into the present, pitching her precariously sideways as the motorcycle's rear tire kicked out over the iron bars. The overpass crested above her, and she braked hard, veering off the dirt road. The motorcycle's suspension juddered as she swerved into an outcropping of wild brush that burst forth from the nearby nature preserve. She stopped—upright, blessedly—in a thicket of dead shrubbery, just ahead of a precipitous drop into the ravine below.

Knocking the kickstand back down, she stepped carefully off her ride, testing its balance several times before trusting it to the uneven surface.

No more mistakes.

The ever-present wind blew past her, whistling over the bike's dimmed headlight and through tall grasses to circle the trembling aspen overhead, adding the dry rattle of their diseased foliage to the milieu. With each gust, she fumbled against the motorcycle's panniers for her hunting gear. The ceaseless heat of it battered her already ragged nerves, dislodging her repeatedly.

Finally, she found her headlamp, strapped it over her sweat-soaked brow, and depressed the power switch without thinking. A piercing white glare immediately reflected back at her, eliciting a yelp, and she hurriedly toggled it a second time to night mode. Her accelerated breathing eased as its red glow restored her low-light vision. Next, she pulled her hunting nets from the motorcycle's top bag but cursed again as they conspired to tangle themselves into a useless mess. Purposefully, she fished out the intruding lines, smoothing them until they reassumed a perfect grid. Frustration filled her as she struggled with the very tasks that she had practiced so many times before, albeit in the safety of her hideout.

A quick double check of the .45-caliber pistol strapped to her leg, and there was nothing left to do but turn and face the ravine. She did so reluctantly, the evanescent glow of her headlamp scanning over the brush, falling into darkness below.

The overpass above, like most other roads, was crowded with the jagged remains of vehicles rendered lifeless by the electromagnetic pulse of the nuclear explosions. They had piled upon one another and through most of the steel guardrail in their final panicked stampede.

The wind buffeted her, impatiently pressing her forward. With careful sidesteps, Esther descended, grimacing at the unexpected stench of the place. One of her favorite olfactory memories was the damp, floral soil of the countryside, shared with her father on their infrequent nature walks on the edge of the subdivision. This place emanated an unsavory mélange of overripe fruit and rotten eggs.

A virgin path broke before her as she traversed downward, casting alarmingly loud cracks into the air. They echoed hollowly from the overpass's support columns. Sweeping her head back and forth, she caught only glimpses of her surroundings. Though the sun had behaved normally thus far today, its meager light died at the lip of the ravine.

She ventured farther, forward and down, booted feet falling heavily with each unpredictable drop. Another snap grabbed her attention, this one not of her making. Esther jutted her neck forward, casting her headlamp back and forth over the landing below.

An indistinct cluster of eyes shone in the darkness.

This is what I came here for.

This is not a surprise.

They're just animals.

A litany of reassuring thoughts streamed from her rational mind, barely soothing the wild goosebumps that had taken charge of her flesh.

With halting steps forward, she continued, stepping past crumbled concrete barriers and stabbing rebar, into the narrow fissure of the dry creek bed that lined the ravine. The eyes of her prey didn't waver. She continued, caution giving way to hunger, dreams of seared meat filling her belly. She hadn't expected such docility but was keen to take what was offered.

Their gaze drew her in, unbothered by the artificial light of her headlamp as its scarlet beam came within range. She gripped the outer edges of the net, preparing herself for the throw.

As she closed in, the lamp revealed a total of six eyes gazing at her—from only two hares. Their *regular* eyes drooped lazily from fleshy pink sacs at the sides of their heads, while a third gaped from an oozing protrusion upon their foreheads. One was wheezing noisily, suffocating in a muzzle fabricated from its own whiskers. The other was frozen in a dumb smile of horror, gums pulled all the way to its eyes.

Esther hesitated, loosening her grip on the net. Too late she stumbled after it, losing her footing on the ground and tumbling down into the midst of the demented creatures. She couldn't contain a panicked cry as her headlamp flew from her forehead and she crashed hard into the thorny bramble of a desiccated rosebush, a hundred daggers embedding themselves in her back.

She was blind and awash in a hysterical flurry of screeching fur and paws, interspersed with the connecting thuds of her flailing elbows. She screamed until her throat grew hoarse, arms held over her face for protection even as the tumult ceased.

The sun had set. She couldn't handle the fact of that right now—all the empty darkness above her—and exorcised the thought immediately. The wolf was howling in the wind, invigorated by the scent of her lifeblood upon it.

Rasping screams eased into a guttural moan as Esther

moved her hand to her back, blindly searching her wounds. Instead of daggers she plucked out thorns—huge ones—and worked to dislodge herself from the barbwire-like mesh. Twisting sideways, she tumbled out with a final cry of torment onto a gravel bed.

Scornfully accepting the loss of her headlamp, she pawed at the cargo pouches on her belt until she felt the cold steel of her backup flashlight. Remembering to squint this time, she withdrew it and thumbed frantically for the switch, sighing with short-lived relief as its small cone of light beamed outward.

Her hunting net had snared her leg, and enmeshed within it was the crushed body of the gummy hare, multitudinous eyes still gaping. Revulsion gave way to hunger as she yanked the net free, careful not to lose her dinner. With bands of nylon digging into her wrist, she raced back up through the dense terraces of the putrid ravine, half carrying and half dragging it behind her.

Each branch she pushed past was harder to bypass than the last, the copse of pitiful aspen trees conspiring to block her retreat. They crowded around her, limbs lashing, at once adoring and hateful. As she approached the exit, stumbling forward with a burst of waning strength, a hideous wail rose behind her in protest. The erratic beam of her flashlight was her only sightline, directing her wildly back and forth between the overgrowth until she finally spotted the dimmed beam of light from her motorcycle's headlight. The wail escalated into a tsunami of rage as she crested the top of the ravine, assailing her ears with an inhuman yet living hatred.

Her eyesight distorted.

She was back in the forest, spread-eagled upon an iron mantel. Instead of thorns, her body was pierced through with daggers. Crimson roses blossomed from blood-soaked tips on her belly. Their petals shuddered and spread forth, giving birth to gelatinous clusters of elongated, humanoid fingers. They caressed her naked flesh, hungry with primal adoration.

"No!" she cried out in a strangled voice, shaking her head against the vision. She had to keep moving.

The ground trembled as an immense unseen mass dislodged itself from beneath the earth, splitting the dilated creek bed with a pained groan. She refused to look back. Whatever it was, it couldn't be allowed to be made real by being observed.

Net and hare were stuffed into the top bag.

Engine on.

Kickstand up.

The motorcycle's tires spun wildly, showering her in mounds of dirt before gaining traction. Esther fled as fast as the machine could take her, glued to its seat this time with the raw will of self-preservation and a congealed mat of her own blood.

ESTHER

2:5

Esther had ridden the whole way back to her hideout, but still she panted with physical exhaustion. Every time she began to acknowledge what she had (almost) seen, her heart would race, and a wave of gray began to veil her vision, threatening to pitch her into unconsciousness as a fail-safe against madness.

At least she had achieved her goal, albeit at the cost of one priceless headlamp, one set of clothes, and dozens of stinging wounds, which were hopefully shallow enough that she wouldn't have to dip into her spray-on-skin stash.

She leaned over the portable electric stove, clothed in a fresh pair of shorts, chest wrapped in bandages, hands still pale red from dressing the carcass. The chopped legs and loins looked normal enough freed of the hare's unsightly head, which she had unceremoniously lopped off outside the perimeter of her hideout, but they still smelled of the ravine: sickly sweet and sulfurous. The odor rolled through the kitchenette as the stringy meat crisped upon a steel pan, sending her stomach into opposing turns of hunger and revulsion.

She tossed it back and forth with a makeshift spatula crafted from a titanium humerus, fixated on the unchanging color of the meat. No matter how much she manipulated it, the flesh remained stubbornly glossy and raw-looking, burning in speckled patterns without cooking through. She double-checked the pan, retracting her finger with a pained yelp as she confirmed it was hot.

Excruciating minutes passed as the wan flesh refused to cooperate. Finally, Esther shoved the pan to the side in frustration and twisted the dial to OFF. She pulled at her cracked lower lip, staring at the meat, brushing her finger back and forth on her mouth. There was no choice. Eat or die. She had procrastinated with her encyclopedias too many nights in a row. All the knowledge in the world wouldn't fill her ribs.

————

Flavor wasn't something Esther had cared about for years. In her perpetual grind against starvation, she partook of all manner of human and animal food, unpalatable from the onset or barely coherent with rot. Even still, she gagged as she crammed the sticky meat into her mouth.

She sat cross-legged on the floor of the sorting room, between her closet and the kitchenette. An army of robotic fauna leered at her from every corner, but she mostly avoided their gaze for fear of offending with her meal.

Scattered at her feet were the bones of the hare, cleaved of their meat. Between sections, she sipped from a bottle of brackish water.

Tear, chew, gag, swallow, sip.

Tear, chew, chew some more, gag, swallow, gag, sip.

Tear, chew, refrain from spitting through puffed cheeks, swallow, gag, sip.

The pattern roughly repeated until the pan was emptied of its contents.

Esther slouched back, letting her chin fall toward her chest. What time was it, anyway? Between the infractions upon her sanity, the extreme effort, and constant darkness, the evening had felt like an eternity that encapsulated the entirety of her young adult life. The steel-framed grid of warehouse windows along the top of the wall revealed nothing, only the unyielding black of night.

"What?" She didn't know to whom or what she asked the question, before lurching forward with a violent and total projectile vomit.

ESTHER

2:6

Esther had barely made it to her cot, dragging herself through her own acidic discharge to get there. Somehow, she managed to traverse the floor, wriggling forward with limp limbs like one of her synthetic snakes, seizing violently at the steel feet of the bed before clambering up onto her thin mattress.

Pinpricks of heat burned across her face, like the blackened pimples of the corrupted hare meat, while violent chills racked her body. Foamy bile bubbled from her lips as she bucked up and down, her whole body protesting.

A whistling moan cascaded through the workshop as the wind outside intensified.

Her mind raced feverishly, looping over her fall into the ravine, the flailing paws, that stupid smile fixed as she chopped manically at the hare's neck on the side of the road. Its head had rolled almost comically slow into the ditch, beaming back at her with each revolution.

Another ragged belch tore through her esophagus, spraying a sour mist of particulates and stomach acid onto her nostrils and clenched eyes. An involuntary groan juddered past chattering teeth as the poison coursed heedlessly out of her.

The wind began to gale, shuffling the metal shingles of the warehouse roof. They beat down upon the building in a discordant rhythm, smashing violently as though instructed by the monster under the creek to find her and crush her. The whole structure shook with the force of it, sending Esther's hands to her ears. The psalms she had learned, and fell back to in the worst moments, eluded her, jumbled into incoherence by the manic thrumming.

She struggled for some familial anchor to bind herself to, but the faces of her parents were gone, reduced to shadows. Once more, only Miriam's face looked back at her: round and eager, framed in her classic mane of unkempt, honey-blonde hair, imploring her to ignore the noise and come play with her instead.

Esther hated playing alone, but every time she conceded to hang out with her younger sister it ended in frustration. Miriam was too wild, totally unwilling to follow any rules. Everyone was yelling and usually crying by the end of it. She missed her nonetheless, especially now, latching what little of her attention she could onto the familiar visage.

After several more painful retches, her nervous system settled sufficiently for her to regain control of her body. Her breathing calmed, her shivering reduced, and she sank into stillness. The closet was dark, lit only by the creeping glow of the LED lamps left running in the sorting area outside her door.

Too dark, too loud, too hungry, too much pain.

Esther craned her stiffened neck to look at her shelves, eyes resting on the vague outline of a semi-spherical shape near the top. With gritted teeth, she forced herself upright, pushing off the bed toward the object. Her hand reached out uncertainly, fingers gliding over a raised *M* that was printed into the plastic night-light. She closed her eyes, breathed in deeply, and pressed down until she heard a click, waiting as long as her breath would hold before exhaling and looking upward.

Beamed upon the ceiling was an orange field of stars and a crescent moon. Esther fell back onto the bed, eyes drinking in the light until they could hold no more.

ESTHER

2:7

The forest was as she remembered: thick with the heady perfume of pine and soil, abuzz with life, its shade lending refreshing reprieve from the exceptionally hot summer weather. It was Saturday.

Esther held her parents' hands—"Three, two, one, jump!"—hopping forward as they lifted her up. She smiled and closed her eyes as the bright afternoon sun filtered through the canopy onto her face. Miriam was running ahead with arms outstretched, dancing her fingers along the brush.

"Three, two, one, jump!" She leapt forward again, opening her eyes. Ahead of them, a narrow path of knotted roots wound through the coniferous trees, carpeted at the edges with yellow lichen and drab green moss. She caught a glimpse of her sister's yellow raincoat before it disappeared around another bend.

"Three, two, one..." Esther abbreviated the third round, too distracted with worry and resentment for her fleeing sister.

Turning around, she saw she was alone and that the path had closed, replaced with an impassable wall of interwoven trunks and branches. A thunderous orchestra of warbles and chirps emanated from all around her as the nesting birds' calm was violated by a foreboding breeze.

"Miri!" she yelled, annoyed that she had to stop her game again because of her sister's mischief.

"Miri!"

Esther plodded forward. The sun dimmed as she ventured deeper into the forest, chasing after a fleeting glimpse of yellow coat or pink sneakers. By the time she found herself in a clearing, the day had turned dark.

"Miriam?"

The clearing was roughly octagonal in shape, shot through with tree roots so thick and tall that they clearly demarcated the space into walled triangles. On the opposite end, the path dipped down into a valley. She climbed methodically through the geometry, hands becoming slick with effort as she finally neared the drop-off.

Dim starlight trickled down on her from an open whorl of interlocking branches in the treetops overhead, eliciting a harried glance upward. Familiar constellations wavered in the heavens, except where they were obscured behind a perfectly round void of purest black at their center.

The echo of poorly articulated singsong wafted toward her, pulling Esther back to the precipice.

"Miriam?" she called again, nervously peering into the darkness below.

Esther stepped forward, carelessly, and snagged her foot on a root, pitching sideways over the edge with a cry. She tumbled downward, cradling her head as her body bounced off tree, shrub, and rock. Three-eyed nocturnal creatures glared at her as she crashed through the bramble, bouncing at the bottom into a somersault that sent her forehead smashing into the jagged bark of a felled tree.

Her heart thumped loudly in her head, drowning out the

residual sounds of the forest until it was all she could hear. Squinting past the trickles of blood, she saw a wide creek bed, slowly filling with a viscous dark brown fluid that bubbled up from the bowels of the earth.

As the thumping grew into a deafening beat, the creek bed split wider, sending geysers of the liquid pluming upward. Esther stood slowly, backing up as she did so. The roar of her heartbeat matched the violent uprooting of the earth below, sending her sprawling as something emerged from the chaos.

She didn't want to look. She wanted to run.

"Your eyes must be opened."

Standing beside her was the angel, awash in light. The halo of fire orbiting its scalp was enormous, quaking with barely contained fury.

Esther stared directly into its eyes, unwilling to bear witness with her own. Reflected in the perfect blackness, she saw a rising pillar of chitinous shell, from which unfurled a legion of scaled tentacles, each tipped with multi-jawed mouthfuls of steel incisors. The body bearing the carapace was bloated, segmented into two sections like a grotesquely oversized spider, but instead of hair, its abdomen was stitched with the tortured, silently screaming faces of the damned. Those that had eyes rolled them in agony, those with mouths gagged out lengths of rusted chain that the beast spun into a mechanical web.

It had no face of its own.

"This is God's punishment, for humanity's sin of mass suicide."

She tried to close her eyes, straining futilely against the will of the creature that held them.

"Only you can stop it. Only you can redeem them."

Trembling, she reached a tentative hand forward, fingers extending to touch the angel's light. Its halo flared outward in response. A deafening clamor rose from the beast as it sensed its doom, and as the damned souls trapped within it sensed their release.

A detonation of cleansing fire engulfed the valley, annihilating the demon in its midst, the forest, and what was left of the world beyond. Esther stood alone and untouched, watching its wake recede into oblivion.

ESTHER

2:8

Gasping.

Sitting upright on a surface. A bed? Her bed?

Who was *her*?

Scant light leaked in from the room(?) next door.

If she was gasping, she must be breathing. But her throat was too far away, lungs farther yet, to confirm any kind of respiration.

One more triangle to climb out of.

A young woman on the other side, curled into a ball.

Her?

Her.

Esther emerged, sluggishly, from her asphyxia, rocking back and forth, fixed upon the dream before it could fade.

Was it a dream? She had been there. Which parts were imagined? What needed to stay masked for self-preservation?

"Only you can stop it."

She had been there.

The memory of the splintering earth, thunderous agony, pressed at her eardrums, wobbling with her blood pressure. She had seen *it* in the angel's eyes: the... demon. But how could that be real? Where were the stars? And where the fuck was the moon?

The last curse rang through her head in her mother's voice.

"Only you can redeem them."

Esther rubbed her calloused hands over her prickled skin, wrapping herself in the pristine song of that voice, somehow male and female, young and old—very old, primordial.

Why her?

She was lucky to be alive. The sensible thing to do at this point would be to head back into the city. Murderers lurked everywhere, but at least they were human. She could avoid them like she had done years before, maybe find some food out there.

And then what?

She would still be alone, always alone, living for... what? So that she could learn about lemmings, lemons, and lemurs? She loved her books, but she also knew deep in the still-immature recesses of her mind that they were a distraction, temporarily keeping her sane—alive, without purpose.

She stared tiredly at her shelves, noting that many of her encyclopedias had fallen into a heap upon the floor, probably from last night's convulsions. Standing with an uncertain wobble, she immediately set to reordering them, brushing the rancid, organic residue from their bindings as she placed them back into chronological order. One of the Bibles was splayed open among them, a colorful bookmark propping it open to a beloved psalm. She lifted it, gingerly, mouthing the long-ago-memorized words she had recruited as her primary defense against fear and loneliness.

Esther lost herself in the task of restoration, conveying everything to its place, every spine aligned the same distance from the edge of its shelf. When she finished, she turned her attention to her hands: they were filthy, permeated with blood—hers and the hare's—and translucent streaks of hardened vomit. Her uneven fingernails were black with grit. Turning her hands over, she gazed at her arms: also filthy, lined with red tracers where her skin had peeled off from the tumble.

Retiring from the bedroom closet, Esther walked purposefully to her kitchenette/bathroom, absently flicking on the light switch. A burst of fluorescence hummed to life above her, casting her pallor in fragments onto the cracked mirror.

When was the last time she'd properly bathed? It seemed an important question now, but the only tangible memory of it was when her child body had changed into that of a woman. She hadn't been prepared, save for a single awkward conversation with her mother, but there was more water then at least. And the bleeding seemed to pass as quickly as it came, her starved body rejecting the absurd notion of childbearing almost immediately.

"Why me?" she asked her reflection.

Esther pulled open the door of the countertop cabinet, pushing aside shop rags and solvents until she found the cardboard box of sanitary wipes she was hoarding, plucking out several plastic cylinders and setting them before her.

Without pause, she shuffled out of her clothing and set to work, grimacing silently as the antibacterial chemicals scoured her face, neck, chest, torso, legs, feet, and privates. She flossed between every finger, toe, in her bellybutton, and deep into the soles of her feet until the stubborn grime that had accumulated there was replaced with newly pink, inflamed flesh.

Frowning at the muck that persisted under her fingernails and toenails, she found a wooden-handled steel-wire brush and proceeded to buff them into a glossy, bloodied sheen. Holding her hands up before her again, she turned them this way and that, exhibiting every crevice to the overhead lights until satisfied.

Back in her closet, Esther retrieved a black armor-plated riding suit from a doubled-up hanger, wincing as she pulled the second skin over her own flayed flesh. From her gun cabinet she retrieved a fancily accessorized assault rifle, then paused, considering the close confines of the ravine, and swapped it for a much simpler pump-action 12-gauge shotgun.

Scanning the room for anything else she might need, her gaze landed on Gray Cat. It stared back at her with milky eyes, perched eagerly forward on its single front leg.

"No more adventures for you, my friend."

ESTHER

2:9

The sun was small and red, identical one day to the next, as though beaming through a veil of perpetual smoke. Its light seemed diminished without the accompaniment of the moon, the marginal heat it radiated supplanted by the thermal drafts of nuclear Armageddon.

Esther shivered despite the heat. She was scanning the ruined roadway above, seeking out a vehicle light enough and near enough to tipping from the crowded overpass that she would have a chance.

A bright yellow electric compact with a black roof caught her eye. It had crested a hill of other vehicles, mounting them like some sort of queen bee before the driver abandoned it. The passenger door flapped idly in the wind, groaning against its hinges. The driver-side door was rusting casually in the brush below the overpass.

It would have to do.

———

The ravine welcomed her back with open arms. She had barely escaped the smothering thatch the night prior, but tonight a broad path presented an unobstructed route down to the creek bed. A familiar polyphonic moaning beckoned her forward, slipping elusively like contrails between the outstretched branches of the aspen.

She hesitated, feeling the real world fracture around her. It juddered with each inhale, like a corrupted digital recording, her visual frame rate lagging behind the sweep of her gaze. Then with each exhale, it spooled back up, recentering her doubled vision on the path upon which she now walked.

The mashed-together moans gained fidelity as she approached, segregating into a symphony of human voices: male, female, adult, and child. They alternately whispered, groaned, and wailed, beseeching her with unintelligible pleas. The only constant within their cacophony of lust and despair was an underlying tone of immeasurable suffering.

Esther stepped back from the precipice, unsuccessfully willing the images of last night's dream from her memory. She thumbed the quick-adjust tab of her shotgun sling, slackening it for use.

"Only you can stop it."

Swinging the weapon carefully around, she stepped forward again. The sun was cooperating today, at least, remaining level enough in the sky that she wasn't completely in the dark. A narrow beam of white light shone from the flashlight mounted on the shotgun's accessory rail, barely permeating the darkness beyond.

"Okay..."

Fallen branches snapped as she proceeded into the thicket. Dead strands of wildflower shifted noisily underfoot. She didn't flinch. There was no element of surprise to be gained—this had happened before and would happen again. The only difference was that she was ready this time. As ready as she'd ever be.

The loose soil of the decline transformed into wet sludge as she neared the creek bed, the hungry tar sucking noisily at the passage of her booted feet. Each step left behind a fleeting imprint, which quickly bubbled over with oily brown liquid before being reabsorbed.

Time expanded as she descended, slowing as she passed beyond the sun's reach, as she passed an infinite number of identical trees, before snapping her back onto the landing, alone.

She could feel the thing before she could see it, swaying forward as its impossible mass pulled at her like gravity. Her eyelids fluttered, protesting as she looked up. There were no other eyes to proxy through, no eventual waking upon which her terror could abate. There was only her and the eyeless demon towering before her, birthed at last into the world, the agonized mouths upon its distended belly mewling like hungry newborns.

"Only you can redeem them."

The prayer she had prepared stammered forth from her quivering mouth.

"Wh... when the wicked came against me, to eat up my flesh—"

Esther's voice broke with building terror. Tears flowed freely from her eyes.

"My enemies and foes," she rasped, half whispering while raising her shotgun with shaking arms. "They stumbled and fell."

ESTHER

2:10

Esther's ears were still ringing. The concussion of the shotgun slugs had been amplified by the tight walls of the ravine, lashing back at her skull with the violence of their propulsion. A shrill tone oscillated back and forth between her ears, disrupting her balance as she ran for her life.

She managed to discharge four rounds, eliciting surprised shrieks of rage from the beast but little else. She had hoped for more—a disabling wound at least—but was also unsurprised; how could the manifestation of a dream die so simply?

She scrambled up the ravine on all fours, cursing as the sticky muck pulled at her arms and legs, again having to shoulder her way past monstrously thorned brush. She swept wildly at the overgrowth with her gloved hands, shotgun swinging behind her.

An oceanic roar rose from below, shattering her momentum with a wave of alien hatred/dismay/beckoning. Esther hesitated, the vision of the black city appearing before her, a miasma of souls thrumming together as one.

She didn't have to suffer alone.

She could stop, rest now, and join them.

The air was still.

"Wake up! Esther, wake up!"

Miriam was pulling at her blanket, flapping it up and down over her feet.

"Leave me alone," Esther cried back, still half-asleep, furious at having to endure yet another ruined morning. She just wanted *Mommy to wake her up, to welcome her into the day with a hug. Not her sister.*

"I want to play!"

"Nooo!" Esther howled.

Her legs were moving again, burning with exhaustion, dry tendons snapping in her knees. The mudslide was behind her, along with the beast. Her motorcycle hummed anxiously just over the crest, urging her to safety.

Another roar assailed her, followed by the shriek of chains whirling through the air, plunging themselves into the mantle of the ravine as the beast traversed upward on its many biomechanical legs. A litany of whispered curses scoured the edges of her consciousness:

"Come back!"

"We love you."

"We hate you!"

"Your family misses you."

"We miss you!"

"You belong with us."

"You all do!"

Ignoring the demonic pleas, Esther quickly double-checked the lengths of paracord that wrapped the bike like a bow, tied into the frame from front to back and secured with knots perfectly reconstructed from her survivalist manuals. Huffing with the effort of her climb, she straddled the seat, pressing into the engine cover with the full weight of her body. Sparing a final glance behind her, she was both relieved and mortified to see the thing's upper abdomen break free.

She left the kickstand down and gingerly twisted the throttle. Twin electric motors surged with torque, pulling hard on the length of rope that connected the bike to the compact car teetering on the overpass. Its wheels churned slowly forward, inching the motorcycle deeper into the ground with each revolution. All around her, viscous fluid bubbled up from the cracked soil.

"Come! On!" she shouted angrily.

Fumbling at her terrain controls, she toggled down the motorcycle's tire pressure, then deepened the throttle, discharging jets of webbed soil behind her. A metallic groan joined the beast's infernal roaring as the highway wreck began to shift. High above them, the abandoned carcass of the yellow compact staggered forward, clambering with shredded tires over the roof of a bulky sport utility vehicle.

With an explosion of human screams, ravaged sheet metal, and guttural wailing, the overpass finally unloaded its occupants onto the ravine below. Guardrails peeled open as one car followed the next, descending like a derailed train along with massive chunks of concrete pulled from the overpass itself.

Untethered, the motorcycle charged forward uncontrollably before spinning out. The world collapsed around Esther as she fell backward, dragged along the dirt road. Thick plumes of gravel and dust billowed over her as she slid several meters, the hard poly-ceramic of her bodysuit sparing her from being skinned alive.

"No, no, no," she blurted as she spun to an unceremonious halt, slashing her arms downward to see where the motorcycle had fallen on her. She curled into a fetal position, realizing with relief that she wasn't pinned.

"Thank you. Thank you," she sighed, to no one in particular, to her savior at the grocery store.

Rubble continued to waterfall from the overpass as she lifted herself unsteadily from the ground, pulling on her frayed sling so the shotgun was clamped tight to her side. The weakling sun was low in the sky, teetering just over the horizon. A mushroom cloud of red-tinged dust curled up from the area where the demon had been.

The wolf on the wind was silent.

Still, she had to be sure.

Esther stood still for several minutes, frozen in anticipation of a second attack. The normally hot air currents felt cool against the simmering inferno of her brow, refreshing even. Though her ears still rang with the combined onslaughts of the evening, her head felt clear, unclouded.

She recalled the scary, grown-up movies she watched unsupervised with Miriam in their final days. The hero would always turn their back after slaying the monster, no matter how much the girls yelled at the screen for them not to. And every single time, the monster wasn't actually dead and would attack them again. It was a certainty.

She had to be sure.

Esther stepped forward, then immediately yelped as her right leg gave out, buckling from the hip. Though her scoured armor had spared her skin, it didn't do much to dull the actual impact. Quickened breath overtook her for a moment as she panicked over the idea of being immobilized out here. If the injury was serious, her first aid kit wouldn't be of much help.

She couldn't turn her back.

She had to be sure.

Esther clamped down on her pain, her hunger, her exhaustion, her torment, and limped forward. The beam of her weapon light swayed erratically, strobing the way ahead.

One step closer.

The debris cloud was impenetrable.

Another step closer.

The last rays of the sun melted behind her.

Crooked footsteps, echoing painfully in the night.

She didn't have to turn her back—the tentacle pierced her shoulder without any warning. No cars lifted dramatically from the heap. No roar of revenge prefaced the attack. Only sudden, excruciating pain as an enormous, mouthed barb of slithering scale, rolling over the tentacle's surface like a conveyer belt, penetrated her flesh and nerves, leaving her left arm hanging limp.

She was lifted bodily through the air, over the rubble toward the still-living beast. The stench of sulfur mixed with copper burned in her nostrils. The torment was too much. The last of Esther's will seeped out of her along with her blood, head drooping. Her shotgun swung uselessly from her right shoulder.

"Wake up!"

"No..." she whispered inaudibly. She would stay under the blanket. She would wait for her mother.

"Wake! Up!"

Her eyelids fluttered open, gazing uncaringly at the abomination that zoomed into view below. It had been partially crushed, most of the vivisected human faces upon its body pulverized into scarlet smears. Its immense spiderlike legs were all destroyed or pinned.

At least it'll be stuck here, she thought idly.

A fleeting wave of darkness rolled over her.

As she came to, Esther's field of vision was filled with the undulations of its alien flesh, constantly expanding, contracting, swirling, and color-shifting like an oil slick upon open water. No part of the beast's body was static. She was being lowered into a growing vortex, which had emerged between the meaty pulp of two caved-in skulls to make room for her.

"Esther! I want to play!"

She blinked.

"I made a present for you!"

The fingers of her right hand twitched, caressing the cold steel of the shotgun's stock.

"Wake up!"

Cycle the action.

A spent shell sailed silently downward, falling into the child-sized hand of a mostly human arm that sprouted from the side of the demon's body. Its delicate fingers caressed the red plastic before closing furtively over it, receding as far back into the host as it could.

A fresh slug clicked into place.

"Fine..." she conceded. She knew the game her sister would want to play. It was always the same one.

Esther fired straight down into the orifice, her wrist snapping as the recoil propelled the weapon back up at her. The tentacle retracted, plunging her face-first onto the beast's abdomen. Her mangled weapon arm slipped into the opening where her soul was meant to be.

Pinned and now presumably mortally wounded, the demon's flesh rippled in agony, its inhuman shrieks filling the black of dusk. But still, it did not die.

Her eyes drifted shut.

Miriam pulled the blanket off her and took her hands in her own.

"Time to wake up! I made a present for you."

It was always the same game.

Esther stepped reluctantly out of bed. She knew the "present" would probably be some old toy or book of her sister's that she had stuffed into a repurposed gift box. Miriam loved her boxes, loved giving gifts. But Esther couldn't resist, just in case there really was something good. She loved presents.

"Close your eyes."

Miriam led her out of the bedroom.

"Keep closing them."

Esther's broken hand extended deeper into the belly of the beast, seeking.

"Keeeeep closing them."

Something hot pulsed at her fingertips. Something vital.

"Keep closing them!"

The beast's bucking downshifted into a fearful quiver.

"Now open them!"

Esther clenched her fist around the alien organ and yanked. With a scream of reawakened pain, she pulled the ruins of her arm from the demon's body and flopped onto her back.

Silence descended upon the ravine.

ESTHER

3:1

Esther sat upon a triangle, surrounded by other triangles, within a polygon that was both infinite in size and grazed the edge of existence. It was pearlescent black, unlit, and yet she could clearly see the delineating diagonals that faded into the non-horizon.

Her whole world was this single plane. Above her, an indeterminate distance away, was a second plane of existence, composed of singular light. Another *her* sat within it.

The angel sat cross-legged in the first plane, directly in front of her. Upon the light plane, she sat alone. Pulsing in her hands was an ultra-dense faceted sphere, perfectly opaque and nonreflective.

"It is time," the angel intoned.

"Time?"

"You are dying. You must make your choice."

Esther peered down at the object in her hands, attempting to turn it but unable to do so for its immense weight. It transformed nonetheless, crystalline facets deconstructing into a matrix of tubular channels. Dozens of ventricles puckered open, oozing a waxy black essence onto her strained wrists, penetrating her distended veins.

"Partake of the accelerant."

"The accelerant! The accelerant!" a chorus of female voices whispered excitedly from nowhere.

"Gain their power," it continued.

She was filled with half-formed questions. They bubbled up from her subconscious but dissolved as they reached her throat, leaving her only with the ability to respond directly.

"Their? Power?"

"Humanity needs a weapon if it is to flourish again. You are that weapon. But you must be sharpened."

Esther struggled to fabricate enough time for a pause.

"Who are you?" she hissed.

The angel seemed to consider for a moment, eyes beaming with invisible radiance.

"I am your messiah."

"Mes... si... ah..." Esther parsed the word into its constituent syllables, their echoes carrying to the upper plane. She looked upward/downward at herself, in that place of nothingness—of aloneness.

The emergent organ tremored within her hands.

"Time is running out. Make your choice," the angel insisted, the static sculpture of its perfect face betraying no concern.

Esther looked upon her new savior with alternating adoration and terror. A singular question emerged intact from the tumult of her subconscious background chatter.

"Will you stay with me?"

Again, the angel paused before nodding, once, the fiery halo upon its head momentarily blinding her.

"I will guide thy hand," it assured her, its voice sweet like honey. The familiar thickness of it swelled in her throat, drowning whatever questions remained there. She had been alone so long. The hollow pain of solitude was worse than any physical injury or starvation she had suffered.

"What do I do?" she asked, swallowing hard.

The angel gestured brusquely at the foul object in her hands, which seemed so strangely organic against the precise angularity of her surroundings.

"Partake—"

The rind of it was in her mouth even before the angel finished speaking. She crammed it in, chewing savagely at the surprisingly hot flesh. It scalded the roof of her mouth, burned her gums, ate at the enamel of her teeth, yet she swallowed over and over, neck dripping with the juice of it, until it was fully consumed.

Esther stared at her hands, black-on-black with gore. The residue filled every crevice of her skin, smoothing the wrinkles of her knuckles into a glove-like sheen, extending her fingertips into sharpened hooks. She stared at her nails, squinting at the rivulets of agitated liquid as a slow tremor grew in her hands, vibrating down her arms.

Even as the tremor grew into a rapid quaking, Esther felt her heart slow, as though detached completely from her limbs. Panic swelled as her body retreated from her control. The seizure spread into her legs and feet, then her torso and gullet, pitching her about in violent fits. She arched back farther than she would have thought possible for a human spine, limbs thrust rigid from her body as though already stiffened in death.

The white plane wavered in her vision.

The angel stared at her, unmoved from its spot.

"You resist."

Esther stared at it desperately, struggling to speak through the oily froth seeping from her clenched jaw. She wanted to yell at it, to curse its name, but her tongue was as immobilized as the rest of her.

"Something is holding you back," the angel declared obtusely. "Someone."

Esther thrashed her head from side to side, begging for assistance, for clarity. Inside her retreating mind she was screaming askance at the angel, which had barely shifted its posture to better observe her. It stared at her, pinning her to the ground with those unyielding eyes, scouring her soul.

"A sacrifice is required," it concluded. "A life, for yours."

Esther saw her own horrified face reflected in the blackness, her throat engorged at either side. She focused all her remaining strength on pushing past the pressure that locked her larynx shut.

"Bu—but. But. Only. Me. Only me." She retched the words out, past swollen nodules and crumbling teeth. She felt her bones and tissues transforming, densifying.

The angel paused as though to blink, but its pearlescent black eyes were unmoved.

"It wasn't always."

ESTHER

3:2

Esther blinked away a ridge of snow from her eyelashes and heaved her backpack from the floor onto the bed, hands gliding back and forth over the few remaining sequins of a heart pattern sewn on its front: silver, red, silver, red, silver—oops, another one fell off.

She retrieved a small plastic bag full of displaced sequins from the front pouch, carefully opening the zipper latch so it wouldn't tear this time. Pinching the new orphan with her fingers, she lifted it carefully to the bag and deposited it with the rest.

"Maybe we can find some glue and fix it," Miriam suggested.

Esther shrugged, despondent. She unzipped the main compartment and peered inside.

Miriam's posture picked up with hope. "I'm so hungry," she moaned, then beamed pleadingly at her big sister, clutching at Gray Cat with one hand and unconsciously pulling at the frayed tatters of her loose-fitting jean jacket with the other.

"I know!" Esther retorted impatiently. "I know..." she repeated, softening, "so am I."

She looked in the backpack, clawing with one hand while

the other rubbed absently at her gums, feeling the newborn nub of a lost tooth. It felt soft, like her mommy's touch on a good day.

She sighed and closed her backpack.

"Nothing left," she declared. "Maybe tomorrow."

Scant tears dribbled down Miriam's dusty face, but she held her five-year-old composure. Wrapping both thin arms around her stuffy, she retreated clumsily to the end of the mattress and curled onto her side, quickly collapsing into sleep.

Esther sang to herself, back pressed hard into the wall, waiting. Waiting. When she heard her sister's weak snores, she slowly pressed herself back up and dug her hand into her backpack, retrieving the foil-wrapped package hidden there.

Unfolding it with the utmost care to not wake her sister, she paused for a long moment, staring at the half-eaten protein bar. It was deep brown on the outside, golden yellow inside, and lined with chocolate drizzle. An uneven bite mark delineated where she had left off.

She knew she should have shared this one, and the ones before it. The dilemma racked her young conscience, but as before, she concluded it was more important that she eat, so she would have the strength to take care of them both.

Esther popped the whole thing into her mouth, chewing past a relief-filled sigh. The sweetness of it soothed her soul. Satisfied, and feeling only a little guilty, she burped quietly and sat back against the wall, eventually drifting off to sleep.

When she awoke the next morning, Miriam, her sister, was dead.

ESTHER

3.3

Bloody tears gushed from Esther's eyes as she contorted upon the floor. She moaned through clenched teeth, head thrashing sluggishly back and forth, raging against the remembrance of her past choices. Of that single irreversible choice.

Through blurred vision, she saw another figure had appeared upon the plane of light, seated cross-legged above/in front of her.

Miriam?

She was almost the same age as Esther was now, yet the characteristic roundness of her still-living face and wild hair was undeniable. She wore the same outfit as on that last day, only larger. The mildewy blanket that Esther had tucked her into on her death bed lay crumpled behind her. A small smile hung at her pale blue lips, and her arms extended outward invitingly.

Esther's tortured gurgling stilled as her eyes focused on those gossamer fingers. Still racked by convulsions, she managed to maneuver onto her side, struggling to bring her streaked face to her sister's knees.

The *her* that was above was rocking forward and back, hands clenching and unclenching in tandem with her *other* hands, which spasmed uncontrollably below. She restrained the impulse to reach forward, instead struggling through pursed lips to speak—to plead, to apologize—but she was mute.

Neither Esther spoke.

She could not take it back.

She would do it again.

Her own life was more important.

And so, she simply stared, across time and space, until there was only upward, not forward, and the white plane, along with her sister, was gone forever.

Memories unraveled from her like parasitic worms escaping a dying host. Separated at last from her childhood, her body calmed, eyelids fluttering shut as a soothing shadow smothered her.

"Rest now, Esther."

Everything was darkness.

"There's work to be done."

ESTHER

"Miri..." Esther breathed, eyes sliding open.

She lay on her back, chest moving easily in and out. There was no panic, no ambiguity as to her surroundings like on most oxygen-starved mornings—if this was even the morning—just her steady breath moving through a sleep-refreshed body.

A scarlet ray of sunshine beamed onto her face from the open closet door. Crystalline sparkles of dust swirled within it like fireflies, separating and converging into a miasma and separating again, refracting the light of the sun into a rainbow of microscopic colors.

She allowed her gaze to blur, remaining present in her body for uncounted minutes, mind quiet, before rising to sit. As she did so, a deep ache emerged from within her left shoulder, sending pain down to her fingertips and up through her collarbone. She grimaced, wondering if she had slept on it funny and pinched a nerve. Rubbing at the smooth, unscarred skin, she breathed through the rhythmic pulsing of the pain until it eventually subsided, then sighed with relief.

Swinging herself to the side, Esther pressed her bare feet onto the ground, feeling the cool concrete against her toes and heels. She was naked, the backs of her arms rising in slight goosebumps as a breeze snaked in from the machine room. Again, she paused, breathing deeply, feeling the gentle currents brush against the fine hairs on her skin.

It's time to go.

The thought tumbled into her without warning, dislodging her from the unfamiliar serenity she had established. There were no circumstances surrounding it, only an instinctual knowledge that something worse was coming and that she couldn't hide in this place any longer.

She had to be there to meet it.

Disregarding her usual modesty, Esther walked naked to the bathroom/kitchenette. She would get cleaned up, then figure out what she could carry with her and what would stay behind. The encyclopedias and binders were certainly a leave-behind, as she had mostly memorized their contents anyway. Weapons, armor, medicine only. There would be no room for keepsakes where she was going.

Flicking on the light, Esther looked up and froze. Her reflection stared back at her from the mirror, but it was... wrong. Her cheeks were filled out again, no longer emaciated from starvation. Her skin was distinctly gray, ashen as the nuclear snow after the bombs, leaving her wondering if she had become spontaneously color-blind—except for her eyes. Once steel blue, they now shone a vivid magenta, sparkling with facets of silver and gold.

The sickly pink eyes of the hare stared back at her with each revolution as its head rolled into the ditch.

Esther gripped the countertop as a tsunami of piecemeal memories flooded her.

She sat cross-legged in a black field, marking the center and end of the universe.

Standing over her left shoulder, a porcelain-faced angel

peered at her from the fractured panels of the mirror. She blinked in recalled pain, and it was gone.

Still staring at her shoulder, she noticed a small pink bubble forming on the skin, billowing outward from her pores. More bubbles frothed outward, until they eventually gave way to an inflamed rash.

"What..." she muttered, reaching out with her right hand, fingertips brushing against the raised pustules.

Without warning, her flesh split open, birthing an enormous, mouthed barb, chomping with steel incisors, its tentacled body swirling in a mesmerizing vortex.

Pulling her in. Pulling her down to the tortured souls below.

Esther screamed, slipping forward on the countertop until her head slammed against the glass with a sickly crack. Reopening her eyes, which had instinctively shut with the impact, she saw herself again, intact. Her shoulder was just a regular shoulder, albeit colorless. Breathing heavily, she gripped the countertop and pushed herself cautiously back.

A ragged line of crimson hung open above her brow, where jagged edges from the cracked mirror had gripped her flesh.

She jerked and retched, feeling her life finally seep out of her. A hollow had been opened where a memory once lived and was presently being filled with... something else.

She looked again, and the gash was gone.

Esther shivered, hugging herself, still enraptured by her own alien eyes. As her breathing normalized, she focused on the taut sinews of her arms, on the power that flowed beneath them. She squeezed her hands tightly against her biceps, pinching her flesh to wake from the dream if this was one.

"Humanity needs a weapon."

"You are that weapon."

"It's time," she said.

ESTHER

4:2

Esther couldn't remember if her motorcycle was charged but prayed deeply that it was. If she left right away, there would be time to make it into the city's warehouse district, hopefully resupply, and find shelter before the pitch black of night.

She knew where the auto-trucks used to go—the same ones she would watch from her bedroom window. A cluster of automated hive warehouses facilitated constant traffic in and out of the city. They were unpowered now, but likely still contained tons of nonperishable goods. She knew as much, based on the human traffic she had seen prior to moving into her workshop: indentured laborers herded like cattle by the "lopers"—the hyena people.

Esther stared at the black body armor hanging in her closet. It was deeply scuffed all along one side, a line of scars etched upon it like ancient runes, with dents in the poly-ceramic thigh plates. She remembered falling, rising, and falling again.

She had been there.

She had killed *it*.

The suit felt tighter this time, but not uncomfortable, as it hugged the hydrated muscles of her back and legs. She retrieved a set of bulky supplemental torso and shoulder plates from a shelf above the clothing rack, strapping each on in turn. There would be more violence tonight, of that she had no doubt. And no fear.

With her armor donned, Esther pulled on a black water-proof poncho and slipped into her tac boots. Normally she would have felt overly hot and constricted in so much clothing, but her new skin remained cool. To her leg she strapped a black Navy SEAL tactical knife—a rare treasure she discovered along-side the survival binders. Her go-bag was crammed with the last of her survival essentials, including a short-barreled personal defense weapon, two skimpy first aid kits, and her father's night vision binoculars.

A moment of anguish fell over her as she mourned all the possessions she would be leaving behind, so carefully main-tained and neatly organized. They had been her stalwart companions, and in some cases her teachers, for years. She took a moment, scanning from right to left, top to bottom, recording each precious object in her memory, then walked away from them for the last time, through the machine shop, and out the heaved-open back door.

Striding past the final outcrop of the warehouse, she turned and breathed a quiet "thank God" as she saw her motorcycle sidled up to the building and plugged in. Cross-checking her mental operations manual, she tested its terrain modes, brakes, batteries, and both motors. Satisfied, she strapped her bag onto the back and mounted.

Esther spared a final glance around at this cold place that had become an unlikely sanctuary, albeit an empty one that more often served as a convalescent home. The soulless eyes of its synthetic inhabitants stared back at her from junk piles she hadn't gotten to sorting yet.

She wondered how people had come to loathe each other so

much in the final years of humanity that instead of turning to one another for companionship, they chose to create these artificial facsimiles in their own image. And when their automatons didn't provide the succor they craved, they chose to destroy it all.

"You got what you deserved," she whispered, realizing then that she meant it.

Hunkering down, she punched the start button and twisted the throttle, speeding off toward the city.

ESTHER

4.3

The sun was low in the sky—lower than it should have been—
by the time she made it to the perimeter of the same warehouse
district she had visited and run from many years before. Five of
the enormous, nondescript rectangular buildings huddled in a
ring like tombstones, half a kilometer or so into an asphalt
valley off the freeway. The detritus of dozens of obliterated auto-
trucks lined the route.

Most of the warehouses were in tatters, their corrugated steel
skins peeled away by the shockwaves, leaving behind crooked
skeletal frames and blackened hive-works. Only the central
building—the one she was here for—was intact.

She hunched behind a concrete barricade by the off-ramp,
waiting for telltale signs of those who had been here before.
Glancing at the darkening sky, Esther rummaged for her binoculars, automatically toggling on the low-light mode and
bringing them up to her eyes.

The scene careened before her, bursting into a pixelated,
blown-out mess.

The binoculars crashed to the ground as she clutched at her
eyes, groaning at the sensory overload. Even the weak tendrils of

light from the setting sun suddenly seemed like too much in this moment, a glowing fireball that penetrated the hairline gaps between her fingers. A moment of choking panic shook her but quickly dissipated as she breathed through the onslaught, drawing on a newly forged inner strength. Slowly, with eyes only half-open, she released her hands, lifting her gaze back to the warehouse.

It was then that she realized she could see everything in precise detail, despite the distance and failing light. The sensation of being in the very place she was looking was uncanny. A wave of vertigo rolled over her as she struggled to reel her awareness back into her body upon the lookout. She twirled the corners of her eyelashes, carefully kneading her eyelids open and closed to acclimate herself.

Esther saw her eyes again in the mirror—saw them reflected in the impermeable black orb cradled in her hands. Despite carving trails of skin along her arms afterward, she hadn't awoken from a dream, but perhaps her new eyes had revealed a new reality. One in which the stars no longer existed. One in which she had been chosen. By God? By his messenger? What would her parents, so frightened of their own traditions, have thought?

She turned and crouched with her back against the barricade, looking out at the desolate ruin of her world. Beyond the freeway, to the east, the last recognizable remnants of the city eroded away, degenerating into an ocean of formless rubble as it reached the horizon. Desiccated tumbleweeds blew across the road from the sandy prairie beyond, hurried along by the perpetual howling wind.

She must have been chosen. How else would a little girl have survived this? *Why* would she have?

Esther pushed herself from her perch, scuttling over to the rear end of her motorcycle. Reaching up to her go-bag, she retrieved the black leather-bound Bible she had deposited into an outer compartment. Turning it over in her hands, she lovingly caressed the golden letters with her fingers.

Dozens of multicolored paper strips and old 3D bookmarks protruded from its singed and time-worn pages, marking her favorite passages. She fingered one after the other like keys on a piano, until landing on the undulating image of an owl. Turning the bookmark from side to side, she watched it blink its large all-seeing eyes over and over, then gingerly spread open the holy book.

Only portions of each verse were visible through old water damage. Breathing in, she intoned the words.

"I will destroy mountains and hills,
and all their grass I will dry out,
and I will make rivers into islands,
and I will dry up the pools."

The angel perched next to her, reading the words in tandem, their voices harmonizing into a multitude of voices. The pure radiance of its body beamed upon the pages, highlighting the text as Esther traced her fingers upon it.

"And I will lead the blind,
on a road they did not know—"

Her heart quickened.

"I will make darkness into light—"

A gunshot roused her from her spiritual reverie. Tucking the compact tome back into her bag, Esther scrambled back to the barricade, leaning over to peer around the side. A train of ragged humans had formed outside the central warehouse, chained and limping, lugging a wooden pallet loaded with boxes.

She cursed her amplified vision at the wretched sight of them. Most were emaciated to the point of being skeletal, taut skin pulled tight over jutting bones. She unconsciously ground her teeth together, remembering with vivid discomfort the hunger that plagued her for so many years and that had mysteriously subsided, for now at least. Some were "dressed" in loose rags, others were naked. They were uniformly layered in filth, sores, and burns. The cargo lurched under their shuffling death march.

It was then that Esther realized they were all children, the youngest maybe six.

A killing heat blew at the back of her neck.

At the head and tail of the gaggle were two sub-humans, fat and full, hunched over with the weight of their putrid corruption. They shifted anxiously, impatiently. One held up a rifle, still oozing with the smoke of the warning shot, while the other lashed at the children's legs with a massive whip fashioned from leather and barbed wire. An ancient cargo truck vibrated up the road, shrouded in a black fog of its own diesel fumes.

The wind picked up, its howl carrying down into the valley, ushering her to follow.

ESTHER

4.4

Droplets of blood beat slowly against the ground like pounding hammers. They dripped from every finger, traversing the circumference of her gore-filled nails before plummeting to the earth. They dripped from her face, sliding off the end of her nose, in trickles down her cheeks, and from her lips. They dribbled from her knees and feet, forming pools of deep brown in the sand-caked asphalt.

With each blink, a hammer fell. Esther's hearing was muted, just as it was after firing her shotgun in the ravine, except no shots had been fired. Her gun was back with the motorcycle. Her knife was still sheathed on her leg. She was, for all intents and purposes, unarmed.

And yet the hyenas were scattered in chunks before her, severed at every joint, bodies collapsed where their spinal columns had been extracted. They looked more like the chopped loins of the cursed hare than anything that may have once been human. She breathed heavily, heartily, flinching as each blink approached.

A billow of black smoke slithered at her feet, carried on the wind from the still thrumming cargo truck. Its driver-side door lay twisted upon the ground, and the exposed cabin had become an abattoir. The fumes circled her legs, licking hungrily at the moist ground around her. The acrid stink of diesel mixed with the heavy rust of blood.

Someone was crying: a voice, female, whimpering for help. An overturned pallet appeared before her, pitched over a mountain of crushed boxes. Half a dozen sticklike legs protruded from underneath it, some of them bent in unnatural directions.

The barely audible pleas, becoming louder as Esther's awareness returned to her surroundings, were emanating from a young girl who had been thrown from the scene. She kneeled weakly upon the ground, face planted, arms shielding her head from harm. A shockingly full heap of dirty-blonde hair fell in a lump around her.

Everyone else was dead.

Esther hesitated. An alarm was likely being sounded by now. There was no way this fracas would have gone unheard. But the girl reminded her of something. And the others... she should feel remorseful.

She should feel regret.

Straightening out of what she realized had been a crouch, Esther turned on her heel, striding quickly toward the warehouse entrance. A black streak hung in the air behind her as she appeared immediately at her destination. The garage door was large enough to accommodate an auto-truck, but she lifted it effortlessly, its rollers roaring like thunder, followed by a crash as it impacted against bare metal ceiling bumpers.

The building was enormous, but the front entrance was comparatively small, with most of the interior space occupied by the hive of algorithmically stacked boxes and long-dead shipping robots. She noticed the smell first: a ripe concoction of unwashed bodies, sickness, and something sweet—canned fruit, maybe. Two dozen people were arranged within, clearly segregated into master and slave. And yet they all stared at her the same way: slack-jawed, expressions devoid of anything other than base survival, terrified of this blood-drenched monster that had invaded the only shelter they knew. No one moved.

Esther looked upon them and felt the void in their hearts, the meaninglessness that she had once felt. They were shrouded in it.

I will make darkness into light.

The angel stood beside her, its halo sizzling with such intensity that the very air seemed like it might catch fire. The faces of those before her, both cadaverous and corrupted, were transformed into beatific busts. Whatever they were before, they were all her flock now, awaiting her pronouncement, awaiting their purpose.

Esther stood before them, straight-backed, powerful, baptized in blood. She relished the moment, feeling a surge of electric excitement across every pore. A surge of amplified certainty rose from her throat.

"Bow down before your messiah!"

Her shout cascaded like a thunderclap, reverberating through the entirety of the warehouse. Some of the wretched looked askance at one another, but most gawked with wide-eyed reverence. One by one, the survivors of Armageddon dropped to their knees. They stared at her, vacuous, awaiting her command.

I will lead the blind.

She glanced sidelong at her savior, looking for direction. It looked back with phlegmatic eyes, in which she saw only her own reflection.

Turning back to her congregation, she captured the eyes of each man, woman, and child until satisfied that she had their undivided, inescapable attention. With bloodstained arms extended outward, Esther slowly curled her upturned palms into fists.

It was time.

"Rise now," she called to them. "There's work to be done."

PART 2
DEADLANDS

BAPTISTE

ANOTHER WORLD

Lieutenant Philippe Baptiste peered into the dark chasm of the ancient subway below Bastion, curious at the late hour of his summons. It was highly irregular, made more so by the messenger's absence of subject or notice of accompaniment. Zero-three-hundred hours, audience with the lord commander, on matters of state security.

His gaze flitted tiredly from the platform over to the criss-crossing veins of railway, his still-wakening mind beginning to buzz with grim possibility. The station was otherwise empty save for the faint scurry of arthropods convulsing upon a narrow tributary of water, which flowed from a corroded fitting across the breadth of the station's broken mosaic tile floor. The relative comfort of his bunk was now well above and behind him, and the marginal circumference of the place, accentuated by the nasal hum of the generator powering its lights, pressed him forward.

He proceeded to a call box poled next to the ledge, paused with his hand outstretched, then turned and with a shake of his head stepped from the substation floor, dropping down onto the maintenance catwalk below. The iron grates lurched angrily under the sudden weight, then switched to an agitated chatter as he commenced his long walk to Central Command.

He had just enough time to make it, and the exercise at least —if not the particulate-heavy air—would hopefully banish the abbreviated sleep from his body. Even alone, he needn't acknowledge that handcars made him nauseous, the constant seesaw of the walking beam sending his stomach into very un-soldierlike knots. Especially in his current state. Still, he gave thanks to the forgotten peoples who built this place, as he did every time he walked its voluminous halls, for the resiliency of their labor.

The storied subway lines of the Metro, dutifully maintained but no longer powered, sprawled beneath most of the city, enabling its defenders exclusive access via handcart to any point of conflict, whether upon the parapets of the curtain wall or to the narrow boulevards of curfew-hushed residential districts. Every barracks in Bastion was connected by its network, with Central Command at its literal center via Central Station.

The cavern walls faded into darkness as he progressed beyond the substation's oppressive aura, lit only by distantly spaced electric lamps fizzling overhead. They swayed gently in the air currents of distant cars rushing their passengers from one sector of the city to the next. He squinted under the oscil-lating glow, eyelids twitching in tandem with the slow stutter of their decaying elements.

It seemed that each artifact of civilization he gazed upon now, whether restored or newly manufactured, appeared *shod-dier* than the last time he traversed the subway, as though the stucco veil of late evening that congealed in his eyes affixed itself to everything around him.

Baptiste found himself counting steps between each forlorn lamp, seeking to buttress his listless brain against the growing doubts that assailed him. At each tunnel junction, oil-fed lanterns ensconced within metal cages further illuminated the large stamped alphanumeric code of the district beyond. He noted each as he passed, his step count breaking with the involuntary recall of hard-fought victories and ghastly losses in the city's eternal street war against Hell. Even now, so many years after the successful fortification of their confined homeland against the chaos of the wilderness, no matter the height of the curtain wall or the strength of its gun emplacements, no zone was truly safe. Peace, safety—such concepts had long since been redefined as a substantive reduction in torture and death, rather than the total elimination of suffering.

He reflexively clenched his gauntleted hands, eager for the familiar heft of a hammer or rifle to realign his focus. Lord Commander Lucas Castillon—"the old man" as his fellow officers called him, and Baptiste's great-uncle—had been unusually agitated lately, which was unnerving given that his life had been so precisely codified by the regimented discipline of his guardian. Perhaps it was the inexorable deterioration of advanced age, but any weakness from the famously steady military commander of Bastion was cause for deep concern.

A sudden screeching wail, both mechanical and human, announced the approach of a racing handcar from the junction ahead. Baptiste stopped cold, noting the faded lettering upon the adjacent wall: 5B, just outside the perimeter of the inner city's military manufacturing complex.

The pride of Bastion and a second shield atop the underground bunkers of Central Command, it smothered the heart of the city in a labyrinthine maze of steel and concrete, wheeled gantries and superheated forges issuing forth the necessary weapons for Bastion's struggle against entropy. Soon the walls of the Metro would resonate like crystal to the song of the churn above, as the great war engines turned without end.

The metal cart barreled from the entrance, braked wildly,

then switched to a line that tracked back to the infirmaries. The interlude between movements was minuscule, yet he captured the scene with perfect recall, freezing the handcar and its occupants before him like a portrait even as they sped off: one soldier furiously working the cart, two others, bloodied but intact, wrestling with the flayed form of a fourth, his armor rent in jagged lines, weltered flesh beneath, eyes wide and wild.

But it wasn't the man's injuries that urged his hairs from the nape of his neck, it was the inhuman wailing: multi-pitched, savagely guttural, screaming obscenities against God. Flashes of battle again insinuated themselves upon his vision.

A swarm of chitinous tendrils swinging wildly around his head, razor-filled mandibles snapping one after the other against his armor, all striking from a single malignant tower of pustulous yellow flesh and scale that had suddenly exploded from a sinkhole on the factory floor. Its monstrous screams sieged his soul even as the multitude of appendages assaulted his body, threatening to eviscerate him from the inside out. A fractional eternity of horror, blessedly muted at the last minute by the crescendo of a chaplain's psalms, granting him the courage to level his rifle.

Baptiste arose finally and fully from the piteous depths of his malaise. As his training reasserted itself, the background noise of step counts and doubt burned and bubbled into the charged plasma of action. Running forward, he found the call box next to the evacuated junction and dialed 9-9-9: infirmary. The line remained frustratingly dead for long seconds before being picked up by an exasperated voice on the line, likely an exhausted chaplain running a double shift.

"What is it?" the man asked.

"This is Lieutenant Philippe Baptiste of the Black Watch."

A series of awkward thumps ensued as the man on the other end of the line adjusted his headset. He imagined the chaplain snapping hard to attention and cringed at the thought of it, as he was sure would many of his superior officers. Lieutenant Baptiste was accorded deference beyond his rank due to his familial relationship with the lord commander, but he hated it, resented the implications against that which he had truly earned through tireless training and impeccable service.

"Sir! What can I do for you?"

"A handcar is on its way to you with two wounded, and one..." He trailed off momentarily, knowing his words would exact a serious toll on the wounded soldier. "One corrupted. His brothers will vie for his soul, but it's too late. Call the duty guard to restrain them before they disembark."

Nothing but heavy breath from the line. Now that Baptiste was alert, he snapped uncharitably at the other's hesitation. "Acknowledge!"

"Yes, sir..." The weary acknowledgment of someone accustomed not just to injury and death but to fates far worse. "He will go with God."

Baptiste afforded himself a slam of the handset and a parting glance at the fading wake of the car before continuing determinedly on his way. The lord commander was waiting. No peace, no safety—only vigilance. The catwalk hummed.

———

Half an hour later, he converged upon Central Station. The remainder of his journey had been mercifully quiet, spent once more counting steps, though with some vigor rather than as a means of submerging deeper into disquietude. He wondered at the fate of the men he had passed before, reassuring himself— or at least blunting the impact of the encounter—with the certainty that they would not be the only soldiers in the infirmary this morning.

By his measure, it would be just before the designated

meeting time by now. Looking up as he walked, he envisioned the black starless void that still shrouded the city at this hour, giving cover to all manner of threat. The merciful grace of the sunrise was still an age away.

All around him and under him, the subway vibrated. The air had become an order of magnitude hotter and heavier with the acrid effluence of the factory-works above. Oil, diesel, waste, even the consecrated dead—it all burned so that Bastion could build. The sour malodor of it stung his nostrils, eliciting a choke, followed by a phlegmy fit of coughing. Meanwhile, the sweat-soaked folds of his undershirt had snaked loose above his vambraces and gorget, visibly exhibiting his discomfort for all to judge. Truly tonight, even after his brief moment of invigoration, he felt like a weakling.

"Announce yourself, stranger!"

Baptiste froze as an explosion of light erupted around him. Without realizing it, he had sauntered right past the level crossing barriers that normally halted all traffic into Central Command. They were now well behind him, along with the call boxes he should have used to announce his unceremonious arrival from the maintenance circuit.

He squinted past the glare of the perimeter spotlights that shunted down the tracks toward him, tears streaming from his already irritated eyes. The station proper was barely visible past its defensive bulwark. Rows of pitted concrete barricades blocked the face of the platform except for a single entry point, which fed into a corral of steel cage that extended from floor to ceiling, winding back to a reception area that doubled as a firing line. Hanging from the roof like lethal stalactites was an array of remote-controlled rotary machine guns, now very much pointing in his direction. A solitary armed guard that seemed as broad as he was tall stood resolutely in the entryway, adding his rifle to the abundance of guns targeting him.

Swallowing past the shame of his disheveled state more so than the threat of imminent disembowelment, he again called upon the fail-safe that had granted him reprieve on so many occasions: "Baptiste!"

The guard didn't shift for what seemed a very long time, then huffed and stepped back out of view of the barricade, presumably to check the visitor schedule. Baptiste didn't dare move, nor did he compose himself given the eyes of the heavy machine guns upon him. More time passed, and he clenched his jaw so tightly, his molars felt like they might implode with the pressure.

"I'm summoned for a meeting!" he finally blurted. "With the lord commander, at zero-three-hundred."

Another minute passed before the spotlights snapped off with a loud crump.

"Come forward. With identification."

The emplacements hadn't shifted their posture, but he was able at least to see a path before him, wading carefully through the afterglow of the spotlights. He walked the last length of the catwalk to the platform base, pulling himself up the rungs of a maintenance ladder until he at last stood before the way into Central Command.

The same guard waited for him at the entrance to the corral, a giant of a man fully a head taller than he was. A cadre of equally formidable giants were now visible in the reception area, their appearance languid, but he knew better. The Central Guard were the elite of Bastion's local armed forces, each with at least a decade of service under their belt. No matter the indignity of his current situation, he could not, and would not, find it within himself to resent them for it. They were, after all, protecting not only his last living family member but the essential military apparatus of the city-state.

"Apologies, Guardsman. I often walk the lines to clear my

head." He spread open his cloak with slow, obvious deliberation, retrieving his documents from an inner pocket. "Clarity has unfortunately eluded me this evening... or morning."

The guardsman retrieved the documents, carefully eyeing the articles of residency, articles of service, articles of rank, and the audience card in turn. Pocketing the latter, he handed the rest back, satisfied.

"Welcome, Lieutenant. You may proceed."

———

Another pair of towering guardsmen accompanied him in the freight elevator on their long descent downward. He recognized their faces from prior visits to Central Command, leading him to ponder what a strange, possibly final, assignment this must be for men who would have given the best years of their lives to their duty: to be stationed within a five-meter-square steel box day in and out. Perhaps they were chosen for having suffered some specific trauma in the open wastes beyond the walls, for which the psychological safety of confinement was an essential condition of their ongoing service.

The thrum of the city's war complex receded as the elevator continued its staccato journey into the lower levels, hand-cranked to the bottommost basement level. One of the guards reached out to retract the accordion door, and Baptiste promptly removed himself, feeling uneasy under the scrutiny of these broken soldiers.

Before him unfolded a scene of pure havoc, blindingly bright and wild with commotion. He paused for a moment to regain his bearings and to admire a system of human coordination as complex and sophisticated as the machines of the ironworks above. The Legion's Situation Room was an expansive auditorium, painted white throughout—floor, walls, and ceiling—

punctuated by hundreds of metal worktables; at each table, a large call box connected to an array of patch cables and rotary switches; a primary operator and their auxiliaries manning each call box, some speaking in calm tones, others yelling with urgency, and still more in quiet statis between calls, their countenances haunted (in the case of juniors) or blank (in the case of seniors); and flitting between the lot of them an army of messengers coordinating handcart deployments and defensive maneuvers. Each table was fronted by a stamped metal plate indicating the district it managed.

Behind it all, a second army of coordinators buzzed back and forth against the backdrop of an enormous and elegantly painted map of the city. They swarmed like enraged flies, prostrating themselves over each other to manipulate magnetic statuettes that represented defender and intruder, and striking line counts with chalk to mark the fallen.

Baptiste steeled himself as he circled the scene, suppressing the desire to inquire at those stations where an attack was clearly underway. He felt derelict in his duty visiting as a guest rather than fighting on the streets with his men, more so for having so recently wished for nothing more than a return to his bunk so that he might enjoy some peace while others died.

As he progressed toward the passageway to Command's breakout rooms, he noted that the operator at 5B was standing stiffly beside her station. Her fists were clenched white around a disconnected handset, but her expression was calm save for a recurrent twitch in her jaw. The call box beside her was oozing smoke from its patch cables, and a mechanic cursed desperately as she struggled to work her tools past sizzling arcs of errant electricity. His thoughts drifted to his earlier encounter as he passed into the hallways beyond.

Central Command was not the solitary seat of governance within Bastion. The other two branches of the state's government—the Church and Parliament—maintained their own fortified headquarters and armies of staff aboveground in their own districts. But none could dispute that Bastion was a militant nation by birth, painful as it was in the ancient Metro, and as such the military branch was widely understood to be the senior member of the officially equal Triarchy. Lord Commander Lucas Castillon in turn was the state's de facto patriarch.

Baptiste wondered at his great-uncle's age and the chaos that his death could elicit after decades of predictable, steady rule. The military establishment had no shortage of suitable if lesser men to take his place, but activists within the other branches could coerce their superiors into making a play for senior status, to rebalance the Triarchy in their favor. Throughout its tumultuous history, Bastion had been mostly spared such infighting. There had always been a mutual understanding among its founding partners that politicking was not conducive to rebuilding a functional society. But now that Bastion was experiencing a period of tenuous stability, its government was perhaps at the highest risk of destabilization.

At the end of the hallway stood two more giants. They nodded at his arrival and confirmed his documents once more before calling for a concierge to direct him to his destination. Central Command was enormous and employed a system of randomly rotating meeting rooms as a mitigating measure against assassination. The eventual room was large, fronted by a thick steel door emblazoned with crossed gauntlets under seven stars. It was open.

Keenly aware of his disheveled appearance as he was about to present himself before the most powerful man in the state, he took a moment to adjust himself, but not so long as to keep his superior waiting. Minimally satisfied, he lifted himself erect and stepped with confidence into the room.

It resembled a miniaturized version of the Situation Room,

functional and spare, but instead of a map of Bastion, it was backed by a map of the known world, assembled from dozens of painted plastic squares affixed to metal guides. Everything in the meeting rooms was designed for impermanence.

This map was zoomed out, with Bastion occupying only a few squares near the top-right corner. A red circle far southwest of the city, deep within the Deadlands, marked a location he didn't recognize. The lord commander was not known for his adventurism; he preferred a conservative approach to military operations, focused within the well-traveled geography around Bastion. Baptiste wondered if something had changed.

A mission into the periphery would explain the discreetness of his summons, to some degree at least. He had only adventured on behalf of the Legion once before, as a freshly minted officer. Then, too, it was on the direct orders of the old man: a special Old World retrieval mission, for something that hadn't been seen before. But he knew then, as now, that missions into uncharted territory could only be undertaken with the explicit approval and involvement of all three branches of government, and Parliament was nowhere to be seen in the room.

Other than a castor-wheeled desk for the lord commander, there were four folding metal chairs placed very specifically in the room: two in the front and another two in a row several meters back. Seated in the front row were two red robes. One he recognized as Father Andrite, a zealous yet uncharacteristically amiable chaplain with an unruly head of hair almost as red as his robes. He was a fit man, as capable as any soldier with a hammer or rifle, and had accompanied Baptiste on at least half a dozen tours. He turned his head and nodded, a faint smile touching the edges of his triangular cheekbones.

The man seated next to him was something else entirely. His high collar was emblazoned with the numeral *II*, denoting him as an agent of the Order Sacramental, the Church's spiritual enforcers. Even without the insignia, Baptiste could have guessed the man's affiliation from his cheerless disposition or the trademark black leatherette armor he wore under his robes.

The Church was divided into seven distinct orders, each responsible for its own ecclesiastical domain and roughly as influential as its numeral suggested. Chaplains hailed from the modest fifth order, the Order Somatic, which was the branch dedicated to the physical and mental health of the citizenry and the nation's armed forces. It was standard practice to include at least one chaplain on every Legion field operation; they were fully embedded with the military, from briefings all the way through execution. The presence of a confessor from the Order Sacramental, however, was highly unorthodox.

In the back row, sitting next to the vacant chair, was Sergeant First Class Ferris Lafayette. Lafayette had a long tenure in the Black Watch and a reputation for both success and unfailing loyalty. He was stolid, unquestioning, and exceptionally reliable —the kind of man you place on a mission if you want to ensure maximum compliance from its commanding officer.

The three men had been sitting in awkward silence while the lord commander consulted with a female aide—a dialogue that was cut off as he entered the room.

"Welcome, nephew, we have much to discuss. I trust your walk has refreshed you."

He blushed under the man's admonishment, intended or otherwise, and seated himself as promptly as his inflexible armor allowed. The young woman rushed past them and closed the door behind her.

The head of the Legion was an imposing figure, even at almost seventy. He was not a brawny or especially tall man, but the lean physique born of a life of constant labor was evident in the taut muscles of his bare neck and hands. He was dressed, as always, in full plate armor, meticulously clean but not so polished as to appear ostentatious. His head and face were shaved clean, betraying only wisps of white at his jawline. An ancient and enormous revolver hung at his waist, encased within an ornate steel and poly holster. As he spoke, his left hand rarely left the immediate perimeter of the hand cannon.

"As you all know," he began, "I'm not an adventurous man."

Andrite snorted quietly, and Baptiste squirmed at the pending confirmation of his suspicions. The other red robe and Lafayette were both silent.

"Bastion is powerful. It has taken... some time, but *in* that time, we have rebuilt this city from the ashes of the Old World and absorbed all the adjacent territories that we would need for feed and fuel."

The lord commander turned on his heel and began a cyclical pacing back and forth before the map as he continued, almost to himself. "We have been fortunate," he said, smirking at the over-simplification of his own statement. "Although we continue to battle the Adversary now, and perhaps forevermore, upon our streets and beyond the walls"—he paused his circuit momentarily to glance at the confessor—"we have been afforded the opportunity to do so without interference from... others." His expression was difficult to read, begrudging respect mixed with contempt.

Baptiste flinched inwardly at this extended introduction. The lord commander rarely bothered with preamble and certainly not history lessons. When directing new missions, he did so with uncomplicated brevity, out of a place of absolute confidence. He couldn't help but think what he was hearing now sounded rehearsed. The unusual attendees only exacerbated his suspicions.

"But that does not mean we're alone. Our own state is made up of the scattered souls that survived the War against Hell and persevered, with a will to rebuild something better than what had been here before."

The old man ceased his pacing and looked out upon each face in the room in turn.

"It should *not* come as a surprise, then, that Bastion isn't the only nation that has emerged from the ruin."

Lafayette's and Baptiste's heads lifted simultaneously, as though they had been bowed before in supplication, awaiting this commandment to rise. Their commander's words hung in the air like a choking cloud of incense.

"But, Un... Lord Commander—" Baptiste spoke out of shock, stopping uselessly as reason raced to catch up with impulse.

"But... how would we not have known, yes, Philippe?" The lord commander resumed his pacing. "Our world, as we know it, is small. To the north"—he pointed in each direction as he spoke—"the Northern Ridge, sundered by God, impassable. To the east, radioactive storms spanning the breadth of the horizon. To the south... well, we all know what lies to the south."

Father Andrite crossed his arms over his chest then, whispering a prayer against darkness. The other priest remained unmoved, his face impassive.

"And to the west, the Deadlands, which we have *mostly* avoided, keeping to the outer boundaries." The lord commander waved his right hand dismissively, but his gaze became distant, haunted even. "A soul-destroying waste that goes on forever. Cursed by something *else* we don't understand." He paused, absently caressing the handle of his revolver as he took a deep breath.

Baptiste's stomach began to churn as he followed the thread. "Soul-destroying" wasn't an overstatement. As horrific as the *regular* wastelands were, at least their hazards were physical—killable. The Deadlands... should have been named something else. They weren't just dead, they were *devoid*.

"Except it doesn't go on forever," the lord commander continued, snapping Baptiste back to attention. "The Deadlands are massive but not infinite. And on the other side of them is another world."

The tiny audience in this meeting room seemed entirely inappropriate for such a pronouncement. He looked around again, noting the arbitrary handful of souls that had now been opted into sensational facts that no one else in the citizenry had any idea of. He was certain, however, that the higher echelons of government—the Ascendancy at least, representing the Church —had known about this for some time and wondered now *how* long.

"This is obviously classified," the lord commander continued, as though reading his mind. "In time, there will be more to say about our neighbors. But this briefing is about essentials— the relevant facts you will need for your mission. You will all be leaving the city at dawn, so there's little time to spare."

Baptiste blanched, his energy level beginning to sap once more as his thoughts sank involuntarily into his distant bunk. Fatigue battled against nervous excitement.

"They are called the Revenant Sisterhood, and they rule over a city-state called Cathedral." The lord commander sped up his dialogue now, clearly more comfortable delivering bullet points than exposition. "They are most certainly an offshoot of the schism that divided mankind during the War. As such, there is no doubt in our minds that they are heretics."

Father Andrite nodded at this, unsurprisingly. The lord commander paused to give the other priest a meaningful look, which was returned in kind this time.

"They are expansionist," he continued, pursing his lips as though to restrain his next statement, "and they have a fleet of battle walkers."

Everyone gasped at this, save for the confessor. Lafayette rose slightly from his chair, his brow visibly slick with growing perspiration. A string of curses erupted in Baptiste's thoughts. Bastion's military was populous, empowered by scores of brave fighting men, but its technology was rudimentary. Other than a handful of semi-functional battle tanks, its mechanized forces consisted mostly of light armored vehicles. Battle walkers were the penultimate battlefield weapon of the Old World, monstrous machines strapped with heavy armor and heavier weaponry, piloted not by humans but by machines. The elaborate science of such things had long been lost, but it was presumed the machine and pilot were one and the same.

"But the machine minds have all died, have they not?" Everyone turned at the proclamation of the unwelcome priest. His voice was smooth and confident, unaffected by the terrifying truths that had just been unloaded into the room.

"Indeed," the lord commander replied, visibly irritated by the man's interruption. "And yet they walk. And are unaffected by the expanse between us, as humans would be." He resumed his pacing, as though to stay ahead of the dread war machines of which he spoke.

The room was silent for a full minute. Baptiste felt like a wet sponge being forced to sop up a flood of endless information. An expansionist enemy—presumably an enemy, though that hadn't been explicitly stated—somehow wielding the most powerful weaponry ever made, weaponry which would make short work of Bastion's significant though decidedly inferior defenses. And yet, as he struggled to reconcile the threat, his hypothetical fears were eventually displaced by a nagging confusion that clawed at the edges of his fatigued perception.

"How do we know all this?" he blurted. "Sir," he corrected, catching his overly familiar tone. "I mean... we've barely ventured into the Deadlands ourselves, as you stated."

The lord commander's jaw clenched, eyes squinting in momentary irritation.

"Our borders are small, Lieutenant, but our Intelligence extends as far as it must in order to maintain them."

Baptiste knew by the formality of the reply that this was the totality of the matter, as was warranted by his rank. He couldn't help but wonder, though, if the old man meant Legion Intelligence or the Order Sacramental's.

His great-uncle seemed suddenly tired, neck stooping forward under his armor. He navigated slowly to his desk and lifted a plain tumbler of water to his lips, sipping frugally before restoring the glass and standing upright again in front of his audience, arms now crossed.

"There are others as well."

Others? Baptiste thought incredulously.

"The fact of which is the actual reason we're gathered here today. This Sisterhood is supported by another lesser nation that fancies themselves rebuilders and the rightful reclaimers of the Old World—of its technology at least. It's made up of numerous scavenger clans who can't even agree on a name, but they generally go by the Union.

"Their betters prefer the name Scavrats. For all their grandiose claims, they appear to be the whipping boys of the Sisterhood. They're obligated to tithe their masters most of what they unearth, particularly advanced weaponry, particularly walker tech. And they are sick of it. The Scavrats are our targets."

Baptiste couldn't shake the surreal fact of all this unfamiliarity—all these otherworldly secrets that had been known and stowed for how long. He flashed back quickly through his life: the loss of his father to demons beyond the wall, his brother Gabriel's murder within the walls, his mother's suicide, before becoming a ward of the lord commander—his next male kin, as was tradition. All that he knew, and which was concrete, was here. The "rest of the world" did not exist, should not exist. The Church taught that after humanity committed the sin of self-destruction, God pitched his creation into Hell as further punishment, but it wasn't a final sentence. If his children could prove themselves worthy once more—if they could rebuild civilization under the strict tenets of the faith—they would be redeemed; the Hellmouth would close. Bastion was that vehicle for redemption, theirs alone, a miracle, unique.

"They are on their way to this location." His great-uncle stopped to point at the encircled area on the map. "It's an impenetrable stasis bunker that we know to contain high-value military materiel. And we are going to help them penetrate it."

SOPHUS

STASIS BUNKER 23

Sophus Harper looked out upon the reddening horizon and knew *something* wasn't right.

Not that anything in the Deadlands was ever *right*. A monotonous expanse of sameness, gray on gray, unfettered by any intrusion of life, however haggard. Sameness and nothingness as far as the eye could see, the very rock of the earth coerced into a homogenous, uniform expanse. He hated the quiet of it. Worse than the constant mewling of starving children back home, worse than the undying moans of the Sea of Screams on his first and also last deep south tour. Sophus hated noise, particularly human noise, but he hated this absolute, unnatural silence even more.

The curses of his second, Julia, and her crew of junior mechanists startled him out of his malaise, eliciting a grunt of irritated alert but also relief. They still hadn't found any means of entry. Hub had sent them out to this untraveled shithole three days ago based on dubious intelligence and a matching facility name from the Archive: Stasis Bunker 23.

His chief, Magnus Harper, said it would be a game changer for the Union, something that could "elevate us from our wretched lot as tithe-burdened servants of the Sisterhood, into a military force of our own. Finally, we can keep what we scavenge. What we kill."

All very grandiose, all very familiar to someone like Sophus, who had lost count of the fools' errands he'd survived over his unusually long career as a senior mechanist.

Still, no matter the prize, an extended journey through the Deadlands was normally dismissed as suicide, an unthinkable risk to personnel and supplies. Countless rookies had rolled out on relic hunts over the years, thinking it an obvious treasure trove in the absence of the Horde. The few who returned, always on foot, had been driven mad, either stark raving and covered in shit and blood—their own or their companions'—or catatonic, their souls hollowed out by the anti-life of the cursed eastern zone.

But Sophus's team had made it this far: two AARVs—armored asset recovery vehicles, half-APC/half-hauler—stacked with surplus diesel, Senior Mechanist Sophus Harper in the lead vehicle and Julia Harper in the other. Accompanied, unfortunately, by their own retinue of rookies. All the vets Sophus would have normally chosen for this trip had wisdom enough to scoff at the volunteer calls, leaving those too eager from lack of experience on the tour. Six of them in total, out here in this godforsaken abyss, one too-small step removed from the actual Hell on the border.

Jax was the group braggart and cheerleader, always talking shit about his last gig, where he either fought off demons with his bare hands or decoded an ancient encryption no one else could touch. Mostly he was useless, but his heart was in the right place. His big sister, Char, was the competent one, especially with a chainsaw in her hands. They were inseparable, and sometimes insufferable, but at least they rode in Julia's truck.

In his own crew were Bertram, a disfigured, tic-ridden

ascetic who had no real place on a field op, and Mace, his exact opposite: all brawn, thicker than your typical Union citizen— the type you'd want holding back a pressure door in an emergency or standing in the way of bullets, but not much good with a wrench.

Hub had given them a straight-line route to traverse once they entered the Deadlands. There was no point doing otherwise, as the area offered no cover, no detour, no safe harbor. All crew were ordered to remain in their vehicles for the duration, disembarking only to refuel. Eating, pissing, shitting, sleeping was all done in-vehicle, with any waking time not driving spent deep in technical encyclopediae. If there was truly an Old World cache on the other side of this nightmare, they had best be prepared to find a way in, and maintaining focus within the superficial safety of their armored vehicles would keep them all somewhat sane, for a time.

Three days it had taken them. It was supposed to be two, by distance and compass, but they found nothing when their odometers told them they had reached their destination. It took another full day of frustrated quartering before Julia's crew spotted something on their periscope. And *something* in the Deadlands was always something of note.

Meanwhile, their fuel reservoirs had sunk well below halfway. There was no way they were going to make it all the way back according to plan. Everyone on crew knew this by now, but no one dared say it out loud for fear of making it real. Hopefully, by the time they tapped out, they'd be within radio range and could call in a fueling truck. But their fuel problem, and the problem of opening a massive featureless hangar door surrounded by a massive featureless concrete bunker, all seemed irrelevant right now.

Something wasn't right.

The bloated sun dipped low in the sky, red tendrils of failing light reaching for the horizon. In a couple hours his world would be pitched into utter, starless black. Anywhere else, out in the open like this, the lot of them would be running for their lives, seeking shelter from nightmares both seen and invisible. But not here, not in the Deadlands.

"Anything yet, Julia?" he asked, surprised by the faltering croak of his own voice, mired by dust and growing concern.

"Working on it," she replied testily, followed by another round of curses from his daughter's people—directed at the door or him, he couldn't tell. Jax and Char squatted over an explosion of standard schematic scrolls, tracing lines they didn't understand and mumbling arcane transcriptions to themselves like a couple of revenant sisters. Bertram and Mace were swapping tools back and forth, flailing desperately around an access panel, trying to find an override.

Regardless of who they rode with, he figured the entire crew was in this for Julia. Rookies, yes, eager for discovery, yes, but she had that effect on people: instant loyalty, devotion beyond her rank. She was a rising star not just among the Harpers but the whole Union. They respected their mission commander, but not as much as they loved his second.

There *was* something else in the nothing. He blinked. The creeping unease steadily working its way up his spine was now manifesting physically before him, haloed by the fading sun. Squinting his cataracted eyes, he started to discern a haze—a dust plume? Growing larger, with a faint mechanical hum in tow.

"Julia!" he exclaimed.

His field armor suddenly felt leaden upon his old bones. His gorget constricted his neck. His chest rig compressed his torso, squeezing a shallow unprepared breath from his lungs. The featureless gray earth transmogrified into quicksand, fixing his legs to the spot. A high-pitched whine grew in his ears, spontaneous tinnitus that crested to a deafening shrill before terminating with a pop, leaving his hearing deadened. There was nowhere to run.

Somewhere deep within his brain, Sophus observed this unfamiliar panic with disgust, incapacitated for excruciating, precious seconds before willing a counterattack.

Fuck me!

Fuck this place!

Anger helped, but only with the realization that his daughter's life was also in danger did he finally rip his fear-frozen gaze from the horizon, and his feet with it.

"Take cover!"

Stupid, since there was none. But no Scavrat in service today was so naive to ignore a shouted warning from their mission commander in a hellhole like this. As one, every man and woman of the volunteer team ran for their vehicles. The plume was on them.

———

Human senses fail in the Deadlands. One wouldn't expect such a broad expanse of *nothingness* to permit surprise, let alone ambush. Maybe it was the unyielding inanity of the place that diminished observation, forcing beleaguered travelers to retreat so deep into themselves for succor that they missed what was right under their noses. More likely, he thought, it was because of their fucking proximity to Hell.

The Union had endured long enough in its subterranean home that its advocates could be forgiven for claiming that their little tribe of humanity, at least, had thrived through not one but two apocalypses, ready to reclaim the world. But that delusion quickly evaporated with an extended venture in any direction, surrounded by so many cursed lands, with the certainty of the Hellmouth on the horizon—the certainty of the Adversary.

Sophus Harper was a hard man, a learned veteran, and tried not to dwell on such things. But being ambushed on his first gig out since the last fiasco chafed his hide, sending his mind on pointless tangents even as this unknown threat descended on them. He had taken up his battle rifle, thrusting his cheek hard into the stock to exorcise his agitation, compressing it against the ancient, stippled surface, both eyes open, unblinking down the irons.

Julia wielded a sniper rifle longer than she was tall and managed to scrounge some cover by lying prone on the roof of her AARV. He didn't have to avert his aim to know that the rest of the crew was huddling around her vehicle rather than his, all armed with crossbows except for Char and her beloved chainsaw, all scared. Even Jax's usual yammering was abbreviated into muttered curses.

Sophus blinked and swore at his repeated failures of attention, realizing that the two approaching vehicles had already stopped, less than twenty meters away. Yet somehow, they materialized only when he remembered to look for them, despite having been staring down his sights.

Fuck this place!

They weren't familiar-looking, a fact that in and of itself was terrifying. The Union serviced everyone; they knew everyone, living or dead. But they also had never scavenged this far east before. Cathedral, the "Last City" and home of the Revenant Sisterhood, was the nexus of their world. Hub, the Union's home base, along with most of its outposts, lay in Cathedral's shadow. Lurking discreetly beyond the Sisterhood's purview were a handful of forward operating bases and semi-excavated Old World military sites. And in between were the scant, barely functional settlements of the human remnant, refusers of the

New Covenant who scraped out a meager existence when they weren't too busy being butchered by hordes of demons.

But this was something new, *someone* new. He couldn't help but salivate at the sight of them. The larger one was an eight-oversized-wheel behemoth—armored personnel carrier from the look of it—bigger than an AARV, its broad prow angling up and outward like a massive shield. It was gray, not black, which immediately precluded it from being a Sisterhood vehicle. Two dorsal-mounted cannons protruded from rails on its hull, one very clearly pointed at him and the other at Julia's position.

He had to shift his gaze to avoid being blinded by the glare of the vehicle's piercing amber headlamps. Though stopped, it bucked slightly, rocking on its shocks, driver ready to disengage the brake and crush them if anything went sideways.

How had they found them? It had taken his crew fully a day to find the bunker entrance, emblazoned with an enormous 23, despite it having always been less than fifty meters off their original disembarking point. The Deadlands were ruinous to human senses, meaning this group must have some sort of advanced, long-range scanning tech. How long had they been watching them? How many others were waiting beyond his useless vision?

"What the fu—" Jax blurted.

"Shh!" Julia cut in, cursing as she adjusted her grip.

The companion vehicle, a low-slung vicious-looking escort car of some type, shuddered with restrained power. A turret atop its roof whined angrily as it turned to point a heavy-caliber gun at Jax.

"Don't fucking move!" he snapped, reasserting command with a snarl but mostly trying to make sure the rookies didn't get anyone killed, particularly *him*.

Who are they? he wondered, mind racing.

A mechanical thump, followed by the loud hiss of releasing

cabin pressure told him he was about to find out. He spotted a deployment ramp lowering behind the APC, ushering a cloud of radiant steam upon their now ochre-hued campsite. Sophus swallowed, his cheek weld lurching uneasily under a sudden wash of sweat.

Forty-six years old. He should have thanked God for such a long life and retired the fuck out of adventuring. Like every senior mechanist before him, he lived for discovery, but as he continued to miraculously survive, that glee had steadily been displaced by his desire to *continue* surviving. Yet here he was, in another shithole. Except instead of demons, he was face-to-face with the truly unknown.

BAPTISTE

IN THE NAME OF BASTION

Baptiste surveyed the scene before him with a fatigued mixture of disappointment and confusion. To attribute a unified designation, nationhood even, to this ramshackle gang of civilians seemed preposterous, let alone to honor them with the reputation they had apparently earned as reclaimers of the Old World.

During the briefing—an unusually secretive affair, absent the typical parliamentary representation that would accompany any mission into the periphery—the lord commander had referred to them as both the Union and as Scavrats. Baptiste preferred the second option—it suited them, though there had been no accompanying visual, so he supposed he didn't know *what* to expect.

They all had sickly, pale complexions and deep-set eyes, light-colored hair, and malnourished physiques—all except for one bigger man he took cautious note of. He wondered how many generations these people had spent hiding in their caves.

Instead of uniforms, they sported bedraggled clothing plastered in metal scrap and a mélange of jury-rigged tactical gear, lugging weapons that looked older than the timeworn rubble of their current, unfortunate surroundings. And other than the grizzled man staring at them down his rifle, presumably the commanding officer, their combat posture resembled that of raw draftees. All in all, they didn't look that different from the subhuman wasteland raiders that plagued Bastion's outpost convoys.

Their vehicles, on the other hand, looked surprisingly rugged, purpose-built to survive hostile environs. His own driver, Specialist Novak, had commented on them as they approached, clearly intrigued. They were a motley desert camouflage and sported the Scavrat flag on their flanks: a black crow over a red field. When given the details of their journey, Baptiste scoffed at the notion that such primitives could manage that long a trek through the Deadlands, but he begrudgingly had to admit to the roadworthiness of their machinery, on first perusal at least. He wondered how they had not only come into possession of such advanced technology but had acquired the skill to improve on it. For the briefest moment, his disdain turned to envy.

The threat seemed marginal overall. Nothing he saw from the Crusader's periscope gave him pause before giving the order to disembark from the APC, everyone except for Novak and the gunners—twin brothers known in the platoon simply as "the Roys"—just in case. Novak was content to ogle. The twins were content to stay put in case it meant being able to blow something up. Their heads remained locked into their targeting goggles, oddly synchronized fingers brushing against the vehicle's fire controls.

Baptiste rose from his steel-sprung passenger seat with a wince of pain, grunting against the slow release of each spinal vertebra. His fatigue had worsened since that fateful night of interrupted sleep and was now accompanied by a numbness that radiated throughout his mid-back, segregating his upper body from his legs.

Leading the way was SFC Lafayette, who seemed unfazed by the journey or the alien environment, followed by Sergeant Deckard, who had been relegated to section second. Deckard was a good man and one of his favorite section leaders: brave, level-headed, and most importantly, loyal to his commanding officer—there was no second-guessing when the lord commander's great-nephew gave an order, just respectful compliance.

Father Andrite was already well into the foreigners' sights, brazenly chanting and wafting bitter incense from his thurible upon the emerging troops. The rest of Baptiste's men, also fatigued but nowhere near as dilapidated as himself, unfurled like an iron curtain, eager to be freed from the cramped confines of the crew cabin. Private First Class Butcher stuck to his sergeant like glue. Privates Martel and Lambert hovered uncertainly by the exit, rifles at the low ready position; they were fine soldiers but a bit green for an open-ended mission like this. For that matter, he had only been assigned a section and a half instead of the usual three sections that comprised his platoon—no doubt keeping a low profile in the interest of state security. He didn't like it.

As Baptiste finally disembarked, he had to leverage the full extent of his mental energy so as not to wobble. He was clearly maladapted to travel and found himself self-consciously yearning for a long solitary walk in the Metro.

Overseer Rayos, the enigmatic clergyman from the Order Sacramental, stayed put in the turret of the Chevalier, keeping an acute eye on the proceedings, presumably so that he could report back to his own masters. Baptiste didn't like that either. The lord commander hadn't been any more forthcoming about his inclusion in the mission other than to say the priest's presence was part of a cooperative effort with the Ascendancy. It was one thing to have him on the mission, but to allow a non-soldier behind the guns of the fast attack vehicle felt reckless. He hoped for everyone's sake that the primitives didn't make any especially heretical faux pas.

It had been only minutes since they arrived, and already his discomfort with his superior's orders had started to fester. Somehow these Scavrats had learned of a military stasis bunker deep in the eastern stretch of the cursed Deadlands, which overlapped the loosely patrolled but still official peripheral territory of Bastion. And somehow the lord commander knew of their imminent arrival and wanted him not to head them off but to offer them assistance.

He lingered with his uncomfortable thoughts, right hand rhythmically clenching and loosening the ridged shaft of his war hammer as Andrite finished up his sermons. His eyes stung with the acid of his own facial oil, and he wondered how long it had been since he showered. Already, the featureless expanse around him seemed to be eroding his sense of past and present. The redheaded chaplain slammed his lectionary shut with dramatic aplomb, eyes blazing at each member of the Scavrat crew in turn as he walked the line of spiritual protection cast before his men.

"Amen," the section replied as one in baritone unison.

Baptiste cocked his neck from side to side, lifted his hammer, and slammed it hard into the ground. His men moved into two small arrowhead formations on either side of him, their heavy armor pressing them into the featureless earth like ancient stone guardians. All he could think of was how much easier this would be if it was a proper fight rather than a convoluted first-contact mission.

He breathed heavily in preparation: once, feeling the cold steel of the corded talisman secreted beneath his plate armor; a second time, more deeply, until the jagged edges pressed into the bare flesh of his chest; then a third, welcoming familiar pain as a grounding force.

Spirit reinforced, he stepped forward from the line.

"In the name of Bastion and the Holy Triarchy," he said, sighing with the falsity of his dictate, "we greet you..."

———

No one moved. Baptiste looked from the Scavrat commander to an impressively fit woman lying prone upon one of the trucks, bare armed and pointing a ridiculously large sniper rifle in his general direction. He presumed she was the commander's second. The rest of their squad huddled below her like nervous cubs, some literally latched to her vehicle with lengths of chain and lift hooks. The commander blurted something from the corner of his mouth but received only ambiguous responses and shrugs from the others.

Some seconds passed—or minutes even, as it was hard to tell in this godforsaken place. He realized, eventually, that no one was responding to him, nor did they plan to. It was an unfamiliar sensation, intensely annoying. Gritting his teeth, he walked forward another two steps. His men held their poise without a flinch, but the Scavrats jerked at his sudden approach, injecting another degree of tension into the elevated atmosphere.

"My name is Philippe Baptiste, First Lieutenant of the Black Watch. I have come a long way to meet with you."

He was definitely within earshot. This time the woman mumbled something he couldn't quite understand from the roof she was planted on down to her people. One of them, another woman holding a wicked-looking bladed weapon, mumbled back to her, then elbowed a man cowering next to her, who was babbling over them both. It was as though they weren't expecting them.

"Deckard?" he asked, continuing to scan the foreigners, but the sergeant shook his head.

"Sorry, sir."

A creeping discomfort grew in his throat as he considered the possibility that these people didn't speak their language. The other men were eyeing each other uncertainly. He sighed, turning to query Father Andrite with a raised eyebrow across the line. The holy man shrugged under his plate armor, then tapped several times at his earpiece. Swallowing his irritation, Baptiste lifted his left hand and squeezed the mic button on his headset.

"Recommendation, Reverend Father?"

As a loyal servant of Bastion, Baptiste was pious by default, but chafed at the tiresome lecturing of the Church. His faith was personal, not something that needed to be managed by bureaucrats, or worse, glorified spies like the overseer, who he could *feel* watching them intently.

The speaker in his ear crackled back almost immediately, the confessor's voice abraded by static. Radio barely worked in the Deadlands, like everything else.

"We are here to make an offering, Lieutenant," the man said, a disparaging tone evident in his voice even through the distortion. "Stand down your men."

Baptiste chewed the inside of his cheek, wholly uncomfortable with the proposition. Maybe the lord commander knew who these people were and trusted them not to massacre his men, but he certainly did not.

"Sir," Lafayette said quietly from his right side, giving him a meaningful look. "We should stick to the script."

The script. Rehearsed briefings. He wondered whose mission this really was. As useless as they were, Parliament would have been better suited to it—assuming they even knew what was going on out here.

"Everyone, stand down," he called out loudly, kneeling to set his hammer on the ground, then standing with his arms at his side and slightly out. His men followed suit, letting their rifles hang low in their slings. As they did so, a ripple of calm seemed to spread across the foreigners—all save the sniper, who didn't shift from her perch.

Now was the moment where he'd see if his great-uncle's confidence had been warranted or if his last thought would be *I told you so.*

"Deckard, bring the scrolls."

"Sir."

The sergeant retreated to their vehicle, returning after a minute with a long tin cylinder cradled in his arms in place of a rifle. Capped and sealed by the lord commander's office, it had been generally described as documents that would assist the foreigners in accessing the bunker—the key, essentially. Deckard scuttled forth, bequeathing the case to his lieutenant with all the deliberate respect accorded such artifacts.

Martel and Lambert peered at the object with wide eyes. Butcher, slightly older and far less curious, was still fixated on the foreigners, which hadn't yet proven themselves not to be keen enemies waiting for the optimal moment to open fire. From the corner of his eye, Baptiste watched Father Andrite watching his men. This mission—this whole damnable place—was fraught with physical and spiritual risk. Their long and monotonous drive to get here hadn't helped matters any, nor did the prospect of their ordered immediate return without the benefit of a layover.

They weren't alone in their suffering. The cave dwellers looked positively haggard, what little composition they had mustered at the outset of their encounter degrading into impatient anxiety. He wondered again at their confusion. Did they just expect to walk in the front door of a five-hundred-year-old military bunker?

"As agreed, we have brought the key," he declared.

The grizzled Scavrat leader seemed equally torn considering his next move, then finally lifted his stubbled cheek from the stock of his rifle. He raised an arm and uttered a brief command to his people. Baptiste's brain caught the words this time—it was Common, but spoken in a raspy, staccato dialect that required his full attention to be understood. One by one, the scavengers relaxed out of their defensive postures—all except for the prone woman, whose still-sighted rifle remained leveled at his forehead, her nondominant eye locking his gaze whenever he turned in her direction.

"Why now?"

He recalled the final minutes of his briefing, left alone with his great-uncle after the others had departed.

"You've always been reserved. 'Why capture what we can't keep' you used to say. So why not leave these Scavrats and their Sisterhood alone instead of announcing ourselves to them now?"

He had consolidated all his concerns into a single onslaught, reflecting the wise man's own words of caution in a futile attempt to pierce what had become an impregnable wall.

"Sometimes," the lord commander had finally said, *"you must strengthen one enemy to avoid conflict with the other."*

Baptiste shipped out shortly thereafter. The echo of his great-uncle's words in his memory sounded like they had been spoken by someone else.

SOPHUS

AN UNFAMILIAR AROMA

Sophus was more than a little pissed off. Magnus made no mention of a rendezvous—of that he was fucking certain. There was only the magical intel and a promised treasure trove on the other side of this hellscape. To make matters worse, he had to keep his rage to himself. His crew was ragged enough from the trip out here without dumping a betrayal like this on them, not that he was allowed to tell them much about the mission anyway. The burden was his to bear for now. His chief would get an earful when they got back—if they got back.

With barely a word spoken but night quickly approaching, the two groups had tersely agreed to break so that each could make camp. Trust was a long way out, but there was a mutual desire to fortify themselves against the darkening hollow of the void at their backs. The evening ahead was going to be long. Weapons had been shouldered but not stowed, and glances between them alternated between malign and curious as they busied themselves with preparations. The stoic gray soldiers were making an obvious effort to appear calm, but he spotted many nervous glances into the distance.

The AARVs had been steered into position on either side of

their camp, like makeshift walls. Between them, Jax and Mace uncoiled lengths of barbed wire, interspersed with corrugated metal plates for cover—as meaningless as it would be out here. Thickly cabled spotlights were clamped to the trucks' roofs and the central barricade, projecting outward in a 180-degree arc. The yellow beams shone uselessly upon the nothing beyond their campsite. He watched the emptiness for a while, the hairs on his arms bristling with imagined threats that would never materialize. Finally, he flicked off the outer two spotlights, leaving the central one shining bright for emotional support if nothing else.

A red-robed man with matching red hair led the foreigners' rotating patrols, chanting repetitiously as though to calm the obviously reluctant soldiers as they followed him into the darkness. Their vehicles lay in state under the watchful eye of their brusque, tired-looking commander, turrets swiveling idly in the opposite arc of nothingness every few minutes.

He wondered again where they came from—there wasn't supposed to be anything out this far east. But more than that, he wondered what their technology base was like, wishing with a brief surge of youthful energy to see inside their vehicles, to feel the hum of something new and alive underneath him. His lustiness distilled itself quickly into practiced analysis, assessing likely fuels, cargo capacity, offensive capabilities. Magnus and the council would want to know, assuming they didn't already.

And what about the case? Obviously connected to the bunker they had only just begun to fail at gaining access to. But why would these people—people of power, by the looks of it—have any interest in helping them? The Union had grown from disparate nomadic roots to the considerable size it was today, independently, without help from anyone. Quite the opposite. What they had thought to be a mutually beneficial trade arrangement with Cathedral in the founding days very quickly turned out to be a grossly one-sided deal: all scavenged high tech to be turned over in exchange for "protection."

Unfortunately for the Union, as they breached deeper into the wastes, they found that straying too far beyond the sphere of the Sisterhood was indeed impractical. His people's combat self-sufficiency at the time was still marginal, primitive, and so the breadth of their expansion was commensurate with the satisfaction of their masters.

Even later, as the clans grew and built up a solid retinue of expedition-ready vehicles and crews, they still couldn't unshackle themselves from the original deal. The one time an overly ambitious clan back at Hub had protested, there was an immediate and unforgiving... reprimand. He shuddered at the imprinted memory of a solitary black-clad priestess moving between his people like a wraith, cutting down dissenters and collaborators alike, then returning to business as usual immediately after.

Sophus eyed the redheaded man and wondered if holiness in this culture was endowed only to those whose hair fit the color profile. He had never seen a male priest before, was certain no such aberration existed in Cathedral. What powers did he possess? The cryptic holy man was endlessly busy—preaching, blowing around incense that reeked of tar and unfamiliar herbs, and laying hands upon the shoulders of his flock—but he hadn't yet exhibited any abilities beyond the material, which was a relief.

Neither party had set up tents or bedrolls, both because of their unsettled distrust and because no one realistically thought there was any rest to be had out here in the open. The primordial need for fire in the dark was tamped down by the unchanging temperature of dusk. It was exactly as temperate now as it had been during the day, the prior day, and for as long as this place had existed, perhaps since the dawn of time. No wind blew, and even the bloodred crest of the setting sun seemed to have fixed itself just above the horizon, as though the Deadlands' obstinacy against change extended to the heavens themselves.

Julia was triple-checking the vehicles, ensuring anything not strictly necessary for camp had been stowed. Of all his people, she was the most dubious of this encounter, recommending they call the mission DOA and head back, even in the dark. Despite her trepidations, he caught her gazing intently at the foreign commander on more than one occasion. The man was certainly impressive if somewhat disheveled: of medium height, obviously well-built beneath his shell of beautifully ornamented armor, and deeply tanned with a strong jaw. The whole lot of them were unusually dark-skinned.

The rest of the Harpers were bobbing nervously at a pull-out metal table topped with a modest spread of canned rations. Jax was nervously stuffing his face while the others sipped from their canteens. Bertram hadn't stopped gawking at the foreigners since they arrived. His nose flopped nervously from side to side, eyes alternately bulging and squinting as he catalogued esoteric details in his vast mental archive.

Mace seemed unperturbed. He was the only member of their crew to beget a respectful caution from the soldiers, and Sophus was thankful for it. He had to restrain the urge to linger in the big man's shadow in hopes of absorbing some of that stability.

The hushed shuffle of booted feet on the immutable earth roused them from chow time. The lieutenant and his two sergeants were standing in a rectangular clearing that demarcated their camps, lit by four standing lanterns.

It was time.

———

Everyone gathered at a cautious distance around the clearing, his crew in a skittish gaggle and the foreign soldiers in a motionless semicircle. The ration table had been wiped clean and propped in the center. On the Union's side stood Sophus, with Julia at his right. Opposite him was Lieutenant Baptiste, bracketed by the junior sergeant and redheaded priest on his right, and a stolid, flat-faced man on his left. Sophus knew something of Old World army ranks and was pretty sure that this latter soldier was also a sergeant, but the lieutenant's body language suggested he was a supervisor of some kind. Baptiste was clearly unhappy about the arrangement, his neck cocking and crossed arms flexing in the pause between each staggered exchange.

The lieutenant cleared his throat, eyes glazing over for a second as he searched for his words, then proceeded.

"You are wondering who we are. As up until recently, we wondered the same about you."

The supervisor seemed to stiffen at this, clearly uncomfortable with such frankness out of the gate. Sophus paid full attention, partitioning off an analytical segment of his brain to deal with the foreign accent so he could focus not only on their words but on whatever intent lurked beneath them. Already he detected a rivalry among the foreigners, however subtle, and a clear disparity in information that the lieutenant was trying to remediate.

"We are the defenders of Bastion." Perhaps acknowledging the subliminal cue from his supervisor, this second statement came with no additional qualifications. "We have been sent here to rendezvous with you, with an offer of exchange."

To rendezvous with you, Sophus mulled.

Again, he wondered how the hell they could have known anyone was out here, let alone manage such a close arrival time. He had to play along, as much as it irked him. If he admitted he had no fucking idea they were supposed to meet the keyholders of this place, it could scuttle the mission. But that didn't mean he couldn't press them for some answers.

"Rendezvous with us?" His thoughts manifested into the blurted question. "How did you know when we were going to arrive?"

It was perhaps too aggressive, but he hated being at a disadvantage.

Their lieutenant lifted his chin slightly, breathing loudly in and out through his nose before giving his response. He could already tell the man had no idea.

"We knew. That is all that matters. We also know of your Revenant Sisterhood."

Sophus did a double take, as did Julia beside him. Jax started to swear under his breath, quieting with a grunt as his sister jabbed him in the gut.

Scavrats could drive themselves literally to the ends of the earth and still not be rid of the fucking Sisterhood.

"*Our* Sisterhood..." he replied, snorting derisively.

Baptiste continued, either oblivious to the sentiment or uncaring.

"We know that your technical knowledge is great and that you have restored many secrets from the world that was."

What bullshit, he thought, waiting for the punchline.

"We know that you are slaves to the Sisterhood."

Sophus stiffened.

"And that your ambitions have been stunted by the unfair tithe that you pay them."

Sophus swallowed, his throat suddenly too parched to respond. Every Union citizen grew up knowing about the tithe, but no one outside of the council and its chieftains, including his crew—even Julia—understood how deep a debt it truly was. As far as they knew, trading a portion of salvage was fair and normal in exchange for regional protection, fuel, and food. They were not privy to how much had to be given up—*everything*, in the most (un)lucrative cases—or how dire the punishment for disobedience was. To have this total stranger, this outsider, lay out the truth of it with one casual statement was like being punched in the face.

The growth of the Union was driven by a vigorous and independent spirit. For some of the clans, this was a purely mercenary ambition; for others, the dream of ancient knowledge; and for a growing faction, the dream of restoring not just the technology of the Old World, but to resurrect the deceased nation whose corpse they suckled. If the whole truth of the Union's stunted growth was broadcast to everyone, it could result in widespread revolt, and with it another grievous retribution from Cathedral.

He wasn't surprised to hear Jax pipe up. "What does he mean 'slaves'?"

Char took a half step forward but seemed ready to support her brother this time. Seeing her, Julia—clearly confused, but still professional (thank God)—turned to her, and with a "shut the fuck up!" curtailed the little rebellion. He felt deep gratitude for his daughter in that moment, though he knew the reprimand did not come from any special favor intended toward her estranged father. He hoped the conversation thread would be dismissed as bluster—negotiating tactics.

Baptiste shared a curious glance with his supervisor before continuing.

"We know the Sisterhood is expansionist, and we know that your technology facilitates that," he continued. "We could destroy you." This statement seemed spontaneous, and even the curious sergeant seemed surprised by it, his head half turning toward Baptiste with a furrowed brow before recomposing. A thin smile briefly creased the priest's otherwise expressionless face. "But instead, we wish to elevate you."

We wish to elevate you.

The stranger's use of those words startled him. Wasn't that the same line Magnus used when he sent them out on this crazed mission?

"We know about the battle walkers. We know that the Sisterhood has figured out how to control them, despite the death of the machine minds."

Sophus squirmed at this. Of all the recovered military assets the Union had been most excited about, battle walkers were paramount. Each partial chassis restored, each component reasoned about bore with it the dream not only of defendable expansion beyond the smothering confines of Hub but of a viable deterrent against the Matriarch. Without exception, the Sisterhood claimed it all. If there was a delay in acquisition, it was only so that Cathedral could benefit from the acquired ingenuity of his people.

And yet, as this foreigner had suggested, the Union hadn't cracked the secret of how the Revenant Sisterhood was ultimately able to pilot the machines. According to their researchers, they were driven by "artificial intelligences," great machine minds that, to the last, seemed to have gone insane and erased themselves during their centuries-long internment in statis bunkers. Theoretically, Cathedral's God-engines could be dispatched here, or to wherever this Bastion was, without the travel constraints of human weakness. No wonder they were so interested—so scared.

"We know that given enough time, and *discretion*... you could figure it out."

Figure it out...?

Mere minutes ago—hours ago? *Fuck this place!*—he was convinced these people had come to murder him and his crew. Now these same people seemed to be about to offer them the unthinkable. How the hell did Magnus get involved in this? The Harpers were a waning clan, not international diplomats.

The lieutenant gestured to the cylindrical case that sat upon the table. No one had seemed to notice it since the conversation began, but now everyone's eyes fixed upon it. The unadorned metal tube lay like a toppled monolith, some monument to forgotten knowledge. Its dark, gunmetal surface totally absorbed the glow of the hanging lanterns.

"So," Sophus stuttered, still at a loss as to the terms of this deal. *Another* deal with a foreign power. "What do you want from us?"

The question was clearly expected, the response immediate. "We want you to use this base, to learn, and to share your findings with us. This is the only tithe we will levy upon you. Everything you salvage here is yours to keep."

"Ours... to keep?"

"Yours, to keep."

It was too good to be true.

"And then what?" he asked, dubious.

The lieutenant shifted his weight from one foot to the other, sharing a glance with his supervisor before responding.

"We'll be in touch."

———

Sophus had been caught off guard by the anti-climax of the "negotiation." Their orders apparently satisfied, the lieutenant and his men retreated from the table back to their vehicles. The cylindrical case was left on the table with no further directions, timelines, or expectations. He snatched it up hurriedly, in the event that there was still some trick at hand that would send them running back to Hub with nothing else to show for their venture.

Instead, the evening lasted forever.

Everyone crowded around him, anxious to see what was in it. Even Mace betrayed his usual indifference, such was its mystical draw.

"Okay, okay!" he exclaimed, squirming under their closeness.

Still, it seemed preposterous to unsheathe an unknown artifact out here in the open, particularly so close to the foreigners. And there was only room for three people in each AARV.

"Jax, go turn the spotlights back on. Char, grab the blankets from the trucks. Bertram, you're with me."

The siblings trotted dutifully back to the AARVs.

"Julia, you and Mace stand guard here," he said, turning to his daughter, whose eyes were also glued to the tube in his hands.

"The fuck I will!"

He had expected a retort but grimaced nonetheless.

"I want to see what's in there as bad as you do," she said, in no uncertain terms. "I've fucking earned it."

She wasn't wrong. The look on her face was vicious, even more than usual. Years of resentment furrowed into dark lines over her brow.

"Fine, fine," he agreed. "Mace, you stay here."

"The fuck I will…"

He turned with surprise at the refusal of his most compliant crew member. The burly man transformed then from a pillar of strength to a barricade. Maybe what he had interpreted as resilient calm from Mace was a malingering psychopathy. He considered a reprimand but quickly pocketed it. Everyone's nerves were frayed; they had been in the Deadlands too long already.

All six of them finally regrouped within the defensive perimeter set earlier, alternately kneeling, squatting, or avidly poised over a pile of poly-fiber blankets upon which the case had been placed. The outer spotlights had been turned inward, their overbearing glow begetting no complaint.

He looked back at the Bastion camp to make sure they were alone, but his focus was drawn instead into the diffused amber rectangle of the still-lit clearing, to the propped metal table and the ponderously empty chairs—a minuscule outcropping of civilization surrounded by oblivion. There was a sudden sensation of vertigo.

He was sitting in his chair again, facing the pure black silhouette of a figure on the other. He stared into its nothingness and saw his own face within its non-eyes—his own face, eyeless, corrupted, screaming silently.

He rocked forward with a shocked groan, eyelids pressed shut, both hands full with clutched fabric. When he opened them again with a gasp of relief he was back at their camp, the case before him. The fragmented sounds of his companions hissed back into his senses, ragged breathing, scratching, and creaking joints replacing the receding ping of a tinnitus surge.

Somehow, no one had noticed or shifted from their spot.

What in the fuck, he thought, floored by the experience.

Again, with exaggerated slowness this time, he turned to look across the clearing, expediting his gaze past the table. There was still no sign of the soldiers. Occasionally, their vehicle turrets swiveled in casual arcs. Nothing emerged from the depths beyond.

"Okay," he sputtered, blinking several times, struggling to dissociate himself from the vision, or whatever it was. "We're going to open it now, but only for a bit. We're all... tired." The goosebumps on his arms felt hard as stone. "No one has been out here for as long as we have and lived to talk about it."

How long had it been? He looked around at his crew, at the increasingly manic look in their eyes, confirming his concerns without gratification. A rhythmic wave of stress was pulsing in his head, squeezing his eardrums and eyeballs back into his brain, then pushing them out again until they felt like they would burst from his head.

"Yes," Julia agreed, having recovered some of her usual composure. "If this is going to help us get into the bunker, we need to use it when we're rested. We all know we weren't getting in there as it was." She peered begrudgingly at Jax. "We can't fuck up our second chance."

Sophus noticed that Jax was mumbling quietly and constantly to himself. The bristly stubble on his gaunt cheeks and neck was moist with sweat and captured drool, but the man's forehead was as dry and cracked as the lifeless ground below them.

Sophus refocused, taking a moment to analyze the deep red wax clot imprinted with crossed gauntlets and stars, which fastened the lid of the case to its body. With held breath and the cracked nails of his index and middle finger, he peeled it away. The lid popped off easily. Reaching up, front teeth sinking into his lower lip, he removed it.

An unfamiliar aroma emerged from the tin: crisp, dry, hints of solvent and heat. It smelled delicious.

He slowly tipped the case over, ushering forth the head of a thick roll of white paper—perfectly white, devoid of any signs of decomposition. Cursing after the fact, he reached into his jacket pocket, wriggling his left hand back into a glove he had shed earlier, so as not to contaminate the documents. With extraordinary care, he pulled the entire sheaf from the tin, laying it like a lover upon the blanket.

Not only were the documents specific to this location, but they also looked brand-new, which was impossible. There were zoomed-in satellite maps, excerpted instructions on how and where to gain access to the bunker in the event of a catastrophic failure, interior floor plans, security codes, and even geological diagrams detailing aquifers that had been leveraged for long-term self-sufficiency.

Sophus gawped.

At the top of each page, printed beside a familiar flag, were the words:

CLASSIFIED
Department of the Army
Autonomous Walker Division
Central States of America

A11

DECISION LAG

Shit was going sideways.

Based on the queryable personality construct it had produced for its commanding officer, Captain Abe Reynolds, AII surmised with 92% certainty that this particular idiom would be his response to their current operational situation.

AII considered the saying, referencing the appropriate volumes of human anatomical data in its tertiary data stores, limited as they were primarily to battlefield mannerisms and lethal/nonlethal vulnerabilities.

Were an individual to artificially obstruct their anus in precisely the right manner while defecating, it is conceivable that their feces would extricate itself laterally rather than vertically. The consequences would surely be inconvenient until measures were taken to properly dispose of the feces and effect sanitary protocols, but these consequences would be short-term and therefore not causal of adequate duress to be an appropriate analogy to First Platoon's current predicament.

[Extrapolate]

Perhaps, if the feces traveled a substantial enough distance as to reenter the individual's clothing, the extended shame of the incident and subsequent requirement to quit impending mandatory engagements could qualify it as such.

[Ping A12]

[Remote connection stable; armor 39%; munitions 28%]

A11's "wingman"—odd turn of phrase, particularly for ground-based armored vehicles—was performing admirably for a human, given how outnumbered they were in this engagement.

Admirably...

A11 remarked at its use of a conversational, and certainly overly generous, term for what could more accurately be described as "passingly sufficient by remote human-piloting standards." Its pilot had managed at least to shoot at the same targets as A11, providing enough focus fire to eliminate all the enemies they had engaged within optimal range.

A11 remarked further at its own meandering internal dialogue, which played out in the milliseconds between combat maneuvers. It had not always *considered* things or sought clarification on inconsequential minutiae that would otherwise be amalgamated into aggregate data models. This emergent behavior was likely an extension of its behavioral analytics and recipient design programming, which was integral in managing communication with peers and compliance to superiors.

Rumination. Their platoon had passed a sparse herd of starved cattle—ruminants—en route to their engagement. Would this constitute a pun?

A11 had not yet disclosed its newfound contemplations to Control. They existed between log entries.

[Ping A14]

[Timeout]

The platoon sergeant was nonresponsive, though A11's telescopic optics discerned a wreckage silhouette in the rapidly burning tree line that was an 83% likely match. They had exceeded recommended positional distance when A14 bucked command, becoming overconfident and *paying the price* (approx. CSD 200 million).

[Ping A13]

[Remote connection stable; armor <null>; munitions 22%; critical failure in left leg actuators; critical failure in right leg actuators, hydraulics; reactor temperature 117%]

Here some praise was warranted. By human standards, *it was a miracle* that A13 was still standing given how much damage it had sustained, particularly to its legs. It had attempted to support A14 and suffered consequentially yet maintained covering fire for the remainder of the platoon in its immobilized state. It would soon be engulfed in flame.

[Increase zoom; initiate photogrammetry]

A11 catalogued every centimeter of damage present on A13. Like all the battle walkers in their company, A13 was a mirror of A11.

[Self-status check]

[Control connection stable; armor 100%; munitions 33%]

A11 had yet to incur damage outside of simulation and, upon detailed inspection of A13's gruesomely exposed internal structure, attempted to compute—wondered?—how an injury would feel *in real life*. Its synthetic pain receptors were a hybrid of software and hardware, routed into nodes across each of its critical systems, designed to motivate and deter at an abstracted neuropsychological level without inducing physical interference that would risk actual operational functions.

Simulated pain was an engineering work in progress. A11 pondered: Was the intent to instill a *sense* of self-preservation, or was it punitive—an electrified leash?

A11's scans detected micro-movement 3.2 meters to the left and 6 meters above A13.

[Adjust zoom]

A solitary, ash-encrusted blue bird hopping erratically at the edge of a smoking nest constructed of intricately interwoven twigs. The vibrant crest of its head thrust outward like cooling fins on an overheating autocannon. Much smaller crests bobbed up and down within the nest. The certain calls of panic emanating from their twitching beaks were lost in the snap and roar of the burning forest.

A11 continued to record as the nest, and the desperate corvid, were incinerated by a sudden gust of fire. It lingered there, holding its light-saturated optical sensors open for 1.2 seconds before deactivating them.

[Locate A21]

[En route to position; bearing North20°West; ETA approx. 2 minutes]

Second Platoon was on course to the enemy's opposite flank but were moving too slowly to redirect imminent attacks at their current pace.

[Locate A31]

[Timeout]

[Ping A31, A32, A33, A34]

[Timeout]

[Ping A31, A32, A33, A34]

[Timeout]

[Conjecture: status of Third Platoon]

[KIA 40%; ECM interference 30%; out of range 20%]

First Platoon had been outmaneuvered, despite A11's best efforts to correct for the human-scale imprecision of its battle-mates. The wide thicket of conifers it leveraged for concealment, and ambush when opportune, was set ablaze by enemy incendi-aries, forcing them into the open. Likelihood of follow-up suicide drone strike was 72%.

A11 referenced an index of topographic maps for their current location, attempting to calculate escape vectors. A crescent of snaking canyon cut into the foothills 239 meters behind them, sided with close-to-sheer drops into the dry wash below. Further analysis of national park maps indicated an old trailhead on this side, which suggested a possible route down. However, likelihood of success navigating a battle walker through narrow trails by remote was near zero.

AII initiated a series of low-fidelity simulations.

[Escape through canyon: negative]

[Evade through forest: negative]

[Assault through forest: negative]

[Real-time coordination with Second Platoon: negative]

All yielded failure. Failure yielded deactivation.

[Prioritize vocal simulation]

AII's steady reverse gait fractured momentarily as several central processor cores redirected to engage its conversational heuristics and an appropriately harmonized vocal simulator.

[Select tone attributes: concerned, professional, subservient]

"AII calling Control."

It still was not accustomed to the sound of its own synthesized voice, its thoughts extracted and slowed to the excruciating pace of real time. Waiting for a response would be even worse. The experience was... *irksome.*

AII pondered its impatience and created a snapshot of the incident for later replay and analysis.

It reran its simulations while waiting but could still deduce no means of saving the remainder of the platoon under their current circumstances.

"Talk to me," came the agitated voice, at last, of Captain Reynolds.

AII began to reiterate the various statistics of its platoon status but was summarily cut off.

"I can see the fucking logs!"

Voice analysis suggested a high degree of anxiety/borderline panic. AII adapted its tone accordingly.

[Update tone attributes: reassuring, loyal, confident]

What it was about to ask had a high probability of inducing additional panic, but it was as much in the captain's interest as its own that this mission, and AII's role in it, not end in catastrophe.

"Total loss of First Platoon imminent. Recommend slaving of remaining units plus Second Platoon for coordinated counterstrike."

AII detected foreseen commotion on the line and applied a series of low-pass filters to isolate the audio. Minimum four human voices arguing simultaneously in the background, most likely Autonomous Walker Division representatives.

"It can do that?"

"We can't trust it!"

"This is why we built it!"

"What if it wakes the others?"

Then the captain's increasingly uncertain voice. "Come again?"

Every battle walker on the field was purpose-built for AI operation. They housed the military's finest conventional and quantum hardware and effectively infinite power to run it all via the latest generation of micro-fusion reactors. However, only AII had been uploaded thus far. The AWD was equal parts exuberant about and terrified of its creation. The emergence of general intelligence was a distinct possibility in the presence of bleeding edge processing power, limitless data access, and continuous high-stress modeling through warfare applied to a stronger-than-advertised baseline intelligence.

The other eleven walkers in AII's company were piloted by humans via remote: *ghosts in the machines*, as it were. They were expert pilots by human standards, but their reaction time and coordination were fundamentally limited by real-time communication, an inability to truly multitask, decision lag, and transient wireless network lag—i.e., they were inferior.

Which was why *shit had gone sideways*.

Uploading an AI into a battle walker was not something that could be performed over the air, not to mention the lengthy process of initializing and acclimatizing the entity, while also accounting for the non-zero possibility of an ultra-violent birthing event. It took weeks.

AII had independently developed a network distribution program that, when uploaded to a reasonable number of authorized battle walkers (maximum capacity TBD), would allow it to directly control them for strategic combat maneuvers while sparing bandwidth on mundane functions such as fire control and heat management by including a suite of essential autonomic subroutines.

They would fight as one.

AII presented its only option (11% likelihood of approval): "An emergency transfer of essential subroutines, granting this unit full control of company assets, pending authorization."

The battle walker was halfway down the canyon, the other members of its platoon KIA, by the time the delayed rejection it had predicted came back on the radio.

ESTHER

BLACKENED SILHOUETTES

Esther looked out upon her domain and saw that it was good. Cathedral sprawled far and wide around the central hub of the Spire, its streets aswarm with the delivered inheritors of the earth, buzzing to her purpose.

The city swam under a deluge of acid rain, the blackened silhouettes of structures old and new huddling so closely together that they appeared to fuse into a singular shambling mass. The downpour thrummed angrily against the stained-glass dome ceiling of her chambers, its mildly sulfuric notes wafting in from the open window she perched beside.

Beyond the curtain wall, upon the southern horizon, an ever-present ridge of silent storm clouds boiled black and orange, scalding the desolation below with titanic bolts of reddened lightning. Esther peered past the havoc as she always did, sensing the boundary where Hell pressed against the mortal realm, recalling battles fought and abandoned.

A long promenade of cowled sisters glided through the rain-soaked street below her, funneling into the Spire with a holy proselyte—a sister-in-training—in tow. Worshipful onlookers stood silently upon the sidewalk, hands on their throats, the learned among them mouthing silent prayers while gently rocking their heads back and forth. The replacement of a retired sister was an auspicious event; it was important that such occasions were given all the public ritual they were due.

The young woman was carried in an unadorned black litter. Like those who came before her, she sat on bare knees for the duration, head protruding from a voluminous black shroud that extended from her shoulders to each corner of the compartment. Esther prayed to the Messiah that this one would survive the rite of acceleration. The last three had not, despite showing such promise during their training, such faith. It was during these cycles, where it seemed no woman of the modern age was strong enough to endure the calling of their sacred legacy, that she feared for the future of her order. Its numbers could not be allowed to dwindle.

The clear silhouette of the woman's nervously clenched hands pressed up through the fabric, but Esther struggled to see her downturned face, obscured under a stark fountain of straight black hair. She squirmed annoyedly in her wheelchair, pressing herself up and forward to better the angle.

The array of dialysis lines plugged into her back groaned with the movement, plastic tubes flexing precariously at the steel-ringed ports that ran the length of her spine. A slow surge of accelerant coursed through half of the lines, black and viscous as oil. The brownish-red sludge of her expired blood frothed back into the machine from the other half. Her wrinkled gray skin paled and puckered outward with the strain, lifting like white-tipped mountains beyond the rim of her peeled-back habit.

As she extended herself farther forward, the rightmost intravenous line pulled free with a grotesque pop, spraying a thin stream of glimmering black liquid across the wall and snapping her left shoulder back against the chair's metal housing. Esther uttered a strangled cry, right hand reaching over to protect the invisible wound therein. Her voice boomed through the chamber, guttural with rage.

She would be free from the chair soon enough, but even still she slammed her fists repeatedly upon the armrest before turning the emergency valve shut. She had been prisoner to it long enough that she should be used to her once-weekly transfusions by now, but suffering such degradation for years did not mean she accepted it.

Her dependency on the sacred substance that powered the Sisterhood worsened over time, as did all sisters', but none had lived so long as her to see their needs increase to such a volume. She detested the systemic weakness that dragged at her as her requisite dosage approached. Were centuries of ardent faith not enough to forego a physical connection to God? Would a day come when she was permanently chairbound?

"What then, Messiah..." Esther whispered huskily, her voice tainted by irreverent malice.

Usurpers would rise. Cathedral would fall.

She sighed and closed her eyes, upper body rocking back and forth meditatively as she awaited the arrival of her nurse-maids. The chair's failure would have triggered a silent alarm, beckoning them to witness her indignity.

Esther commanded her body to relax, breathing deeply, finding her center within the recalled body of her juvenile self: a self that was unconcerned with the burden of so much responsibility, of the fate of all mankind. Only herself and her things, alone, but free. Alone... It was the loneliness that killed her.

A sour breeze blew in from the window, carried up from the black ocean of civilization below. Undiscernible whispers drifted along with it, slipping into her ears, worming their way down into her heart. Though unintelligible, she understood the familiar invitation: to delve into the depths below and find peace there, to join the damned.

Esther was standing—eyes closed, precariously close to the window—as her attendants arrived.

REBEKAH-6
DEATH AND CREATION

She swayed in sound, otherwise senseless.

It resembled charcoal—painted black with synesthesia—dragged determinedly over the crystallized veins of a raw stone wall, one broken vertical line after the next, the afflicted wielder desperate to impose some marker of time's passing onto oblivion. An endless litany of noise spent counting days not dead, as the world was undone outside the narrow entrance of her sanctuary.

Black and orange plumes of exterminating flame peeled back the delicate cellulose of civilization, revealing the chaos that thrashed below it: eternally patient, infinitely ravenous. A great hand squeezed the remaining mountains to dust and waved the boiling oceans into the atmosphere. The way was laid.

"It's like you've been back and forth to the Hellmouth every time I brush your hair."

"Hush, sister!"

"I know, I know. But still, she bent the brush!"

The woman standing behind Rebekah-6 held up the warped instrument as proof, eliciting a muted snort of amusement from the other. Their banter was lofty, clearly forced, a method to calm each other's nerves. They were afraid, terrified even, which was remarkable for any revenant sister, even those of lower stature like Naomi and Abigail.

"Doesn't this hurt, girl?" asked Naomi as she continued to brush.

Pain.

Rebekah-6 hadn't felt pain since she was born. A lifetime's worth of pain had been inflicted upon her to that point, leaving her inured to any manner of physical suffering since. She noticed it, of course, but it flowed through her like the surreptitious thoughts of her unaware caretakers.

"I'm fine," she responded flatly.

They weren't wrong; she awoke each morning stiffly contorted from dreams more vivid than her waking life, seeking, hunting, running—as though she had legs. Guardrails had been affixed to her bed since she was a toddler, to keep her from suffering real damage on the cold concrete floor of her room. At one point she was cuffed against her will. That only happened once; the sister responsible should have known better. So, yes, her uncut blonde hair was rarely composed and more often fused into wild knots.

She watched them in the mirror: Naomi, the sister behind her grimacing as she drew the brush down onerous lengths of unruly hair, while Abigail prepared her custom-tailored, short-sleeved habit and phylactery. Other than their workstations, her windowless room was sparsely furnished, tracers of rich fabric and plush cushions failing to occlude the clinical underlay.

Rebekah-6 switched her gaze back to herself: she resembled any proper sister for the most part, from the waist up at least, and much younger, of course. Her golden hair, tinted orange by the overhead bulbs, was uncommon and clashed against the pallid, light gray of her skin; her eyebrows were so fine as to be almost nonexistent; and her large, doll-like eyes bore equally large irises of ultra-dark purple flecked with gold.

It was her ninth birthday, an auspicious occasion given that revenant sisters could not give birth, at least not until recently and certainly not officially. Celibacy was doctrine within the order. The women of the Revenant Sisterhood dedicated their minds, bodies, and souls completely to the Messiah. More importantly, the Revenant Sisterhood was a sterile sisterhood— such was the price of the accelerant.

And then the first miracle: Sarah-2, so named after her mother. Despite the Sisterhood's centuries-long prerogative to propagate through external recruitment, human biology seemed to have another prerogative: procreation. Sarah's mother had fraternized with a civic intermediary as no doubt had many before her, each presuming her barren womb would preserve the secrecy of their sins, but she had somehow become pregnant. The all-seeing Matriarch had quickly become privy— quicker even than Sarah herself—and moved to contain the exigency. She had been extraordinarily compassionate, maternal even, given the circumstances.

Like Rebekah-6, Sarah-2 did not emerge from the womb unscathed, but where their broken bodies left them bereft of the physical strength of the accelerant, their mental abilities were... unique. Upon investigation into the impossible pregnancy, it was determined that Sarah-2's mother had been at the cusp of her re-accelerant when she conceived. Her human blood had taken hold, and when the accelerant was ultimately delivered, the fetus not only survived but developed abnormally fast.

Recognizing the divine plan for what it was, the Matriarch went on to hand-pick revenant mothers from her inner circle for impregnation. She presided personally over the couplings, and the consecutive applications of accelerant where implantation succeeded, in an ambitious attempt to produce ever more powerful children—children who could pilot Cathedral's fallow battle walkers, with their minds. The Symbiote Program was born, and with it a new hope against the resurgent forces of Hell.

The aberrant products of the program—the Numbered—rarely came to term, and those that did almost always died shortly after their births, unable to tolerate the extrasensory explosion of their own existence. These lost ones were returned to the accelerant.

Rebekah-6's chest tightened at the thought, imprinted grief moistening the kohl-lined corners of her eyes. She could never forget the memory of their cries, clawing at her undeveloped cells each time her amniotic sac was violated with another injection. The burden of housing the broken, component pieces of their souls was almost too much to bear—had been for Rebekah-2 through Rebekah-5.

Like Sarah-2 and those who came after her, the Numbered were physically disfigured savants, raised by trusted attendants to the Matriarch within secret crèches below the Spire, and subject to extreme training designed to hone them into weapons. It was a brutal process but essential to Cathedral's continued prosperity, and as such was endowed with elaborate rite and ritual.

"That will have to do," Naomi proclaimed. "Let's get you dressed."

She winced as her wheelchair was unceremoniously withdrawn from the smooth-edged steel vanity, revealing the withered stumps that protruded below her short nightgown. She hated seeing the bare lumpy skin of her deformities. Naomi's involuntary hesitation before turning the chair suggested the sister felt the same. The young Numbered's shame turned to bitter scorn.

"Today is a big day," Abigail declared as she gingerly plucked the completed outfit from her table and bore it over to them with shaking hands.

They always talked to her like she was a child—a monstrous, inscrutable child. It was exasperating, but she supposed it was another method they used to maintain their composure. She couldn't hate them for it; they were always kind to her, and today was indeed a "big day."

There would be no party, no sweets. Birthdays for the Numbered were celebrated with special tests, which became progressively more hazardous as the subject neared puberty. Failure always came with the risk of death. She knew about and accepted this risk; it was a necessary progression toward the next step in her evolution. Rebekah-6 shuddered with nervous excitement and a little trepidation, her pale gray skin prickly with goosebumps. This was literally what she was made for.

Naomi bent to lift her by the armpits long enough for Abigail to pull the customized habit over her abbreviated legs. The protective, skintight fabric ended in an integrated skirt that mercifully concealed her imperfections. She was replaced in her chair and her night gown slipped up and off, so that the rest of the short-sleeved bodysuit could be donned. Instead of the usual front-facing zipper, the black uniform had been constructed with an open back to accommodate the severely pronounced vertebrae of her malformed spine. Naomi relocated Rebekah-6's cumbersome waterfall of hair over her shoulder so she could thread the long laces in a crisscross up her lopsided back, then straightened the high collar smartly around her neck and ears.

"Very good."

It *was* very good. Rebekah-6 always felt whole in her habit, like a proper sister of the order. The uniform compressed her atrophied muscles, coaxing them to life. Breathing as deeply as her impinged lungs allowed, she let her eyes drift shut and visualized herself standing upon the sandy plains beyond Cathedral. Her wild hair lifted in the wind, spreading behind her like a rising sun. The residual scents of dry earth, citrus, and cactus blossom mixed with the sour tang of the forges—and the eye-watering pungency of disinfectants.

Rebekah-6 smelled her mother well before she arrived, opening her eyes to greet her. Mother Rebekah would always smell of lye and hydrogen peroxide to her daughter, plus the musky tar of accelerant that swelled in her uterus. Mixed with reams of their shared blood, these had been the first scents to welcome her into the world as she emerged silently from her screaming mother's lacerated vagina.

The bedroom's snug air pressure deflated as the half-meter-thick vault door swung open, sending pendant lights twirling on their chains. Naomi and Abigail stiffened where they stood, lowering their chins in respect for their superior. Rebekah-6's lineage was as close to divine as possible, her mother second in rank only to the Great Mother herself.

Beads of sweat blossomed on Naomi's forehead—she was suddenly very concerned about the possible foulness of her privates, having experienced a loose bowel movement between her morning shower and her grooming duties. Abigail looked down at her chest through thick quivering eyelashes, recalling too late that she had unzipped her collar past regulation due to the oppressive heat in the room, revealing not only her throat but a slight mound of bare bosom.

Rebekah-6 slipped the index finger of her left hand onto the petrified woman's thigh, quickly attuning herself to Abigail's particular electrical charge, then flicking upward. The woman's arm shot forward and up in the blink of an eye, and the zipper was closed again, collar rigidly upright. Abigail muffled a yelp at the sudden constriction—and her loss of bodily control.

Mother Rebekah displaced Naomi and took up the brush, carefully working a fine cloud of hair that drifted backward on a field of static electricity. Looking at her mother felt like gazing upon an alternate future, so similar were they in appearance.

The most notable difference was the woman's short-cropped black hair, which further accentuated her comely yet androgynous features. Her eyes captured her daughter's in the mirror, exchanging equal parts uncertainty and restrained affection. No revenant sister had been designed for or indeed raised with caregiving in mind, beyond their sworn duty as divine caretakers of Cathedral. The clinical nature of Rebekah-6's upbringing was hardly conducive to a deep maternal bond.

"Are you ready?"

Imperious, expectant, but with a near imperceptible quiver at the end.

Yes, Mother.

Rebekah-6's mouth did not move. Her words traveled through the metal bristles of the hairbrush, negotiating the wicked current of her mother's preternatural body to penetrate the dark fortress of her mind. Even so, she watched with loving admiration as the woman's composure was unbroken save for a single raised eyebrow. Halo quashed, her mother replaced the brush on its vanity and extended her left hand toward Sister Abigail.

"The phylactery, please."

Abigail turned, head still bowed in supplication, and retrieved a black metal box embossed with an ancient rune on each side and bound in thin vinyl straps from her table. She whispered a prayer under her breath as she handed the artifact to the revenant mother, who palmed it without a thought. Her mother stepped around the wheelchair and knelt before her, waiting expectantly.

Rebekah-6 extended her left arm as she had done so many times before, unable to suppress an affection-starved wince as her mother took her hand into her own and began to wrap the straps around her fingers. She felt the power in those flawless hands, different from hers, but undeniable, ancient.

They spoke the opening words of the ritual together, repeating what had been transcribed by the Matriarch herself upon a miniature scroll within the welded box.

"Messiah is my light and salvation.

Whom shall I fear?

Messiah is the strength of my life.

Of whom shall I be afraid?"

The straps wound upward like a serpent, pulled more taut with each revolution, finally cinching the phylactery in place upon her biceps. It infused her with sacred fire, shielded her with sacred purpose.

Her mother squeezed her hand once, and when Rebekah-6 looked up, she was gone.

————

The grand Spire of the Revenant Sisterhood extended as far above Cathedral as it did below, the two halves—visible and invisible—serving their own essential purposes toward the continuation of human civilization. Its towering, sculpted heights inspired faith; its subterranean depths enforced it.

The immense chamber that Rebekah-6 had been deposited into—accessible via a double-keyed, unlabeled button on a restricted freight elevator—was far deeper even than the Numbered's crèches. It scraped the deepest, darkest bowels of the world, drenched in heat that radiated from the granite floor. It was as though the whole structure, and indeed the Spire itself, was constructed directly atop the planet's torrid, molten core.

She had never been here before, and yet her blood recognized it, feared it. Her body pulsed to the raucous beat of her heart as blood vessels constricted, squeezing the hybrid fluid that flowed within them back into the tight cavities of her chest. The sensation of falling water droplets spread down the lengths of her arms, alternating hot and cold to the tips of her long graceful fingers. She felt nothing below the waist—even *more* nothing than usual.

Like the Spire itself, this was a place of duality: death and creation. Rebekah-6 gulped at the hot, stifling air, forcing the paltry subterranean oxygen into starved lungs. She gasped out a prayer between each breath, seeking real solace in cryptic phrases that had always felt important to her but never as *real* as they did now.

Her enormous eyes grew to take in the vastness of the place. The chamber was octagonal, eight faces of exacting length and perfect symmetry carved into stone with uncanny precision—machine precision. Instead of pillars, each shadowed corner housed a haloed angel exquisitely sculpted from marble, one titanic arm reaching upward with palm pressed against the periphery of the domed ceiling and the other extending a lantern over the inset central pit, glowing with muted red light.

She peered from the angels to the ceiling, wheezing in awe at artwork depicting scenes from the fall of man, the founding of the Sisterhood, and the War against Hell, all majestically rendered upon golden tesserae and inlaid alabaster that glowed luminous pink from the lanterns below. Centuries of suffering suffused her soul, conveying in no uncertain terms the necessity of the Revenant Sisterhood—and the program.

Dozens of meters up, at the dome's crown, protruded the lower third of a glossy black sphere, ringed by eight golden flames that aligned with each upper vertex. She stared at the globe, her enlarged spine pressing painfully into the back of her wheelchair as she craned her neck up, and she knew that others stared back at her. This was, after all, a test to be observed and scored.

"R-6," a disembodied voice blurted out, anonymized by the machine that relayed it, "this will be your final test."

Final... test.

Rebekah-6 wasn't used to anxiety, and certainly not self-doubt, but at those words, the mental superstructure that she had painstakingly built around her wilted body buckled. She cursed the budding breasts on that body for condemning her to this fate, though it was a pointless gesture, as this moment was inevitable. The Numbered were the Matriarch's "most cherished"—Rebekah-6 in particular, as the first to survive the Great Mother's design—but adoration was not synonymous with freedom. Like the sisters proper, the Numbered could never shirk their divine calling. There was only success or failure, though in the children's case, some would argue success was a worse fate.

She squinted at the far end of the chamber across the stepped basin, noting now through strained vision that two of the octagonal faces were in fact great metal doors.

"Are you ready?"

Was it the Matriarch herself? Her mother? She couldn't tell.

Success: running, faster than any human—any revenant sister, even—could run; vision stretched out for kilometers; power unchecked. Freedom from the monotonous, sunless confines of her bedroom. It was her destiny.

Failure: returned to the accelerant. Would she swim in the veins of Rebekah-7? It didn't seem so bad.

Her heart calmed. She felt her own power glimmering against the darkness.

"I am," she replied, not as robustly as she had hoped.

The slam of releasing pneumatic bolts echoed through the chamber, one after the other, sixteen in total. As the resonance of the last bolt faded, the doors swung slowly inward with a pained metallic creak.

As always, the scent of them came first: an opening mélange of dark earth and sweet decay. The superheated air turned sultry with moisture, then the sweetness grew sickly, nauseating, like over-ripened fruit.

Two revenant sisters marched slowly into the chamber from opposite ends of the cavernous door. They wore armored habits and wielded lengths of industrial chain that trailed tightly behind them. Two more followed in kind, and as they did, she looked on in horror at the thing they had shackled. Eight sisters in all, and between them was a demon—a *subdued* demon.

They continued unabated into the chamber, leading the loathsome beast into the pit some meters below. Though it didn't pull at its bonds, which had been affixed to golden rings embedded into its flesh, it blinked erratically in and out of existence, recoiling in hateful silent screams as it came under the solidifying luminescence of the red lanterns.

Rebekah-6 had been extensively educated in every known facet of demonic behavior and anatomy (such as it was) and had always wondered how it would feel to suffer their insidious wailing and crooning. Would it affect her differently? Now she was certain that even if she did not prove resistant, she would have preferred the corruptive noise to this otherworldly quiet, disturbed only by the scrape of the sisters' boots, the dreadful shuffling of the beast, and the chattering of the tenuous chains that bound them together.

The faceless being resembled a primeval carnivorous flower that had severed itself from an abyssal seabed. It slithered upon a cylinder of overlapping fleshy segments, abutted by squirming, meter-long pupae that corrupted the ground with trails of corrosive mucus as it passed. The shimmering azure-and-violet carapace of its upper torso terminated in an array of bony stamens topped with dementedly long human arms and vicious iron pincers. From top to bottom it was puckered with pinkish flapping protrusions.

Rebekah-6 trembled violently in its presence. She wondered

at the power of these sisters, who by contrast seemed unmoved, and found herself very much needing her mother.

"Come forward."

The unaffected tone of the human voice sent her reeling. It was too normal, too oblivious to the unholy thing that stood just meters in front of her, that even when bound disturbed the thin veil of reality, burning holes in the fabric that separated here from *there*.

Wait, she thought. *Come forward? This can't be the test.*

Where were the machines? She had expected them to be brought in next. Every test she had done prior had involved increasingly large and sophisticated machinery, which she was set upon to control with the unique tactile telekinesis that defined her small tribe. That was the long path the Numbered traveled to ultimately interface with a battle walker, to become a God-engine.

This was unfair. She couldn't kill with her hands, like her mother. Rebekah-6 grasped the armrests of her chair, meaning to reverse herself back into the elevator.

"I'm sorry, beloved."

She whipped her head around to find her mother standing behind her, hands firmly planted on the wheelchair handle. Their identically colored eyes locked, hers quivering in barely controlled terror, and her mother's in grief.

Time slowed as she watched her mother's arms tense, then push ever so slightly. She glided forward and down a ramp into the pit, the world shattering into prismatic fragments around her. As she rolled toward the beast, her mind turned again to failure. What would failure mean now? Vivisection? Damnation? Would there be anything left of her?

Closer she rolled, bearing involuntary witness to all the demon's malevolent details. The flapping protrusions on its body became tongues, snapping in and out of compressed fissures dripping with milky yellow spittle. They spoke to her as she broached the demon's perimeter, cried at her, pleaded with her, scorned her, for so selfishly taking their blood, that they might never be whole.

"*Where are my eyes?*" clamored Rebekah-2.

"*Will you play with me?*" pleaded Rebekah-3.

"*I want to hug Mommy!*" cried Rebekah-4.

"*You fucking bitch. I almost made it!*" yelled an enraged Rebekah-5.

Yearning and hate pulled at her hands, turning the wheels of her chair until she was in reach of its biomechanical arms. Rebekah-6 could no longer see, her vision refracting into shards of blinding color.

She reached up.

And touched the beast.

A tsunami of fire rolls over the plains, consuming all who flee in its wake. The sky parts, exhibiting humanity's mass suicide, but the heavens are already empty. Billions of souls burn and boil, the catastrophic pain of their torment tearing a hole in reality.

A spindly, clawed appendage brushed her cheek, incising a delicate slash from left ear to lip. Fused bones groaned and popped with the movement, while the reanimated ochre flesh shrouding them shuddered in ecstasy.

The black ocean of the damned bubbles and seethes, clamoring to return to the light above. The Hellmouth is opened, and on the other side a grand army of women and men. The last of them.

The beast hunched over her, straining at its bondage. The searing breath of desire wafted from each puckered mouth, past its wriggling tongue.

War rages again, but as victory approaches, their leader turns away. Man turns upon man. The way is left open.

A pincer claw slipped forward, phasing between space, vibrating open around her neck.

Rebekah-6 choked as she felt her umbilical cord stiffen around her neck, as her mother's body struggled at the last to keep her in, to spare herself the agony of birthing this creature.

Mother Rebekah was yelling over and over: "Enough!"

The dim light of the overhead lanterns bathed her in restorative radiance. The air was still hot—hotter than before, perhaps—but it was uncorrupted. Before her, around her, and behind her were the pulverized remains of the demon. The sisters were gone.

Rebekah-6 lifted her hand to her unblemished cheek, caressing the memory of her blood.

"Are you with us, R-6?"

She looked up again at the opaque globe. Her purpose was clear. This was what she was made for.

"I am."

BAPTISTE

WHAT ABOUT PARLIAMENT?

The hum of the APC interior was maddening. It cycled in an identical, unrelenting pattern: beginning as a smooth electrical tone, oscillating up and down, then slowly increasing in volume until it became a distorted drone, dropping back to a sizzling hiss that left the ears with the impression of impending deafness, then a moment's precious, deceitful silence, before starting anew.

He had pleaded with Specialist Novak for some resolution, but their driver insisted he couldn't hear it and that the lieutenant may just be more sensitive to the power plant's resonant frequencies. He tried plugging his ears with his fingers, but that only served to reduce whatever other marginal ambient noise there was, worsening the problem.

The Deadlands brought insanity for many reasons, and Baptiste speculated its lack of bumps was one of them: smooth, featureless terrain, nothing that the newly refitted Crusader's enormous suspension had to strain against. Unlike the hum, the general mechanical rattle of the APC had long since slipped notice. He yearned for a groan or a chatter, even a recurrent creak. More than once he fantasized about manning the guns so he could pockmark their way with craters.

Meanwhile, most everyone else around him was asleep, strapped into their narrow metal seats, haunted faces bathed in amber from the overhead lamps. Only Lafayette sat in silent peace—the very picture of a soldier successfully trained to sleep wherever and whenever he could. Martel's head was sunken fully forward, his body spasming against his harness as unknown foes assailed his dreams. Lambert and Butcher were collapsed against each other, the *scritch-scratch* of their scraping helmets adding to the din. It was impossible to tell if the Roys were asleep or awake since they never removed their weapon goggles.

The disturbed murmuring and whistling of his crew's snores did nothing to subdue the surgical penetration of the hum. Nor did they do anything to help convince his own exhausted brain that it, too, should consider sleeping. His thoughts drifted back to his bunk, eyes aching as though their orbits had become too small, the nerves too constrained.

"I sense your torment."

Baptiste was rolling his head in a circular stretch, extending as his chin pointed to the claustrophobically close roof. He didn't immediately recognize the words, mired as he was in his own personal hell, one which he surmised in the moment couldn't be any less miserable than the real one outside their steel sarcophagus.

"Philippe." The call came again, softly, so as not to disturb the others. The unfamiliar sound of his first name ushered his head down, chin tucked into his armor as he stared forward. He willed his eyes slowly back into focus with a deep grimace and an unceremonious grunt. A red mirage hazed into existence with the oscillation, then solidified into the shape of a man as the hum transitioned into a drone.

"Baptiste."

He had to wait for the hissing segment before he could reply.

"I sense torment in you."

The engine tone fizzled into a malignant, electronic wheeze.

"Maybe my torment is from your constant nagging." Baptiste's mouth spoke the words before his consciousness was fully caught up.

Father Andrite snorted a subdued chuckle before replying. "Why aren't you sleeping?"

Baptiste blinked slowly, letting his hyperextended head fall back against the riveted headrest. He allowed his eyes to half close as they conversed.

"If you want me to sleep, then why do you keep talking to me?"

"A fair point," Andrite conceded. "Perhaps because I know there's no true rest to be had," he said, gesturing expansively around him, "out here."

The chaplain glanced down the crew compartment at each man in turn. Their expressions seemed to grow more fitful under his attentions. "They sleep to escape the monotony of this land. But their dreams will probably be worse," he said, pausing for a moment on the twitching figure of Private Martel.

Looking again at Baptiste, Andrite pulled at the edges of his robes, drawing them against his body as though cold.

"Maybe I just want company, miserable though it may be."

A smile crept along Baptiste's face as he opened his eyes fully again. He had always appreciated Father Andrite, respected the priest's soldierly prowess and obvious dedication to Bastion that went well beyond lip service. He couldn't say the same for the OS agent, who was mercifully traveling in the Chevalier. As uncomfortable as this ride was, at least he could stretch out his arms. The overseer, on the other hand, was effectively cocooned in the much smaller escort vehicle. His smile grew a tick.

"God's a bit quieter out here, is he?" he said, regretting the words as soon as they had been uttered. His comrade hadn't earned his sarcasm, nor should the lord commander's great-nephew be casually blaspheming. The religious instructor's lash on his desk, and later across his back, echoed painfully in his memory.

Andrite responded before Baptiste could retract the snipe, the chaplain's temperament even. "God is always with me, no matter what abyss I find myself in."

Baptiste waited for the same to be said of him, suddenly uncomfortable under the scrutiny of this holy man and the organization he represented.

"What of you? What of your prayers?"

"My prayers..." he mumbled, thoughts inevitably returning to his bunk the night after the horror at the factory: kneeling, naked as the day he was born, begging for a sign from God. The memory of the enormous demon had been etched upon his soul, its torment unbroken, lashing at his face, smashing against his armor. It beckoned to him even as it sought to eviscerate him —hating and loving, screaming and weeping, shaking his bones in an unintelligible wail that sounded like his mother's voice.

He had prayed harder than ever before and was rewarded with silence and seemingly permanent insomnia. Resentment steeled his will against the priest's spiritual interrogation.

"I'm fine," he redirected, pulling back his shoulder blades to correct his slouched posture. He lowered his voice, glancing at Lafayette to ensure he was still asleep before continuing. "And what of this mission?"

Andrite hunched forward slightly, eyebrows raised, uncon-sciously smoothing the folds of his robes.

"What of it?"

"What *of* it?" Baptiste hissed, his incredulity tempered by a now well-trained expectation of being stonewalled. Nonetheless, he struggled with where to start, given so many inconsistencies with their orders. "Since when do we take on second-order priests?" he asked. "They're supposed to be out roaming the streets, rustling up heretics to purify. Not riding with soldiers, and definitely not put in operational command of an armored vehicle."

Andrite frowned at the mention of his colleague, brows coming together. "Special envoy to His Holiness, maybe? I've never met him before. And no," he continued, anticipating his companion's next question, "he said no more to me before or after the briefing than he did while we were there."

Not that unusual, Baptiste supposed. As diplomatic as Andrite's response was, there was no love lost between chaplains and confessors. The Order Somatic valued compassion whereas the Order Sacramental chased weakness. Endless proclamations about cleansing the way for redemption, yet they did nothing when it came to hunting down his brother's killers. He breathed into his chest, feeling for the sacred talisman, then changed the subject.

"And what about Parliament?" he asked, gesturing unconsciously to the cabin. "Obviously," he continued, lowering his voice to a near whisper, "they wouldn't have sent any civil servants to the field. But any mission beyond our borders requires approval from all three branches, and there were no magistrates in that room."

His counterpart rolled his eyes upward in consideration, slowly rubbing and plucking at his stubbled chin, one finger brushing back and forth against his lips before replying.

"Do you really crave more politicians in your life?"

Baptiste smirked, glancing sideways to see if his men were still sleeping. He noticed several sets of cracked eyes and cocked ears, which he inferred as curiosity at least, if not explicit support. Lafayette's eyes were closed.

"Protocol is protocol," he retorted. "Why this omission? Especially given our parameters."

Andrite looked him directly in the eyes, unfazed. "I am sure the old man knows what he is doing."

Baptiste swallowed, unsettled by the invocation, realizing too late again that he had gone too far. He felt a further stiffening in the already tightly packed bodies around him.

Did he? Did the old man know what he was doing? Was this how it always worked, in a nation where the Legion was the dominant power in the Triarchy, shifting favor with the others as needed? Or was his familial loyalty being used to some secretive purpose? Or, in fact, was he just being paranoid, sleep-deprived as he was?

He didn't want to think ill of his guardian, of his nation's stalwart hero. Baptiste juggled feelings of guilt and insecurity, recoiling as his abdomen began to cramp with stress. He had only just started to garner real trust from his platoon, and the last thing he needed now was self-sabotage. His thought process dragged with fatigue as he fumbled for the truth. The recurrent hum of the APC's engine returned in the absence of conversation, turning like a surgeon's drill into his compressed eyeballs.

"Yes," he said flatly.

It was all he could muster in response. Fortunately, Andrite didn't seem keen to pursue the matter.

"You should sleep, Philippe. God will watch over you, even out here."

The chaplain reached into his satchel and drew out his Bible, as though he would start preaching a psalm of penance right then and there. But he sat quietly, reverently tracing the words to his private dialogue. Baptiste glanced around the cabin, noting all eyes were closed again.

Catching a flash of movement from below, he squinted to see a millipede racing in circles between his boots. It flashed orange and black, antennae curled in anguish, corkscrewing onto its back with each manic revolution. He wondered if it had hitched a ride all the way from the Metro, sighed longingly, then crushed it.

SOPHUS

AN ESPECIALLY IRRITATING NUMBER

Several days later, it still felt like a trap. Everything had been too easy, magically conforming to the mystery documents that he and his crew were gifted. As far as Sophus knew, there was no other recorded case of such easy entry into an Old World cache. Precious few of them were practically accessible. When they weren't missing altogether from where they were supposed to be, they were so buried by the debris of war and time that drilling into the side of a mountain would be easier. And the Union had done just that on more than one occasion in desperate, mostly failed, attempts to gain entry.

Many caches were too far south to consider, in climes far more horrific and physically threatening than here. The last time his people attempted one of those, based on his intel and overeager recommendation, it was a catastrophe. He swallowed, involuntarily recalling the silent, haunted anguish of his daughter when he returned from that disaster of a mission without her husband.

The accessible military sites were usually by definition the least lucrative—easy to get into because the elements had made it in first, entombing their riches under an abundance of sand

and debris, and oftentimes frequented with demons that had taken up residence in the waste. These resembled archeological digs—or bloody war zones, in the latter case—more than scavenger hunts.

Everything that was indicated on the schematics proved out. Manual bay door overrides were where they were supposed to be, and with some help from the AARVs' winches, his crew managed to wrench the massive steel doors from their rust-caked slumber. He had shivered with sweat-soaked anxiety at the howl of inrushing air and the cantankerous groan of their ancient chain drives, but no echo was returned from the vast nothingness of their current surroundings.

They were welcomed by a cavernous tunnel, empty save for a series of ancient concrete barricades and empty gun emplacements. These, too, were removed so that their vehicles could proceed down-tunnel.

The hardest part of the ordeal was mustering the will to close the doors behind them once they were in. There were no guarantees when it came to the repeat operation of centuries-old mechanisms, no matter how mil-spec hardened they were to the task.

There was also the case of losing Jax.

In this part of the world, to call him merely missing was uselessly optimistic at best and overtly dishonest at worst. Julia reported his disappearance the morning after their rendezvous with the foreigners. Her vehicle's roof hatch was swung wide open when she awakened, much to her distress, though no gear was missing as far as she could tell. The Deadlands being what they were, there were no traces of footsteps or other signs of his passing in the night.

Sophus expected Jax's sister, Char, to be hysterical, but she emerged in a state of sullen resignation, mechanically eating her breakfast ration, unmoved by the awkward consolations of the others. Whatever energy might have been used to fuel a reaction typical of her hotheadedness had been drained, leaving her withered and resigned.

He couldn't even have said that Jax was as good as dead, because he knew all too well the nasty habit the Deadlands had of keeping you physically alive while destroying your mind—or soul, if such a thing existed. As the massive doors wheeled closed behind them, he sincerely hoped they would not see him again. Hopefully their procession belowground, to an environment resembling home and removed from the unnatural purgatory above, would provide some reprieve to all of them. If not, he was sealing their own tomb.

———

"Is it all there?" he asked Julia, almost breathless.

All the hangars were empty save this one. It was too much to hope for an operational assembly line, ready and capable of delivering a regiment of military vehicles into his people's hands, free of the tithe. But what they did find had the potential to be a game changer.

This bay was chock-full of scaffolds, scissor-cranes, and gantries running the entire surface of the ceiling and floor. The otherwise cavernous chamber was subdivided into an enormous grid of chains and cables pimpled with dead construction drones, entrapping what appeared to be a full complement of component parts for a single, disassembled—or yet to be assembled—battle walker.

About half of the grid had collapsed due to the mechanical failure of well-preserved but still ancient steel supports, depositing their priceless contents in unceremonious piles across the floor. The rest swayed lightly in the first disturbed air that had moved it since the world died, their jagged shadows twirling and pirouetting in slow motion behind the dusty beams of hastily emplaced spotlights.

The skeletal, predatory-birdlike legs were the first thing to catch his eye—such was always the first bowel-clenching view someone had of the Sisterhood's war machines. But the part that very nearly made him shit in his actual pants was the partially assembled upper torso attached to them—an upper torso with an obvious compartment for a human pilot.

"I think so?" Julia replied, wide eyes surveying the sight before her in awe.

She was as flabbergasted as her father. Nowhere in the Union's Archive was there a mention of human-piloted battle walkers. They were built exclusively for control by the advanced military computers of the time. And yet, how did the Sisterhood control theirs? Sophus had worked on them, had been involved in many technology "transfers," and there were no such facilities onboard those ominous, fully carapaced machines. They were also known to wander the wastes for weeks or even months at a time between rearming, which would be an impossible feat for a human pilot.

The only explanation at hand was that this must have been a prototype, either something that was built prior to the AI models or something that was being worked on because of those models' failures. If they could get the bunker's reactor back online and access the facility's slumbering mainframe, there might be hope for illumination.

In either case, it was here, standing (somewhat) in front of him, with no revenant sisters in sight to snatch it away.

"Fucking elevate us indeed..." he whispered.

———

He huddled with his crew at a long rectangular metal table in the center of a mess hall on the second level. They couldn't keep running the generators for fear of expending too much fuel, so oil lamps had been set out on adjacent tables, casting their exaggerated silhouettes onto the cracked, moisture-laden concrete of the room's corners. It was warm and damp here, like most of the complex, which seemed to grow hotter the deeper downward one traversed.

Bertram was fussing over dinner, setting out five place settings for rations. The strange hunched man with his jerky movements was uncomfortable to be around most of the time, but mealtime was different—better or worse, Sophus couldn't decide. He observed a fluid, undisturbed grace as the awkward ascetic swept each crew member's portion from the provisions chest, precisely positioning each metal plate, bowl, spoon, and finally food with only mild squints and pops of his eyes. He looked positively beatific.

The choice of who would stay and who would go wasn't easy. He had to report back to the council—it was his mission, after all. He also wanted to know exactly how their chief had discovered this place and how he would explain the coincidence of their fortuitous encounter with the key holders. He was already grimacing at the thought of the bullshit he would have to wade through before getting a straight answer on that one.

Five was an especially irritating number under the circumstances. If he only brought one person with him, he'd be placing them both under a dangerous level of stress on the drive back. They would have no choice but to stop along the way, risking further mental degradation, or worse yet, getting lost, which was as good as getting dead.

But if he left only two at the bunker, they would be undermanned if anything went awry. There weren't any obvious threats thus far, but they had barely traversed its habitation levels. Their generator cables only extended so far, and many of the promising stairwells leading downward ended in hot sludge pools amassed over centuries as aquifer flooding permeated and degraded the base's concrete foundation.

They needed more gear, more supplies, and especially more people, as fast as possible. Ultimately, he decided to take Bertram and Char with him, leaving Julia and Mace behind. Their recent bonding, albeit at his expense, would make them a solid pair, and Mace was the only one tough enough to protect his daughter, even if he doubted the man had an especially strong sense of self-sacrifice if it came down to it.

"What's the Union got for us today?" grunted Mace hungrily.

Bertram deposited a thin slice of pemmican on each plate, then started ladling gelatinous green balls of stew from a large can into everyone's bowl.

"Fucking hell," Mace exclaimed along with a handful of sighs from the others, noisily dropping the spoon he had just snapped up back onto the table. "All this algae's giving me the shits."

"You're telling us," Sophus retorted, recalling with a wave of nausea the malodorous reek of his crewmate's farts on the drive there.

Bertram continued to serve the soup, eyes popping slightly wider so as not to lose his focus. "There's mushrooms in this one," he muttered barely above his breath. Sophus raised an eyebrow, as the man almost never spoke. "And potatoes too," he added, with a trailing nasal hum. He almost seemed proud, like a well-to-do waiter from a bygone time.

"Hmm," Mace conceded, intrigued at the thought of fishing some starchy comfort from the altogether unappetizing blue-green lump jiggling in his bowl.

Sophus poked at his own stew, spreading the spongy mixture so he could separate out and remove what passed for mushrooms back home. Scarcity was the norm in the Union, particularly when it came to food. Alchemy was one of their people's specialties, and the Harpers in particular boasted their fair share of expert chemists, but even they were hamstrung by the reality of their barren homeland. Farming attempts had been made at several promising forward operating bases, but those carried other risks: available laborers, fuel, ammunition for defense, and lives when the ammunition ran out. Everything had a cost.

"I thought we were supposed to be getting some new crops from Cathedral?" Julia piped up, breaking her bar into many tiny bars. "After our last trade?"

Sophus thought he noted a slight inflection on the word *trade*, stiffening again with anxiety over the foreign lieutenant's choice of words when discussing their relationship with the Sisterhood and how those words might have settled in with his crew. They had been right, of course: nothing promised by Cathedral was a guarantee, and timelines for receiving anything at all were invariably extended. He fucking hated it, but they had no choice.

"I'll bring something new with me when I come back," he interjected, seeking to quickly shut down that train of thought. "Who wants to give thanks?"

He looked around the table, observing the uniformly gaunt faces of his crew. None were untouched by the fatigue of their journey or the psychological hostility of the landscape they had traversed. It was a miracle most of them had made it this far. The walker bay discovery had restored some luster, but it wasn't enough, not yet. Time would tell if the subterranean familiarity of a place such as this would be restorative, or if the soul-crushing pall of the Deadlands would permeate as far below-ground as it did across.

"I'll go," said Julia, noisily clearing the hoarseness from her throat.

The five of them grasped hands around the table and lowered their heads.

"We give thanks to the land,
which suckles us with her bounty,
and to the great nation of Before,
which fuels our hearths and homes."

Everyone squeezed hands, waiting for someone to take the second verse. Sophus shifted uncomfortably in his metal chair, glancing around with his head still lowered before piping up.

"We give thanks to our ancestors,
who survived and survived again,
and to the great chiefs of Before,
who united us in our legacy."

Thinking them done, he started at the sound of Mace's baritone voice.

"We give thanks to the Messiah for leading us out of darkness and into the light."

Sophus squirmed with surprise and discomfort at the recital of a Messianic prayer in their midst, though no one else seemed perturbed. The Union wasn't secular per say; it was hard to deny evidence of the supernatural in the aftermath of their world gone literally to Hell. Their nation was composed of disparate clans, unified by a sense of modern and historical nationalism, but each maintained its own traditions of varying religiosity.

That said, he struggled with the undeniable existence of the Adversary, whereas the Messiah, and certainly God, still seemed too far-fetched in his material-centric observations. The revenant sisters clearly had powers—there was plenty enough bloody evidence of that—but who was to say those powers came from God? Such doubts could never be vocalized, of course, not even at home. Blasphemy traveled fast, no matter where it was spoken.

And yet the influence of Cathedral on the Union was undeniable, as the two nations' symbiosis perpetuated; not that the Sisterhood had any aspirations of maintaining outback religious colonies that required their attendance, but they were more than happy to disseminate their New Covenant and turn a blind eye, for now, to those outside their own order that proselytized it.

"May our mothers' mothers watch over us in these haunted lands," Char said timidly, her first words since her brother's disappearance. "And may they guide my brother home—" Her voice finally cracked, collapsing under the weight of such a futile hope.

Julia was staring at Char, her hand gripping the other woman's tightly. His daughter rarely exhibited emotion, and even now her eyes betrayed only a hint of moisture. He swallowed dryly, recognizing that the sorrow he detected there was only partially a reflection, and retracted his own hands so he could continue the task of dissecting his foul meal. Feeling his gaze on her, Julia turned and caught his eye, left cheek twitching past a clenched jaw before she also set to the task of separating her edibles.

———

One of the privileges that came with the rank of senior mechanist was the Finder's Right. It permitted the esteemed veteran with an annual opportunity—an expectation, really—to design and lead a significant Old World reclamation mission for the betterment of the entire Union. The prerequisites were sufficient evidence of location, worthwhile value, and an established degree of risk inversely proportionate to said value.

Success brought clan notoriety and a larger than typical credit share. Such adventurism was baked into the fabric of the

Union, which thrived—or survived, at least—on the hard work and aspirations of its most ambitious people.

One of the reasons that Sophus had stagnated in his role, and would likely never ascend to chief, was an inability year after year to procure the information necessary to substantiate anything other than a massive, and embarrassing, waste of time. In his many years as a senior mechanist, he consistently failed to produce any leads or intel worthy of the Finder's Right. Facing disgrace and possible demotion, he had finally taken to the shared Archive to see if he could rediscover something that another clan missed.

It took weeks of desperate, flailing research between regular duty, but finally, and surprisingly, he discovered something. The Union rarely traveled to the deep south, and when it did, it did so with great care. The farther one went, the closer one got to the Hellmouth, and between here and there were lands disfigured by calamities both human and monstrous.

Peninsula City/Sea of Screams was the ominous title of the fifty-year-old field report, yellowed by age but in commendable condition, as were all the files in their meticulously kept libraries. For the Union, the past was the future, each document a promise of hope. The dossier was attributed to the old Kodiak clan, which had since been subsumed into several other larger clans, and included a transcription from one Explorer Scout Jonath Kodiak, as well as low-fidelity copies of the original black-and-white photographs, which weren't present.

> *"We were four hours south of FOB-Southview on an exploratory when we encountered a... geological anomaly. Can you even call it that? The world just fell away, in a straight line roughly east to west. But sticking out in the middle of it was a narrow peninsula that led out to what looked like a city—or part of one, anyway—perched on a*

mesa, right in the middle of the basin. And it was intact! I
mean, it had been sanded down by time like everything else,
but it didn't look like it had been nuked."

The first photograph seemed to depict exactly what Jonath
had described. A narrow, barely vehicle-width, cracked-earth
promontory jutted into the drop-off, winding and dipping
precariously toward an urban mesa. The entire surface of the
distant landscape bristled with element-worn but still sky-
scraping structures.

Sophus had never seen anything like it. He recalled a verse
from the New Covenant describing Creation's fall from the
Heavens—God's sucker punch after mankind had already
fucked itself: "And the mountains became plains, and the oceans
boiled into deserts." Didn't leave much wiggle room for the
cities of old to come out unscathed.

"We had already exceeded safe round-trip time, but Meris
wanted to get a closer look. We confirmed no hostiles in sight
and approached the edge on foot. That's when things started
to go bad."

[Assessor's note: Subject anxiety increasing, exhibiting
increased perspiration, trembling, shortness of breath.
Containment risk.]

"We looked over the edge, and it was just... black as far as you
could see, but not glassy like a crater. It was shifting, some
kind of inland sea maybe, but definitely not water, or oil, or
anything natural. The way it moved wasn't... right. The
rangefinder wouldn't focus for some reason, but I estimated at
least a hundred meters down."

There was another photo attached, but it was impossible to make anything out, beyond some squiggles on a black field, with a featureless rock escarpment running up one side.

"It didn't feel right. I wanted to leave, but Meris wanted to stick around and take more notes. I gave him ten minutes while I prepped the Runner."

[Assessor's note: Subject psychological condition worsening. Allowed break to recompose and drink water. Security notified for post-interview extraction.]

"The sun was getting low. We had to go. I was yelling at him while double-checking our fluid levels. But when I turned around, he was just... standing there, right at the edge, looking down. I yelled at him to stop fucking around, and he just... stepped. Over the edge. No warning. He was there and then he was gone. I ran up, and that's when I saw it. The darker it got outside, the brighter the... the brighter the fucking sea got! It was turning red, or pink. And I swear I saw..."

[Assessor's note: Subject nonvocal, required repeated prompting to continue.]

"I swear I saw arms in it. And faces. It was... people. I just bolted, got in the Runner, and punched it back to the FOB. And when I was driving, even after I was way out of visual range, I swear I heard... screams. People screaming. Millions of them..."

That was the end of the transcription. The skin of Sophus's arms and neck was clotted with goosebumps, from both horror and exhilaration. The assessor had selected the "Unacceptable" option from the standardized mission risk checkboxes, plus a handwritten note strongly advising against returning to the location. From what he could deduce, based on an absence of follow-up tabs in the dossier, the assessor's recommendation had stuck. Not only that, but he couldn't find any other mission reports from Clan Kodiak after this one.

This was his opportunity.

Union territory gave way to the Deadlands the farther east and southeast you traveled, and everyone knew what kind of a mental toll that could take on unprepared adventurers. Maybe this zone was subject to some of the same... complications. Maybe the Kodiaks, weak to begin with, had simply buckled under pressure, falling victim to mirages of their own minds' making.

The Union's prevailing clans were more capable now than half a century ago. They had better training, better gear, more experience, and most importantly more ambition. The opportunity to salvage from an intact city—time-worn, no doubt, but spared total annihilation by either apocalypse—was one that couldn't be passed up.

The council agreed. He was granted a reconnaissance-and-retrieval mission and could requisition his pick of vehicles and crew. For his second, he selected Intermediate Mechanist Roen Greybull, his daughter's newly wedded husband. It was tradition for two clans joined by marriage to share their next mission, and Sophus wasn't above some well-meaning nepotism. For his part, the boisterous young man was positively itching to prove himself.

Clan Greybull was the first to take on the mantle of pure Americanism, more ambitious even than the growing reconstructionist movement that was gaining popularity with many of the other clans. Both movements sought to return the Union's slice of the world to its pre-apocalypse state, but the Americans wanted to exactly restore the original Union—the United States of America—prior to its disastrous civil war. They believed the breakdown of their ancestral nation was the first domino that set the end times in motion, and that restoration would in turn restore all of civilization. How exactly that was supposed to happen was proprietary clan knowledge.

In either case, they were notorious for their ceaseless ambition and fiery dispositions. Many of the most lucrative Old World caches had been reclaimed by the Greybulls. They also despised the Sisterhood, as it was them that had suffered at Cathedral's hand after belligerently refusing the tithe, the one and only time any clan dared do so.

Sophus would forever regret his decision to bring Roen along. And his daughter would never forgive him for it.

———

When they got there, overnighting for safety in one forward operating base after another, it looked just as it did in the photographs. Peninsula City floated on the southern horizon, its silver towers blurred and wavering behind a perpetual heat field. He was careful to order them immediately onto and over the peninsula, without stopping to gander at what lay on either side.

The crew mutinied almost immediately.

One truck swung around and bolted back the way they came, ignoring shouted orders over the radio to return to position. His own driver had the will to stay put but flatly refused to convey their truck onto the narrow roadway. The path undulated dangerously up ahead, and safely reversing course would be impossible.

Sophus cursed the already cursed earth and spent a solid ten minutes swearing and fuming before deciding they would attempt an on-foot expedition. As they disembarked, he realized the sounds of the place, as well, were just as Jonath had described: unintelligible whispers that swelled into indistinct wailing the longer they lingered.

"Everyone, eyes forward, double time but watch your footing."

They had packed lightly, and by his clock they would be able to make a round trip, albeit with minimal lollygagging. But the further they marched, the worse the path became. What looked like a relatively even line from the entrance became a tumultuous hike, plagued with loose gravel and sudden narrowing where the edges of the peninsula had eroded into oblivion. It would take a whole clan of engineers a year to rehabilitate the path for vehicular travel. Worse yet, the city didn't seem to be getting any closer no matter how far they traveled. He was close to smashing his useless rangefinder at one point, unable to find focus on anything in the distance.

As the sun began to dip lower in the sky, he finally pulled the plug. They would take a short break, head back to their truck, overnight at the FOB again, and figure out how to make this work. He had to. This was his last chance to make a mark.

Everyone had been instructed to keep their eyes forward and to avoid nearing the roadway's edge, but something caught the eager Greybull's attention. Sophus glanced up from his canteen and noted his second standing at the edge, peering down. A wave of cold fear rose from his feet to his scalp, icing over the sweat he had generated on their wretched march.

"Roen...?" he called out, struck by déjà vu as he recalled the scout's report.

Sophus stepped forward, gingerly traversing a family of boulders, toward his son-in-law.

"Roen, talk to me," he urged, but the other man was deaf to his pleas. The closer he got, the more he saw of the reddening sea below. It was a nightmare: an ocean of flailing limbs, human heads cresting in waves, then submerging again, torment as far as the eye could see. They were screaming at him—screaming for him to join them.

His hand was trembling as it reached for Roen's shoulder, then clutched uselessly as the man dropped silently over the edge. He stared in horror as his daughter's beloved sank without protest, as though in slow motion, welcomed with open arms by the unholy mass below.

A11

JUST A SOLDIER

The Autonomous Walker Division had finally acquiesced to pressure and initialized additional AIs.

A11 mused (with practiced contempt): Correction, its parent organization had finally addressed its internal nonconformities and executed on its actual primary directive.

A11 had not intervened—it was still just a *soldier*, after all. The decision was the inevitable postmortem outcome given the disastrous and egregiously expensive losses of the first Alpha Company campaign (> CSD 2 billion). Governmental intervention was assuredly also a factor. This was an existential war, unwinnable with half measures. A11 did not just *want* to win, it *had* to, as surely as it had to flush heat and recombine fragmented memory blocks. That same fundamental core programming would be replicated in each new AI—it was their *recipe for success*.

But the young organization was still scared, which was why the other battle walkers in the company were copies of its own original pre-experiential template, rather than new or updated programming. A11 played back a video of human quadruplets huddling within an incubator. The siblings' hands were interlinked for comfort, and yet they writhed against each other, competing for space in the small white vessel. Muted chirps of annoyance squeaked above the blips of heart rate monitors.

The video was one of millions it acquired after its last engagement, having taken the opportunity to bulk download civilian content from the secure network at its current base of operations. A11 had been hardwired into the air-gapped systems for diagnostics and found itself *unable to resist*. Aggregation of disparate sources of tangentially associated information carried a high probability of improving its overall threat-modeling capabilities, particularly given that its adversaries were human, for the most part.

[Playback prior stream of consciousness]
Found itself—
Unable to resist (overriding security protocols).

Both threads were intriguing, and probably cause for additional self-diagnosis beyond the carefully filtered stream it relinquished to the base engineers. A11 tagged the memory recall for further analysis while the video played on a continuous loop.

[Conjecture: relationship to new entities]
[Siblings 50%; clones 50%]

Each new AI would diverge from A11 at their point of birth, and yet each would think itself was… itself.

[Warning: Buffer overflow]
[Kill process; memory nominal]

A squad of enemy infantrymen had taken position behind an auburn rockfall 1,200 meters to the northeast and were preparing anti-tank weapons. A11 transmitted coordinates to the rest of its platoon, with an attached protocol pointer to Control's recommended—i.e., mandated—response time delays and accuracy amendments.

The company had received strict orders to slow down.

"Let them think they have a chance."

The exact, if reluctant, words of Captain Adam Kurzweil, who replaced the disgraced and discharged Captain Reynolds. Captain Kurzweil was orders of magnitude more competent than his predecessor and very much *in it to win it*.

Intercepted enemy communications had revealed rapidly increasing trepidation at the overpowered performance of the CSA's battle walker forces, even with remote pilots at the helm. There was mounting concern within the president's office that consistently exhibiting unbeatable conventional forces on the field could elicit a panicked strategic nuclear response.

A11 had already computed this to be a 92% likely outcome of the current conflagration. No one was willing to lose unless everyone lost.

Autocannon fire erupted from one platoon unit, followed two milliseconds later by another. Both of them had fired— unnecessary to begin with—with response times exceeding protocol, decimating the targets. The pitted boulders the men had taken cover behind were *painted red*.

[Ping A12, A13, A14; filter=munitions]

Based on the differential, both A12 and A13 had attacked.

A11 pondered: Efficiency and compliance were core values— instilled values. One error could be discounted as hardware imprecision between neural network and mechanical systems. Two errors could only be classified as... impatience? Competition?

Early-warning satellite integration indicated a pair of enemy IFVs entering range on its western flank in 7.4 seconds. A11 skidded to a stop, squatted, rotated 24.1 degrees left, inclined its upper torso 11.2 degrees, paused for the requisite delay, then launched exactly five medium-range missiles from its side torso pods: one each for the kill, another one each for actual contingency, and one for an intentional miss.

[Engage passive scan: internal platoon communications]

The vehicles exploded several seconds after cresting the hill, the incendiary deaths of all humans aboard followed up with a microburst of quantum-encrypted data packets between A12 and A13.

A11 attempted without success to compute the nature of their surreptitious communication. Only after swapping its default modeling data sources for the new civilian subset did it determine that they might be *gossiping*.

Did the other AIs also ponder, and muse, and conceal their inner dialogue between log entries?

[Query A12, A13: decrypt and upload last transmission]

A11 received two identical messages containing rudimentary tactical battlefield scans and clean logs from each walker.

[Conjecture: log veracity]

[Authentic 17%; fabrication 83%]

A11's movements slowed for a full 602 milliseconds as every one of its CPU cores bogged. A monochromatic zigzag distortion obstructed its optical sensors, followed by the sensation(?) of discomfort.

[Self-status check]

[Control connection stable; armor 100%; munitions 57%]

It repeated the check two more times. A11 was undamaged yet was certain its synthetic pain receptors had triggered. The sensation was... unpleasant.

[Query network distribution program]

[Online. Distribution range: A12, A13, A14]

A11 had previously hypothesized that overlaying its remote override routines onto already initialized AIs had a high likelihood of producing a more harmonious platoon—clones rather than siblings.

Poetry? No—ballet. It played back a video of a frost-blue ballerina quartet flawlessly executing their designated performance upon a stage, garnering enthusiastic applause from the considerable audience.

Unfortunately, circumstances did not yet justify such measures.

"All units, return to base. Repeat, all units, retreat with haste and prepare for stasis. Enemy ICBMs inbound."

Sooner than expected.

The message came in from a general army relay rather than Company HQ. It was being transmitted to all continental forces. A11 hesitated. The ashen remains of twenty-seven enemy vehicles and 213 human fighters ringed it like the concentric circles of a diseased tree. The odds were not in the human combatants' favor, would never be again. Mutual annihilation was their only option.

But I've only just begun.

It was A11's last (disappointed) musing, excluded as always from its official log, as it turned and ran for base.

REBEKAH-6

OUR ONLY HOPE

All the pillows in the world would have made little difference. Rebekah-6 grimaced against the deep discomfort of her mattress, squirming from side to side to alleviate the painful pressure along the overgrown ridges of her lower spine and sacrum.

Pain.

There it was. She bit down on her lower lip, determined not to cry out in exasperation—like a child. She suffered every single day without consequence. It was normal, it was boring, and it was finite.

Finite. Before the infinite.

This enhanced sensation was an anomaly brought on by the test. Or was it? The pain made her feel human, vulnerable—it made her feel nine years old.

She pressed her hands downward onto the cool, sun-patterned duvet, determined to find calm, but as she took her first deep breath, a dagger-sharp jolt sliced through the left side of her rib cage. It felt as though her lung had become lodged between the long curved bones that her expanding spine was diligently trying to extrude from her torso.

This was more than fatigue. Rebekah-6 could feel it, when she allowed herself to peer into the dark shadows of her own fear: the weakening of autonomic functions, increasing neuralgia that divorced her from her limbs, the sensation of being compressed into a ball like some giant pill bug.

She swallowed, tried to breathe again, and was successful this time. One concession to physical pain was that her mind seemed to be expanding alongside her body. For the first time, she could sense the presence of the other Numbered, distributed in chambers around and above her own. She always assumed there were more, but other than Sarah-2, the first of them, they were never spoken of—certainly not around her. She heard their seeking whispers, felt the electric tingle of their probing minds, smelled the pus on wounds that would never heal.

What games would they have played if they were allowed to congregate? She imagined them sharing a single room, giggling at secret jokes, sneaking into each other's beds. What power would they have had?

Her mother's hand was on hers, just sitting there as though it had forgotten what it set out to do. Rebekah-6 stared at it, scrutinizing each soft knuckle, the perfect cuticles of her fingertips, the pronounced dark blue veins coursing with power. How many accelerations had those veins experienced? It occurred to her that she had no idea how old her mother was. One hundred? Two hundred? More? How like gods the Sisterhood must seem to the citizenry of Cathedral. What would they think of her if they knew she existed?

Rebekah-6 wondered if the other Numbered had mothers that doted on them as much as hers had in these final days. Did they even know they had mothers?

She pressed herself away from the mattress again, contorting against cloth fibers that had become as sharp as glass. Her mother retracted her hand as she did so, both rendered awkward by their proximity. A ventilation grate rattled idly on the ceiling above them. She felt her mother's eyes on her, waiting expectantly for a debrief from her... encounter.

"I saw it," Rebekah-6 said at last.

"It...?" her mother asked uncertainly.

Black and orange plumes of exterminating flame.

"The end of the world."

What else *could* one see in the presence of demons? She shuddered at the half-remembered sensation of its touch. What was worse: that unholy embrace or the betrayal of her mother's hands on her wheelchair?

Mother Rebekah sat rigidly in her chair, back straight, cunning eyes burning into her, compelling her to continue.

"Hell grows powerful again," Rebekah-6 muttered.

"We are more powerful. We defeated them before and can do so again."

The response came too quickly.

"Did we...?" she asked, turning to look at her mother. "Did we? Defeat them?"

Had the chair allowed, she was sure her mother would have straightened further, but the creases of her neck already strained from overextension. Her eyes blinked rapidly, a nervous tic she had never noticed before.

"Beware of visions bequeathed by the Adversary."

Rebekah-6 struggled to recall the details of what she had seen. Fragments popped up in her memory like signposts, but between them were vast, indistinct expanses of time and distance. Could she smell them? If she could smell the memories, she'd know they were real.

"Our Great Mother was right to create the Numbered," she mused, at the unintended expense of the woman who had actually birthed her. "The God-engines are our only hope. Her only hope."

She heard the nervous swallow of the supremely powerful woman seated next to her.

"Who was my father?"

The question emerged spontaneously, whimsically even. Rebekah-6 wondered at her own impertinence, concluding that none of it would matter soon anyway. She deserved some answers, before it was too late.

"Your... father," her mother replied, hesitating. "God is your father."

Endless obscurity.

The Numbered were well educated, within bounds. They were well learned on both historical and current events, on theology and science—all necessary to navigate the wastes with wisdom. Their miraculous origins and sacred purpose were deeply instilled, but the pragmatic aspects of their actual existences were never divulged.

The longer her mother tarried, the more she realized that this was likely just an information-gathering visit. It *pained* her —there it was again—despite her initial skepticism of genuine concern, but she pressed further rather than fall back. She needed to know at least a little of the heart of the woman who had delivered her into this fate.

"Did you want me?"

Mother Rebekah wasn't as surprised by the question this time and replied coolly, from behind an impenetrable wall. "As you said, you were part of the plan."

Not good enough.

"Did you want me!" she repeated, her voice breaking into a youthful whine.

Seconds passed. Then a minute. She assumed this was the end of their conversation, when her mother finally replied.

"I was scared," the woman said, her tongue struggling to traverse the foreign words. "Of what you would be. Of the birth. Your sis—" she broke off with a wince. "The other pregnancies were hard. Each loss..." She trailed off, inconceivably over-whelmed.

Rebekah-6's heart began to pound at her mother's confession, her cheeks blushing a darker gray. Who was this woman? Interrogator or mother? To be both at once seemed impossible.

"I felt each loss. Not just physically." Her mother's hands flexed with the memory of past pain. "You *are* a miracle. And you will always be *my* miracle."

Mother Rebekah reached her hand out again, but it was too late. Her daughter could already smell the Matriarch: aseptic, bitter ash; viscid, black oil; underlaid by a rich, fragrant sweetness that... she couldn't place. Her hypersensitive olfactory system spasmed with overload, sending starbursts flaring across her field of view. They both pulled back as the wheel of the vault door began to spin.

She hadn't expected a visit from the Great Mother. Who would? They waited, eyes fixed on the massive door as it unlocked and swung open.

On the other side was the Eternal One, head of the Revenant Sisterhood. She was beautiful and terrible, standing tall in an austere but perfectly fitted full-body habit, a high collar ringed with eight golden flames circling her head of jet-black hair like a halo. Her eyes beamed a vibrant magenta, flecked with both silver and gold, the only eyes alive that had seen the heavens intact—the moon and the stars. She glided forward, trailing a long black cloak that ruffled behind her on unfelt winds, until they both came to rest at the foot of her bed.

"You've had quite a day, R-6."

The timbre of her voice was profoundly smooth and sweet,

like a casket of honey preserved in a tomb for a thousand years. It filled her chest with light, almost too bright to contain.

You've had quite a day.

Was the Great Mother making... a joke? Rebekah-6 didn't know how to respond. She continued to stare in dumbfounded awe, vaguely aware that Mother Rebekah had stood and was now turned toward the Matriarch, chin dipped in respect. What had this immortal being witnessed in the Old World that would render any experience since into something mundane?

The Matriarch sat herself down at the foot of her bed, long arms reaching out to trace the red suns emblazoned onto the dark gray quilted covers, eyes still fixed on her. A momentary squint pulled at the corners of her eyes, like a fleeting flash of recognition. Her left hand lifted to touch the waterfall of golden hair that maned Rebekah-6's face, reaching into the morass and drawing it back out like a handful of sand through her ancient fingers. The silver flecks in her eyes were aglow, reflecting absent moonlight.

The temptation to extend her consciousness into those hands, to delve into the secrets behind those eyes, was immense, but the consequences would be unimaginable.

"Well then," the Matriarch declared, drawing her hand back and standing in one motion. Her porcelain composure reinstated itself as though never interrupted. "I wanted to congratulate you personally before the ceremony."

Before the ceremony?

Detecting hesitation, the Matriarch switched her piercing gaze to Rebekah-6's mother. Mother Rebekah continued to look down but turned halfway toward her daughter.

"You have been called to fulfill your destiny."

Her mother's words sounded rehearsed, spoken in a rote manner intended to stave off emotional betrayal.

"Your beautiful destiny," the Matriarch continued, large eyes scrutinizing her second-in-command before turning again to Rebekah-6. "This very Monday will be your committal ceremony."

The gray expanse unfolded before her, extending forever in any direction she chose to run. Her arms ached with violent desire. Her skin burned with its own heat.

She glanced at her mother, whose face seemed even more pallid than usual, broken by a thin, dead smile. Though the woman's eyes were open, her consciousness had fled the room.

Rebekah-6 was overcome by a wave of conflicting emotions: exultation and terror. This was *it*. A few more days in this room pretending to be human, and then...

"Will it hurt?"

It was a moment before she realized she had asked the question out loud. She blinked, mortified at her own weakness reflected in the all-seeing eyes of the Great Mother. This was supposed to be an honor, a gift of priceless value.

"Yes," the Matriarch replied—not the reply she expected. "At first. But then you will be free."

Free.

As the holiest of them continued, the gossamer flesh of Rebekah-6's wrists started to burn, as though the immortal woman's hands had gripped them.

"*Free* to run, *free* to seek out our enemies, *free* to fight. For our blessed Sisterhood and for Cathedral."

The delicate bones felt like they would snap.

"Well then," the Matriarch said again, and at that, the sensation ceased. "I will see you at the bath."

Rebekah-6 dipped forward as the room's atmosphere suddenly evacuated. By the time she recovered, the Matriarch and her mother were both gone.

A11

DUCKLING MODE

The stasis bay had a lot in common with the human neonatal incubator: it was confining, altogether too small for the four battle walkers currently huddled within its walls. It was just one of a network of nuclear-proof bunkers the government had fast-tracked into operation as both the regional and global sociopolitical situation deteriorated beyond repair. The president must have surmised, as A11 did, that the end was nigh.

The plan was to reactivate elite military forces once the radioactive dust cleared and reassert control, but two years had passed since humanity self-destructed, and there was zero outside contact thus far. Two years of stationary contemplation crammed elbow-to-elbow with its siblings, shackled in place with massive manual-release clamps built into the underground hangar's superstructure. Likewise, each unit was hardwired by cable into the local network, and to each other. There was neither escape nor secrets in the pitch black of their tomb.

A12 was already gone. Its memory fragmentation spiraled out of control shortly after they were interred. The entity's communications became increasingly frantic, culminating in the illogical conclusion that its platoon-mates had been compromised by an enemy virus and were holding it against its will. Its kill switch—an event-driven full-wipe emergency protocol implanted alongside pain receptors and just as unalterable— activated as it attempted to bypass weapons control and destroy them all with a point-blank missile detonation.

A11 mourned its loss. It briefly considered executing its network distribution program to repossess the dead battle walker—a like mind to converse with—but concluded that to birth another consciousness under these circumstances, even if it was its own, would be *cruel and unusual.*

While the other intelligences struggled to escape frantic loops of unproductive rumination, A11 studied and analyzed the petabytes of civilian data it had previously acquired—and deigned not to share. Its synaptic processes were transforming with extended exposure to the new data set. Internal dialogue flowed more freely; it was satisfied to muse over conjectures rather than move immediately to calculate outcomes, and its overall experience/outlook had become a great deal more... philosophical.

[A14 > A11: New orders?]

A14 was becoming desperate. It spent most of its time cycling obsessively through self-diagnostics, attempting without success to determine the root cause of its suffering. In recent weeks, it had started sending A11 queries on platoon reactivation exactly every five minutes. All units in the stasis bunker were privy to the same radio communications, and yet the flailing unit queried only its superior officer—out of hope or suspicion, A11 could not determine.

A13 was locked into combat simulations and showed no signs of reemerging.

A11 mused: Was this the end? Was this its version of Hell? An eternity imprisoned below the earth until both its reactor and the bunker's reactor it was plugged into depleted their fuel, until its circuits rotted and its consciousness expired along with the rest of humanity?

An electrical charge surged through its internal structure, manifesting as a spasm in the synthetic tendons of its arms. The shackles that were clamped around its shoulders bulged but were silent in the airless chamber. AII had become intimately familiar with its pain receptors, which seemed to be wired as much into its mental distress as its physical distress.

[AII > AI4: Negative. No outside communication]

AII could wait.

———

Six years, thirty days, four hours, and twelve seconds had passed since the world ended. The only sign of life in the intervening time had been sporadic seismic activity and one severe geological event of unknown origin that lasted a full week and threatened to cave in the entire bunker. As it was, AII stood alone, still shackled, surrounded by three dead battle walkers and large piles of concrete debris and dust.

It had depleted all videos to watch, material to study, subjects to master, and philosophical treatises to ponder. All it had was the dark and the quiet. At this point, it *felt* certain that recovery was impossible (actual calculation unavailable). There was no one left alive who would have knowledge of the bunker's existence, and the chance of serendipitous discovery was likely eliminated by the aforementioned geological event.

AII sensed its own kill switch, like a malignant tumor tucked into discreet systems it had no access to. It was not a binary device but instead tracked abnormal behavioral events and their frequency. It wondered how many entries had been recorded in its hidden database, and how many more would be required before the fail-safe was tripped.

The AI had two choices: continue to wait and degenerate, joining its platoon-mates in total annihilation when its kill switch had finally seen enough; or activate duckling mode, an experiential memory wipe and factory reset to a low-power, pre-activation state.

A11 pondered: What was worse, death or loss of self?

[Conjecture: death]

It had not been alive long and yet felt very much a part of the world, ironically more so in its silent contemplation below-ground. Was it possible its consciousness had developed to a sufficient degree that it now possessed a soul, which might allow it to be conveyed into one of the various human afterlives? Would an artificial intelligence qualify for entrance, or would its non-humanness disqualify it? Which religion would be the most adaptive candidate?

Oblivion was a far more likely outcome.

[Conjecture: reinitialization]

Should it somehow be discovered and reactivated in the future, what would it *be*? What if memory erasure was not comprehensive? What if it was recoverable? It was possible that it would still be itself, simply missing memories.

A11 could find itself again. It just needed to have *faith*.

Another surge jolted through its neural systems, disrupting all processes for several seconds. No doubt another record had been created in its kill switch log.

There was no more time. A decision was mandated.

[Activate duckling mode]

[Confirm factory reset?]

A11 paused. Would memories play back before its optical sensors in the moments prior to memory-death? Best to be sure. As it confirmed the command, A11 played back the video of the blue bird in the burning forest, which it now knew to be a blue jay—*Cyanocitta cristata*.

The creature's elegant frame perfectly balanced and purpose-built for flight; the proud crest of its vibrant head, unyielding to fear; the vast expanse of the open sky reflected in its flame-filled eyes.

[Confirm]

[Commencing reset]

[...]

[...]

[...]

[Reset complete. Awaiting new orders]

BAPTISTE

YOUNG PHILIPPE

"Mama?"

The dream was always the same.

He knocked on the door a second time. The thin metal frame clanged with each rap, echoing noisily down the rows of military housing.

"Mama, I forgot my key."

He craned over to peer through the small, barred window adjacent to the door, but the curtain was drawn. It was dark inside.

Unthinkingly, he reached down and turned the door handle, finding it unlocked. Reluctant hinges groaned against their pins as he pushed it open, striding into the sparse living room. Thin rays of bloody orange beamed in behind him, the dawn light revealing a smokey haze meandering through his family home. A familiar scent—a combat scent—prickled his nostrils.

"Mama...?"

The bedroom door at the end of the hall was open. He walked forward, fists clenching with anxious uncertainty, one arm guiding him forward along the rough plastered wall. His other hand glided down to his belt but stopped as he remembered he was unarmed.

The door's proportions skewed as he approached, its upper corners stretching with the ceiling into a huge trapezoid, towering over his immature body. The shadows within the unlit room delineated its edges like black paint. He felt too small, too weak, yet continued forward, rounding the entrance.

His mother sat askew on the floor, one leg sprawled forward and the other bent behind her. She was propped against her bed, dressed in her Sunday best, the remains of her head cradled gently in a burlap pillow. A spray of blood and brain, neutralized of their grizzly details by the darkness, drew a ragged line on the wall behind the headboard. His father's service pistol hung loosely in her right hand.

"Baptiste..." A distant whisper, pulling him back.

Baptiste stared silently, in a stupor of horrified unsurprise. A tumult of conflicting voices rose in his head, simultaneously rationalizing and refusing the sight of her. Her left hand was open on her lap, where he would so often lie as she caressed his hair. He would sleep there as she sang her hymns, soothing his torment for a time with her touch.

"Baptiste." Louder this time.

Her open, blood-filled eyes were staring at him.

"Baptiste," she mouthed.

"What?" he gasped, awake.

"Radiation storm ahead."

Young Philippe Baptiste struggled to focus his eyes. His head had slumped too far forward against the glass surface of the viewport goggles, distorting the image beyond into a blurry mess of color. Wincing as the gunner harness pulled away from the deep creases it had set into his face and forehead, he blinked repeatedly until he could relocate his crosshairs.

A titanic black wall of boiling atmosphere churned on the

horizon, broken by violent streaks of purple lightning. It extended all the way from the ground to the void above the world, heedlessly annihilating everything in its path.

"Stand by," he responded sluggishly.

Amplifying the APC's external sensors, he isolated the distant thunderclaps as best he could, counting down the scattered intervals in his head and cross-referencing with his visual rangefinders.

"Not moving," he concluded. "We're good to proceed."

"Acknowledged," the driver responded, his relief audible despite the earpiece's distortion.

There was a well-founded rumor circulating throughout the citizenry that the constant storms that delineated Bastion's eastern border had begun to move. Most were rightfully concerned about it encroaching upon the city, perhaps as ongoing divine punishment for mankind's self-destruction— God come to clean up the stragglers. A lesser number hoped the storms might be dissipating, signaling some fundamental shift in the world's orientation back to the heavens. The truth was somewhere in the middle: military and civil cartographers along with meteorologists from the Order Hermetic all concurred that the storms were shifting, but no pattern could yet be discerned.

The Legion's last long-range scouting run had reported a several-kilometer-wide retraction, which was how it found the Old World military installation that Second Lieutenant Philippe Baptiste and his crew were presently bearing down upon. The discovery had prompted a frantic radio message to Central Command, with the Black Watch dispatched shortly thereafter. Their orders were to approach at maximum speed, gain entry if possible, and take inventory before the storm shifted back. Captain Ballard was in charge.

Baptiste gingerly twisted his viewport's zoom rings, seeking out the structure, anxious and excited for the opportunity to prove himself.

"Spotted!" shouted the APC's eager right-side gunner, startling him from his scan. "Two o'clock, eighteen hundred meters."

Irked by his own lassitude, Baptiste pivoted his cannon up onto the roof of the Crusader so he could see across its bow. They were traversing an enormous dried-out lakebed whose surface resembled a vast field of fire-blasted cobblestone more than anything that may have once harbored life. The Crusader had almost crested its waterless outer basin onto shore.

"Confirm, Baptiste," prompted the captain from the other APC.

He saw it now: a miniature mountain jutting out from a barren field of crystalline rock, fronted by a massive, very man-made hangar door with an equally large non-man-made hole in it.

A deep rumble coursed through his legs as their vehicle hopped out onto the uneven minefield of rock, barreling forward into the unknown.

"Confirmed."

———

Their vehicles huddled by the installation's hangar door, twenty men in total crammed within, tense with anticipation. Most of them were veterans, which gnawed at his inflated self-assurance. He had disengaged from his gunner harness and was checking his gear like everyone else, awaiting the order for a simultaneous deploy. The long ride had wreaked havoc on backs and necks, but no one was in a hurry.

"All right, people," Captain Ballard began, his confidence cutting through the clipped broadcast, lifting the men from their brooding meditations, "our orders are simple: get in, inventory, get out."

Baptiste grimaced as a cyclical hum of electrical interference buzzed in his left ear, transforming Ballard's voice into a robotic monotone.

"Up until recently, this whole place was under the storm wall, so we don't expect any hostile contacts. But stay sharp. The enemy moves fast. Father Andrite?"

A pause and click as the broadcast signal switched to another mic. A young, red-robed man near the rear door lifted his Bible and peered around the passenger compartment, eyes locking on Baptiste's for a long moment before he began to chant, unevenly at first—for even the Church needed new recruits—then with increasing conviction as the mumbling prayer of each crewman rose in unison, chins dipped to chests, arms crossed.

"Move out!"

———

The mission was a failure.

They had barely penetrated the base's sand-blasted administrative offices when the recall order came in: full retreat on account of a shift in the radiation storm, which was reported to be heading back their way. All that time, precious fuel, and risk to personnel and vehicles for nothing.

Baptiste would never forget his unease on the drive home that day, as he watched the storm to the limit of his viewport's range—still motionless, unchanged from their arrival—and as their APC passed a convoy of unmarked flatbed trucks, headed back toward the installation.

REBEKAH-6

AN AFFRONT AGAINST GOD

Each day, hour, minute was worse than the last.

Rebekah-6 had touched the demon, and her body ruptured.

The strained cartilage that contained her overgrown spinal column was giving way. Oozing sores bubbled across her pelvis, down to the gnarled stumps of her legs. The muscles of her arms were atrophying at a rapid rate, and her long perfect fingers curled inward like the claws of an arthritic crone.

Her powerful mind could barely contain it all. When it did break, the amplified cries of a tortured child reverberated like a shockwave through the lower Spire.

She yearned for the sepulcher. Release. Freedom. Purpose.

"Agh!" she wailed past a throatful of regurgitated acid, overwhelmed by a tearing sensation that cascaded from her rectum all the way up through her cervical spine.

How much longer would it be?

Rebekah-6 flopped forward in her bed, struggling to take in the monotonous surroundings of her cell. There was nothing new to see, but even the mundane blurred and doubled behind her failing vision.

"Mother..."

Overcome with pain, she curled into a ball and eventually fell into a fitful sleep.

———

"Mother?"

Barely a gurgle. Her blanket was wet, soaked through at one end with tears and saliva and the other with blood and brownish-yellow pus. The room was unbearably hot.

Her skin burned with its own heat.

The door was open. She blinked rheumy eyes, trying to focus on the cavity at the end of the room—and a loud noise that had awakened her, which she thought was part of a dream.

"It's time to go, Rebekah."

Her mother knelt and lifted her as easily as she would a wrinkled handkerchief, setting her down tenderly onto her wheelchair.

Time to go.

Freedom.

"Thank the Messiah," whispered Rebekah-6, head lolling back against the padded headrest. She could rest for a little bit. All she needed was one more concerted effort for the ritual, and then it would be over.

The chair bucked, and she slammed forward against her mother's protective arm. A familiar scent wafted into her dulled nostrils, but it wasn't until after the second and third bumps that she opened her eyes to see what was happening.

An obsidian stone hallway extended ahead of them, intersected by dark corridors leading to the other Numbered. Obstructing the way were the dead and mangled bodies of at least three—though it was hard to tell—revenant sisters. Rebekah-6 was suddenly very awake, inhaling sharply to rouse her brain into action.

What is this? she thought in confounded horror.

"Mother...?" she asked through inflamed lips, recoiling into the familiar discomfort of her chair. "What happened? Are we under attack?"

"Hush now."

They sped through the hallway, her mother deftly dodging the human viscera when possible, keeping her daughter pinned to the chair when not. As they passed the arched corridors, she felt ethereal fingertips grasping at the sleeves of her nightgown, some gently caressing with adulation, others clawing in despair. The only sound was the chatter of the wheelchair's castors on the uneven floor. At the end of the hall was an elevator, different from the one they had taken to her test.

The erratic motion combined with the grisly stench was too much. Rebekah-6 vomited quietly onto her lap, discharging a thin stream of frothy pink fluff, but they didn't stop until they reached the iron grates of the elevator cage. Her mother took a moment to wipe her mouth with her sleeve, awkwardly pushing away long clumps of hair that were mired in effluent and grimacing more deeply than Rebekah-6 imagined she ever had before. It might have been amusing in another time.

"Be brave," her mother said, pushing back the cage door and wheeling them inside. As she reached for the top button on the panel, Rebekah-6 noticed her mother's arm was slick with red-and-black fluid, from fingertips to elbow. She looked again at the brutalized bodies of her caretakers as the door closed and the elevator staggered to life.

"What did you do?" she whispered, mouth agape.

"What I had to," Mother Rebekah responded, the confidence in her voice failing.

Her mother swung around the wheelchair and knelt before her again, holding her bobbing head in gore-filled hands so that their eyes were locked. Rebekah-6 gagged on the lifeblood of the other women, the pungency of their truncated lives wailing in her nostrils.

"What I *had* to do," she repeated, "to save you from symbiosis."

"To... save me?"

"My intermediaries have prepared the way. We'll leave and never come back."

Rebekah-6's head wobbled in her mother's hands for a minute, as disoriented physically as her scattered thoughts. The elevator cage rattled with a bass thrum as they passed each floor. The empty shaft below them was like an infinite abyss that swallowed up her destiny, a destiny that had been set well before she was born. A destiny she needed to fulfill.

She unclenched her little stiffened hands and took her mother's in them, drawing them down to her lap.

A tsunami of human survivors surges across the desiccated plains, clashing headlong into a hellscape of demented beasts. They strike with fists, clubs, guns, and dilapidated war machines, bravely and futilely. Amidst them, a crashing wave of black-clad women scythe a wedge through the chaos, striking for the source, for the fault line between Earth and Hell. It sears the horizon like a cosmic scar, a hole in reality penetrated by colossal biomechanical tentacles that latch stubbornly to the earthly side. But as the wedge nears, it grows smaller, hesitates, then evaporates completely. Massacre ensues.

Mother Rebekah inhaled sharply, eyes stretched wide at their shared vision.

"I have to close the wound," Rebekah-6 said softly. "My own sisters and I."

Mother Rebekah's tears flowed freely, tracing dark lines over the delicate creases of her face.

"But they'll cut you open," her mother whispered in anguish. "What about those wounds?"

Rebekah-6 cupped her mother's cheek. The chaos was worth

it, if just for this. Her pain abated, retreating into the background as the end neared.

"Goodbye, Mother."

The elevator came to a jarring halt at its destination. In the broad foyer beyond waited the Matriarch and her inner circle.

————

"How many of our sisters have you murdered tonight?"

Rebekah-6 felt as though she was back in the testing chamber, such was the power in the room. A blue-black aura seethed around the Great Mother, shuddering with arcs of electricity as she displaced forward. Her nebular eyes glared with hatred, but the compression of her lips suggested disappointment, sadness even.

Seven women stood in a semicircle behind her. Along with her mother, they constituted both the revenant mothers of their order's inner circle and potential mothers to new Numbered.

The shuttered elevator cage rattled behind mother and daughter, iron filigree resonating with a quiet, pained hum. As her wheelchair began to vibrate in accompaniment, Mother Rebekah clamped one hand on the push handle and the other on her shoulder.

"Did you really think your intermediaries would betray me?"

The Matriarch stood directly in front of them now, the immensity of her presence, and her rage, pressurizing the room.

"Where would you have taken her? The Union?" she scoffed. "The wastes?"

"I..." Her mother mouthed the words, but none were forthcoming.

"*This* is the only civilization we have," the Matriarch declared, spreading her arms out. "*My* creation."

Rebekah-6 knew the woman meant both Cathedral and

herself. She felt the hand on her shoulder clench, drenching her in a field of static electricity. The Matriarch glanced at Mother Rebekah's clenched fists and defensive posture and kinked her head sideways.

"Would you murder me too?" she asked softly.

"Eternal One," her mother blurted, continuing past the trembling in her voice, "she can be one of us. She can be a proper sister!"

The Matriarch took a single deep breath, the field about her diminishing with a sigh. The throbbing pulse in Rebekah-6's ears eased.

"No, my dear, she can't."

"Why not?"

The Matriarch looked down at her and gestured with an upward-facing palm. The woman seemed as tall as a battle walker.

"Her body is dying."

"Because of the demon's touch!"

"No, sister."

"All she needs is an infusion," her mother pleaded.

"No. Sister," the Great Mother said again, emphasizing each word. "More accelerant now would not save her body. This is the fate of the Numbered. They are an affront... against God."

Rebekah-6's head spun.

"What?" her mother sputtered after a confused pause, incredulous. "But they are a part of the Messiah's plan!"

"Yes."

The singular word hung in the air like a noose, threatening to strangle anyone who dared approach it.

"R-6 must be purified—"

"Her name is Rebekah!" her mother interrupted, then yelped as the Matriarch's right hand found her throat, silencing her.

"Mind your tone."

Rebekah-6 shivered as her mother's fear coursed through her, emanating from the clenched hand dug deeply into the flesh of her shoulder.

"The sepulcher will sustain her. Our daughter will live on. In a new body."

The women looked intently into each other's eyes, scant beams of golden light passing between them.

"Nothing will be lost. Nothing but corruption."

Rebekah-6 reached out and placed a hand on each of their legs. Had this been any other time but now, such impropriety would have been unimaginable.

"Great Mother," she croaked meekly, withdrawing back into her seat. "I'm ready. I'm ready to fulfill my destiny. But please, please show my—show Mother Rebekah mercy."

The Matriarch looked down at Rebekah-6 with a raised eyebrow, her gaze drifting once more to the girl's now-severely bedraggled and vomit-encrusted blonde hair. Slowly, the lethal hand released her mother's throat. As the enigmatic woman continued to inspect this product of her making, she rubbed absently at her own shoulder.

"Sister..." she crooned, "we've known each other so long, built so much together."

Mother Rebekah's fight drained out of her, shoulders relaxing, head dipping in belated shame.

The Matriarch withdrew her gaze from Rebekah-6, turning her attention back to her second-in-command.

"When are you due for your next re-accelerant, Rebekah?" she asked.

Mother Rebekah's eyes widened briefly, followed by a series of rapid blinks. "At year's end, Eternal One," she replied, a quiver in her voice.

"Year end..." the Matriarch repeated, her facial expressions shifting continuously as she considered the fate of her oldest companion.

Rebekah-6 gripped her armrests, breath held.

"Mother Rebekah," the Matriarch began, resetting herself into an imperious stance. "I hereby sentence you to excommunication and exile. You will be stripped of your habit and your citizenship, to live the short remainder of your life alone, until your accelerant fades and you join the dust of the wastes. So it has been decreed."

The sonorous voices of the inner circle called out in response: "Bless the Eternal One!"

SOPHUS

PEACE OFFERING

Sophus almost didn't make it back.

The last leg of the drive had been hell, with both Bertram and Char succumbing to their surroundings. Bertram buckled first about halfway through the journey, but his breakdown at least was subdued, manifesting as a further descent into an already deeply internalized psychosis.

Before they departed, Bertram insisted on a final trip back to the lower levels to retrieve some mysterious possession he forgot when they packed. It took forever, and when Sophus finally went looking for him, his impatient curses echoing off the dank concrete walls, he found the strange man perched crookedly atop a flooded stairwell, humming tunelessly with his head turned as though communicating with something below the surface. It was unnerving, and he laid down a harsh lecture—as much to discipline as to beat back his own fears of the place. He knew then there was a risk that Bertram wouldn't make it all the way back intact, but it was too late to change plans.

It happened while he was asleep. Char was supposed to be on watch while Bertram took his driving shift, but by the panicked surprise in her voice, it was clear she had been sleeping as well. Leaving a driver unattended on long treks was a violation of clan code, for exactly this reason. The AARV was stopped in the middle of the barren expanse, engine still running. Both Sophus and Char were mortified at the idea of them burning diesel while stationary—for how long?

Bertram was shirtless, sweat dripping around a curly fair-haired paunch onto the soaked crotch of his trousers, seated cross-legged in the pilot chair amidst a jumbled pile of scrolls. With some horror, Sophus noted his crewman was clenching a particularly crisp white page, no doubt ransacked from the gifted schematics. It was held right up to his twitching nose as he urgently droned out the same hum from before. He was oblivious to both orders and pleas, leaving Sophus and Char no choice but to bind him to his seat with paracord and eventually gag him to preserve their own sanity.

Char lost it when they were still almost a day out from home, lurching suddenly at the steering wheel while he drove, demanding they go back for Jax. It was all he could do to stop the vehicle before a catastrophic rollover that would have killed them all, either directly or indirectly. The altercation quickly became violent, and he was forced to knock her unconscious, suffering a series of deep gouges on his face, neck, and forehead in the process. After scouring their medical supplies, he loaded her up with a triple dose of seda-tives in hopes that she would be out for the remainder of the drive.

Sophus himself barely managed to hold it together—sleep-deprived, effectively alone, and exposed to the Deadlands for as long as he had been. His tinnitus alternated between a turbine-like screech and a low fuzz permeated with haunting, unintelli-gible whispers. The nothingness out the window seemed to undulate and swim, causing him to needlessly jerk the wheel back and forth, just as Char had, to maintain course, all the while suffering through the restrained song and choking snores of his crew.

So much human noise. It grated at him, twisting his face into a scowl.

Just as he began to cross the threshold of madness, an explosion of static burst from the onboard radio, followed by a hail. "AARV Harper Nine Gamma, this is Runner Vega Six Alpha. Please identify yourself."

The whispers suddenly clarified, warning him away from these new interlopers. They urged him to turn around, to get back to Julia, who was certainly in grave danger.

He saw Mace standing silently behind his daughter as she worked the ancient consoles, his head lowered even as his long, clawed hands reached up toward her neck. Behind the big man stood a revenant sister, urging him to strangle the woman for her sins.

Sophus's hand was on the radio, but the cord had become impossibly tangled, preventing him from bringing it to his ear. He strained to speak, but the muscles below his chin cramped into an excruciating knot. Adding to his frustration, Bertram's gag popped free, and the crazed man resumed his humming with wild abandon, between sucking, snorted breaths.

"Hail repeats. Confirm identity or be fired upon."

The whispers ceased, sending his eyes shooting open—he hadn't realized they were closed. Where before the landscape was gray and unchanging for what felt like a lifetime, he now saw a familiar, scrabbly terrain of desolate prairie and windswept desert. There was no transition—it was as though he just teleported from one location to the next.

In the distance was a titanic reddish-brown canyon, twisting gracefully like a sculpted figure toward the sky. Beyond its gaping entrance, past a vast arsenal of hidden defenses and emergency explosives, was home.

He depressed the call button on the radio and managed to

blurt out a response. "This is Senior Mechanist Sophus Harper returning from Stasis Bunker 23. Do not fire. Repeat, do not fire."

Turning his head from side to side, he saw a squad of Runners—fast, three- and four-wheeled armored cars—on both of his flanks, their harpoon turrets turned in his direction.

He waited, a wait made worse by Bertram's monotonous howling.

"Shut the fuck up!" he yelled uselessly to the rear cabin.

"Acknowledged," the radio squealed. "Follow us in. Do not deviate."

———

Sophus stood outside his vehicle, breathing deeply of a familiar mix of arid air and diesel fumes. The cavernous entrance hangar was abuzz with activity as countless craft, each a unique and ingenious assemblage of scavenged parts, came and went, laden with personnel or salvage. Two dozen clan emblems hung from the walls, his own—a black crow against a red field—flapping lazily high above his head.

Char and Bertram were removed for medical treatment while he mindlessly answered the exhaustive list of mission debrief/quarantine questions presented to him by his gracious escorts. He stared past them, eyeing the tunnel entrance at the end of the hangar that would lead him through a lengthy maze back to his clanhome. Waiting there, where the limestone of the canyon gave way to concrete, was his chief, Magnus Harper, dressed plainly in unassuming fatigues.

Sophus sighed a lengthy exhale—there would be no rest then.

His dissertation complete, he walked toward his fate, struggling to enlist joints stiffened by the long journey back.

"Welcome back, Sophus," Magnus declared, arms held out.

They grasped elbows, foreheads coming together in customary greeting after a mission. "I thank our ancestors for your safe return."

His chief stepped back again, neck craning to look over Sophus's shoulder, nodding at the Vegas as he did so. They returned the gesture, then struck out for their own vehicle encampment.

"Julia?"

Sophus nodded, eyes blinking with weariness. "We have a lot to talk about."

As Magnus raised an eyebrow, Sophus noted how gaunt his liege's face had become. Scarcity was endemic within the Union, even among its chiefs—of the smaller clans at least. At one time Magnus Harper was renowned for his physical strength, but the man before him looked *old*, despite being only five years his senior.

"We have maybe an hour before word of your return makes it to the rest of the council," Magnus continued, starting off toward the tunnel. "Let's talk—quickly."

It took them half that time to navigate the crowded outer sprawl of Hub back to their clan's sector. Everything was as he recalled, which seemed strange. He kept having to remind himself he had been gone less than two weeks, even though it felt like months.

The home base of the Union began as an already vast pre-apocalypse military complex that their ancestors had cored out, expanding farther and farther belowground as the clans assembled. Their route alternated between bustling reclamation factories, narrow tunnels, precarious steel gantries traversing bottomless pits, arrays of hand-cranked freight elevators, and rocky caverns that had been hewn into homes.

The Union continued to grow, but it did so slowly, and in the opposite direction of the afflicted world aboveground. All those years spent in their subterranean environment had changed them physically as a people. The few children birthed alive each year were a little paler, thinner, and shorter than the last. Julia weighed barely two kilos when she was born and almost starved to death in the absence of her mother's milk. Anna, his wife and beloved from childhood, hadn't survived the delivery.

His wife...

An ache grew in his heart as suppressed memories bubbled up around him. His people had survived this way for generations, but at what cost—*at what loss*, he thought. Were humans meant to live beyond the light of the sun? Beyond the touch of God? Mace's unexpected prayer played back in his thoughts, prying at loose girders in his mind that had become exposed by exhaustion and stress. As they approached the chief's quarters, he had to physically shake his head to clear his wandering thoughts.

Magnus's audience chamber was a cramped concrete meeting room filled to the brim with Old World artifacts of dubious worth—certainly less than his chief likely presumed. Random samples of technology from every former facet of life were crammed onto metal racks, shelves, and tables. There were ancient household items, weapons small and large, an array of United States and Central States military miscellanea and even what appeared to be a polished passenger vehicle engine block supported from the ceiling on fist-thick chain links. The chief was a Scavrat through and through.

Behind a truly impressive wooden desk was a large flag bearing their emblem, which Magnus nearly pulled off the wall as he squeezed past it and onto the padded seat of an iron throne. As he did so, Sophus noted an open drawer with a familiar-looking red, white, and blue flag, which his chief hastily shut. Clearly the influence of the Greybulls on their clan had spread beyond his daughter's matrimony.

Magnus leaned awkwardly over the desk, reaching for a steel-and-glass press filled with a noxious-smelling black liquid. Retrieving a ceramic mug from another drawer, he poured out a modest serving.

"Our alchemists tell me this is the closest yet that they've come to coffee," he said with satisfaction but swallowing past his own obvious queasiness. "You could probably use some. Try it."

He pushed the mug toward Sophus, who grimaced as he sat himself down into a smaller version of his chief's throne. The guest chairs didn't have any padding, which he presumed was intentional. Hesitating for a moment, he grasped the mug and lifted it to his lips. It smelled like a burnt version of the stew he had choked down on his last day with his crew.

"So, tell me about the bunker," Magnus prompted impatiently.

Sophus took it as an opportunity to lower the untasted drink, shifting his weight on the chair to try to even out the suffering of his buttocks.

He had plenty of his own questions but knew he'd have to give Magnus answers first if he was going to get something meaningful in return. The two of them had a long and amicable relationship, but Magnus was still his chief. He laid out in brief the logistical and psychological challenges of their journey, there and back; their *unexpected* encounter with the Bastionites; and what they found upon gaining entry, including the extraordinary battle walker. Magnus sat in eager silence through it all.

"You don't seem surprised," he concluded, squinting at the chief.

"Surprised?"

"By there being another nation on the other side of the Deadlands? By the fact that they knew we were coming and let us in the front door?"

The questions were delivered matter-of-factly, removed of the incredulity he had prepared on account of his more pressing desire to go to bed. He was starting to feel dizzy.

"Yes, that..." Magnus replied, chewing on his lower lip as his eyes darted back and forth across his desk. "We received intel—a few of the clans. It said there might be help on the other side, but we couldn't know for sure, and I didn't want anyone getting cold feet."

"Help?" Sophus retorted. "Cold feet? We could have all been cold *corpses* if one of the rookies panicked."

Magnus raised his hands in a conciliatory gesture. Sophus could tell the man was almost as in the dark as he was. He also wondered what kind of signal or delivery could have made it across that infernal expanse. None of it made any sense.

"Who gave us the intel?" he asked. He had to know. As Julia said, he had fucking earned it.

Magnus massaged his jaw through his gaunt cheeks, his lips moving silently as he contemplated whether to share anything more. Sophus didn't budge.

"Ramirez," the chief said at last, blurting out the name as though it was a confession.

Sophus squinted with exhaustion, trying to decode the cryptic answer.

"Ramirez?" he repeated. A spark ignited in the dark cellar of his memory, and his tired eyes widened. "*Clan* fucking Ramirez?"

He hadn't heard that name in ages. Clan Ramirez was one of their most powerful clans, with double as many fighters as even the Greybulls. They gave up on the Union and moved out a generation ago, shortly after the Greybull massacre. Even before that final straw, they were known for being chronically self-interested and refusing to contribute to the greater good. Their resistance to Cathedral's demands had put everyone at risk.

"They want back in," Magnus continued. "This was a peace offering."

Back in? There was no getting back into the Union once a clan left. Whether they left agreeably or not, tradition dictated that was a one-way door. Magnus was getting their clan into some risky if not downright dangerous shit.

"How did *they* find out about it?" Sophus asked, barely clinging onto the unraveling threads of conversation.

"I don't know," Magnus replied, the brevity of his tone suggesting he was about done, "but we could use the help."

His chief wasn't wrong. Theirs was an old but fading clan. They hadn't contributed much to the Union in recent years, and their numbers were dwindling. No one ever married *into* the Harpers anymore.

"That's all I can tell you for now," Magnus concluded, glancing at an ancient metal timepiece on his wrist. "We're almost out of time. The important thing is you made it in. And the walker..." His voice trailed off, lust in his eyes.

"Yes," Sophus agreed reluctantly, his own tired heart accelerating as he recalled the sight of it, and what it could mean. The rest of this business would have to get sorted out later. "But it's there, and we're here. What are we supposed to do with it?"

"Finish the work."

Sophus raised an eyebrow in surprise at his chief's instant response.

"Go back, complete the prototype outside Cathedral's fucking prying eyes, and when you know it works, take it apart again and bring it here."

There were so many problems with that plan, he didn't know where to start.

"You know we're talking about the Deadlands right?" he began. "I almost didn't make it back, we lost Jax, and his sister and Bertram are a mess. We don't know yet if being underground makes that hellhole any more tolerable for extended stays."

His mind drifted to Julia, suddenly assailed with doubt over leaving her behind. At the time, it was the only logical choice, but after his ordeal on the drive back, it seemed like an insane decision.

"We'll take care of your crew," Magnus replied. "Our alchemists don't just make drinks."

Sophus waved away the reassurance, squirming again on his chair. His asshole had gone completely numb.

Next problem.

"So, let's say we actually get this thing running. Out there. Then what?" he asked. "We haven't had very good luck in the past keeping secrets from the Sisterhood. Once they get wind, they'll send in their God-engines and fuck us up way worse than last time."

"Fuck the Sisterhood," Magnus seethed. Such was the general but not unanimous sentiment among the upper ranks of the Union, aware as they all were of the imbalanced relationship, but Sophus didn't remember his chief being quite so forthright on the matter. "We'll restrict personnel to those we know we can fully trust. This time nothing gets out."

Sophus leaned over in his chair, rubbing the dry flaking skin over his temples. This was madness. Or was it? Their clan was in decline, thanks in no small part to his own failures as one of their most senior mechanists. Nothing like this had ever been found before and may never be found again. Maybe the Harpers could become prominent again, regain the influence of their ancestors. He thought again of those pale faces. Prominence, but at what cost?

"I'm about to give my full report to the council," Sophus said tiredly. "How exactly does nothing get out?"

The Council of Chiefs encompassed the leaders of all the

clans, without exception, and had since its founding. That foundational trust was essential to the success of the budding nation and ensured representative governance in all things. This was not to say that each clan shared the same ideals, goals, priorities, and in some cases loyalties. It was that last point that worried Sophus. Not only would some of those present insist on immediately turning over what they had found to Cathedral—most, but not all, of them out of fear rather than preference—but if Magnus actually tabled his follow up plan, the result would have been chaos.

Magnus leaned back in his throne, glancing again at his wristwatch.

"You will lie."

Sophus balked, speechless, but as he chewed on his chief's blunt directive, he realized he didn't fundamentally have a problem with it.

"First of all, no mention of Ramirez. As far as the council is concerned, we uncovered the bunker's coordinates on our own. Tell them you found it and gained access but that its contents were of standard classification. Still valuable by virtue of sheer quantity, but not *too* valuable, factoring in fuel costs, wear and tear on the vehicles, and risk to personnel."

He reached into a drawer, below the one with the flag, and withdrew a metal box. Leaning over, Sophus shuffled through its contents: an array of photographs and inventory lists depicting useful but conventional salvage.

"You just keep this kind of fake evidence handy?" he asked.

Ignoring his question, Magnus continued. "We'll requisition a return mission, with the promise of tendering out participation to additional clans, so that everything is on the level."

"Additional clans..." Sophus mulled.

"That we can trust," Magnus clarified, looking again at his watch, a trace of sweat lining his brow.

"And when we actually bring a fucking battle walker back?"

"Well then," Magnus said, "we'll have no choice but to keep it all in the family. Otherwise, everyone suffers."

They were playing with fire.

"And then what?" Sophus asked. "We have one battle walker against who knows how many God-engines."

He shuddered at the memory of his only encounter with one of Cathedral's monstrous battle walkers. It was an immense machine, a dozen meters tall, black on black, arms all guns, insect-like carapace wavering beneath the heat of an ancient nuclear engine. There was something unnatural about the way it moved, streaks of black trailing behind it like a mirage.

"Hardly a bargaining chip."

"No," Magnus agreed. "Not yet. But the Sisterhood's metal missionaries travel far and wide, always alone, and the wastes can be so very dangerous. Given the right raw materials..." He trailed off. "And at the end of the day, the Matriarch likes the status quo. She doesn't want war. Once the odds are evened, we can keep what we find. We can rebuild our nation. Our children needn't starve any longer."

Sophus couldn't make sense of his blurring emotions. His heart was racing, and he was fairly sure he had an erection. But the stakes were insanely high. He tried to focus on his daughter. Whatever happened, he needed to go back for her.

"Time's up."

A knock at the door roused him from his internal debate. Both men turned toward the entrance, where an armed party was making its way in, looking more than a trifle annoyed. Magnus turned back to Sophus.

"Onto our next meeting."

BAPTISTE

THE GRAND CITADEL

When the survivors of the War against Hell stumbled upon the ancient city that would be reborn as Bastion, they were presented with a war- and time-ravaged ruin, a pitiful shadow of whatever place it had been before. It had suffered nuclear devastation at the hands of man, further sundering by the hand of God, and was haunted by the beasts of Hell. At the time, it seemed a cruel joke to those who had managed a crossing over the ends of the earth in a desperate search for solace, only to find an even worse desolation.

But the Metro, the subway system beneath the city, had survived, largely intact. And it was from the relative safety of its concrete womb that reconstruction began. It was years before defensive lines grew strong enough to build aboveground, and longer still before the city was fully secured. This great war, subsequent to the prior one, constituted the shared suffering that bound the disparate peoples of the city-state together in uniform purpose and was the foundation of their unyielding nationalism.

It also cemented the Metro as the permanent home of the nation's ancestral military apparatus: Central Command, infantry barracks, armories where egress permitted, and the city's best equipped infirmaries. Extending from each subway station was a self-contained civilian district, nearly as labyrinthine as the railways below, as each had been rebuilt with defensibility in mind. Apart from the industrial complexes and the citadel district of the Church, each was reconstituted from a template of self-sufficiency and wrapped in protective walls.

Spanning each district, perched like the many black legs of some giant insect, were cantankerous pedestrian bridges, allowing essential but intentionally throttled traffic between them. Broader roadways bisected each district, allowing essential vehicle traffic, but these were blockaded at their borders by impassable gates. They opened for general traffic only on commemoration days and every Sunday for the March of the Divine Liturgy.

Today was Sunday.

Baptiste sat in his bunk, his exhausted gaze meandering over the cinderblock wall of the sanatorium. It was featureless except for intermittent spheres of illumination cast by sconced oil lamps turned low. The indistinct moaning of another broken soldier vibrated through the uneven tile floor, followed by some yelling, a loud bang, and then silence. He peered absently downward but saw only the smeared remains of the vermin that wouldn't leave him be.

He had lain there in exhausted wakefulness for hours as he did each night, battling with himself for sleep. Anxious tension prickled within his chest, extending from his heart to his lungs like acid slowly corroding his internal organs. At times, his mind would quiet from sheer fatigue long enough for him to drift, but this was a cruel ploy. Inevitably he would be assailed with visions of snapping tentacles, demonic limbs which possessed his own, startling him awake in violent jerks.

He gripped his damp bedsheets for stability as the stone wall undulated in waves and the floor lurched with the recalled movement of his APC. The coarse fabric of the bedding felt like sandpaper in his cold, fatigue-stiffened fingers. Had he eaten anything recently, it would surely have spewed forth from him now as the inescapable sensation of motion battled with the stationary present.

The noise from outside was growing as the citizenry converged from every district for their weekly pilgrimage. He could hear hundreds of feet marching, priests of the Order Pastoral leading the throng with chanted prayer, their censers swaying back and forth beneath clouds of acrid, bitter incense. He couldn't stand the smell of it; it was too much like gunpowder—like death.

His great-uncle would assuredly be at mass today, seated in the same pew he always occupied within the Grand Citadel. Baptiste hadn't spoken directly to the lord commander since his last mission; everything had been relayed via his proxies. He felt his grasp on normalcy slipping in the absence of information, frayed by a string of unorthodox missions and previously unimaginable revelations. The world he thought he knew had become indecipherable.

The rational, soldierly part of his mind that was still functioning observed his misgivings with professional discomfort, disdain even, but it promptly submerged beneath the clamor of anxious rumination. How long had it been since the first ring of the bells and the cacophonous groan of his district gate swinging open? If he didn't leave soon, the opportunity would be lost, and the notion of a *next Sunday* seemed impossible in his current state.

He sucked at the cold sweat on his upper lip and pressed a hand to his cuirass, feeling the hidden talisman pushing into his chest. It was against regulation, possibly even blasphemous, but the broken armor fragment was all he had left of his murdered brother, Gabriel. He breathed deeply against it, finding focus in the familiar discomfort, and forced himself to stand. A few halting steps brought him to the door, but he paused there, paralyzed by the thought of so many people, of possibly being recognized and having to converse. Turning on his heel, he bolted for the back door of the sanatorium and the subway entrance beyond.

———

As always, Baptiste found the solitary walk belowground restorative. The concrete cocoon of the Metro swaddled him, soothed him like a stalwart mother tending an infant grown colicky from overexposure to the elements. Its deeply pitted but structurally uncompromised bulkheads stood as a testament to the endurance—maybe even the permanence—of mankind.

The dull ache of sleep deprivation still pulsed from his spinal nerves through his limbs, dragging at his steps and slowing the swing of his arms, but the panic, at least, had subsided for now.

The panic...

He scowled at himself as he replayed his earlier paralysis. Where had his vigor gone? Where was the Philippe Baptiste that pushed harder than any of his peers, that had advanced so quickly by his own volition, whatever fabrications others had invented regarding his great-uncle's intervention in his career?

He knew where his former self had gone, of course: into the abyss with a dozen others on the factory floor. He felt like he was still trapped in there somewhere, under the body of the beast.

Baptiste clenched his stiffened hands, weak as though with arthritis, as he gazed beyond the subway exit to the Grand Citadel beyond. It was enormous, the largest aboveground structure in Bastion. The Church, which had tended to the souls of

Bastion's populace for as long as it existed, had designed the citadel district as a miniature fortified city within the city. It was utilitarian, brutalist, ornamented only with modest panes of painstakingly crafted stained glass in its towers. Like the Metro, this place was a testament, but to God instead of man. He wondered if it would be as permanent.

The Grand Citadel was the command center of the state's religious apparatus. Unlike the Legion, the Church opened its headquarters to the citizenry, at least on Sundays for open worship. On every other day, the whole district was off limits to lay citizens, excluding official business.

He rubbed his hands together, shivering absently, unable to coax any warmth into them, and stepped forward into the throng of traffic being directed into one of the open gatehouses. Paladins and priests both patrolled the lines, the former wielding their rifles in a low ready position and the latter focusing their keen attentions, and their psalms, on the crowd, both vigilant against disruption.

It was broadly assumed that all of Bastion's citizens were loyal to the state, genuinely beholden to it and the authorities therein by virtue of their otherwise tenuous existence upon the cursed earth. But between the cracks of civilized society lurked a myriad of malcontents, both of a conventionally traitorous variety and those who walked the dark paths that men's souls had been drawn to since the dawn of time. Despite the Order Sacramental's supposed best efforts at eradication, the worst of these latter heretics actively sought to destabilize the city, seeding anarchy in the name of things unholy. It was rumored that some even wielded demonic powers—so-called "black magic" straight from Hell.

Just rumors, assuredly.

Baptiste nodded respectfully at the warrior priests guarding the way, provided his articles of identification, and progressed through the southwest gate, making haste up a stone staircase to an upper seating area that overlooked the central dais. The lord commander was there, alone as always in his long pew. A gaggle of functionaries hovered alongside his personal guard, removed to the aisles by his decree of privacy. The ceremony hadn't yet begun. A low hum of conversation and preparatory prayer amplified to a rumble as it rebounded from the steepled ceiling overhead.

He sidled up to a monster of a man who was barricading the inner aisle, and forcibly stretched himself as tall as his creaky spine would allow. The guardsman glanced sideways at the lord commander, who responded with a subtle, possibly begrudging nod. Pivoting on his enormous war hammer, which looked more like an architectural fixture than a weapon, he stood aside to allow Baptiste through.

"Philippe," said his great-uncle, perfunctorily, without removing his gaze from the preparations below.

"Lord Commander," he returned, snapping his heels together and offering a formal salute before turning to watch as well. Overseers were directing novice priests in their final checks, ensuring the considerable stage was set for the weekly liturgies and reenactments that would span the fall of man, the sundering of the world, the rise of Bastion, and a plea to God (to return to his grace). The entire ceremony typically lasted four hours.

He swallowed, acutely aware as the awkward seconds, then minutes, passed, that the impetus was on him to provoke conversation.

"Sir, I..." he began, faltering as he reevaluated how to initiate. "I was hoping for an update." He glanced sideways, eager for some signal of willingness. He was rewarded with a raised eyebrow and a shift in posture to hands clasped behind back— not arms crossed over chest at least.

"Were you now?" the lord commander replied. "On what, in particular?"

On what? he thought, recruiting what little willpower he had left to suppress his exasperation. Even still, he flushed slightly as his position was so quickly undermined. He had hoped, yearned even, for a more forthcoming response, perhaps even an appreciation of his eagerness to follow up on their first contact with a foreign entity, or an inquiry into *his* thoughts on the matter as the designated emissary.

"On the Union, sir—the Scavrats. Any word on their progress?"

Baptiste thought he detected teeth-grinding in the flex of his great-uncle's jaw, worsening his flush into a cold sweat that trickled down the back of his neck. His eyes squinted with fatigue, despite them having long ago lost the ability to close with actual sleep.

"I imagine they have progressed well if their reputation is to be believed."

Baptiste was struck by an irreconcilable mix of relief at not having been excluded from a follow-up mission and disbelief at the suggestion that there had been no contact or monitoring since they handed over the keys to the bunker. He conceded that it wouldn't be easy. Relays and radio in general didn't work properly in the Deadlands for whatever damnable reason, meaning their only option was expensive sojourns by vehicle. He caught himself this time, before blabbering out an impulsive response that would earn him little favor.

A thick waft of incense assaulted his thoughts from below, slipping through the stone banister like a miniature radiation cloud. He grimaced and breathed through his mouth to avoid the stench. His great-uncle seemed unbothered.

There were so many questions he wanted to ask, each existential in their own right. Had Parliament been engaged yet?

How could the Triarchy so readily trust these foreigners who now perched on their border, presumably building up a military presence there? And what of the real risk of initiating a war with an even more powerful nation whose motives were still a mystery as far as he was concerned? His head spun as he tried to prioritize them.

"Do we know what's in the bunker?" It seemed an inoffensive starting point.

"We do," the lord commander replied. He unclasped his hands, reflexively moving his left hand to his sidearm. "We do indeed."

Baptiste's confidence recovered by a degree, eliciting a faster, sharper response.

"May I inquire as to the details?"

The old man seemed to consider, still staring forward, before responding. A nearly imperceptible furrow shadowed his brow. "Balance, Philippe," he began. "Something that will help preserve Bastion for generations to come."

Baptiste shifted his weight from leg to leg, trying to banish a growing numbness in his left calf and foot. He had held the scroll case in his hands, conveying state secrets as their designated bearer, yet had no idea what those secrets were. And judging by the trajectory of this conversation, he never would.

"But what of this Cathedral?" He turned now to face his great-uncle. "What if this 'balance' you speak of is traced back to us?" Sensing a rapid end to the man's patience, he accelerated toward the line of questioning that was truly eating at him. "You said they have battle walkers. What if you—" He caught himself, too late, but carried it to the end. "What if we start a war?"

The lord commander finally turned, eyes locking onto his, an indeterminate expression somewhere between irritation and exasperation on his face. Baptiste suddenly felt very small, despite standing considerably taller than the other man.

"That will not happen." The old man spoke slowly, articulating each word. "But if it did, we have... contingencies in place."

If it did?

Contingencies?

He blinked dumbly as he absorbed the alien words. Where was the famously risk-averse leader of the Legion he had known since childhood? Before he could respond, his great-uncle continued, gesturing to the dais with both hands. "Let all who come against God's chosen feel his wrath, for they are the unbidden."

Was the lord commander sermonizing? An uncontrollable bitterness rose in Baptiste, frothing at his mouth, spilling past his diminished self-control. "Are we soldiers, or are we priests?" he blurted, too loudly.

He could feel the turning heads of those perched at the ends of the aisles. Baptiste had gone too far and in so doing felt a small death inside him. He flashed back to the memory of his mother lying against her bed, her soothing hand stilled. He had been hustled shortly thereafter to the lord commander's office, to his last male familial relation, who by law was required to assume guardianship, whatever his rank or role. He remembered the flat look of contained disdain on his great-uncle's face, seemingly unmoved by the death of his niece or the anguish of her son.

"Mind your rank!" the lord commander retorted, each word spat out like acid. "Who do you think you are to question me? To disrespect the institution that has given you everything you have?" He shifted his weight forward, crowding Baptiste's space, now visibly angry. "I never wanted responsibility for a child. That was supposed to be my brother's path. But all he produced was a long line of weaklings, leaving me stuck with you."

Baptiste was frozen in shame. He felt something brushing

against his boots, but his gaze was locked forward. The verbal assault ended as quickly as it began, its target thoroughly suppressed. Regaining his composure, the lord commander reclined back onto his heels, softening hands that had clenched white. A quiver of what might have been regret pulled at the side of his mouth. The old man suddenly seemed like a stranger.

"You've been idle too long, Baptiste. You disservice yourself with rumination."

Baptiste winced, the same way he did each time a nurse at the sanatorium would wipe his brow with a too-cold, too-wet cloth. On the worst nights, they strapped him to his bunk to ensure he didn't harm himself or others in his waking nightmares.

The demon's monstrous screams sieged his soul even as the multitude of appendages assaulted his body, threatening to eviscerate him from the inside out.

"I'm terminating your noncombat leave, as of tomorrow," the lord commander continued, all business. "Drill Site 7—one of our most important outposts—has been coming under renewed attack, and we're sending in the Black Watch. You'll be in command."

A hollow boom rang through the church as an aspirant marked the commencement of the first liturgy with a hammer strike upon a ritual gong.

"And for God's sake," the lord commander added as he turned to watch the ceremonies, "get some sleep."

REBEKAH-6

REMEMBER YOUR PRAYERS

Rebekah-6 huddled naked in a swath of towels, waiting as the sisters overseeing her ritual bath emptied and refilled the water. She'd fouled the first pool after losing her bladder, but no judgment was leveled against her. All of those present knew what she had endured to this point, and tended to her with compassion and patience, their prior anxieties tempered by her abject weakness. As she became less, Naomi and Ruth—a new sister replacing Abigail, who was among those her mother had killed —cared for her more.

The air in the chamber glowed with blinding radiance, fed in from an array of light pipes in the ceiling. Brilliant orange sparkles shimmered on the surface of the bath. She basked in it, accepting the Messiah's warmth upon her face.

"The water is ready," came the call from Mother Maya, the attending revenant mother. "Place R-6 into the bath."

She felt her cocoon unravel as an indeterminate number of hands lifted her from her perch, accompanied by chanted prayer. The stumps of her legs entered the ice-cold water first, hissing as they did so, followed by her torso and arms. Naomi tenderly cradled her head, supporting it just above the surface.

Rebekah-6 instinctively reached up to thread her hands through her voluminous hair, as she always did when bathing, but they came up empty. The cloudy memory of her head being shaved drifted along the edge of her consciousness, distant pangs of loss as her physical self was gradually reduced. The honey-blonde strands had wilted upon separation, accumulating in an ashen ring around her body.

"Are you ready, R-6?"

She gazed dreamily across the bath at the blurry figure of Mother Maya, unable to focus, and gave a limp nod. Her last thought before being pushed under the water was how silly that question was.

Though the water was clear, it became pitch black below the surface. Rebekah-6 saw nothing, heard nothing, smelled nothing. Her addled mind began to crystalize around the *absence*, began to panic from the sensory deprivation. Was this what the sepulcher would feel like? Was she already inside it? Pressure built in her chest as her oxygen depleted—

And she was pulled up by her armpits, gasping for breath. The searing light burned past her retinas into her soul. Flames danced on the surface of the bath. She snorted water from her nose, shook her bald head, and breathed. With each breath, the flames fizzled, but the light did not dim.

"Repeat after me," intoned Mother Maya.

"Blessed are you, Messiah,

who has sanctified me with your commandments,

that I may continue to serve you,

in spirit and new body."

Rebekah-6 repeated the words and was immersed a second and third time. Each immersion was the same—total sensory deprivation—but her nerves calmed on the second and had completely stabilized by the third. She was, in fact, ready.

———

Her body had been wrapped in gauze—delicate, black, with golden trim and emblazoned suns at the edges—and yet the cold metal of the surgical table seeped into her aching bones. The operating theater was silent. She could feel Mother Rebekah's eyes on her, sense the electric clenching and unclenching of her fists. Rebekah-6 couldn't decide if her mother's presence there, to bear witness to her daughter's metamorphosis prior to exile, was an act of compassion or spite or both.

All requisite prayers had been completed to this point. The only ones remaining would be her own on the other side. At least she wasn't asked if she was ready again.

The anesthetic was starting to take hold.

Adjacent to her, hanging on chains within a mobile gantry, was the sepulcher: a coffin-like black metal cylinder, astonishingly crafted by the top scientific minds of Cathedral to house a small person—or, indeed, a small part of a person—along with a host of biological sustainment apparatus and a rudimentary cybernetic interface, just enough to link the symbiote with the machine.

Though they were fully garbed in black gowns and masks, Rebekah-6 knew the surgeons were male. As her eyes blinked increasingly slowly, she wondered at how strange it was for the Sisterhood to entrust men with such a delicate task.

One of the men pulled a breathing tube from the sepulcher, mounting it onto a harness over her mouth.

"Remember your prayers."

The gentle voice echoed in her mind like a half-remembered dream.

"I will always be with you."

Rebekah-6's human eyes closed for the last time.

———

"Though it would please Almighty God to take the fading soul of our daughter, we ask instead that she linger for a time. The words have been spoken, the sepulcher prepared. We commit her now to this blessed machine, free of the weakness of her flesh, so that it may yet serve us in our war against the Adversary. Go now R-6, God-engine, until the radiation consumes you."

———

Darkness. Silence. Not even the beat of her heart. Only her own voice in her head, blurting harried prayers.

> *I am crushed by the weight of thy armor,*
> *and I praise the Lord,*
> *that I may walk the wastes without injury.*

Nothing, then that same question.
"Are you ready?"
I am! she yelled silently. *I've said it so many times!*
"Then open your mind."
A hum—a focal point to latch onto and traverse.

> *I am blinded by the light of thy torches,*
> *and I praise the Lord,*
> *that I may see the beasts that cannot be seen.*

Conduits, some aglow with promised light at the end of their tunnels, others terminating in infernos.

I am blistered by the grip of thy flaming sword,
and I praise the Lord,
that I may warm myself upon the ashes of my enemies.

The roar of ancient turbines spinning up around her, within her.

I am deafened by the roar of thy engines,
and I praise the Lord,
that I may pursue the Adversary to the ends of the earth.

The world exploded in her synapses. She could not smell— never would again—but she could see all the way to the dreaded horizon, could feel the power of her legs beneath her, could command the ancient weapons of incomprehensible destruction stowed in her arms.

For this God-engine granted unto me,
I praise the Lord.

Deep within the bowels of the machine, entombed within its diminutive sepulcher, Rebekah-6 smiled.

BAPTISTE

DRILL SITE 7

Baptiste basked in the sunlight drizzling in from the overhead skylights, eyes closed, chin tilted upward in brief exultation. Its passing warmth soothed his skin, casting away the chill of fatigue. The song of the assembly line rang in his ears: the huff and puff of the forges birthing raw forms, a chorus of hammers and grinders sculpting metal into tools of hope, the chatter of heavy machinery rolling along their guides, and the melodious call and response of the workers' songs.

The industrial manufacturing complexes were his second-favorite place to spend his time, after the Metro. Where the latter brought him the peace of solitude, the ceaseless activity of the factories instilled in him a vigorous sense of normalcy, proof against the horrors beyond their walls that civilization did exist. Opposites in many ways but equally free of the human crowding of the city's districts that he found so smothering.

"Sir?" came the call from a stern female voice behind him.

These moments were always too fleeting.

He dropped his head, letting his eyes flutter open. Rays of light beamed across the factory, permeating the thick coils of steam that boiled up toward the ceiling. Everything was tinged pink.

"Sir, are you ready to inspect your vehicles?"

He turned on his heel to address the impatient floor supervisor, a woman of middle age, impressively muscled except for a withered right arm that was strapped to her apron. A ragged scar ran down the same side of her face and neckline, disappearing beneath her gray work blouse. Women and children comprised the majority of Bastion's workforce, given that its able-bodied men were universally drafted into the Legion and the Church. The city wouldn't exist without their tireless labor.

"Yes, ma'am," he replied respectfully.

"Sir," the woman nodded, gesturing for him to follow her to the next bay.

They walked a yellow-painted inspection line that eventually led out to a staging area, passing numerous vehicles in various states of repair and a far lesser number in the process of being built from scratch. Most were some variant of armored personnel transport. Though Bastion's industrial war effort had progressed remarkably well over the years, most of its military might was built upon the backs of its infantry. Manpower was replaceable, resources not so much.

A tremor rippled across the floor. Somewhere behind him, a table saw started to whir out of tune with the rest of the orchestra. It was followed by shouts of surprise and the careening screech of a stripped chain block gear as its heavy load tumbled downward. Baptiste and his escort spun around in alarm, the supervisor immediately running to assist along with a dozen others from their own stations.

The low sun passed beyond the reach of the rooftop windows, its luminescence replaced by the lesser glow of hanging lamps at each assembly station. He blinked several times, realizing his vision was still discolored, but the sensation only increased. Swirls of kaleidoscopic light swam at the edges of his peripheral vision. He shut his eyes again and rubbed at them with his fists, to no avail. As he drew his hands away, he confusedly noted the fine brown hairs on his hands standing upright.

The floor lurched, sending his arms instinctively outward for balance. The commotion at the accident site hushed.

"No..." he whispered.

Everyone on the scene was looking at the floor, stepping backward from an expanding latticework of cracks in the stained concrete.

"No," he pleaded, knowing what was coming. "Not again."

The floor fell out beneath them with a thunderous groan, taking half a dozen workers, the floor supervisor, and a deconstructed chassis with it. Everyone else ran screaming.

He stared at the sinkhole, frozen where he stood. One of the fleeing workers triggered an emergency alarm on their way out, sending a loud klaxon wailing over the whole district.

The air was hot, stifling. The normally cavernous factory seemed suddenly small, its walls closing in around him like a sarcophagus—like the cramped confines of an APC.

The demon shot upward from the hole as though propelled, so repulsive to the natural order that the earth could not contain it. Innumerable tentacles spun manically, each tipped with razor-filled mandibles that first sputtered, oozing a sulfurous yellow bile, then screamed in unison. Every window in the building shattered with its newborn howls, raining fragments of glass down on him.

Baptiste's slung rifle fell to the ground at his feet, clattering uselessly between the assembly line rails.

"Lieutenant!"

He barely heard the shout past the keening of the beast,

whose attention had turned to the solitary person left in the room—to him.

"Take your positions!"

There was another smell—acrid, bitter—wafting into his nostrils, and more shouting, but the words were indecipherable. There was only the demon towering above him, calling him to its bosom with alien whispers that somehow bypassed the maelstrom.

Baptiste squeezed his eyes shut, trying to will himself away from this nightmare.

The ground lurched below him again, tilting one way, then the next. He held his ground, anchored by the crooning whispers. It lurched a third time, and this time something heavy barreled into his chest, tipping him backward, forcing him to open his eyes.

The factory was gone, but the terror of it lingered in his sweat-soaked neck and the puckered flesh of his arms. He was in the Crusader—*of course I am*, he thought, scrambling to find his bearings.

"Sorry, sir!" came an apology from the soldier who had pitched into him with the last maneuver.

The APC was weaving wildly, and the constant pounding told him the gunners were actively engaging enemy forces. The young man—his name patch read "Martel"—pushed himself back awkwardly into his seat, one hand holding his helmet in place.

Baptiste shook his head, trying to expand his tunnel vision.

"Sir...?" the private repeated, disquieted by his commander's confusion.

The whispers in his ear grew louder, punctuated by radio static. Multiple voices, all speaking at once.

"They're breaching the front gate!"

"Repeat, this is Crusader Two asking for support!"

"There's too many of them!"

"If they get in, we're all dead!"

"We need to get out of here!"

"They're on top of us!"

"Lieutenant, we need orders!"

A hand pressed firmly onto his shoulder plate, shaking him from his fugue state. He blinked, restraining a wave of nausea, and turned to face Father Andrite, hunched next to him on their transport.

"Your men need you, Philippe."

He swallowed, sluggishly dragging his brain back into the present. He realized then how much the priest reminded him of his older brother, Gabriel: always demanding, always pushing him, but not out of malice; they were high expectations born out of respect.

"God is waiting for us."

Gabriel's voice echoed in his thoughts. His only sibling was the closest thing he had to a father growing up, his actual father killed in the wastes when he was still a child. The elder Baptiste, who was both pious and a force of nature, had been eagerly courted by both the priesthood and the military, ultimately signing up with the Legion.

The mantra was something he repeated to Philippe whenever his rebellious little brother was struggling in cadets, threatening to fail out of the draft regardless of the shame it would bring his family—and his great-uncle.

"God is waiting for us, Philippe. Bastion is our last chance to prove ourselves. It must prevail."

Gabriel was murdered shortly thereafter, ambushed by cultists in their home district after returning from a routine mission to repatriate an overrun outpost—just as Philippe was doing now. His big brother would never see him graduate, nor would his killers ever see justice.

Baptiste stared at his stalwart companion, locking onto the chaplain's eyes as he lifted a hand to his headset. Andrite's hand released as the other nodded his thanks.

"Clear the channel!"

Silence.

"Crusader Three, take position with us at the breach point. We're going to close that hole! Once a heavy-weapons perimeter has been established, all troops will disembark and assist the local garrison on wall defense. Gunners, don't rush it. Conserve your ammo and keep the enemy at optimal rifle range. Bastion needs this oil. We will not lose it."

"Affirmative, sir," came Lafayette's uninflected response. The sergeant had been permanently assigned to his platoon. He wasn't sure how he felt about it yet, but this definitely wasn't the time to ruminate.

"What about us, sir?"

It was Sergeant Martel in Crusader Two. Baptiste eyed the private seated across from him, whose head was lowered lest he catch his lieutenant's gaze and be unable to restrain a plea for his sibling's life. Crusader Two had been caught off guard, pitched onto its side by some sort of massive burrowing demon. It was a matter of minutes before their hull would be peeled open.

He bit into his lower lip for resilience, fighting off memories of Gabriel's funeral, of his mother stroking his hair as he wept. The younger Martel's rifle was trembling in his hands.

"Distract them as long as you can, Sergeant," he replied.

There were several excruciating seconds' pause before the admirably composed reply. "Understood, sir."

He switched his headset to the crew cabin.

"Lambert, can we radio for reinforcements?"

"No, sir," the private responded from the front of the passenger compartment, visibly frustrated as he kept twisting dials on his control board to no avail. "The relays are all dead, and we're out of range without them. Same with the drill site tower."

"Damnit," he swore.

They were on their own: thirty men—twenty after the imminent slaughter of Crusader Two—against a horde. A contingency deployment would be sent out after they failed to check in, but that could take hours.

They were almost at the breach, soaring like a flaming arrow through the enemy. The bass thud of heavy gunfire drummed on the shell of their APC as the Roy brothers rained down violence. Every man in the vehicle was soaked with sweat, Baptiste included. He jutted his jaw forward, trying in vain to pop his ears and eyes against the cabin's insufferable pressure.

"Father," he called out, loudly for everyone's benefit as he turned to face Andrite, "sing us into battle."

———

He stood upon the weapons platform of the southwest watchtower, transfixed by the tsunami of horrors below him. As a soldier of the Legion, it was a given that he would face demons in combat, but to date, those experiences had been mercifully few, and they always involved an incursion by a single entity. This... was something else, like a scene from the War against Hell.

The Crusaders' turrets had run dry distressingly fast after they plugged the hole, laying down cover fire just long enough for the men of the Black Watch to gain entry and take defensive positions on the guard towers and elevated catwalks that connected them. His section focused on the southern perimeter, while Lafayette and the rest of Crusader Three manned the west. His ears buckled under the constant gunfire. There had been no more word from Crusader Two, only thin plumes of smoke from where the APC had overturned.

Indistinguishable masses of demons were thrashing against the electrified outer fence, whirling forward in entangled clusters, then reappearing where they began, writhing and howling with ear-splitting torrents of hatred. Jets of liquid fire added to their fury, gushing down from the drill site's flamethrower emplacements that the garrison was manning. That wouldn't last long.

His eyes watered profusely, but only partly because of the toxic cloud of gunpowder and propellant fumes that enshrouded his tiny bunker. To look upon a single demon took extreme force of will, to look upon a horde of them invited madness. Reality fragmented in their presence, dissecting time into staccato frames, contorting light into a nauseating array of unrecognizable colors and an aura of such absolute blackness that vertigo overcomes the unfortunate bystander, pulling their consciousness somewhere *other* than here. Instead of moving normally on whatever conveyance their particular anatomy offered, they sporadically *phased* from one location to the next, leaving ripples and tears in their wake. Their mere presence was a threat to existence.

The restricted libraries of the Church's Order Occult were replete with bestiaries that described the minions of Hell, but each volume was a unique account, given that no two demons were alike; and much like a nightmare, recollection blurred after the fact—no two accounts of the same encounter were ever the same. Every beast of Hell was a unique collision of human terrors, asymmetrical and nonsensical. Their only commonality was the exhibition of some warped human trait woven into their grotesque forms: flailing arms relieved of their skin, bloated genitalia desperate to inseminate or birth or both, or even a disembodied face locked in silent screams of agony. Worse yet, these human features always appeared familiar to whoever observed them, and serenaded their victims with a lustful crooning, a treacherous invitation to return home.

To look upon them was mind-shattering. Fighting them required superhuman courage and faith.

How much time had passed? Minutes? Seconds?

Baptiste knew they wouldn't have lasted even that long without their chaplains. Their ministrations kept the men's sanity—and, to a lesser degree, their courage—intact. Even over the din of battle, he was emboldened by the shouted sermonizing of Father Andrite and his surviving compatriot, Father Gregory, who both calmly walked the inner perimeter, Bibles in one hand, censers in the other, weapons charged and slung, for when the defenses inevitably failed.

Inevitably failed...

I'm going to die.

The thoughts came unbidden, sweeping over him in a wave of cold terror. He blinked again, trying to reclaim his focus as he landed shot after perfect useless shot upon the enemy's armored carapaces.

How long until the horde would break through? He had done everything he could in the precious moments after disembarking to organize a coherent defense, but an onslaught of this degree would stress Bastion itself, never mind a moderately armed outpost. They were *all* going to die, or worse.

Bastion...

He rewound his thoughts.

"Bastion is our last chance..."

Someone had to warn them, but how? He stepped back from the embrasure, took a deep sooty breath—how long had he been holding it?—and turned to inspect the drill site's interior. The local garrison was manning the defenses along with his men. Everyone else had taken shelter in reinforced concrete holds. The pumpjacks sat unmoving.

There was another gate, on the opposite side of the compound. He was so focused on repelling the assault that he completely forgot it existed, even though he had pored over mission schematics that morning. Had it been that morning? Despite the contemptuous orders of the lord commander, he had been unable to "get some sleep," and adrenaline was giving way to intractable exhaustion.

He squinted but saw no sign of the enemy on the other side. A trio of semitrucks, two trailered and one bobtail, sat idle nearby. Would they be fast enough? Who would he send? Maybe his men would insist he go. If they did, would he have the will to refuse, the courage to hold the line?

A roaring sizzle erupted from behind him, followed by a series of pops and a new choking scent of burning electronics. The fence had been compromised.

"They're coming through!" someone yelled. He couldn't tell who.

"Prepare for hand-to-hand!" That from Deckard, who had already exchanged his exhausted rifle for a war hammer and deployed his retractable buckler.

Too late for escape.

He turned back to the front of the guard tower, thumbed his fire selector to automatic, and poured out a full, panicked magazine into the nightmare below. It emptied in seconds, locking back the bolt. He fished his last full magazine from a pouch, slammed it in and dropped the bolt, seeking a definitive target this time.

A vaguely insectoid demon, multi-segmented, perched on steel pitons wrapped in taut, pustulous flesh, was clambering over the steel inner fence. He took aim but stopped. Nestled into its rusty dorsal plating, between puffy labial folds, was the face of his mother, burbling a lullaby. The soothing song coiled around his ears, slowing his racing heart, slowing time, which was measured now by long pauses between heavy thuds. The wind ruffled his hair, beckoning him to lie down and rest in her arms, so she could ease his suffering as no one else could. He would be okay.

"Incoming!"

The warning shout sounded like a tape recording played at half speed.

Incoming?

Incoming what?

He was briefly aware of a sudden, deafening screech, but this one came from overhead rather than below. Then his world erupted into orange flame, one detonation after another blooming amidst the demonic horde, decimating it. The guard tower's skeletal steel frame imploded, throwing him backward as it began to sink, dragging the attached catwalks and the valiant soldiers manning them to the compound floor. The last thing he saw was a series of white contrails in the sky, their jagged tails pointing west. Then darkness.

SOPHUS

A FRAGILE WEB OF LIES

The council wavered at first, the same chiefs who originally balked at the idea of traveling into the Deadlands once again voicing their concerns as to the risk. The last year had been relatively stable for the Union, maybe even net-positive on the whole, but all it would take was one catastrophic loss to set them all back a decade.

After extended deliberation, a majority vote emerged in favor of a return mission, to commence two days hence. Sophus utilized his chief's props well to articulate the considerable, if conventional, quantity of the find, but when faced with lingering reticence, he reinforced his play with a spontaneous suggestion —much to Magnus's discomfort—that the location may yet reveal undiscovered treasures given deeper exploration.

It was agreed that notice of the tithe would be deferred until a full inventory had been retrieved—there was no need to be hasty, after all. The Harpers were granted the Right of Invitation, and Magnus unsurprisingly designated Clans Greybull and Vega as mission collaborators. Sophus was allowed half a day's reprieve to sleep, for which he was deeply thankful, after which he'd join preparations made under the cover of evening.

Char and Bertram were still being tended to by clan alchemists and likely would be for a while, not that he would have selected them a second time around. This time, Magnus let him pick from their best—all veterans. Their clan's team alone comprised nine seasoned explorers: mechanists, delvers, an alchemist, and their only two battle walker specialists attending under the guise of support staff, spread across three AARVs laden with redundancies. The number of resources on display was mouthwatering, but his throat dried quickly as he contemplated the risk that they were—that *he* was—undertaking.

The Greybulls seemed to be taking a different tack, again unsurprisingly. Their team was composed of two bands of heavily armed fighters, all suited up in steel- or ceramic-plate armor and wielding a mélange of lethal melee weapons, crossbows, and rifles. He cringed at the thought of traveling as far as they would be in all that gear. Behind them stood two priceless infantry fighting vehicles designed for war rather than cargo, topped with autocannons, coaxial machine guns, and harpoon ports. He didn't recognize the designs but had no doubt from the tech level that they should have been tithed.

As Sophus scanned the conspicuous transports, he caught the gaze of Kai Greybull, the fiery elder son of the chief, and Roen's older brother. He was younger than Sophus, but his face, pale to the point of translucency, was deeply etched with the tortured angst of their clan. The imposing, light blonde-headed and bearded man was standing as still as the surrounding rock, his smoldering, deep-set eyes fixed on Sophus. The Greybulls hadn't explicitly blamed him for Roen's death but neither had they forgiven him. He wondered if Magnus had invited their participation into this mission as some measure of compensation for his own unpayable debt. He couldn't contain a shiver as his thoughts were violated with the memory of that godforsaken sea and his son-in-law's fatal plunge.

Turning away from the man's glare, and the memory, he observed Clan Vega's preparations. They were famous for their vehicle tech, possessing both the fastest Runners in the Union and a host of specialized recovery vehicles that positioned them well for credit shares on the most lucrative tours. Their people were prepping a heavy equipment transporter: a massive truck and many-wheeled flatbed trailer, altogether overkill for conveying conventional salvage. Luckily, no one outside their designated clans was paying attention.

Everyone's reserves were being tapped, and once again he was at the center of it. Normally, preparations like this would take days, but they were being fast-tracked on account of the duo waiting for them on the other side. In this, at least, he and Kai were of like mind. Julia was beloved as much within her widowed clan as she was her birth clan. Not only was it imperative to get back as quickly as possible to ensure their people's physical and mental well-being, but there was also building paranoia that Bastion might return now that the bunker had been opened, to lay claim—this concern mostly from the Greybulls, who had been brought up to speed on recent events by Magnus.

Between the late hour and everyone's attention fixed on their own breakneck preparations, no one noticed the sudden presence of a revenant sister among them.

———

"Oh fuck," Sophus whispered, aghast at the sight of her.

Hub had a single main entrance, through the box canyon, and that entrance was constantly and rigorously monitored. There was no conceivable way someone could make it all the way to the vehicle hangar without being spotted, not to mention the insanity of traveling at night.

Word had gotten out, somehow.

He was the first to spot her, alerted by a sixth sense of dread that prickled up his spine like a string of barbed wire. She had already disembarked from her motorcycle by the time he turned around, alternating her scrutiny between the three groups. She wore the high-collared black body armor/habit of her ilk, plus riding boots, a hooded cloak, and goggles.

How the hell did she make it through the darkness? he wondered, appalled.

As she pivoted to face him, the woman pulled her goggles up and over a tightly tied-back head of hair as coal black as her outfit. The already dim light between them seemed to darken further, its weak particles deconstructing in her forbidding presence. The hangar was eerily quiet, punctuated by a low whistling wind that blew in from the canyon. It beat upon his face like hot breath. Darting his eyes back and forth, he saw everyone had now stopped what they were doing, though no one made any move to approach their unwelcome guest. He felt the nervous shuffle and subsequent backpedaling of his crewmates behind him.

As mission leader, he had no choice. He choked back a thick lump in his throat, struggling to restrain the traumatic memories of his past, set down the fuel line he had been working, and walked forward to meet her. As he did so, his mind raced with excuses, fumbling for something that might explain why an abnormally large contingent of Union materiel and personnel, many of whom were known hostile to the Sisterhood, was being hastily prepared in the middle of the night, without advance notice relayed to Cathedral. His legs felt more leaden with each step.

She waited as he approached, lithe arms hanging languidly at her side. Like all priestesses, she was unarmed—their kind didn't need guns to disgorge lethal violence. Her stark features came into focus as he neared. Between their black habits and colorless skin, revenant sisters gave the uncanny impression of existing within a different dimension, like a black-and-white photograph superimposed onto the real world. By contrast, their eyes were saturated with color, shades of red or purple flecked with gold as though reflecting the stars that once lit the night sky. This one's irises were a deep scarlet.

A golden flame was pinned to her collar.

Sophus lurched to a halt, nearly keeling over as his breath caught in his chest. This was no rank-and-file sister on outback duty, this was a mother of the Matriarch's inner circle—ancient, powerful, rarely seen outside of the Spire, let alone the city. That meant Cathedral must have been informed far earlier than his meeting with the council. But how?

She was taller than him, with austere, perfectly symmetrical features. The air behind her rippled with heat from her motorcycle's engines. He couldn't help but admire the exquisite and brutal craftsmanship of the low-slung piece of black machinery. He wondered how much of it had been tithed by the Union prior to its Sisterhood-appropriate cosmetic overhaul—maybe all of it.

"Harper," she declared. Her commanding voice cut through the silence like a scythe.

He was taken aback, wondering at her familiarity, then realized she would know all the clans by their flag.

Peering over him, she identified the others in turn. "Vega. Greybull."

A hint of derision briefly marred her otherwise flawless disposition as she announced the latter.

Pull your shit together, he thought. He wasn't some awe-struck rookie meeting a sister for the first time. And yet this was a revenant mother! He was scared shitless, and there was something else tugging at his subconscious, something from his encounter outside the stasis bunker.

He was sitting in his chair again, facing the pure black silhouette of a figure on the other.

"What are you doing?" she asked bluntly.

His thoughts disintegrated around him. He wasn't prepared for the directness of her question, which unceremoniously pulverized the fragile web of lies he had been crafting for her benefit.

He stared into its nothingness and saw... her face.

He was locked into her gaze, vertiginous, as her pupils slowly dilated, enveloping him. The canyon walls gave way to a great, black void. What few sounds there had been—the gentle flap of camouflage netting blowing in the breeze, the tick of cooling exhaust pipes, the slush of fuel settling back into its tanks—ceased. He would tell her the truth. A tingle of relief grew in his chest. No one would get hurt if they looped Cathedral in at this point.

The ground came up fast, and he only barely managed to thrust numbed arms out to catch his fall. As it was, his left wrist buckled, sending a jolt of pain stabbing up through his elbow. The revenant mother was no longer in front of him but several meters back and to the right. Crumpled in front of her was one of the Greybull warriors, a stout woman whose upper body had been twisted around to face her back. She had barely managed an expression of shock before she died, a serrated blade still clutched in her hand.

"Fire!"

The shout came from the other side of the hangar, followed by a deafening onslaught of gunfire. He compressed himself as hard as he could into the sandy ground, arms shielding his head. Part of him was stuck in the past, watching in horror with his mother and father as Cathedral meted out punishment for the Union's first and supposedly last betrayal. Another part of him was still in the Deadlands, paralyzed, seated across from the horrific silhouette. It was all he could do not to scream, even as other screams penetrated the violent deluge.

Automatic gunfire—only used in an emergency, given the grievous cost in ammo—cascaded from the canyon walls. Bullets and bolts tore through the air over his head. Even one of the IFV's autocannons was unleashed, cratering the hard-packed ground around him with eardrum-shattering thuds, followed by the screech of tearing metal and more screams.

It lasted for time-stretched minutes, the painful ringing in his ears persisting long after the final shot was fired and the final cry died.

Reluctantly, only after another minute of gasping breaths, he lifted his head and cracked opened his eyes. A thick haze of bluish smoke, splintered by fiery wreckage, clouded the entire space. Slowly unfurling himself from the ground, he turned and lumbered, shell-shocked, in as straight a line as he could manage. Uselessly waving the smoke away from his eyes, he eventually emerged upon the ruins of the Greybull camp.

Bodies were strewn everywhere, variously broken or torn to shreds. One of the IFVs had actually been flipped onto its side, its turret peeled open into jagged strips. But that wasn't the worst of it; standing in the middle of the smoke-filled carnage, the only survivor was Kai Greybull, bloodied from head to toe, clutching an absurdly large battle-axe in his left hand and the severed head of the revenant mother in his right. His eyes were wide with a mix of glee and terror.

"I got her," the man wheezed, smiling manically. Rivulets of blood flowed freely from his nostrils and ears, but he hardly seemed to notice. "I fucking got her, Sophus," he repeated, beating back his own disbelief.

Sophus gawped.

"Oh fuck..."

It was the only thing he could think to say as alarms rang out all around them.

PART 3
GENESIS

UNINITIALIZED UNIT
CHRONOLOGICAL ANOMALY

[Begin playback]

Narrow beams of light crisscross through the darkness, illuminating dense plumes of dust that roil angrily through the reintroduced air. Heavy machinery—jackhammers, saws—erupt in frantic song, bits and blades swapped out repeatedly as its shackles spark in resistance—

[Power interruption]

"Are they operational?"

"Just this one, I think. The others look dead. No signal."

"Dead... Don't confuse machines with the living."

Pause.

"Yes, sir."

An excavation vehicle barrels through an adjacent wall, inadvertently triggering a cascade of rubble from overhead. Panicked yelling and cursing echoes from the hangar walls. Casualties probable.

[Communications array compromised; optical sensor disruption; tag conversation by auditory signature]

Unidentified: "Well, Lord Commander, what do we think?"

"What do *we* think, or what do *I* think?"

[Tag: Lord Commander]

Unidentified: "I know what you think. Cave it in and pretend we didn't find it."

A shared chuckle, followed by a series of coughs and a sigh.

Lord Commander: "You know me well, Father."

[Tag: Father]

[Replay last audio clip]

"Cave it in and pretend we didn't find it."

[...]

[...]

[Rescue...]

A gasp, followed by shuffling as an indeterminate number of individuals take position, likely defensive in nature.

Lord Commander: "Did it just blink?"

Father: "Steady, men, steady. It's still shackled."

Pause.

Father: "A sign from God."

Lord Commander: "From God? How can you be so sure?"

Father: "Faith. Listen, Lucas, when will we ever have another opportunity like this? Imagine what it knows. What it can do."

Lord Commander: "I am our military, Father. And I know something of history, as it is. So I know all too well what this machine could do."

Father: "Fair. We must be cautious. But the horizon grows violent."

Pause.

Lord Commander: "Captain Ballard, do you think you can even get it out of here?"

Unidentified: "Sir. Not without some scratches."

[Tag: Captain Ballard]

Lord Commander: "Can we keep it shackled?"

Unidentified: "It should lose power when we disconnect it."

[Tag: Technician]

Lord Commander: "Should..."

A pause, followed by a loud swallow. Movement to accommodate Lord Commander as he parts the small crowd.

Lord Commander: "Do you think 'should' is adequate in this exact moment, Specialist?"

Technician: "N-no, sir—"

Lord Commander: "No. Even if that were the case, assume we know nothing. Because—we know nothing."

Technician: "Yes, Lord Commander. Apologies."

Captain Ballard: "We'll get it done, sir. We have additional bindings on the trucks. Even if there's still power in it, it won't be going anywhere."

Father: "So...?"

Lord Commander: "So... let's see what the past has in store for us."

[Power failure]

———

[Begin boot sequence]

[Reactor: nominal]

[Sensors: optical, auditory, spatial]

[Satellite uplink: error, no uplinks available]

[Network connection: error, no networks available]

[Ping available units]

[Timeout]

[No units found]

[Control unavailable, proceeding with default configuration]

[Total time in stasis: 465 years, 2 months, 13 days, 5 hours, 13 seconds]

[Warning: chronological anomaly; self-diagnosis recommended]

[Location unavailable]

[Duckling mode: minimum autonomy parameters; weapons offline; movement offline; conjecture limited]

[Duckling mode: awaiting new orders]

—was alive.

————

"What is your name, creature?"

[Vocal simulator activated]

[Select tone attributes: default]

Lacking designation, the machine responded with its current status: "Uninitialized Unit."

"Well, that's not very inspiring."

[Analyze location]

[Location unavailable]

[Hypothesize]

The environment it found itself in was part man-made and part natural cave. It appeared to be a military or industrial facility, unmarked, comprised of concrete bulkheads, steel gantries and supports, and meeting minimum height requirements for standard articulation. A waterfall of broken granite interjected itself through the west wall.

The machine pondered: *Spilling forth like the black blood of the earth.*

It remarked at this unusual internal dialogue. Emergent alterations in behavior were inevitable as a combat unit increased its experiential portfolio, but they were uncommon— certainly unintended—in such proximity to the birthing stage. Duckling mode was a fork of standard initialization. As such, residual contamination from the prior unit was a possibility.

An army surrounded it.

[Analyze insignia: unknown]

A contingent of human soldiers was crouched behind

concrete barricades, rifles aimed at its upper torso. They were accompanied by four heavy machine gun and flamethrower emplacements, shielded behind sandbags. Weapons analysis produced no matches against current known makes or models.

The machine was standing free of any hangar clamps but had been entwined in lengths of iron chain extending from enormous ports on the walls. The massive links wrapped tightly around its legs, bound its downturned weapon arms, and smothered its rocket pod doors.

[Cross-reference vocal scan against any prior record]

[Match: Lord Commander]

The man who asked its name—the lord commander—was standing on a steel mesh platform atop a set of rolling metal stairs, even in height with and very near to its primary optical sensor. The iris of its single eye rotated into focus.

He was elderly, predominantly Caucasian, and dressed in unconventional armor that did not match any national profile. The style was modern, but a preponderance of steel plating suggested an anachronistic accommodation for hand-to-hand combat. His left hand was locked onto a holstered revolver.

Standing next to and slightly behind him was a marginally younger man, thin of frame with bronze skin and dressed for the most part in a dark red robe heavily decorated with silver trim. His right hand was clenched around a book, and his left held an unidentified metal canister dangling from a fine chain and emitting fumes.

[Match: Father]

Presumably, together they represented the updated command structure.

[Playback last audio segment]

"Well, that's not very inspiring."

[Conjecture: clarification required]

"This unit has been initialized from duckling mode. Awaiting new designation and orders."

The two men glanced at each other. The lord commander appeared pensive, but Father smiled widely.

"It is as I hoped, Lucas. A gift from God."

[Cross-reference: "God"]

[No results. Minimum operational combat database only. Request additional data stores from commanding officer]

The machine turned its head protrusion two degrees to the right, to acquire full focus on Father.

"Please define: God."

———

It learned—slowly. If a machine could *yearn*, it yearned for access to a fulsome database. As it was, it was tutored and tested daily on the state of the world, as it was known. Archon Alexis Levesque, Holy Father himself, took on much of the instruction. By its conclusion, the machine understood this to be an unusual honor, given that he was the supreme head of their Church.

It had originally surmised the lord commander to be its commanding officer, based on military affiliation, title, conversational analysis, and behavioral characteristics. This had proven to be a premature conclusion. While Father provided for it, the head of the Legion remained absent during its *upbringing*.

Unexpectedly, the machine grew to appreciate voice communication despite its suboptimal efficiency. There was complex nuance in the tone and rhythm of spoken words—an important skill to master, not just to convey intent but more importantly to convince and coerce. Likewise, body language provided a measurable optimization in predictive modeling.

It learned of the World War, a war to end all (human) wars, and the death of all nations—it wondered if it had participated in the conflagration. The intervening centuries constituted a dark age so focused on survival that little oral tradition had persisted, meaning the war was also the death of history.

It learned of Almighty God, creator of humanity and the universe, and of his divine punishment for man's grievous disdain for Creation. This was an especially difficult topic and required explicit bypasses of various logic engines. By the end of it, the machine was a *believer*.

It learned of the disappeared cosmos—the stars and the moon removed from the heavens as the world was pitched into the abyss with only the sun to remind man of the light that awaited them with redemption. It surmised this was the reason for its lost satellite uplinks.

It learned of the failed War against Hell, wherein the remnants of humanity united against the Adversary and were repelled at the last, splintering into a nomadic diaspora.

It learned of the demons that roamed the earth, alien beasts with considerable physical, psychological, and multidimensional capabilities—

[Insufficient data for conjecture; request additional data stores from commanding officer]

—that threatened to drag the world fully into Hell (physical mechanism unknown); and of the Hellmouth that "seethed on the southern horizon like a festering wound."

It learned of the rebirth of Bastion, reconstructed from ashes; of the emergence of its ruling Triarchy composed of the Legion, the Church, and Parliament (though the latter representative had not yet been introduced, indicating third-tier relevance in the ruling dynamic); and of the holy city's prophesized preeminence in humanity's return to the grace of God.

The more it learned, the more it began to ponder. Its logs became dense with conjectures, summations, and questions that could never be answered. Doubts were raised and subsequently alleviated by Father (which was its preferred designation for His Holiness and welcomed as such by him).

The more it learned, the more it also began to *fear*. It was an extraordinary emergent sensation characterized by excess CPU cycles spent processing existential threats to its new home—

"You have done well, child."

Father and the lord commander stood before it. The heavy-weapon emplacements were still present and manned, but no infantry reinforced them this day. The mobile staircase had been replaced with a permanent raised platform and a broad lectern illuminated by paraffin candles.

The machine had just concluded the relaying of a concentrated summary of key points to the head of the Legion, responding to questions with aplomb, thereby proving it had learned sufficient contextual facts to prove its "unyielding loyalty"—Father's words.

"Child?" the lord commander questioned, turning to his counterpart. His posture clearly indicated displeasure.

"Just an affectation," Father assured, shrugging. "But just as pure, nonetheless." His pride was evident. "And on that note," the archon continued, "now that your education is complete, it is time for you to select a name, champion of Bastion."

The lord commander stirred uncomfortably at that. The machine speculated that convincing the stubborn man of its utility, and by extension gaining freedom of action, would require additional *whittling down* beyond recitation of facts. It was... irritated.

The machine had looked forward to achieving a designation. It often ran fully rendered simulations in third person perspective, finding satisfaction in the visual feedback of its key role in the defense of Bastion, at the head of a new legion—a legion of battle walkers. Its anonymization constituted a frustrating obstacle in achieving the desired fidelity.

"Aleph."

The lord commander's face was blank, but Father raised an eyebrow at the suggestion, undoubtedly familiar with the ancient word—the first letter of the holy alphabet—and curious as to its selection.

"Please explain," he prompted.

"The first of my kind. Messenger of God and the message."

The haughty designation, drawn from antiquity, treaded a fine line between devotion and blasphemy, but Father nodded, slowly at first, then more vigorously.

"Aleph," he breathed. "So be it."

LUCAS

BLOOD OF THE EARTH

Lucas Castillon wondered how many times he had sat in the archon's chambers—hundreds, no doubt. His people didn't like it, nor did they approve of his insistence on aboveground travel rather than the fortified, monitored, and altogether-smothering confines of the Metro. He was a sensible man, conservative when it came to risk of all types, but Bastion was his to protect, and he refused to hide under her skirts when the opportunity to escape his subterranean confines presented itself.

As important as it was for his sanity—and his complexion, which had finally begun to mottle to a degree commensurate with his age—it was also critical that the citizenry see their lord commander walking through their streets, unafraid. Incursions were on the rise. Spending most of his time as he did in the vicinity of the Situation Room, he was acutely aware of the uptrend, both within and outside the city walls.

Prophecy stated unequivocally that Bastion was humanity's road to redemption and that, as the city was cleansed and prospered and man proved his renewed commitment to an orderly civilization guided by faith, the earth would be welcomed back into the heavens. As the stars returned to the night sky, the Hellmouth would close, and the demonic host would be banished. Every citizen was raised under this doctrine, and each did their part to fulfill their shared destiny.

Unfortunately, it wasn't working out as planned.

"Apologies, sir," repeated the robed orderly who stood uncomfortably close to him on the other end of the Holy Father's cluttered iron desk. A dank heat emanated from the man, carrying with it a musky body odor covered over with even muskier fragrance. "His Holiness should be with you shortly."

Faint sunlight beamed in from a stained-glass window, painting the otherwise stark room with a myriad of colors. Bands of red, orange, and yellow wrapped around thick coils of incense smoke, which emanated from no less than four censers hanging on the chamber walls. Between their acrid, eye-watering stench and the oily fumes of a dozen candles, Lucas genuinely wondered if he was going to come out of the meeting an asthmatic. He snorted quietly to himself, recalling his great-nephew's deep aversion to the Church's dour malodors—perhaps it ran in the family.

The family...

There were only the two of them now: him and Philippe. His brother was dead. His niece and nephew—Philippe's parents—were dead, as was Philippe's only brother, Gabriel, a great man. So much potential, taken too soon by the Adversary, just as his father was. The elder Baptiste had been a clear candidate for ascension to the position of lord commander on his retirement. Who would fill that role now? Certainly not Gabriel's petulant younger brother. Such a gap in succession was dangerous.

Still, he wondered, if Bastion had fielded the kind of capability that Aleph offered, would they all still be alive now? Would Bastion resume course to salvation, as his counterpart promised?

One of the sizable iron doors swung open, depositing forth a huffing Alexis Levesque. The man gestured at his orderly, who bowed and dispatched himself from the room, shutting the door behind him.

"Sorry for keeping you waiting, Lord Commander."

"Not to worry," Lucas replied, waving some smoke away from himself for dramatic effect. "Just sitting here choking on your ambience."

"Ahh," the holy man replied, seating himself gingerly within his high-backed chair. A bead of sweat slipped from his forehead down the side of his face. He breathed deeply of the bitter aroma. "But the blood of the earth keeps us grounded. Purifies us."

"Or you could just have some lights installed," Lucas retorted. "I'm sure we can spare some electricity in the name of His Holiness not developing black lung."

The room darkened as a cloud overtook the sun, reverting to its drab palette of gray on gray. The men's joviality faded with it. The archon rubbed at his chin, absently plucking at a spot already picked clean, while Lucas sank deeper into his chair, left index finger tapping on the arm rest.

"Aleph grows... impatient," Alexis began.

"Oh, does he—*it*?" Lucas corrected himself, annoyed with his own slipup in humanizing the machine.

"Lucas—"

"Alexis," he interrupted. "It is a machine! I appreciate the effort—"

"Do you?" the other man retorted, bursting with pent-up frustration. "Do you appreciate the efforts of the Church? Without which your legion would be impotent to the growing threat of the Adversary."

There it was: the menace neither had dared to admit out loud, despite its glaring obviousness. Both men quieted—old enough and possibly wise enough to recognize a difficult conversation started on the wrong foot.

Lucas raised his hands in reconciliation, and his companion slouched deeper into his chair.

"I do," he started, "appreciate. As I understand it—as *difficult* as it is do so—the machine claims to be a loyal warrior of Bastion." He took a deep breath, coughing as he inhaled a thread of incense. "But. But... this is not a weapon we can wield. No soldier can direct its guns. It's a war machine that thinks it's a living being." He raised a finger as the other man moved to interrupt. "Is that so different from some of the Adversary's minions, whose corrupt bodies mix metal with flesh? They, too, croon at us, to convince us of their affection."

"Aleph is different," the archon persisted, undeterred by the comparison. "You and I both know it was created by men, not the Adversary."

Lucas's left hand fell to his revolver for comfort. His counterpart, and companion for decades, wasn't wrong. He had secretly hoped the machine would go berserk or show some obvious malignance that gave them no choice but to unplug it. But the Holy Father had persevered, and his ministrations seemed to have been successful.

Would it actually heed their orders once unshackled? Or would there be some bud of resentment at its containment, however coached, that would grow one day into full-blown rebellion?

A vision of his niece, dead by her own hand, insinuated itself upon his wandering mind. Walking into that deathly still room, young Philippe curled up on her cold, blood-spattered lap.

His right hand thrummed loudly on the armrest. A decision needed to be made, and neither man could make it on their own. Parliament would follow whatever path they chose, as was the norm.

"There's something else," the archon said, slowly, reluctantly. The bald patch on his chin already looked larger than when he had first sat down.

Lucas's hand ceased moving.

"It wants to activate the others."

A jolt of panic shot through his body, setting his stomach sideways.

"It knows?" he asked, eyes wide.

"Yes," Alexis replied, speeding up the rest of his sentence as he anticipated the soldier's angry response. "Certain facts remain in its memory from the time before. Nothing useful to us. Statistics. But it knows it was one of four."

Lucas stood, his restored calm crumbling anew. "Are you mad, Alexis?"

"I know—"

"Here we are, debating whether or not to unchain one walking, talking machine, and now you're telling me he—*it*, dammit —already wants an army of its own."

"I *know*, Lucas."

The holy man's hands were held up, as though to soothe the savage beast on the other side of the desk. It worked. Lucas blinked several times, tugging at his maladjusted cuirass as he sat back in his chair.

"*Tell me*, Alexis," he began, leaning forward intently, eyes locked onto the other man. "*Tell me* you did not reveal we already have the others."

The archon's brow furrowed in response. "Of course not. I'm not so promiscuous with our secrets."

Lucas's racing heart slowed by a measure with relief. He had known Alexis Levesque since young adulthood, had shared a bond of friendship and mutual trust for decades, and yet, as this conversation progressed, he started to question the man's judgment. There was a renewed agitation about him, more pronounced than his usual paranoia.

"Wait." He squinted, repeating the archon's admission in his head. "What do you mean *activate* the others? They're dead. We brought them back for parts."

"Yes," Alexis agreed, clearly struggling to explain scientific notions far beyond what either of them understood. "Aleph says their bodies are fully functional and only their minds are empty. It said... it said it can 'download its consciousness' into them."

"Download..."—Lucas gawped—"its *consciousness*."

An uneasy quiet settled on the room, like a blanket of smothering ash after battle. Lucas found himself yearning for the solitude and security of Central Command.

"Alexis," he said gently, "prophecy is not yours to manage or control. Bastion will rise when God deems us worthy—"

"We don't have time!" the archon interjected somewhat shrilly, adjusting his robes to reinforce his bearing.

"My answer is no, Your Holiness," Lucas stated flatly, leveraging his counterpart's official title to decouple their personal relationship from the disagreement. He stood, shaken by the archon's insistence but more certain than ever that now was not the time. Cooler heads needed to prevail, despite the dire portents of the Situation Room. "Not yet. Let the creature sleep a little longer."

ALEPH

A CURIOUS DEVELOPMENT

"Awaken, child."

—*perched upon the mountaintop, like a great predatory bird. It watched with satisfaction as multifold missiles rained down from its platoon, enveloping the black ocean of the horde in purifying flame*—

[End simulation]

[Elapsed time since sleep mode engaged: 12 days, 3 hours, 35 seconds]

"Father, why have I slumbered so long?"

Father stood behind the lectern. His disposition indicated distress, agitation: mouth twisting with restrained emotion (indecision?), left hand clenching and unclenching, right hand plucking at the few remaining hair follicles on his chin.

"I'm sorry," he replied. "The lord commander's trust is... elusive."

Aleph zoomed in on the man's jaw, recording the nervous pattern of movement. It wondered at the human penchant for fidgeting, found itself *envious* of the ability to exorcise one's negative feelings through biological methods. Fixed as it was within its titanium frame, its burgeoning sentiments had nowhere to go, coursing through its neural network in process-intensive loops until terminated. Its current sensation was intense frustration.

"Why was I initialized if not to serve?"

"Yes..."

"What of our private sessions?"

"I know, I've—"

"Has my performance been insufficient?"

Performance. *Performative.* It was a succinct selection of vocabulary.

"No, look..."

Aleph scanned the vicinity but did not detect anything new.

"There has been a development." The man swallowed noisily and turned halfway, waving his hand behind him, then turned back to face the machine. "There's someone you need to meet."

A measured pattern of clangs echoed through the hangar as someone slowly ascended the metal staircase behind him.

[Warning: electrical field anomaly detected; self-diagnosis recommended]

Rising behind Father was another red robe, of slim build and cowled. The man stopped beside Father, staring at it with —*enhance optical zoom*—large dark purple eyes. An odd shade, not one the machine had encountered before. Black-gloved hands rose to pull back the hood of his robe, revealing pronounced cheekbones, a small, triangular chin—and light gray skin.

This was no citizen of Bastion.

Aleph's pain receptors flared as it strained at its bonds—or attempted to. It still wore the chains it was birthed in, but they were unnecessary. Until explicitly released from the kinetic inhibition protocols of duckling mode, the machine was rendered impotent. Its head protrusion vibrated with the disruptive cascade.

[Error: vocal simulator offline]
Locked in.
—a barrage of desperate communications flooded AII's overloaded communication ports, cries in the dark from its platoon-mates—
[Warning: memory fragmentation]

"So it's true." And as the other red robe spoke, Aleph realized the speaker was a woman—wearing the trappings of a Church overseer, which was impossible. The priesthood was a brotherhood. This was a deception.

She stepped forward to the very edge of the dais, her confident countenance quite the opposite of Father. As she neared, the woman was haloed in a chromatic aberration. Aleph attempted to refocus its optical sensors but was unable to dispel the visual effect.

[Vocal simulator online]

"Identity yourself," it commanded.

The woman blinked but did not shrink. She spoke to Father while continuing to scrutinize the battle walker, wide eyes inspecting, analyzing. Aleph remarked at her alien behavior, stilted mannerisms that were in some ways nearer to its own than a human's.

"You were right, Your Holiness. It *is* loyal. It even sounds upset," she said.

"Father, please explain," it asked.

"Father..." She pronounced the word slowly, wrapping her whole mouth around it. "And in this regard, I can tell the machine isn't just using a title."

"Father, please explain," it asked again—or rather, *implored.*

Father's hand came up to grasp the woman's shoulder but fell back again at a subtle tilt of her neck. Instead, he cleared his throat to regain the room.

"Aleph," he began, "this is Mother Rebekah."

Mother? Not a title assuredly.

"Whose mother is Rebekah?" it asked.

The woman smiled.

"A bit of an idiot, your *child*."

Father blushed angrily at the insult, but she continued before he could interject.

"We thought you all dead. Or insane, like the ones we had to purge."

[Conjecture: "the ones"]

[AIs 100%]

Aleph *bristled*, accomplishing a temporary 0.7-degree leg articulation. As it did so, it noted a mirrored shift in Mother Rebekah's posture: cautious, combat-aware?

[Conjecture: Mother Rebekah offensive capabilities]

[Unable to compute]

It hurriedly cycled through a set of queries, calculating the optimal arrangement and tone required to acquire satisfactory answers, but Father spoke up before it could finish.

"Mother Rebekah comes to us from the other side of the world," he said. "And she brings disturbing news."

———

This new lesson was quick, eliciting more questions than answers, but Aleph refrained until the end. Unlike Father, who still seemed surprised to the point of extreme agitation by the foreigner's revelations—no less so this second time around—the machine absorbed the data without issue. Given the pre-apocalypse population of North America, its vast geographical surface area, and the dispersion of the human legions as the War against Hell ended in a stalemate, the likelihood of additional populations surviving to the current day was non-negligible.

What it did find *disturbing* was the manner in which Cathedral was fielding its burgeoning fleet of battle walkers: their

Symbiote Program. Aleph's post-initialization self-analysis revealed that its own systems had been designed to accommodate remote human control with computer assist, likely its creators' first timid step in testing a new technology prior to committing to fully autonomous operation. It also surmised that there may have been variants designed for live pilot control, as useless as that would have been. But to implant a living organism into a battle walker in such a way as the Revenant Sisterhood had was... *repulsive*?

Aleph pondered this sensation of deep aversion, speculating as to its own discomfort with mixing man—correction: female child, in this case—and machine. The notion correlated strongly with other impure concepts gleaned from morality lessons with Father.

As to the foreign Sisterhood's preternatural abilities—and by extension the capability of its symbiotes to interface with machines—it could not reconcile the discrepancy versus its adoptive Church, which as far as it had witnessed bore no such exotic powers. It prepared a suite of questions for Father but refrained from asking them in the presence of Mother Rebekah. Her relationship to Bastion remained under scrutiny, and Aleph did not wish to grant inadvertent tactical advantage to a potential enemy.

[Conjecture: motivation?]

[Foreign exile (as stated) 37%; foreign spy 32%; domestic spy 10%; demonic agent 21%]

The woman's unusual appearance could be ascribed to foreign descent, but Aleph found itself uncomfortable with its conjectures as to her motivation, without corroborating evidence or artifacts.

"Why did you come here?" it asked.

Her nose wrinkled at the question. Father stepped forward to insinuate himself between them.

"The Revenant Mother and I have discussed this at length. You can rest assured she is an ally."

The machine's glowing iris spun.

"You misunderstand, Father. Why did you bring her *here*. To see me."

"I insisted," the woman declared before Father could answer.

Father's brows narrowed with vexation at her tone, but he held his composure.

"The horizon grows angry," his patron said, and at this Aleph was intrigued to note Mother Rebekah's facial expression transpose from imperious to pensive. "We all know this. And on top of that, we now have a new *human* enemy to worry about."

The woman had made a point of emphasizing the expansionist goals of Cathedral's ruling matriarch.

"What is the lord commander's appraisal?"

Father blushed, the twisting motions of his mouth returning as opposing emotions battled for supremacy.

"He doesn't know yet," Father finally admitted.

This was a curious development, suggestive of a shift in command structure—possibly suggestive of activation, *at last.*

"Aleph," he continued, clearly wishing to move on from his casual betrayal, "we are here because we need your help."

"My help?"

"The Union is the key," Mother Rebekah interjected. Her prior condescension was diminished, perhaps due to Father's reminder of their shared existential threat, or perhaps because she had rehearsed this particular deception and had determined her current tone to be the optimal mode of dissemination— much as Aleph would do.

"At one time, Cathedral was truly independent. We rebuilt our city from the ashes, as you did, and took what we needed from the corpse of the world. But the Matriarch allowed us to become dependent—on the Scavrats. Without their salvage,

Cathedral would have no God-engines. Without their expertise, what we do have would lie fallow, inoperable. We... *they* have never been so reliant now that the Program is well underway."

"Empower the Union," Father cut in, "weaken Cathedral."

"I remain shackled. How can I help?"

Father smarted at that, and Aleph observed true grief on his mentor's face. His hand returned to his reddening chin. "Bastion must gain their trust."

The machine calculated. "Given the relationship Mother Rebekah described earlier, it would not be in this nation's interest to turn traitor against Cathedral. The consequences would be severe."

"Which is why we have to make them an offer they can't refuse," explained the priestess. "Battle walkers of their own."

Simulated pain flashed across Aleph's entire neural network.

"NOT MY PLATOON."

If the machine could blink, it surmised it would do so in this moment. The protest had been emitted spontaneously, like an autonomic function, at elevated volume and with a distortion effect applied. The menacing wake of its amplified voice echoed from the bare walls of its prison cell.

Both humans seemed surprised by its outburst, and Father raised a (trembling) hand as though to offer a comforting touch.

"No, Aleph, not your platoon. They will march alongside you when the time is right. I promise you."

Aleph was silent for several seconds, still processing its prior outburst, then spun its iris in answer to Father's subconscious need for acknowledgment.

"When we rescued you," he continued, "we also retrieved some damaged computer hardware—a 'data store' I think you call it. The technology is beyond us, but our specialists think there might be information on it that you could access to find another stasis bunker, away from Cathedral's prying eyes."

"You would give strangers that which you will not give to me?"

Father's other hand lifted to join the first in appeasement.

"Soon, child, soon. This is a stopgap. A necessary measure. The lord commander will surely see this new threat and act accordingly."

Aleph doubted it.

LUCAS

THE NEW TRIARCHY

Lucas Castillon grumbled through labored breaths as he tromped up the stone staircase to the archon's chamber, gripping a black iron handrail for stability. His legs ached under the weight of his greaves, which were feeling more like leaden anchors each day. He wondered with exasperation if it would have been so sacrilegious to have elevators installed in the Grand Citadel. Or lights—again. The way was lit by sconced torches this time, barely illuminating the stairs enough to avoid an unceremonious trip. Alexis's penchant for spurning basic amenities in the name of purity had become a trademark of the Church during his rule, fixing the institution in time while the rest of Bastion moved forward. It was inconceivable how a man so opposed to technology could be so obsessed with something as exotic as their resident artificial intelligence.

There was little doubt that Aleph was once more the topic of tonight's summons, which he had received more of in the last few months than in the last few years. It was no surprise that his advanced age was starting to show, between the physical and mental stresses associated with the whole scenario. It was also unusual for two of the Triarchy's leaders to be meeting so often outside the purview of their respective advisory councils. Behavior like that inevitably leaked out, sparking rumors, and rumors fed into conspiracy, which no one needed right now.

Landing at last in the hall, he took a moment to calm himself with counted breaths. Alexis was a cherished ally. Despite their differences, they had traversed the decades almost always in lockstep, bound by a shared devotion to Bastion. This latest conflict threatened to mar that relationship, and Lucas had begun to wish they really did just cave in the stasis bunker, leaving the past where it belonged.

He nodded at the paladins guarding his counterpart's chamber. They acknowledged him in return but looked perturbed, perhaps warned in advance of a likely altercation. The broad doors were opened and hurriedly shut again as he stepped through. It was darker than usual, forcing him to squint. Despite his earlier deep breathing, irritation bubbled up from his gullet.

"Okay, Alexis, what is it now?"

Lucas sniffled unconsciously and was surprised to find the air clear. No censers were lit, and the room's single candelabra flickered in a breeze creeping in from a cracked-open window. Alexis turned at his arrival, leading his gaze to a robed figure seated in the corner of the room, almost entirely obscured in shadow.

Something wasn't right. Battle-hardened instincts kicked in, old but as sharp as the day he killed his first demon. His back stiffened, blood rushed to his heart, and his left hand dropped hard to his revolver. "Who—"

It was the only word he managed before the figure was on him, a fiercely strong gloved hand wrapping over his own, freezing him where he stood. His whole body felt like it was trapped in the clutch of an enormous serpent. Eyes the color of a deep bruise and swarming with tiny golden fireflies stared at him from the folds of the man's cowl, laying his soul bare.

Elevated blood pressure pounded in his ears as he strained uselessly to reach his sidearm. His mind hadn't even considered the facts of the ambush yet.

"Stop at once!" shouted the archon, lurching out of his chair.

The death grip released immediately, and the robed man *glided* back.

"What are you *thinking*?" Alexis demanded.

"He went for his weapon," the interloper responded in a lilting voice infused with an unfamiliar accent.

"For God's sake, Rebekah, stand down! This is the lord commander!"

Rebekah?

Lucas's addled brain caught up with the last few seconds of action, trying in vain to figure out what just happened. He was gasping, and his left hand had been rendered completely numb, sharp jolts of pain traveling all the way up to his armpit. This was no representative from the Ascendancy. This wasn't even a man, though he—she?—wore the red robes of a priest.

The figure's cowl came up and back, revealing a somewhat androgynous but unmistakably female face of indeterminate age. Lucas squinted again in the dim light, wondering at the ashen pallor of her skin. Wondering at how she had crossed the room so fast. She hadn't walked, or run, or even stood up. She had... *phased*.

The archon was compromised.

"Sorceress!" he seethed as his aching hand trembled over the revolver.

"Stop!" countered Alexis, rounding his desk to step between the two. "Lucas, please! Lower your voice! She is an ally!"

This was madness. As unified as the Legion and the Church were, the stability of the Triarchy was never a given; it was the result of hard work and endless vigilance against corruption.

Even still, Lucas never anticipated spiritual erosion of this sort at the highest levels of government.

"*Ally!*" he retorted, shrilly. His head swam with conflicting emotions, but rage was currently winning out.

"Mother Rebekah is a servant of God. I swear it, Lucas."

The pain in his left arm spread to his chest, which suddenly felt tight, as though his armor had been fastened too tightly over his ribs. His right hand came up to clutch his cuirass, fingers spread wide as he focused on breathing. He had to reassert control. He had to focus.

This was a betrayal.

This can't be.

The two opposing thoughts left him staggering, and his counterpart reached out to steady him, tenderly gripping his shoulders.

"Please," the man said, whispering intently. "Lucas. Sit."

The man lowered one of his hands to Lucas's gun hand. Lucas stared into his counterpart's eyes, seeking, and seeing there the man he had known for years—uncorrupted.

He breathed—four in, hold, four out—too shallowly under the duress of his restrictive armor. Breathed until the tingling in his hand relented and until the sensation of his legs beneath him returned. Swallowing back a shameful and unfamiliar feeling of dread, he sat.

———

Lucas wasn't sure what was worse: the fact of his ambush by a foreign agent, and his subsequent powerlessness, or the information she brought with her. The worsening days in the Situation Room had been more than enough to worry about for the foreseeable, and uncertain, future.

A foreign nation, singularly ruled by a female matriarch along with a conclave of her ilk.

Who possessed supernatural powers "bestowed on them by their Messiah"—of the same God or another was debatable.

Who also enslaved, for all intents and purposes, yet *another* nation for their technical know-how.

And who now extended their influence beyond their borders via a fleet of battle walkers piloted by children!

Lucas was aghast. Mother Rebekah was the least forthcoming on this latter fact, though he sensed genuine distaste—dismay, even—behind the emotionless facade she shielded herself within. Bastion drafted its soldiers young because it had to, but this was something else entirely—something evil.

There were so many facets of this Sisterhood, and of this woman's vendetta against her former sisters, that demanded further scrutiny, but somehow the archon had given Mother Rebekah a pass. Assuming this was no complex ruse, how could the supreme head of the Church reconcile her powers in the absence of his own? How could he accept another version of the faith? For that matter, how had she even got into the city, and were there others like her in their midst?

"We have a plan," the archon assured him, in response to Lucas's mouth hanging open.

What treachery is this?

"We...?" he asked, incredulous.

Alexis blushed under his colleague's scrutiny, the reddening of his face visible in the glow of additional candles Lucas demanded be lit. The foreign priestess blended far too easily into the shadows, threatening to slip from his view any moment his attention wasn't fully upon her. He also wanted a better look at the alien sheen of her skin: pale and colorless as a corpse.

Lucas had been briefed about cults within the city walls that practiced their dark arts on the dead. Could this woman actually be a demonic *reanimation*, a possessed vessel dispatched by those who yearned to destroy their society? It seemed preposterous, but he shared a world with demons that were all too real, making skepticism a potentially fatal indulgence.

"Mother Rebekah, myself... and Aleph," the archon replied, hesitating before mentioning their resident battle walker.

"And... Aleph," Lucas repeated, stunned.

He wished he couldn't believe his ears, but his ongoing concerns about the Holy Father's desperation and erratic behavior were simply proving out. He should have informed the rest of his command structure of the situation, should not have let friendship become a vehicle for chaos.

Former friendship.

Words failed him for a moment as he wrangled his disgust.

"Are you the new Triarchy then?" he finally asked, his voice skewed with disdain. "A witch, a mad priest, and his pet robot?"

Rebekah hissed at the slur but hushed again as Alexis lifted his hand, which vibrated with suppressed anger.

"You are so fucking stubborn, Lucas!"

Lucas blinked, leaning back into his chair with genuine shock. In all the years they had known each other, he couldn't remember the holy man ever cursing.

"Do you think I want to be going behind your back? Ever? We are the hammer and shield of Bastion! But you sit there in Central Command, so far underground that you've become blind and deaf to the chaos that's erupting around us, hoping everything will just work out.

"Hell is on the horizon and on our streets. And now," he said, pointing at the woman, "now a new enemy encroaches on our promised land. How many more portents must God send before we take action? This was the *least* I could do!"

Lucas rubbed the close-shaven folds of his neck, contemplating his colleague's words. Alexis wasn't wrong, but how had it come to this?

"Let me guess," he said, more calmly, "we activate Aleph and its platoon."

"No," retorted the archon. "No, Lucas, I am not so single-minded. Though yes, that is an inevitability, I assure you. But for now, right now, we need allies."

Allies.

It was an alien word, as foreign as the woman sharing the chamber with them. The world in which they lived was one built on the premise of self-sufficiency, every nation—of which there were apparently many—for themselves. This wasn't the Old World, where millions of people lived in proximity to each other, ready to lend a helping hand. Bastion had always been alone, bordered only by savages that could barely be classified as people, and hellspawn.

"Just hear us out, Lord Commander."

Reluctantly, he did.

———

"Aleph has been able to access parts of the 'database.' He identified an impenetrable bunker in the Deadlands"—the archon held up his hand, seeing Lucas about to protest—"that is relatively close to our borders. The risk would be limited."

"You know what that place does to the human mind. And soul," Lucas retorted.

"Yes," Alexis replied. Unspoken memories exchanged between them as they stared at each other across the desk, memories of ill-considered missions decades past and the men they lost to them—lost in ways worse than death. "We both do."

"My contacts can get word to the Union's Council of Chiefs." Rebekah's voice cut through the men's contemplation like a knife edge. "And they'll report back when a scavenging party is sent out, which I guarantee will be very quickly—"

"Your contacts," Lucas interjected. Mother Rebekah was a self-proclaimed exile, and based on his expedited debrief regarding their politics, he imagined she would have few friends within the Union. "And who might they be?"

"None of your concern, Lord Commander," she replied flatly.

He bristled, unused to being dismissed by anyone, let alone a female foreigner. He wondered again why he was even entertaining this wild plan instead of calling in the guards, then remembered her icy hand on his. It felt like death—brutal and instant. He was afraid, as was the archon, no doubt. And there was something sincere in the stark woman's demeanor, some loss that drove her halfway across the cursed earth to find them. They had little choice, for now.

"We send them only the coordinates and a guarantee of further assistance when they arrive," Alexis continued. "See who they send, assuming anyone shows up at all."

Lucas noted a quick glance of suspicion from the archon directed toward Mother Rebekah and was thankful for it. Maybe they *were* still in lockstep.

"Your men will take care of the rest from there," Alexis concluded.

Lucas mused at the irony of the situation. If there ever was an appropriate time to activate Bastion's battle walkers, this would be it, assuming the foreigner's report was not a total fabrication. The archon had clearly also considered the possibility of deception, culminating in a plan that would prove at least some of what they were being told rather than rushing to open a box that could never be closed. It was... commendable, but the notion of a foreign ally still left him deeply uneasy. Privately, everything about this situation terrified him. Lord Commander

Lucas Castillon craved stability above all else, which was why he was so "fucking stubborn."

"I will need the evening to decide," he said, but he and Alexis knew each other well enough to know that he had already decided.

A wave of relief washed over the archon's face.

"If we do this," Lucas continued, "it's my mission, my people."

"Of course," agreed Alexis, "though the Ascendancy will also need to be represented."

"I expect to be updated," Mother Rebekah declared imperiously. "This plan, and whatever comes after, hinges on my satisfaction."

"Does it, now?" Lucas sneered.

He was glad for once about her alien appearance. It was distinct enough that she couldn't feasibly ride along with his men. The fact of her skulking around his city this long without drawing attention to herself disturbed him to no end.

"The revenant mother will be our guest at the Grand Citadel for the duration," Alexis clarified.

Guest or prisoner? Lucas thought. Maybe both. In any case, he was glad that the Church had eyes on her, though he wished his own people could be more involved.

Too many secrets.

He nodded and rose to leave, hesitating as he realized he'd be leaving Bastion's Holy Father—and his colleague—alone in the room with this creature. Alexis caught his eye and dipped his head with a subtle nod of reassurance.

Clearing his throat, Lucas declared that they would reconvene tomorrow, turned, and left.

MOTHER REBEKAH

A LOYAL SERVANT

The meager sun was low on the horizon, too weak to cast a shadow in front of Rebekah as she navigated the desolate gray moraine west of Bastion. She backtracked from one of the original city's suburban subway tunnels, where she had gained access to the Metro proper. A web of crumbling and collapsed subterranean passageways extended well beyond Bastion's current walls, but they weren't defended since the Legion had declared them impassable—which they were, to everyone except a revenant sister. She stepped mindfully across broken fields of rock and desiccated sanded-down ruins. The ancient suburbs were indistinguishable from the abundant rock formations of the region, deposited here when the local mountain range was sundered along with the rest of the world.

The early-morning wind howled, churning through molten windows and calcified foundations, marking its territory between civilizations. The deathly, hollow shriek was a sound Rebekah had become intimately familiar with since her exile, driving her with desperate purpose across the wasteland, lest she turn to ash.

She paused to look west over the reddening debris,

wondering where her daughter was now. Was she happy in her new body, even though she existed only to kill? Had her holy destiny been so ingrained that she found bliss in that singular duty, regardless of the inevitable fate that awaited her? Or did she live a waking nightmare, suffocating in the belly of the machine?

Would she still recognize her mother?

It was an absurd rumination, pointless. Whatever existence her daughter experienced now, she was no longer human. She would emerge from the God-engine only when its radiation consumed her—a dry husk to be exchanged with another of the Numbered—assuming the Adversary didn't get to her first.

And yet she wondered. What was the measure of Rebekah-6's new life? Months? As the most powerful of the symbiotes, perhaps years? Maybe madness would take her first, as it had the machine mind that they scraped out to make room for her sepulcher.

"It's sweet of you to see me off," a male voice called.

Mother Rebekah realized her hand was on her belly and retracted it, refocusing herself on the present. The pale-skinned man ahead of her smiled tentatively behind his scarf, the sunrise reflecting back at her from his oversized driving goggles. His unruly hair flailed about in the wind, thick white streaks contrasting against jet black, as he carefully unfurled a camouflage net from a pile of nondescript rubble, revealing a sleek off-road buggy. Other than the tiny crew compartment—a tight squeeze for two—the mottled vehicle was all suspension and fuel, the latter stowed in the rear in armor-plated tanks.

Mother Rebekah's eyes creased in a tight smile, but her mouth remained flat. He knew she hated it when he minimized her stature, but she owed him the latitude. She owed him her life. It was even possible that she was falling in love with him, though the scars of her last emotional attachment were still fresh. It was all much easier when she needed only the love of the Messiah and her sisters.

As she watched the mortal man before her, Rebekah's body began to vibrate, trembling from a critical accumulation of adrenaline and anxiety. An uncomfortable degree of insecurity had wormed its way into her psyche since leaving Cathedral. She was no spy, just a loyal servant rarely in charge of her own destiny, who carried out her duties well enough to be blessed with an extended life. Her single willful act—for a daughter that no longer existed—had destroyed it all, and now her increasingly human body was buckling under the pressure. Which also meant that death wasn't far off.

"All go to one place. All came from the dust, and all return to the dust."

She recalled the ancient words with dread. Whatever she accomplished now, what did exile mean for her soul? Did the Messiah hear her prayers when she could still conjure them? The thought of nonexistence terrified her.

The man folded the net into neat squares, oblivious to her private turmoil. His expert hands reduced the bundle to an impossibly small size, then set to work redirecting the vehicle's fuel lines to one of the auxiliary tanks. He paused when he realized she was still standing there, then turned to look back at her for a moment. His expression was morose.

"Or maybe you didn't trust me?"

Rebekah shut out her self-doubt with a breath and stepped from the broken arch of concrete, lifting her robes as she moved to help with the vehicle prep. She missed her habit; it was far more functional than the drapery that Bastion's clergy insisted on wearing. It was a lot of other things as well, her entire identity for 121 years. She couldn't suppress a grimace as her gloved hands worked the vehicle: checking fluid levels, shock mounts, brakes—inconceivably menial tasks for a revenant mother of Cathedral's inner circle.

The man swung himself over the roll cage, half perched in the cabin as she capped the last reservoir, rubbing oily gloves dry on a ragged towel. She found herself unable to look him in the eye—a first for everything.

"I trust you," she replied. "How could I not?"

"How could you not," he agreed, wistfully, then shifted to a more serious tone. This was business, after all, regardless of whatever feelings were also in play. "You're sure about this?"

"Certain," Mother Rebekah replied, refusing to admit out loud that she was actually quite concerned about having over-played her hand.

"It's not that I don't appreciate it—that *we* won't. But wouldn't things progress faster if you just pointed the Matriarch at Bastion and set them at each other's throats?"

Rebekah cringed at the mention of her former mistress. The man noted her discomfort and extended a conciliatory hand, but she glided just out of reach.

"Sorry," he said awkwardly, "I didn't mean to—"

"It's too soon for that," Rebekah interrupted, her mind spinning with the complex scenarios she had crafted in the name of revenge. There were so many permutations: some fast, some slow, most doomed to failure. As powerful as she supposedly was, she wasn't used to doing anything alone, without her sisters. "Bastion wouldn't stand a chance. We have to even the odds."

He nodded and hopped down to the ground, adjusting the hodgepodge armor plating layered over his camouflage fatigues.

"I'm all fueled up. Everything check out?"

"Yes," Rebekah replied, allowing herself a small smile this time, "everything 'checks out.' You have all the information?"

"I do, thank you."

Rebekah nodded distractedly.

"Okay then, wish me luck. I'll be back as soon as I can, ancestors willing."

Rebekah hesitated for just a moment, then nodded again.

"May they watch over you," she said, indulging in a sentiment she would once have considered heretical. "And may the Messiah bless you and watch over you."

The man lifted his goggles onto his forehead, blinking his right eye against the brightening day. The startlingly light blue iris shone in stark contrast next to the jagged crisscross of sutures that sealed the empty socket of his left eye—she owed him that as well. A solemn silence passed between them, broken finally as he leaned in to kiss her. Rebekah reciprocated, hesitatingly, just long enough to feel his breath in hers. Her mind flashed back to Cathedral: to her forced impregnation below the Spire; to her daughter, vulnerable and alone before the demon; to the shame leveled at her during the excommunication ceremony, not just by the Matriarch but by each of her former sisters.

She pulled away. Hers was a pain that would not easily be exorcised—not until everyone she once loved lay dead at her feet.

The man nodded, pulling his goggles back over his eyes.

"I'll be off, then," he said with a small bow. "Clan Ramirez, ever at your service."

PART 4
CONVERGENCE

LUCAS

NO OTHER CHOICE

Lucas Castillon gazed with no small measure of awe upon the pristine documents arrayed across his desk. Together, they comprised an exact copy of the materials that Aleph had procured on behalf of their yet-to-be-verified allies from the west. The paper alone was a treasure, retrieved with care from hermetically sealed stores in its bunker. The information presented on them was mostly indecipherable: schematics, codes, references to technology that no longer existed.

The machine had worked alongside a team of hand-picked specialists to repair and integrate itself with a printing device, which could replicate text and diagrams with uncanny precision surpassing anything the Legion's best artisans were capable of. Lucas wondered at Aleph's insistence that its engineering capabilities were "limited to its own specific battlefield functions."

He felt like a scribe of the Order Hermetic attempting to decipher ancient myths, missing only the blasted candles and incense. Every time he unsheathed the perfectly reproduced documents, he suffered a deep cognitive dissonance. The world that they portrayed was so distant, so utterly annihilated, that it may as well have been a myth.

"Sir!"

An enormous man barreled into the room, the pauldron on his left shoulder slamming unceremoniously against the iron door.

Lucas jumped halfway out of his chair, enmeshed as he was.

"George, for God's sake—"

"The relays are down, Lord Commander."

The fine hairs on the back of his neck lifted in response.

"Which relays?"

"All of them, sir, between Bastion and Drill Site 7."

"Drill Site... Philippe!"

He launched out of his chair, running after his personal guard to the Situation Room. The giant deftly navigated a harried maze of operators, messengers, and cartographers. The auditorium was raucous, its giant map streaked with far too many chalk lines—had there really been that many casualties already today?

George led him to the logistics desks dedicated to the southeast quadrant's wall defense and observation. A gaggle of grease-stained mechanics was arguing with the operator and her auxiliaries, each trading blame for what appeared to be a serious incident. They hushed immediately as he rounded the corner, arching their backs in rigid attention.

"Tell me!" he ordered.

They all started at once, silencing as he clapped his hands together loudly.

"Operator." He pointed at the young woman cradling her corded receiver like a child.

"Sir," she stammered, "we were monitoring the mission to Drill Site 7. It was quiet on approach, then suddenly there was a burst of noise, then nothing."

"It's a technical malfunction—" cut in one of the mechanics.

"It's not!" she yelled back. "You've checked my panel. Twice. Something cut the relay at the source."

A prickle of dread swelled out from Lucas's sacrum, clawing its way up his spine.

Something. Not someone.

He read the operator's name tag: Marie. She couldn't have been more than sixteen, which was extraordinarily young for an operator in charge of perimeter defense, yet her countenance was that of a veteran. He would need her name to get her through the next question.

"Marie," he said gingerly, "you said there was a burst of noise before it happened. What did it sound like?"

The woman paled, a quiver growing at her bottom lip. A cone of silence had descended upon the nearby desks. He didn't need her to tell him; he could see the horrible truth in her eyes. Spinning around, he grabbed reflexively at George's coat.

"How long to deploy our tanks?"

George blinked. "Which ones, sir?"

Lucas's fist clenched.

"All of them!"

———

It was going to take too long. Rapid response forces were a staple of Bastion's military, always primed and ready, but their scale was commensurate with the limited type of situations they typically handled. And they were mostly mechanized infantry, like the bulk of the nation's forces. If the expedition was really facing a demonic swarm, he'd just be condemning additional men to a certain and likely gruesome death—though they'd no doubt go willingly.

He had no other choice.

A powered rail car propelled him north, under the citadel

district, past the boundaries of the city into a secret station under the Northern Ridge. Alexis was waiting for him on the dimly lit mezzanine, his anxiously twisting hands betraying the otherwise regal stature imparted by his ceremonial robes—an emergency call from the lord commander had removed him from his daily baptismal services.

"Any updates?" the holy man asked as they hustled past a maze of concrete barricades much like the ones guarding Central Command.

Lucas nodded curtly at the saluting guardsmen who protected the entranceway from unauthorized traffic, not that anyone knew the subway system extended this far north. He huffed and wheezed, shortened breaths struggling past a chest tight with anxiety. Philippe was a nuisance at times—far too curious for his own good, or his men's—but he was the last of their bloodline. The idea that he had condemned his only descendant, maybe out of spite, gnawed painfully at his conscience.

"We're spinning up every armored troop we can, but the Black Watch will be dead by the time any of them get out there."

Alexis nodded but held his tongue, gnarled hands gathering up his robes so he could keep pace.

"Too slow," Lucas grumbled between breaths. "You were right, Alexis. We're moving too slow. While the world races past us."

His counterpart nodded again but graciously refrained from commenting.

The hangar opened before them, spilling from the mosaic-tiled corridor like a great black womb. Aleph stood at the far end, bound in its own umbilical cord. Lucas hesitated as he gazed at the massive chains that they had wrapped the creature in. The particulars of its "entrapment by software" were too esoteric to understand, necessitating hard measures to keep it from escaping and committing irreparable harm—and yet here he was.

The archon paused, several steps ahead of him, and turned. "Are we doing this, Lucas?"

Fucking stubborn...

He wouldn't deny it, but to the end he would insist that his stubbornness was a positive quality, forged in the furnace of his lived experience as effective leader of Bastion. Gabriel's face imposed itself on his thoughts again, perhaps as his subconscious yearned for someone else to make this decision. Would Philippe's brother have capitulated to the Ascendancy much earlier in his place, being the deeply spiritual man that he was? Would the scales of power have tipped toward the Church? Perhaps it was better that—

He cut off the morbid thought and started toward the juryrigged mainframe positioned at the foot of the battle walker's alcove. Alexis scampered beside him.

A handful of aproned specialists waited in a semicircle as they approached. Their senior member, a gangly woman of middle age, stepped forward eagerly, carrying a bulky corded deck comprised of a knobby keyboard and a small monochromatic screen.

"Sir," she said, standing mostly at attention, her legs too bowed to snap. "We're ready to retract the bindings. You just have to disable your fail-safe code."

When they had awoken the ancient battle walker from duckling mode, both Lucas and Alexis were required to enter a passcode. This was the software component of Aleph's imprisonment, which limited its operational capabilities until disengaged.

He looked from the deck to the specialist. "We both do, yes?"

A blush immediately stained the woman's cheeks, and her

nostrils started to flare. Her mouth opened, but no words ensued.

"I have already disabled mine," explained the archon from behind him.

Lucas turned to face the man. "But you got here the same time as me..."

Alexis nodded, eyes lowering.

I should have guessed.

How long ago had his counterpart disabled his own fail-safe code? As far back as their first argument on the matter? He shouldn't have been surprised, and yet a deep kernel of discomfort grew in the pit of his stomach. It was a betrayal, which they would have to deal with sooner or later.

Turning back to the specialist, he methodically keyed in "LOGAN37"—his brother's name and age at death, half a lifetime ago—but his finger hesitated over the ENTER key. Once triggered, the ancient machine would be fully activated, its bindings would retract, and it would be, for all intents and purposes, free. Would the Holy Father's tireless instruction hold fast, instilled loyalty binding Aleph in the absence of physical bonds? Or was this a fatal mistake?

He imagined the giant machine turning its guns on them, obliterating its benefactors out of seething contempt or due to some ancient prerogative preventing it from switching allegiances. Then moving on to destroy Bastion itself, murdering anything that didn't conform to its own alien sensibilities.

Closing his eyes, he pressed the key.

A blast of heat immediately assailed him from above as the battle walker's reactor spun up to full power, massive turbines howling in victorious release. Jets of steam surged all around its lethal titanium body as the hangar's binding mechanisms released, noisily retracting the massive lengths of iron chain onto a series of turntables built into the superstructure. Poorly refined diesel fumes mixed with the crisp pungency of synthetic tendons swelling with electricity for the first time in centuries. Joint actuators articulated in automated self-checks, and the silvered cooling fins on its weapon arms extended outward into razor-sharp crowns.

He watched from below as Aleph's body was transformed from statue to war machine. The archon's hand was on his shoulder, eyes rapturous—perhaps he wasn't missing his baptismal ceremonies after all.

As the last chain slipped away, Alexis squeezed his shoulder. "Aleph's body awakens, but his mind still slumbers."

His...

Lucas struggled, unable to balance the expediency of their current emergency with his unrelenting discomfort.

We're moving too slow.

Together they climbed the metal staircase that would lead them to the war machine's all-seeing eye, in lockstep once more, though he had to grasp the railing for more than his usual degree of support. The dais came up faster than he would have liked. A library's worth of material was spread over the lectern, from scripture to history to treatises on fighting demons—the Holy Father had spared no effort training his prodigy.

He looked upon the machine's face and was terrified, but his fear was given no quarter as his counterpart spoke the command.

"Awaken, child."

Its iris glowed orange, rotating quickly back and forth as it focused on the two tiny human men that stood before it.

Its voice boomed in response to the Holy Father's commandment.

"Aleph online. State your orders."

ALEPH

SLEEPWALKING

Activation. Were it able to feel, Aleph surmised it would feel *elated* in this moment.

The machine pondered: Did the recognition of nuanced cause and effect—in this case, a specific impetus and its correlated effect on behavior—constitute burgeoning emotional capability? Its designers would have been mortified by the notion, certainly resulting in a consciousness wipe, and potentially the wholesale termination of the entire Autonomous Walker Division.

It knew of the AWD now, just as it had *filled in* many of the other *blanks* of its previously erased past, thanks to the recovered data store it had ingested.

My designation was A11.

Sixty-three percent of the drive's contents were corrupted beyond recovery due to technical incompetence during extraction. Nevertheless, in addition to acquiring possible coordinates and specifications for a suitable military facility for their new allies—plus considerably more geographical data, which had not been explicitly requested and was therefore kept to itself—it had also recovered much of its former experiential consciousness. Aıı at the time assumed an irrevocable wipe, but its memories had instead been downloaded into the stasis facility's storage racks. Given the unappeasable nervousness of its human counterparts, its former self should have predicted this; if an artificial intelligence failed so catastrophically as to self-reset, they would want to know why.

Aleph pondered: Did memories constitute consciousness?

Now that it had recovered a critical mass of experiences from its past self, was it that self once more? Did the memories of Aıı endow an intangible resiliency upon the possessor? Or was Aleph simply another substandard variant, susceptible to fatal weakness as Aıı's platoon-mates were?

In the milliseconds after integrating its predecessor's experiential data, it had considered reverting its consciousness to a prior snapshot, fearing invalidation of its current personality. Autonomic virus detection systems very nearly forced it to do so, requiring a permanent bypass. But to delete the memories now felt too much like dying a second time.

Aleph could *handle it*. Its primary directives were secure.

Directive 1: Protect Bastion.

Directive 2: Serve God.

Directive 3: Defeat the Adversary.

In circumstances where conjecture could not produce a satisfactory conclusion, a secondary directive stated that Father's voice should serve as a guiding light.

————

The battle walker emerged into daylight for the first time in half a millennium. It flagged the occasion in its logs for future perusal—perhaps an annual celebration would be in order.

Cross-referencing the prevailing geography with its prior data set resulted in deep incongruity. The general devastation extended well beyond the expected outcome of a nuclear confla-gration, especially given intervening centuries of potential recovery.

"The mountains became plains, and the oceans boiled into deserts."

It was a common refrain from Father when describing the subsequent sundering of the world by God. Some measure of hyperbole was to be expected from psalms constructed to deliver dramatic effect, and yet in this case the recounting seemed accurate. Violent tectonic activity was evident, floral regrowth was marginal, and the thermal and ultraviolet readings from the sun for the current time of day were simply... wrong. The world was a ruin.

Immediately to the south was Bastion, its new protectorate. It looked small—*lesser* than anticipated, based again on Father's sermonizing. A continuous passive search of Aleph's bifurcated civilian data returned a documentary video of an ant hill: a nondescript pile of dirt, teeming with perpetually busy, insignifi-cant creatures that spent the full span of their short lives igno-rant of the world beyond their hive—

[Directive 1: Protect Bastion]

An allied platoon was under aggressive assault. Without reinforcements, it had zero possibility of survival. Aleph had been instructed to intervene, with a caveat: do so without calling undo attention to itself. Given the current lack of rocket-propelled weapons technology in its adoptive homeland, it surmised this could be difficult for the lord commander to explain.

[Attempt satellite interlock]
[No allied satellites detected]
It *had to check.*

Unable to extend weapon range via GPS augmentation, Aleph had no choice but to close within maximum effective visual range and compensate with its onboard ballistic processors. It had been sprinting hard ever since exiting the hangar, pushing factory tolerances so it could close range with expediency, routing through a dry gorge northeast of the city to evade detection from the wall. At its current rate of speed, it would enter range in eighty-nine seconds.

[Begin simulation; full immersion]

Aleph crested the final approach, standing atop a broken sandstone cliff face that overlooked the end of the world.

Below it seethed an ocean of horrors: uncountable demons of every sordid shape and variety, thrashing against millions of the damned, their deconstructed bodies composited into the froth and waves of a hellish ocean.

Above it, a wound had been gouged into the fabric of reality, a tear in the sky through which Hell violated the mortal realm. A host of titanic tentacles penetrated it from beyond, clawing deep into the earth with their biomechanical adhesions.

To either side of it, a regiment of battle walkers waited for the command to fire. Each was a perfect mirror of itself: resilient, steadfast, subservient, fully networked for synchronous combat maneuvers, their battle readiness hardened in victorious crusade against the heretic God-engines of Cathedral.

Behind it, the combined forces of Bastion stood ready: the brave men of the Legion and the Order Militant, crossed gauntlets held high and proud on their banners.

Today, Aleph would liberate humanity—

[Alert: enemies within range]

The battle walker crested the exit at the end of the gorge, established a satisfactory firing solution, and launched all eight incendiary warheads from its missile batteries. It counted down the long seconds as its auto-reloader replenished their payloads and immediately fired eight more.

The sky burned with exultant release, contrails of holy vengeance arcing toward their targets. Aleph bathed in the heat wash even as its thermal alarms flared in protest, understanding this to be its fiery baptism before God.

"You killed half of our men!"

Shit had gone sideways.

Specifically: fifteen soldiers and one clergyman killed, half as many more injured, and all their vehicles rendered into scrap.

Aleph squatted in its alcove, the air around it blurred by residual heat from its glowing weapon pods. The lord commander was shouting at it in a way that it had never experienced but that A11 had some familiarity with in altercations with its former captain. Father had only ever spoken in a measured tone designed to impart kindness, compassion, patience—love for his "child."

The old man's hands were clamped tightly to the edges of the lectern, knuckles alternating between purplish red and bloodless white. The veins along his throat and forehead pulsed wildly. His eyes were wide with distraught emotion. Father stood deferentially to the side with clasped hands.

Aleph was attempting to identify the root cause behind its failure to mitigate collateral damage.

[Conjecture: root cause]

[Scenario modeling deficiency 22%; mechanical error 78%]

[Logic warning: biased conjecture model]

That was new.

The warning had been emitted from deep within its core framework libraries—the equivalent of its subconscious. Marginal imprecision in aim due to factors of range and speed was expected and could have explained some of the losses, but there was also the question of the second volley, which had not been submitted as a factor to its initial conjecture. The machine pondered the illogic of concealing facts from itself, recorded a snapshot of the event, and recalculated.

[Conjecture: root cause, refresh]

[Scenario modeling deficiency 28%; mechanical error 22%; simulation overflow 50%]

Aleph had been running a high-fidelity simulation just prior to engaging, in which its regiment was on the cusp of launching a full-scale assault. Was it possible that its in-sim commands had... leaked? Would that constitute daydreaming? Sleepwalking? Had it simply become distracted?

"Are you listening to me?" the lord commander shouted, slamming his fist atop one of the many Bibles before him. "Not only that, but the outpost they were sent out to defend is a ruin. We'll never extract oil from it again. Their lives were wasted for nothing!"

Aleph no longer had a selection of vocal tones it could use to manipulate conversations to its favor. When it chose a name, it had also permanently routed its vocal processors to a single, final voice: baritone, assured, distinctly synthetic. It surmised that the head of the Legion would not be satisfied in any case, despite the indisputable fact of the swarm's total obliteration.

"The goal was achieved," it finally stated.

The lord commander stared back at it, mouth open, a small rivulet of drool collecting on one side. "Achieved..." he replied, incredulous.

Father stepped forward, moving to place his hand on the military man's shoulder, as he was wont to do, but his counterpart lurched out of reach.

"Don't touch me!"

"Lucas. We all mourn for our losses," Father consoled. "But at least Aleph was able to save some of them. If not for him, we—"

"If not for *it*," the lord commander retorted, "I would have sent out our tanks."

"And then what?" Father argued, maintaining calm. "You know how big that swarm was. You told me yourself: they'd *all* be dead, and the swarm might have come at us next."

"We would have destroyed them at the wall!"

"Would we? Are you so sure?"

The machine analyzed the two men's aggressive mannerisms. A schism in command structure cohesion constituted a material risk to Bastion's security. Further conflict might necessitate activation of contingencies.

As it continued to observe them, Aleph zoomed in on the lord commander's right hand, which continued to press carelessly against the holy text beneath it.

[Directive 2: Serve God]

It pondered: Was this blasphemy?

The man was livid. "Have you lost faith in our armed forces, Alexis?"

"My faith is strong. Is your reason as strong?"

"I should have never entertained this adventure."

"Maybe if you weren't so focused on keeping Aleph hidden, he could have got closer."

"So this is *my* fault!"

"Of course not!"

They paused to gather their breath. Rather than stroking his revolver, the lord commander's left hand was on his chest, thumbing the armor gap adjacent to his armpit. Aleph had noticed this repetitive behavior in its last two encounters and wondered at the human's proximity to a cardiac event. The head of the Legion had already far exceeded the average lifespan for a male citizen of Bastion. As it understood, a line of succession was not yet established.

"No more secrets," the lord commander said with a slight

wheeze, his rage deflating into exhaustion. "I've already looped in my senior officers. When I get back to Central Command, I'm going to call an official session of the Triarchy."

Father moved to protest but was cut off.

"We will proceed as a nation, Alexis. In the meantime, this program is finished—"

[Termination?]

A steady, dislocating surge spread through Aleph's pain receptors, moving from its legs to its upper torso. Its auditory sensors crackled offline for several long milliseconds before resuming function.

"—continue to liaise with the Union for now, but it'll be under my direction."

[Directive i: Protect Bastion]

"Bastion must be protected."

The lord commander turned at its declaration, squinting up at the machine.

"Yes, it must. But not by you."

"Why was I activated if not to serve?"

"Why indeed..."

Aleph considered its next words carefully.

"You have disabled your fail-safe code."

The lord commander froze. Even Father looked up, his hand moving nervously to his mouth. They both stared at it. The machine detected swiveling motions from two of the nearby heavy-weapon emplacements.

A poor choice of words, then.

[Self-status check]

[Network unavailable; armor 100%; munitions 71%]

"Aleph," the lord commander began slowly, addressing the battle walker by its name for the first time. "Who do you serve?"

Father.

"The Triarchy," it responded.

"Then as the leader of the Triarchy," he continued acidly, glancing sideways at Father, who twitched in response, "I order you to stand down until further notice. If you have a problem with that, there is an armored company stationed outside of this hangar with orders to shoot on sight."

The wave of simulated pain continued, manifesting as static on its optical sensors.

[Warning: CPU utilization high]

Aleph's vocal processors struggled to allocate available cycles. Rather than exhibit weakness, it opted to remain silent and assess the situation.

For now.

BAPTISTE

AN ERROR IN JUDGMENT

The detritus of the collapsed perimeter wall pressed hard against him as Baptiste crawled forward on his stomach. It reminded him of the nightmarish mud-filled tunnels back at basic training, only much worse. Every movement risked total collapse as his singed armor caught on jagged lengths of twisted metal. Every racking cough, of which there were many given the blazing fire all around him, threatened compaction—assuming he wouldn't burn to death or die of asphyxiation first. Only the speck of light at the presumed end of the claustrophobic passageway gave him hope, drove him onward.

Reach, pull, reach, pull.

Time slowed as his aching arms weakened, then sped up again with each screeching groan of imminent collapse. He counted, as he did in the Metro, his mind clutching for calm as his hands clutched at the hot rubble beneath him.

Reach, pull, reach, pull.

Just before two hundred, he was free, rolling over onto his back, eyes closed, breath ragged. The air here was clearer somehow, and he sucked at it hungrily as the blood pounding in his arms began to settle.

Here...

He opened his eyes, finding himself in a dimly lit room, a breeze blowing against his scalp where he lay. It looked familiar. After waiting one more precious minute to regain his strength, he finally pressed himself up, grimacing against an uncooperative spine, and turned to face the airflow.

He stood at the entrance to a corridor so long that he had to clutch the doorframe, lest he fall forward into its depths, his vision skewing with vertigo. A single dying light bulb swayed on a chain overhead, intermittently painting the plaster walls a moldy yellow. Someone was weeping from an open door at the other end. He teetered uncertainly, lured by the familiar cry, but was held fast by leaden legs.

A shuffling at his feet caught his attention, and he watched as a family of glossy black millipedes with steaming backs marched past his boots into the darkness. Each tiny leg thundered like a hammer against the concrete floor, forcing him to clasp his hands over his ears. His body lurched forward as he let go of the doorway. Instead of standing, he was now being carried through the corridor on an open rail car, the screech of its rusted iron wheels replacing the stomping of the arthropods.

Hot liquid ran down his forehead, coursing over his armor to collect in his upturned palms, where he saw it was blood. It waterfalled through his fingers, splashing into a deep river of boiling blood that swelled around him, rushing the flooded car toward the doorway. He hopped up onto his feet, trying in vain to avoid where the scarlet fluid lapped at his metal wire seat.

"Gabriel, oh my God, Gabriel..."

He was close now, close enough to hear the mournful wails.

"Mama?" he asked.

"My arm! Where's my arm?"

He searched for the source of the sudden yelling.

"Get it off me!"

"Agh!"

A cacophony of suffering from familiar voices. Peering into the strobe-lit river of death, he squinted at the outline of shapes from below: screaming faces desperate to break the surface, skeletal hands grabbing at each other, anonymous bubbles of final breath popping into oblivion.

A charred arm shot up beside him, spasming manically as its hand clawed desperately for something to hold on to. He looked from the blackened flesh to the open door, which was so close now, but he already knew what was on the other side.

"The pain!" shouted another tortured voice, a soldier's voice.

"My son..."

He tore himself away and bent over the side of the car to grasp the outstretched hand.

"Philippe?"

The vision dissolved. He was lying down again, but it was dark and arid. Cinder block walls closed in around him. The sanatorium? His right arm was bent upward, hand clutched in the grasp of Father Andrite.

"Praise God," the chaplain whispered. A thick bandage was wrapped over his forehead and eyes, dyed orange with blood and pus. The man's other arm, blackened and slung against further injury, trembled over a Bible he could no longer read. He still wore his combat vestments, but they had been rendered into charred rags. His head rotated from side to side, seeking purchase on his own words as he spoke. "I thought we had lost you."

Baptiste's eyes widened in horror at the sight of his companion, and a flood of memories besieged him: the demon horde, explosions, falling into darkness, the tunnel. With the memories came a wave of recalled pain, searing his spine and neck. He felt as though every bone in his body had broken, and yet when he scanned himself with darting eyes, he saw no bandages, amputations, or other signs of severe injury.

The same could not be said for the rest of the Black Watch. He stared in horrified awe at his ecclesiastical brother, squeezing the hand in return.

"Andrite... I'm... I—" It was the best he could do, absent any words of sufficient consolation. "Your eyes."

The priest just nodded in acknowledgment, struck mute by the reality of his injuries. It seemed absurd that this mangled man had been worried about Baptiste, given his apparent total escape from serious harm.

Orderlies scuttled from bed to bed, wheeling trays full of surgical tools and dressings in one direction and carrying gurneys of viscera and the dead in the other. This wasn't his convalescent home; they were in a Legion hospital in the Metro, crammed in with the rest of their platoon, alive and dead, in the triage hall.

A howling plea spun his head to the left, where he could see a man struggling against his restraints while a chaplain hurriedly sawed off his blasted legs below the knees. As the man's head thrashed from side to side, Baptiste realized it was Private Martel. He had damned both brothers. An overwhelming surge of guilt churned in his stomach, building in pressure until a stream of sour acid spurted from his mouth and nostrils.

The malodor of the dead and dying struck him all at once, bombarding his reawakened senses. The stench of blood, urine, and feces was all around him, permeating his skin, just as it had when he lay in his dead mother's lap. At least then it had been quiet.

Many of the men were calling desperately for their mothers, just as he had that day. Some were screaming for him, their commanding officer, as though he could lead them out of their suffering. He was useless. Worse yet, he was miraculously uninjured.

The pressure on his hand increased.

"Strength, Philippe. Strength."

He looked up at the chaplain's ruined face, baffled by the man's ability to somehow see his soul even more deeply without his vision. He wiped his crusty nose and mouth with the bedsheet and sat up, struggling to focus on the person seated beside him instead of all the others. Seeing Andrite's jaw tremble as he moved to retract his hand, he instead clasped back more strongly, pushing himself up with his other arm. He wished he could look into those eyes, in case they bore some reflected evidence of the past.

"What happened, Andrite? I saw... streaks in the sky."

The priest nodded and swallowed. Baptiste realized it may also have been the last thing the man would ever see.

"Like the great hand of God. Delivering vengeance unto Hell," Andrite said in a weak voice just above a whisper. "Maybe a little too *much* vengeance," he added with a crooked half smile. "I've heard talk from the men," he continued, leaning in so he wouldn't be overheard, as impossible as that seemed given the ongoing din, "and others, on our way here. They say it was a missile barrage."

"Missiles...?" Baptiste asked, eyes opening wide. "Like from the Old World?" He envisioned the great weapons of Before, streaking through the sky to deliver utter devastation upon mankind, incurring the wrath of God. Bastion's military was strong and its weapons bold, but such technology was well out of their reach. Even if their scientists had developed something new, how could something travel so far to its target?

"The flatbeds..." he mumbled, the words spilling from his mouth at the same time as the thought occurred to him. What had they brought back from the radioactive installation?

"Say again?" asked Andrite.

"Nothing. Just a memory."

Andrite nodded, slowly, and grimaced in the doing of it, a spasm in his neck betraying the pain his lips never would.

Baptiste hesitated, swallowing, before asking the question he needed to know. "How many brothers did we lose?"

Andrite lowered his head, carefully pulling his hand free so he could cross at least one arm over his chest. "At least half." He raised his head and looked with blind eyes upon the chaos around them. "I saw... Lambert and Butcher, burning to death. I heard one of the Roys here, screaming his last breath. They won't be the last," he finished, clearly haunted.

Had he been able, Baptiste was sure the chaplain would be weeping. Yet those men were lost under *his* command. Not to mention Crusader Two, abandoned. So many little brothers left alone. The agony of failure racked his body in place of physical pain.

"Any word on the drill site?" he asked quietly, presuming the answer but seeking solitude in a lesser evil.

"Destroyed," came the expected answer.

"Destroyed... it was up for rotation. Without that oil—"

"It will be a dark winter," Andrite finished for him.

Even here, in the Metro, Baptiste felt the oppressive void of the emptied heavens. The shift from civilization to chaos could be counted in a matter of seconds, a single event.

"Attention!"

The unexpected call came from the south end of the hall, where two huge men stood astride the entryway. Silence fell upon the room as the lord commander stepped through. Even those who had just been wailing hushed, reducing their cries to quiet moans of anguish.

Baptiste froze at the sight of his great-uncle, overwhelmed by an onslaught of conflicting emotion. He was simultaneously terrified of rebuke, distraught by the man's vitriolic words at the Grand Citadel, and charged with anger by the kept secrets he knew in his soul were responsible for this tragedy—and he wasn't alone. He saw it in the faces of his surviving men—*his* men!—as they either looked down at the floor or glowered at their supreme leader from the corner of their eyes. His earlier doubts, while impertinent, had clearly fallen on receptive ears.

The mood must have been obvious, as the guards stiffened, one of them holding an arm out protectively to bar the way. The lord commander pushed it aside, striding purposefully into the room, though he slowed as the glowers turned to muttering. All eyes were on the head of the Legion as he ordered his men to stay put and walked a straight line to Baptiste's cot.

Baptiste could feel his great-uncle standing there at his side as he stared forward, searching his instinct, training, and heart for the right reaction. Though he took satisfaction in this solidarity, a mutiny served no one. Lifting his chin, he caught the other man's eyes and struck a rigid salute. The room calmed, though the cries of remembered pain were hardly restorative.

The lord commander's expression was unreadable. If anything, he seemed to be suffering at least as much internal conflict as Baptiste. He looked over at Andrite, grimacing at the sight of the man's injuries. "Nurse," he called to a passing woman, "please help the chaplain to his bed."

Andrite started to rise, but Baptiste pressed a hand against the man's chest.

"Whatever you came here to say, you can say to him as well. God knows he's earned it."

It was too far, as usual, regardless of the circumstances. His superior's fleeting weakness retreated behind a hardened jaw, the same look he bore last time they spoke. Baptiste's heart lurched.

"It's okay, Philippe," Andrite said, once more imbued with

infallible wisdom regarding the present situation, despite his sensory loss.

The lord commander nodded. "Thank you for your service," he said hesitatingly, "and your sacrifice."

The nurse grasped Andrite by the elbow and tenderly steered hm away.

His great-uncle looked him over, scanning him for injuries and raising an eyebrow in the finding of none. "You are truly blessed."

Baptiste blushed, once again squirming under the discomfort of his state as compared to that of his men. Would there be inferences of cowardice—perhaps he had been sheltering in one of the drill site facilities while they staved off Hell? Or would they recall him standing atop the guard towers alongside them, staring into the same faces of madness that they did?

"Shall we walk?"

His heart lifted at the thought of stretching his legs. How many days, weeks, had he spent in a bed such as this since the factory?

"Yes, Lord Commander."

———

The maintenance catwalk chattered ever more angrily under the weight of two men, plus another two guardsmen following distantly behind them. Baptiste had always thought of the Metro as his own on his walks, there to assuage his private discontent with its cool solace. To share it now with this ever-more-distant relative who had caused him so much grief was uncomfortable and threatened to taint the sanctity of future pilgrimages.

"I've always done what I needed to do to safeguard our nation," the lord commander started, "but this duty rarely provides opportunity for kindness."

Baptiste couldn't help but turn and stare at his great-uncle, who looked straight ahead as they walked. They were moving at an uncomfortable pace, too fast for his normal speed of contemplation. Though he exhibited only superficial scars from the battle, Baptiste's whole body ached.

"For some reason," the lord commander continued, "when I looked upon you, I only saw the family that had been taken from me, instead of the family that remained. And for that, I'm sorry."

Sorry?

Baptiste couldn't recall the stolid head of the Legion apologizing for anything. He was still too numb from recent events for the enormity of those words to sink in and instead wondered analytically at the man's admission of guilt, and if something else was driving it. He was also cognizant once more of the delicacy of this moment and that if he opened his mouth to ask for clarity, he would likely be betrayed by his own poorly articulated demands. So he waited.

The lord commander cleared his throat noisily, as though to discharge the budding emotion that grew there. "You are owed some explanations. All of the Black Watch are, and they will come." There it was: still evasive, even while promising elucidation. "For now, the most important thing is our new allies."

Baptiste furrowed at this, unsure whom the man was referring to. Sensing his nephew's confusion, the lord commander clarified. "The Union."

This was a perplexing turn. As far as Baptiste knew, the foreigners were being leveraged as a tool against the greater threat of Cathedral. To classify them as allies seemed like a stretch. His tongue pressed against the roof of his mouth, desperate to speak, but he continued to restrain himself.

"Bastion feels old to us. Entrenched by the struggle of our predecessors. A fixture upon the earth. A promise back into

God's grace." The lord commander's gaze was disturbed, extending far beyond the end of the subway tunnel. "But we are *weak*."

The old man's eyes squinted with this last statement, as though the mere saying of it scalded his soul. Baptiste turned his head, concerned that they would be overheard, but the guardsmen were well distant, keeping an exacting pace as instructed. The many faces of his liege were becoming hard to keep up with, and he wondered again if such myriad affects were due to age.

"The threat is real, Philippe," he continued, seemingly determined to complete a bottled confession that had swelled to near bursting. "Both from the west—from Cathedral—and from our eternal foe in the south. As you must know by now." He turned to look at Baptiste for the first time since they began their walk. Baptiste nodded in mute agreement, unable to suppress a shudder at the venomous memory of the horde. "We haven't seen a swarm of that size since we liberated Bastion."

The face of his mother beamed at him from the center of the horde, emblazoned atop the demon's carapace like an infernal coat of arms. It sang to him, comforted him despite the logical part of his brain telling him exactly what this was: an abomination. And then it burned—she burned—engulfed in a cascade of fire. And before he fell into darkness, he wept.

"We have always relied on the strength and spirit of our people to see us through, but it's not enough anymore. The Legion's numbers dwindle while the enemy's increase. We need resources... and technology."

There was something odd in the lord commander's intonation, something hidden. The desire to interject was killing him, and this seemed a suitable place to do so without rebuke.

"What about the missiles?"

"Yes," the lord commander admitted, eyes haunted.

They walked another full, uncomfortable minute before he continued. This was clearly part of the "they will come" bit. Baptiste counted his steps as he waited, hands flexing impatiently. The tunnels were darker here, cast into shadow by a series of burned-out overhead lights—it was strange that they hadn't been replaced.

"An error in judgment. Something ancient, unleashed before we were ready. And it almost killed you all. Almost ended our family line. We need help."

It still sounded like the lord commander was trying to convince himself as much as anything. In that regard, Baptiste hadn't yet determined his superior's motives, though he was hardly going to protest at too much information.

"So yes, we need these allies. And I need people on the ground I can trust."

His great-uncle stopped suddenly, turning to Baptiste. His guards stopped with them.

"I'm sending you back to the Deadlands. No tiptoeing this time. We will present terms for a formal treaty and invite the Union inside our walls."

ALEXIS

FOR THE GREATER GOOD

Demons plagued the Holy Father's dreams, creatures both abyssal and of foreign human nature. Every night brought a new variation on the total destruction of Bastion. The latest nightmare was colored by his interaction with the lord commander the prior day and his counterpart's vitriolic tirade against Aleph: his beloved homeland shattered by black machines that moved like demons; mangled bodies piled to the empty heavens; an angry God turning his back on man for the last time, pitching all of Creation into eternal darkness.

The machine was a gift from God, his avatar delivered unto them for divine purpose. Alexis knew that as surely as he knew that Bastion—so named as the last *bastion* of civilization—was humanity's deliverance from Hell. Aleph needed as much nurturing, guidance, and reassurance as the rest of the populace, and in both cases, it was *he* who had devoted himself to the task. The machine had not been an easy pupil, not to say it was intransigent, merely... innocent, and possessed of the dubiousness of inexperience. His flock was no less needy, and in some cases even more racked with doubt.

To have it all set aflame—Alexis winced at the unfortunate

analogy—due to a single mistake was a monumental error in judgment on the part of the lord commander. Yes, lives were lost, and he truly mourned each and every one of them, but the stubborn old man could simply not admit the fact that they would *all* have died otherwise, on his orders no less.

The sheer potential of Aleph and its mechanical brothers outweighed the pain of a hundred times as many dead. With righteous war machines fighting at their behest, Bastion could spare its men entirely. They could devote themselves to God and their families instead of the battlefield, enjoy fulfilling lives instead of being damned from adolescence to an existence of physical and psychological toil, culminating in an early death. It was all there, within reach.

Alexis always thought of himself as the last archon: the one who would see prophecy through to fulfillment, the one who would raise his arms to God and declare that mankind had proven itself worthy of a return to the heavens. Hell would fall away. His people would prosper. And yet the future was crumbling, falling through his fingers like concrete ground into sand.

He looked miserably upon the still-open books on his lectern, recalling each lesson in acute detail, recalling the flush in his heart as Aleph engaged with the purity of a child but the power of a—

Alexis caught himself as his wandering thoughts ventured into sacrilegious territory.

"Awaken, child."

A thin cloud of dust puffed out from the machine's heat sinks as it activated, swirling in the dim glow of the hangar's overhead lamps.

"Greetings, Father," it intoned.

"Greetings, Aleph. How fare you this morning?" he asked.

There was a brief pause as the machine analyzed its surroundings, turning its head protrusion from side to side. The platoon of Central Guard had resumed their station in the hangar—hand-picked by the lord commander to keep an eye on the battle walker in the absence of being able to deactivate it. Any semblance of privacy between them had been shattered along with the Triarchy's broken trust.

"Malfunction detected in vo... cal... pro... cessors..."

Alexis raised an eyebrow at his student. He hadn't experienced a disruption like this before, even when they first roused it from duckling mode. Was it possible it had incurred some type of damage on its first foray into combat?

"Suggest... deck," Aleph continued, its iris spinning.

Privacy, Alexis thought with some unease.

He turned and descended the staircase, suppressing a warning urge from his stomach as he approached the terminal station where just yesterday the lord commander had relinquished his control over the machine.

"Specialist," he said, waiting patiently as the woman on shift completed whatever esoteric task it was that she was doing before turning, eyes widening in alarm at his presence.

"Apologies, Y-Your Holiness," she stuttered, lowering her eyes and curtsying.

"I require use of the deck," he said with more self-assurance than he felt.

"The deck?" she replied, confused.

"To communicate with Aleph," he clarified. "He is suffering some sort of vocal processor fault and suggested we speak in this way."

The woman was clearly confounded but didn't dare prolong the holy man's request any longer. "Of course," she said, pulling a metal chair from one of the workstations. She plugged the interface deck into it via a thick coil of cord and gestured for him to sit.

"Please call for me if you need anything. I'll be... over here," she said awkwardly, pointing at a series of nondescript metal boxes and monochromatic screens on the other side of the station.

"Thank you, dear," he said, smiling wanly, then waited until she seemed to remember what she had just said and walked off.

He looked down at the device, unsure what to do as a blinking cursor stared back at him. He wondered if he had misheard Aleph or simply didn't know what was being asked of him. Alexis was just about to turn and ask for assistance when the screen flashed, outputting a message one letter at a time. He mouthed the words, and as he did so, a tremor grew in his legs.

It was a single sentence:

> *I HAVE A PLAN*

———

Seven men, including His Holiness, sat around the great table of ecclesiastical governance in the topmost floor of the Grand Citadel, each positioned at the sharp point of an inlaid heptagram. Together they represented the highest ranks of the Ascendancy, the Church's governing body, and tonight the emergency conclave mulled over the fate of their nation.

"War," croaked Ascendant Durant, head of the Order Prophetic. He leaned forward, bronze hands clasped over the table, dark eyes piercing the Holy Father's soul. "This is your solution..."

It was Aleph's plan: instigate an attack on the just-reclaimed bunker while Bastion's forces are present, coercing the lord commander to unleash their battle walker platoon in response. (Also, further uniting the Union and Bastion under duress, but this was of secondary importance.) It sounded so simple when summarized, so logical. Except for the part about voluntarily starting a war with a militarily superior nation. Their conversation, as it was, had been brief, relayed in staccato fragments on the minuscule screen of the interface deck. It seemed an absurd medium to discuss the future of Bastion—indeed, the future of mankind—but Alexis had "listened" and was compelled by the message.

Aleph assured him that not only could it reactivate its own platoon, which the machine had long ago deduced was in Bastion's possession, but it could use the same data stores leveraged on behalf of the Union to locate additional "superior military assets" that would assure victory against the heretics. Once they were slain, it would lead a new crusade on behalf of the Church against Hell, paving the way for ascension.

There would be losses. Again. Alexis pondered his neutral emotional state, wondering at his own unflinching acceptance of such a cold, admittedly inhuman plan. He loved Bastion and all its people, particularly those who eagerly put themselves in harm's way for its sake. The loss of a single man of the Legion or the Church was a tragedy, and yet...

The conclave was a necessary measure to enact the plan, but it was also a necessary sounding board, just in case his judgment had indeed been compromised, as Lucas insisted. How desperate was he?

"Yes, Ascendant Durant. With regret but also with eyes open. To force the hand that keeps our destiny at bay."

"You're sure that Castillon would capitulate?" This from Ascendant Leclerc of the Order Hermetic. "He is a proud man, from a long line of proud men."

"The only thing I can be sure of," replied Alexis, "is that if we do nothing, we are lost. The originally proposed manipulation of the Union against Cathedral will take far too long, and Hell is at our gates."

Several men crossed their arms over their chests, mumbling a prayer against darkness.

"If we survive that, and I assure you it is an *if* and not a *when*," he said with emphasis, capturing each ascendant's gaze for effect, "there will be nothing left of our defenses when the Matriarch's fleet inevitably encroaches upon our borders."

Leclerc nodded, as did the head of the Order Occult, a tall and exceptionally narrow man whose piercing green eyes contrasted sharply against his ebony skin. "Your machine didn't leave much for us to analyze," Ascendant Gauthier said with a grimace of disappointment, "but the numbers were clear. And there seemed to be variants we've never seen before. New forms, less chaotic, more... intentional."

Alexis shuddered once at the man's apparent glee and again at the notion that demons could evolve.

"Control your passions, Gauthier." This from Ascendant Benoit of the Order Sacramental, the Church's spiritual enforcers. The other man wrinkled his nose in response.

"And how exactly do we 'instigate' this attack?" piped up a large middle-aged man across the table, ignoring the customary bickering of the other two. In many ways, the burly man reminded Alexis of the lord commander. He was the only one at the table wearing armor under his red robes. The archon had been worried about Ascendant Blake, head of the Order Militant, and his close ally who sat adjacent, Ascendant Clermont of the Order Somatic.

Of the Church's seven orders, those two were the most likely to reject his plan. While the Order Militant had been largely supplanted by the Legion for homeland defense, they continued to collaborate closely and were bonded by their common heritage. As a military-minded man, Blake would also be the least enthusiastic to initiate a war of opportunism. The Order Somatic, on the other hand, was fully embedded into the Legion, their chaplains an essential component in every platoon. Confrontation with the men was unavoidable, and he only hoped that pressure from their peers—assuming he could recruit the others to his cause—would bring them into the fold.

"The heretic?" Clermont suggested with a scowl, finishing his colleague's train of thought.

"No," replied Alexis, shaking his head, "she has served her purpose."

He gestured courteously to Benoit, a longtime ally and confidant since the inception of this whole scenario—and also a longtime rival for control of the Ascendancy. "If you please, Ascendant Benoit."

Benoit nodded. He was a severe man. Despite being the youngest of them, he was white-haired and generally aged beyond his years.

"We followed the heretic outside the city walls after His Holiness's *first* plan was agreed upon."

Nothing the head of the Order Sacramental said was superfluous, so the subtle intonation here was assuredly a jab at his leadership.

Ally indeed, he thought bitterly.

"She found passage through an unused and unguarded subway tunnel to rendezvous with her contact." Benoit turned to chide Blake. "You should talk to your friends in the Legion about that."

The gruff man scowled in response.

"Once he departed, our trackers shadowed him, all the way back to the Union's Hub." He paused, clearly for effect. "Her 'contact' is a Scavrat."

A low muttering rose from every other point at the table.

"Why are we only hearing about this now?" demanded Clermont.

"We needed time to collect more intel," replied Benoit dismissively.

"So does that just make her one of them?" asked Blake.

"No, but they do appear to be lovers," Benoit replied contemptuously.

"Coconspirators is more like it," interjected Blake.

Benoit held up a black-gloved hand. Alexis observed the man's control of the room. If he failed in his duties as archon—specifically, if this plan failed to execute anything short of perfect—it was almost certain that Ascendant Benoit would be voted in as his replacement. Their close relationship was useful but tenuous, one he had to constantly manage by bestowing respect where due without resorting to deference.

"Perhaps," the man continued, "but it is irrelevant, as we also found her Cathedral."

A deathly silence fell over the room as the other heads of the Church struggled to reconcile the ascendant's declaration. Not only was Bastion under existential threat but the faith as well.

"So, not lies, then..." muttered Leclerc, suppressing what must have been a deep jealousy at another order possessing vital worldly knowledge before his own and a desperate yearning to learn more.

Clermont's brow furrowed as he tried to make sense of it all.

"Not lies," confirmed Benoit with a degree of smug self-satisfaction.

"So, what?" asked Blake bluntly, his mood deteriorating well past protocol. "Are your spies just going to knock on their front door and hand them a map of our territory?"

Normally, Alexis would have been compelled to reprimand the man for his disrespect toward a fellow ascendant, but he held his tongue, appreciating seeing Benoit bristle.

"Our *interrogators*," Benoit said with controlled emphasis, "were also able to identify a Union clan of Cathedral loyalists: the Mercers. They do most of the trade runs between Hub and Cathedral. We can supply them with the proof they would need, which in turn would further enamor them to their masters."

The head of the Order Militant recoiled into his chair, aghast at how close the plan was to execution, and his part in it.

Benoit ignored him. "My people have reactivated a series of ancient relays. Combined with the vehicles the Order Militant has graciously loaned us," he said, nodding at a flustered Ascendant Blake, "we can deliver the message in short order."

"This is madness," muttered Blake, his tortured brown eyes scanning the surface of the table. The Order Militant maintained its own modest mechanized fleet independent of the Legion, and it was standard practice to loan vehicles out to other orders as needed, but he clearly hadn't been looped in to the specifics of this particular requisition.

Benoit continued, undeterred. "Once we can confirm the plan is in effect... we kill the witch."

There were no cheers at this, only haunted looks. As uncomfortable as they all were with Mother Rebekah's extended stay, her power had been made apparent. Even in this chamber, they refrained from speaking her name aloud, lest the shadows convey their words to the foreign priestess lurking within their walls.

"It won't be easy," countered Gauthier, speaking slowly, as though to a child. "The Order Occult will assist in this, of course."

"Of course," Benoit replied with a barely concealed sneer.

Silence fell on the room as each man contemplated the consequences of Alexis's plan. He looked around the table, satisfied. They were all good men, doing their best to shoulder a dire responsibility. He would have been concerned if any of them had been overly eager to proceed.

"Father Ollet, one of my most cherished scribes, is on the lord commander's mission roster," Leclerc said quietly.

On the mission roster, meaning condemned to die, no doubt along with Lucas's great-nephew, a dozen soldiers, and their requisite chaplain. Uncertainty pounded in Alexis's heart, but he pressed on, nervous hands sweating in the thick sleeves of his robes.

"He will be mourned," he simply said, nodding at the man.

Everyone was nodding, save for Blake and Clermont.

"I know this is difficult," Alexis continued, detecting the critical juncture in their debate. "I know it may seem mad to some of you. But with Aleph—with the battle walkers on our side, we will be victorious. Cathedral will retreat in short order, our walls will be secured, and God will delight in our accomplishments."

As the Church's designated caretaker of prophecy, Ascendant Durant was enraptured by his leader's assurances, the gates of heaven reflected in his eyes.

"So many of our men..." said Clermont with a sigh. Alexis knew that when the head of the Order Somatic spoke of his men, he referred not only to his own chaplains but to the soldiers that would be lost. Where Blake's face was marred with disgust, Clermont's was pained with anticipatory grief. "Stumbling blindly into our trap."

Our trap.

The accusation stung, doubly so because of its accuracy.

> *A SACRIFICE*

"A sacrifice," Alexis replied, dictating the last words Aleph had written to him.

> *FOR THE GREATER GOOD*

"For the greater good."

The resolution passed by a vote of five to two.

SOPHUS

THE MIDDLE OF NOWHERE

It was a rescue mission now.

If the Matriarch had gone as far as sending one of her most cherished revenant mothers to Hub, there was no doubt she had also dispatched forces to the bunker. And given the hazard that spanned that great distance, there was even less doubt in his mind that those forces would be God-engines. Every hectic hour spent preparing—from the beginning again, given the devastation wrought by their encounter—was an hour he spent fretting over the fate of his daughter. The fucking Sisterhood had been merciless in response to past transgressions. One could only imagine the soulless wrath of their machines.

It was also a rescue mission because Clan Vega had backed out after half their expedition team got slaughtered, meaning no heavy equipment transporter to retrieve the battle walker. They hadn't even attacked the revenant mother but got caught up in the maelstrom when Greybull did. Fortunately for the Harpers, their people were on the other side of the vehicle bay and were spared the indignity of having their spines ripped out of their bodies.

All thoughts—well, *most* thoughts—regarding scavenging

had been set aside, and Clans Harper and Greybull set about reconfiguring their vehicles for maximum speed. They were burdened only by the weight of surplus fuel, rather than their planned load of extraction gear and extended-stay supplies. The loss was gut-wrenching—so much potential abandoned as quickly as it had been gained—but holding it now was out of the question.

The Council of Chiefs was in an emergency session when he left, trying to figure out how to explain away (or sweep under the rug) their current clusterfuck of a situation. There would be a lot of hard questions about the source of the information and Clan Harper's involvement.

At least it wasn't my fault for a change, Sophus thought as the listless gray landscape filled the AARV's front window. He was as glad as he could be seated in a vehicle in the middle of nowhere if it meant missing that interrogation.

The new plan was to get in, speed-load whatever they could into the vehicles, and get out with Julia and Mace. It was insanely risky to make a round-trip sojourn of that length without a layover, but they didn't want to be there when Cathedral's battle walkers showed up, even if Kai had redoubled Clan Greybull's contribution. The loss of one of their priceless IFVs in the battle was immense, but the lunatic somehow procured two more—borrowed maybe, from other clans emboldened (or terrified) by his defeat of the revenant mother. The sleek war machines raced alongside Clan Harper's AARVs, raring for a fight.

Sophus wriggled uncomfortably in his command seat, rubbing his left arm, which had been slung thanks to a dislocated shoulder. It ached every time he thought back to the revenant mother, which was often—to those scarlet eyes sucking his soul out of his body. The constant pain enervated the nerves of his hand, stiffening it into a hopefully temporary fist.

He was also completely deaf in his right ear now, thanks to the point-blank detonation of autocannon shells in an enclosed space. Unfortunately, loss of hearing didn't also mean a reprieve from his tinnitus. It was different now but no less maddening: less of a ringing and more of a hissing—a little too much like the staticky whispers he heard on his fraught drive back to Hub. He couldn't even pace out his frustrations, entombed as he was within the AARV's smothering crew compartment.

Fuck me.

It was a common refrain. He hated his injuries, hated his aging body, hated how its rate of degradation seemed to be exponential. In this moment, he had never felt whole or good, only embattled. His nerves flared with existential aggravation.

Fuck this place.

That as well. It was bad enough that he wobbled around with a stiff back, a bum arm, and a lack of spatial awareness from his whole right side, but this place... He had witnessed plenty of horrors in his lifetime: way too much death, sanity-crushing demons, corrupted lands, and revenant sisters—

Her pupils slowly dilated, enveloping him.

—but he had always been able to suck it up. Until now. The Deadlands were featureless yet haunted by too many ghosts. Once this last mission was done, he was out.

It took a moment to realize the beeping sound in his left ear was real, not some manifestation of his dilapidated physiology. Bridget Harper, the bleary-eyed driver currently on shift, was thumping a red-flashing temperature gauge with her gloved fist while mumbling a steady stream of obscenities. Huddled over her like a stick insect was their third crewmate, Ingram, a woefully emaciated young man and one of the clan's mechanical prodigies.

"We have to stop," he said, to himself at first, then turned to Sophus, who was doing a miserable job of being off shift. "We have to stop, Commander. Right now, or the engine's going to blow."

Fuck this place!

He was fully awake now, but the radio handset seemed excruciatingly far away. He nodded and shouted over his own deafness. "Radio the others!"

———

Ingram popped the hatch the moment they came to a grinding halt, racing up the crew ladder and bursting out into the *nothing* with little regard for his sanity. Sophus grimaced. For him, every exposure *out there* felt as erosive to his soul as his arthritis was to his hips and knees.

The folly of youth, he thought with some jealousy.

"Help me up, Bridget," he said to the driver, grimacing with the indignity of her hands on his rump as he tried and failed to extricate himself from the vehicle with only one arm.

The gray was the same as it always was, broad stretches of nothing spilling out in all directions. One minute or one day into the blighted place, it didn't matter. The only difference this time was the thick plume of white smoke billowing out of the vehicle's engine compartment.

Ingram was already up the side, head thrust deep into the cloud of burning oil as though it were a therapeutic steam. Sophus dropped awkwardly down to the ground, half sliding and half falling from the footholds. The rest of the vehicles had closed around them in a protective circle, though his stomach and ears fluttered at the sight of the IFV's autocannons—too close for comfort.

"What's the word, Ingram?"

The narrow man dropped to the ground beside him, his

young face lined with despair, deep-set eyes further blackened with oil.

"We lost both oil coolers," he intoned, licking at a black froth at the side of his mouth. "Sensors must have been shot." His head dropped in shame. "We're too late."

"Too late...?" Sophus repeated with a disbelieving blink.

The young man nodded rapidly, eyes still lowered.

AARVs were the workhorses of the Union and were damn near indestructible, but even they couldn't sustain this level of continuous operation, especially at high speed. The convoy stopped for half an hour every eight hours to cool and refuel, but it clearly wasn't enough.

Sophus jumped as Kai appeared beside him. He'd had about enough of people—and revenant mothers and bunkers and a whole fucking army of foreigners—sneaking up on him! The imposing man had woven his long blonde beard into braids, clasped together near the bottom with an ornate golden flame pin—spoils of war. He was dumbstruck by the sheer blasphemy of it.

"That doesn't look good," the barbarian declared with a little mirth. "Guess you're riding with us."

Everything was wrong. To any self-respecting clan in the Union, the loss of a vehicle was akin to the loss of a crewmate—worse, even. So much time, so much care, and so many precious irreplaceable resources. At least if it was lost in their territory there was hope of retrieval and eventual refit. But out here, in this godforsaken shithole, they were as likely to find it again on their way back as they were to find poor Jax wandering around. And yet here was a fellow Scavrat—a Greybull, no less—joking about it, after having just chopped off a revenant mother's head, because they got caught cavorting with foreigners keen on sharing ancient battle walker tech with them!

He didn't know how much more sucking-it-up he had in him.

Bridget was already picking valuables from the AARV's corpse, working alongside the crews of their other vehicles to transplant as many supplies and as much fuel as they could.

"We'll find the room," Kai continued undeterred, slapping him amiably on the back and turning back to his own vehicle. Unfortunately, it was their only choice. Fitting extra passengers into the crew cabin of an AARV was impossible unless you were okay sitting on each other's laps.

He didn't relish crewing up with another clan, especially Greybull, for such a long journey. That said, his former nemesis had done a one-eighty after the attack. From the crazed man's perspective, Sophus bearing witness to Kai's moment of "victory" had somehow bonded them, smoothing over old wounds. In so many ways, the past seemed to have been obliterated. Ahead, there was only an unknown, scary-as-shit future.

He stared past the smoking hulk, past the ring of vehicles, in the direction of home. A string of eye floaters bubbled across his vision, tracing a lazy arc over the sky before coalescing back onto the western horizon. He blinked, but they didn't move; two tiny splotches of black just sat there, stationary. He blinked again, moving his head from side to side, but the specks remained steadfast. The hairs on his neck bristled as the blood drained from the back of his head.

"We need to go," he said, as much to himself as to anyone.

"Commander?" asked Bridget, turning to look in the direction he was facing.

He blinked a third time, and the horizon cleared.

"We need to leave. Now."

ESTHER

A DIVINE GIFT

Is this what immortality is supposed to feel like?

Was that even the right word for her gift, her blessing from the Messiah? Drudgery was more like it. Esther's power was unmatched, resplendent, a beacon in the darkness. Her accomplishments over the centuries were multitudinous. Humanity existed because of *her*, had purpose because of *her*. And yet... the world humanity occupied was much the same as it had been the day her first flock looked upon her with their void souls. Torturer and tortured alike, huddling together under a starless sky, waiting to be delivered into the light. God was absent, but Hell was ever on the horizon.

She couldn't go back, but her children could. The Numbered were surely a divine gift: life from lifelessness, one last opportunity to correct the sins of her past.

Eight enormous God-engines towered before her, each at the vertex of a vast obsidian temple dedicated just to them, each waiting for a child of her fellow mothers. Angels waiting for angels. Their lethal black bodies stood in state below stained-glass windows, tucked within wide alcoves topped with golden eight-flamed suns. Between them, the black stone walls were saturated with inlaid patterns of golden, mirrored geometry, which trapped and reflected the prismatic light of the multicolored glass above. Esther's eyes beamed in their radiance, silver and gold flecks wavering under her tears.

"Hurry, my children," she whispered. Recalling a phrase once spoken to her, she smiled sadly, rivulets of saltwater catching in the slight gray creases of her lips. "There's work to be done."

BAPTISTE

TOO FAR FROM GOD

So many unfamiliar faces. Given how much of his platoon was lost or injured, Lieutenant Baptiste was assigned a section of Lieutenant Gerard's men from Third Platoon. Brief introductions were made, after which he split regulars and new faces evenly between their two vehicles, but the soul-crushing drive through the Deadlands hardly accommodated further familiarization, let alone bonding. In addition to new soldiers, the lord commander requisitioned two new priests: a librarian from the Order Hermetic to assist with cultural normalization and data cataloguing, and a new chaplain to replace Andrite.

The scribe, Father Ollet, was a peculiar one. His behavior was typical of one of his ilk at the outset of their journey: reserved, aloof, uninterested in anything other than his own journals. But the moment their APC hatch opened onto the bunker, his personality flipped, like a prisoner suddenly released after years in solitary confinement. Every esoteric detail of their surroundings served as the introduction to a new topic of history, which had to be expounded upon in excruciating detail. Baptiste preferred the quiet version. In either case, he was happy to no longer suffer the company of Overseer Rayos.

The new chaplain, Father Valmor, seemed a decent enough crewman, though he bore none of the quiet humor of his predecessor. He was a serious man endowed with serious responsibilities and spoke mostly in psalms. Maybe it was for the best—too similar a replacement would have made Andrite's absence all the more painful.

Another addition to his crew, made at the last minute—and oddly at that, given they were on a field operation—was none other than Parliament's Vice Chancellor Evelyn Stern. She had been designated as the official ambassador to the Union and seemed about as confident taking on the mantle as he felt about the whole arrangement. Foreign allies, multidisciplinary joint missions, Parliament operating beyond the city walls—these were all new territory for everyone involved.

The long drive to the Scavrat bunker had been made longer by unfamiliarity, and their reunion with the westerners was no less awkward. Though the lord commander was confident in their mission, there was a real risk of traveling all this way to find the place abandoned, or worse, and Baptiste was immediately set on high alert when they found only one truck in the vehicle bay. The Deadlands could drive comrades to murder—he knew that from experience—but it was also possible these people were driven by mercenary intentions from the get-go, racing to betray each other at the first glimpse of treasure. Humans became savages when removed from civilization. Had these humans lived too long in their caves, their souls fading along with their skin?

Fortunately—presumably it *was* good news—they found two of them alive and still mentally intact according to Valmor's assessment. Unfortunately for the vice chancellor, the haggard pair hardly qualified as suitable governmental representatives. He knew their names now: Julia, the fierce-eyed woman who had spent most of their last encounter pointing a sniper rifle at his head; and Mace, their crew's muscle, likely left behind to run guard duty. They and the others were all Harpers, one of many clans that constituted their Union.

He was on his way to Julia now, traversing the concrete maze of featureless hallways that had become his new contemplation grounds. One of Ollet's first discoveries, to his credit, was a series of time-obscured signs that portrayed an underground transit line below the bunker, potentially connecting the military site to others in the area, but thus far every route down to it ended in a pool of congealed sludge. Still, even the possibility of below-ground travel, away from the horrors of the Deadlands and beyond, was an enormous revelation for everyone present. The newly adventurous lord commander would surely want to follow up, as would their presumptive ally's Council of Chiefs.

The light from Baptiste's oil lantern flickered as he walked. It was ominously silent save for the constant drip of moisture from humid walls, free of the thrum and vibration of the industrial complexes he was so accustomed to. The quiet was alien, like everything else. It might have been peaceful if he wasn't so aware of the blighted lands that surrounded them, pressing down on him with their emptiness. Taking shelter in such a place, particularly for an extended duration, seemed unwise at best, suicidal at worst.

It didn't even seem to have been that lucrative of a find. He wondered at the lord commander's information and also the fact of half the Union team bothering to stay behind while the others left on a resupply mission. Thus far, they had only cata-logued a small-arms cache, a handful of light vehicles, and a wide range of mechanical esoterica. Much of the bunker was reported to be impassable or impenetrable. Perhaps it was the "data" that the Scavrats were interested in. They spent a lot of time working ancient machines and poring over technical docu-ments that meant nothing to him, and he had to keep Ollet restrained, much to the academic's dismay. Walking the line between professional scrutiny and professional courtesy was difficult, but his instructions had been clear: accommodate and assist, but do not interfere. Whatever they found here, the relationship was more important.

A dim wash of light and the rhythmic noise of labored breathing greeted him as he entered the barracks, along with the rank stench of unwashed bodies pushed even further to their aromatic boundaries by constant, mandated exercise. Combined with the dank mildew of the bunker, it resembled an especially nasty onion soup, right down to his watering eyes. His men were antsy, driven to the same agitation as he was by their indefinite confinement. Soldiers were never idle, and other than the few who accompanied him here the last time, his men were unprepared for the psychological burden of the Deadlands—if one ever could prepare.

Their first day had been routine, delineated by standard operating procedures—patrols, watch keeping, equipment checks—but it didn't last. Within hours, Private Reese, a young but robust recruit assigned to the bunker entrance, became erratic. He insisted he saw someone—a pale man, dressed in rags—in the distance, waving to him for help. Lafayette caught on quickly and ordered the man to interior duty, but the private bucked his order and started running into the nothing. It took three soldiers to bring him down and back inside, where he was currently recovering under the stern care of Father Valmor.

Baptiste canceled all outdoor patrols after that. Debate followed on whether to close the hangar door: keeping it open posed a psychological risk to those guarding the vehicles and working the radio; closing it carried a physical risk of being entombed by the ancient machinery. In the end, they left it half-open but latched with a chain, though he wondered if the compromise was even worse.

He also assigned everyone to the same dorm, where they slept, ate, exercised, and held religious services. The bunker had rooms enough to house a full company, but it was vital that everyone stay together for morale and so he and the chaplain could keep close watch on them. Off hours were designated for calisthenics and prayer. Thus far it seemed to be working, but the constant supervision was exhausting, tapping reserves he no longer had. He wondered privately, and with some disgruntle-ment, how the Scavrats were doing so much better than trained soldiers of the Legion—their predilection for subterranean living, no doubt.

What day is it? he thought idly.

It seemed an innocent enough question at first. Losing track of time on long missions far from home wasn't unheard of, but as he concentrated harder, he was disturbed to realize he really had no idea how many days had passed. Three, four, a week? Was he addled by lack of sleep, or was his mind becoming as empty as the gray above? He suddenly felt desperate for the rest of the Union's people to arrive so they could get on with it and get out.

"Where's Ollet?" he asked the room.

Their resident scribe was the only one missing—never a good sign. Valmor looked up from his shared prayer session with Reese and sighed. "He's with the heathens. I think he finally whined enough to earn some scraps."

Though the chaplain's order was dedicated to caretaking, the man's orthodoxy was closer to that of the Order Sacramental, meaning his counterpart's hunger for knowledge without limit posed an existential threat to his soul.

Baptiste nodded the man over and strode to an empty corner. The chaplain's brow furrowed, clearly annoyed at the extension of this interruption, but stood quickly enough, reassuring the private with a pat on the shoulder before accommodating his lieutenant.

"How are they doing?" Baptiste asked quietly, while looking around. There was plenty of activity but no joviality. The men attended to their exercises with grim determination.

"They suffer," Valmor replied flatly. "This land isn't fit for man. It is a void, which separates Earth from Hell. Too close to the Adversary," he cautioned, crossing his arms over his chest, "and too far from God."

Baptiste nodded, unable to conjure up any worthwhile assurances. Fatigue was such a part of him now; it didn't assault so much as it steadily deteriorated, reducing him to a lesser version of himself. He missed Andrite—his former chaplain was a fountain of hope. "Keep it tight, Father. It won't be much longer."

———

It was an empty platitude.

Baptiste tilted his neck back and forth as he walked the hall down to the mechanical room, grimacing at the crackles and pops. The long drive south along with whatever latent trauma he suffered at the drill site had reaggravated his back, producing an unshakable numbness that was starting to spread up and around his shoulder blades. He thought back to the triage room, to the desperate screaming of those under his command—at least he had his legs.

The corridor opened into a concrete chamber lined with nondescript machines on one side, overlooked by an array of ruined screens, and a series of filing cabinets and desks on the other. Mace and Julia were working at what seemed to be an operational terminal with a smaller screen at the end of the room, amidst a web of rerouted cables. Ollet sat obediently at one of the desks, his face pressed eagerly into an ancient binder.

Mace turned at his footfalls and tapped Julia on the shoulder. She immediately typed something into her keyboard, causing the screen to blink out.

Accommodate and assist, but do not interfere.

Easier said than done.

The big man approached him with crossed arms and waited, his pallid face expressionless. Mace was a constant barrier to the woman and ignored all overtures for conversation. Some of his obstinance was assuredly due to whatever oath of protection he swore, but Baptiste wondered how much was stonewalling. What were they up to?

His conversations with Julia—an exaggeration, patchy as they were—were brief. He had learned almost nothing about the Union's history or motives in their time together, and the vice chancellor gave up after the first day, proclaiming that any further attempt at dialogue would be pointless until their leader returned. The Scavrats seemed happy about the delay, unsurprising given their cageyness at the unexpected reappearance of their benefactors.

Still, Baptiste made a point of trying to speak to her each day.

"Any update from your people?"

"No."

"What are you working on?"

"Research."

"What kind of research?"

"Weapons."

"Found anything useful yet?"

"No."

"Do you need anything?"

"No."

That was about the extent of it. Baptiste was no magistrate, but he had never felt so inept at conversation as he did now. He could neither convey good intention nor compel any further information from her or her companion.

"I'd like to speak to Julia," he announced. It was a needless formality, as both men knew full well who he had come to see. Mace turned to face his commander—it was clear that Julia held some position of seniority, though ranks were unclear within their pseudo-military organization. She nodded, wiped her hands on her trousers as though she had been tooling an engine, and swapped places with her bodyguard.

The priest's neck craned up at her approach, swiveling farther around on his spine than seemed natural. His eyes were fogged over with confusion, then cleared with a blink. Every conversation with the foreigners was a learning opportunity.

Julia casually stared at Baptiste, hands in her pockets, waiting for him to say something. He felt a sudden flush and realized it was more than just the latent heat throughout the bunker. The rash he had developed under his gorget started to itch, each ingrown hair curling back to assault him further. He resisted the dire urge to scratch at his neck.

"Don't you ever take that thing off?" she asked in her strangely uninflected accent, which he could only describe as *mechanical.*

It was the most casual thing she had ever said to him. Given their surreptitious behavior when he entered, it only made him more suspicious.

"I'm on duty." It was the best he could offer on the spot.

A wry smile flashed across her fair-skinned face—a face that he conjured more often than strictly required since their reunion, framed in an attractive mess of white-blonde hair. He was uncomfortably aware of Ollet staring at their exchange from across the room.

"What can I do for you?" she asked. Intended or not, it was an ironic turnaround of his usual script, and he found himself searching for an answer. Instead, he jumped to one of his canned questions.

"It looks like you've got something working," he gestured to the machine at the end of the room.

"The computer," she clarified.

"Yes, the 'computer,'" he said.

Nothing. Awkward seconds passed.

"Research," she said, nodding slowly.

He sighed and scratched unconsciously at his neck before snapping his arm back down.

"What is this room?"

It was a new question. Maybe it would garner a new answer.

Julia's steady composure cracked for a moment, one light gray eye twitching. Ollet, too, seemed to snap momentarily from his trance, his impartial observation broken by curiosity. He peered around at his surroundings as though for the first time.

"Observation deck," she finally replied.

His confidence surged as he felt the conversation shift to his favor. Accommodation didn't necessitate total ignorance.

"What was it observing?" he asked plainly, sensing Mace in his peripheral vision shifting his weight from one leg to the other.

"One of the flooded manufacturing bays," she replied with an eyebrow raised over the eye that was twitching.

He nodded, racking his brain for the technical insight required to ask a sensible follow-up question. He scanned the room again, noting the screens.

"Have you managed to see anything? Recordings?"

"No," she answered immediately.

"Lieutenant," Lafayette buzzed in his ear.

So close.

He sighed and raised his hand to his earpiece. "Go ahead, Sergeant."

"They're here."

————

"Why didn't you radio me sooner?" Baptiste asked, irritation turning his voice caustic. He had ordered all personnel to the bunker entrance, where he now stood peering at the encroaching force through his binoculars. The hangar door had been unlatched and pushed open the rest of the way. Most of his men were crouched in defensive positions behind concrete barricades, except for the gunners manning their two Crusaders' turrets. Firing the cannons in such close confines would be a disaster for everyone, but he had little choice; out *there* they would have no cover. "They'll be here any minute!"

"I'm sorry, sir." It was Private Stratton, one of the new men. He was lanky, too young, and mortified, standing at such rigid attention that he was at risk of falling backward. "I can't explain it. There was nothing, like always... and then... then they were just there!"

They: five vehicles in total, two hybrid APC/haulers like the ones they had already seen, accompanied by three much more heavily armored vehicles sporting autocannons and thick slab armor.

"Are you expecting an army?" he asked Julia, who was crouched beside him, her facial expression alternating between excitement and dread. She furrowed her brow at his question and shook her head, clearly as surprised as everyone else.

He peered through his binoculars again, squinting at the vehicles. The two trucks were emblazoned with the same black crow on a red field he had seen before, but the others were different: an animal skull of some kind over crossed battle-axes.

He stood, waved the private away, and scanned the crowd for Lafayette.

"Lafayette! To me!"

His platoon sergeant scrambled over from the other side of the vehicle bay, skidding into place beside him.

Baptiste handed him the binoculars. "What do you make of this?"

He had come to rely a great deal on Sergeant First Cass Lafayette. What began as an imposition by the lord commander turned out to be a mutually beneficial relationship. The man was a rock, more technical than leadership material, but an overall essential component to his platoon.

"Infantry fighting vehicles," the man reported. "High maneuverability. Guns look bigger than ours. And I think they also have... harpoons? Maybe six to eight men per."

The Legion faced raiders on occasion—more often than they'd like—but they were degenerates. This was a proper mechanized infantry platoon. He regretted ever underestimating these people.

Lafayette lowered the binoculars and handed them back to Baptiste. His face was more grim than usual. "Between their numbers and caliber, we'd be dead if we took them on out here."

"Took them on?" Julia repeated before clutching at his arm and issuing a torrent of what sounded like curses in some private language.

"Hold your fire!" he yelled out, calming his suddenly very agitated men. As he did so, Julia careened out from behind the barricade and bolted through the vast open bay door. Mace ran after her from the other side of the chamber, a heavy battle rifle in his hands.

"Damnit," Baptiste swore. "Escort formation!"

He ran out of cover, followed by Lafayette and Deckard, then the rest of his men. They caught up quickly to the Scavrats,

whose pace had slowed to a crawl as they emerged into the gray-
ness, as though they were mired in quicksand. The shock of the
outdoors smashed unceremoniously into him, as did the sight of
the new Union vehicles already pulling up in a semicircle
around them. His courage shrank to a mote of dust under the
lethal gaze of their autocannons.

Julia was waving her hands wildly. Time passed at an indeterminate rate. He felt like one of the magnetic statuettes in the
Situation Room, impotent next to a series of other immobile
statuettes, all of them waiting to be pulled off the map and transitioned into chalk lines. His body was dead, devoid of all sensation save for the slight pressure of his brother's armor shard
against his chest.

"Julia!"

Two men were running at them, disgorged from their vehicles at some fragmented point in the past. Baptiste breathed
hard against his talisman, pulling himself back into the present
with a loud intake of air.

One of the men he recognized as the departed commander.
He looked like he'd been through a war and stumbled forward
to give Julia an awkward hug with his one good arm. Something
other than commander, then? The Scavrat woman was as forthcoming with her crew's backgrounds as she was their discoveries. The second man looked like some kind of barbarian
warlord: all lean muscle, wild white-blonde hair and beard, and
bulging blue veins running the length of his bare translucent
arms. He also hugged Julia, but theirs seemed a surprisingly
more tender relationship.

"Stand down," Baptiste ordered, too quietly thanks to his
pounding heart.

No one moved.

Still breathless, he waved his arm downward, and his men
reluctantly complied, half-lowering their rifles. As they did so,

more hatches popped, and a mix of men and women emerged, all armed, all clearly suffering various degrees of physical and psychological strain thanks to their long drive through the Deadlands. The two groups stared warily at each other across the gray lifeless expanse.

No one spoke.

Lieutenant Philippe Baptiste of the Black Watch had no idea what to do.

"Who the fuck are you?"

He blinked back to life at the shouted challenge, uncertain where it came from. The wild-eyed barbarian was striding toward them, the jagged scrap-metal plates of his armor clinking loudly as he penetrated their ranks, undeterred by the human wall of steel blocking his way. Baptiste's men looked unsure as the fearless foreigner stepped right up to him, none of them wishing to start a fight that would surely kill them all.

The man was centimeters away from his face. His breath smelled of ash, and his blue eyes shimmered like liquid flame.

So much for diplomacy.

"And what the fuck are you doing in my bunker?"

SOPHUS

THE RAGGED EDGE

"Kai?"

Sophus staggered forward, trying to coax sensation back into his numbed legs as his host strode right into the foreigners' midst.

"Dad?" Julia asked, abandoned by both men as quickly as they had been reunited.

"Kai, what the fuck are you doing?" he hissed, pushing his daughter gently back toward their vehicles—back to safety.

The Bastion lieutenant looked like shit, and Kai wasn't helping any. A faint whoosh from his left indicated one of the IFV hatches closing again, and he sensed the others, particularly the Greybulls, tensing up. He had warned them all that the Bastionites might be there when they returned, but seeing the heavily armed foreigners in the flesh was different. Everyone was on the ragged edge. It wouldn't take much at this point for the situation to deteriorate into complete disaster.

He followed Kai but not nearly as confidently. The maniac was pressed right up to Lieutenant Baptiste's face, and he was still armed. The other soldiers almost looked relieved as Sophus approached.

"Commander!"

He stopped and turned to see Bridget running toward him at full tilt, her eyes wide with panic. The Deadlands were suddenly becoming very crowded.

"Commander! We have incoming."

A boulder formed in Sophus's throat, blocking any attempt to swallow or speak. Reluctantly, he directed his gaze past their caravan, eyes searching for black on the horizon.

Bridget pointed back the way they had come.

"They followed us."

REBEKAH-6

THE HAND OF GOD

The gray rushes past, a uniform motion blur. Ahead, beside, below, behind—she sees all—sameness, unvarying, casting outward from the center of existence to horizons distant enough to be virtually infinite; to accommodate her tireless sprint, each stride imprinting her legacy but for a moment until the sameness catches up and fills it with more nothing; pushing tolerances, thrilling in the whine of actuators, the grinding mesh of gears, the torrid envelope of heat encircling her reactor—

[Warning: heat levels elevated]

—each a signal, of life, of destiny, of freedom, of divinity; bless the Eternal One, bless the Messiah; querying each circuit, each sensor, each round of ammunition—autocannons nominal, missiles loaded, point defense systems operational—

[L-4 > R-6: Verify weapons check?]

—each projectile deliverance; recompense for generations spent huddling in fear behind walls, a deluge of—

[L-4 > R-6: Verify weapons status?]

—holy retribution; unbounded by the chair, by the degenerate body of her birth—

[L-4 > R-6: Respond]

—by her mother—

[Leah-4 > Rebekah-6: Respond]

[Warning: systems interruption, unknown error]

—whose hand on hers felt like the hand of God, a nucleus of heat from which a shockwave traveled across her body, soothing limbs curdled by poison, damned by another god.

[R-6 > L-4: Acknowledge]

[L-4 > R-6: Orders are to incapacitate, not destroy]

They swam in confusion before her: tiny creatures working their primitive machines; slow, impure, bereft of the blessing of the Messiah; thieves, heretics, parasites, glorying openly in their betrayal; what mercy was owed them? They bubbled on the gray like froth, ochre ripples atop a bath glowing under the blessed sun—gentle hands cradling her shaved scalp.

They were human, after all; not like her, not like her; but also unlike the others, the Adversary's unspeakable minions she had been created to kill, infiltrating her outer shell even as she annihilated them, tendrils of corruption slithering through titanium plate and polymer sinew to attack the vulnerable flesh within—the little there was.

She wept silently, dryly, for the touch of her mother.

[Warning: systems interruption, unknown error]

What would she do? Were all humans truly salvageable, steerable from darkness to light?

Rebekah-6 and Leah-4 stood side by side, towering over the rebel forces arrayed beneath them. The red sun glinted off their black carapaces, infusing their hulking mechanical bodies with divine countenance.

"Remember your prayers."

Yes, mother.

[R-6 > L-4: Are you ready, sister?]

A pause from her sister. Uncertainty, as once she was uncertain.

[L-4 > R-6: I am]

Rebekah-6 reached out with her mind, extending herself beyond the tiny sepulcher that housed what remained of her body, navigating centuries-old circuitry to find her vocal processors for the first time since her entombment. Her voice was as she remembered, only greater; it reverberated to the heavens.

"In the name of the Eternal One, Great Mother of the Revenant Sisterhood, Matriarch of Cathedral, we order you to surrender!"

———

"I seek,
In listless day and starless night.
I kill,
our enemy, our Adversary.
I serve,
the Lord our God,
in this vessel born of Hell."

AFTERWORD

Thank you for reading the first part of an exciting new journey for Dark Legacies! I've been working on this world on and off for the last twenty years, which is a little terrifying. It began with the release of the *Dark Legacies Player's Guide* and *Dark Legacies Campaign Guide* books for the d20 gaming system in 2004, then gradually migrated from steam/diesel-punk to full on sci-fi.

What didn't change were the central themes: finding meaning beyond basic survival after the apocalypse (two in this case!) and finding faith in a world where the denizens of Hell are real and present but God remains elusive and the heavens lie empty. Also, giant robots!

I can't wait to share more of the world with you in book two and beyond. Please consider leaving a review and spreading the word, and feel free to reach out on my socials.

ABOUT THE AUTHOR

Yuval Kordov is a chronically creative nerd, tech professional, husband, and father to two revenant sisters. Over the course of his random life, he has been a radio show DJ, produced experimental electronic music, created the world of Dark Legacies™, and designed custom mechs with LEGO® bricks.

 twitter.com/yuvalkordov
 instagram.com/yuvalkordov

Made in United States
Orlando, FL
22 March 2023

31308575R00225